GREED

THE SEVEN SINS SERIES

BROOKLYN CROSS

BROOKLYN CROSS

GREED

THE SEVEN SINS SERIES

ALSO BY BROOKLYN CROSS

The Righteous Series

(Vigilante/Ex Military Romance - Dark 3-4 Spice 3-4)

Dark Side of the Cloth

Ravaged by the Dark

Sleeping with the Dark

Hiding in the Dark

Redemption in the Dark

Crucified by the Dark (Coming Soon)

Dark Reunion (Coming Soon)

The Consumed Trilogy

(Suspense/Thriller/Anti-Hero Romance - Dark 4-5 Spice 3-4)

Burn for Me

Burn with Me (Coming 2022)

Burn me Down (Coming 2023)

The Buchanan Brother Duet

(Serial Killer/Captive Romance - Dark 4-5 Spice 3-4)

Unhinged Cain by Brooklyn

Twisted Abel by T.L Hodel

The Battered Souls World

(Standalone Books Shared World Romance- Dark 2-3 Spice 2-3)

The Girl That Would Be Lost

The Boy That Learned To Swim (Coming Soon)

The Girl That Would Not Break (Coming Soon)

The Brothers of Shadow and Death Series

(Dystopian/Cult/Occult/MFM Romance - Dark 3-4 Spice 3-4)

Anywhere (Coming Soon)

Seven Sin Series

(Multi Author/PNR/Angel and Demons/Redemption - Dark 2-5 Spice 3-5)

Greed by Brooklyn Cross

Lust by Drethi Anis

Envy by Dylan Page

Gluttony by Marissa Honeycutt

Wrath by Billie Blue

Sloth by Talli Wyndham

Pride by T.L. Hodel

WARNING

This book is a Fictional Paranormal Romance story and is intended for mature audiences ONLY, as defined by the country's laws in which you made your purchase.

This book may contain some violence, strong language, intimate content and scenes that some readers may find descriptive. Please be aware that this book has dark humour and may not be suitable for all audiences.

Like most other content rating systems this is only used as a guide.

ACKNOWLEDGMENTS

I'd first like to say a huge thank you to the other authors in the Seven Sins Series. Billie Blue, Drethi Anis, Dylan Page, Marissa Honeycutt, Talli Wyndham and T.L. Hodel.

The Seven Sins Series is the first collaboration I've done, and it has been an amazing journey that I'm sad to see come to a close. I know that there will be more fun and exciting collabs in our futures, but this one feels very close to my heart. I want to tell you all how much you mean to me, and how special you made me feel when you asked me to be a part of this project and entrusted me to kick things off with GREED.

Secondly, I'd like to say a huge thank you to my amazing PA Julia Murray, my Beta Team, Street Team and Arc Team for all of your hard work. It truly takes a village to write a book and bring it into the world and each one of you play a critical role in the process.

Lastly, but certainly not least, I'd like to thank the Bloggers, Reviewers and Readers that took the chance on reading this book. It is only with your continual support that indie authors like myself are able to keep writing.

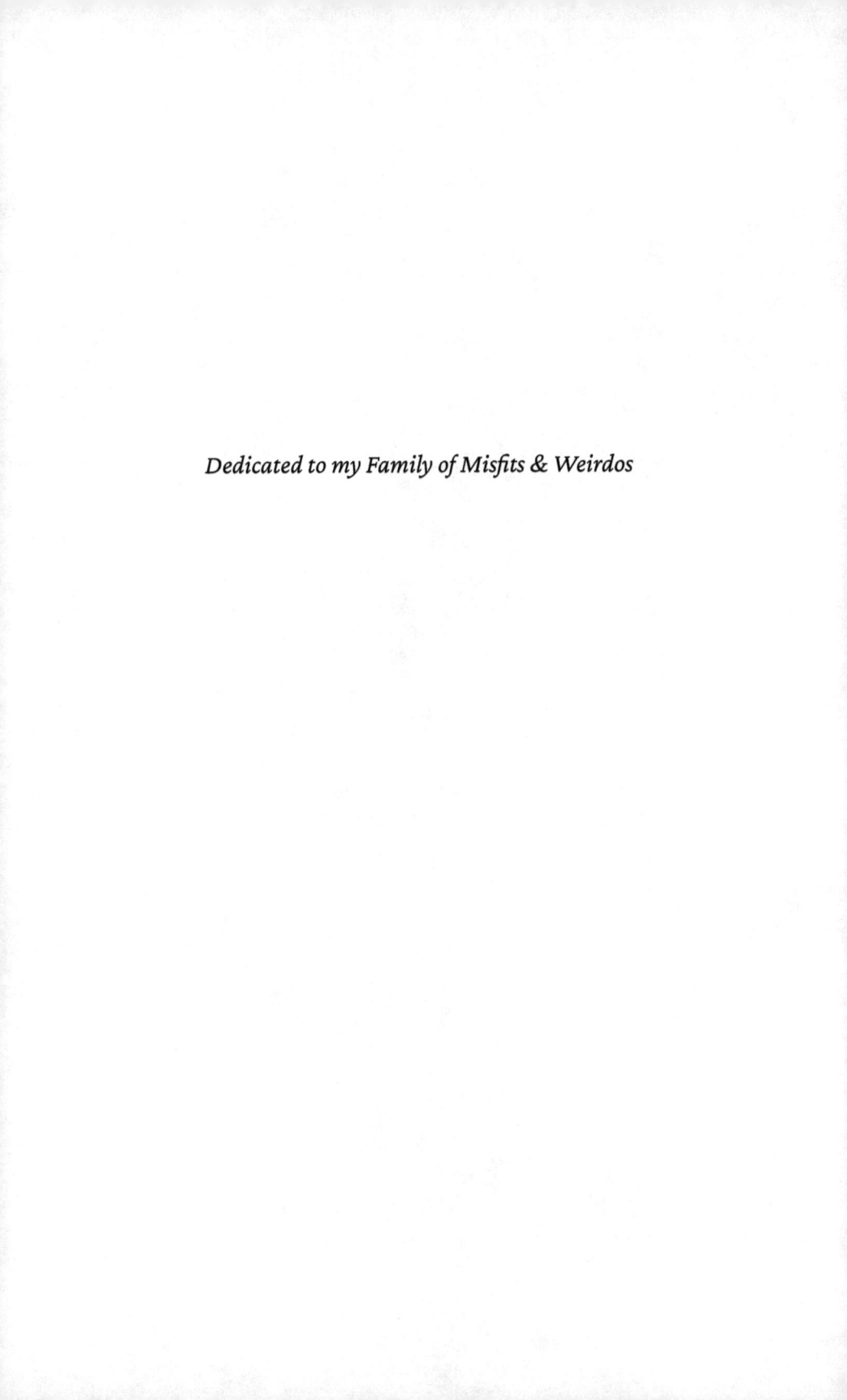

Dedicated to my Family of Misfits & Weirdos

Playlist

Way Down We Go - KALEO
Glitter & Gold - Barns Courtney
The Motto - Tiesto & Ava Max
INFERNO - Bella Poarch & Sub Urban
Hellfire - Barns Courtney
Money - Pink Floyd
@ my worst - Blackbear
Goosepumps - Travis Scott
Electric Love - BORNS
I WANNA BE YOUR SLAVE - Maneeskin
Counting Stars - OneRepublic
Highway to Hell - AC/DC
Heaven's Gate - Fall Out Boy
Forget to Remember - Mudvayne
Demons - Imagine Dragons
Take On Me - a-ha
The Reason - Hoobastank
Locked Out of Heaven - Bruno Mars
Kryptonite - 3 Doors Down
Angel - Sarah McLachlan

Humanities' first fall began with the snake and the apple of Eden.

As the apple was devoured, the sin of Greed was born.

ONE

HEAVEN MANY MOONS AGO

MADDIX

I soared above the clouds, my wings skimming the puffy whiteness cutting pretty lines with the thick, white feathers. Dipping my tips, I flicked the magical fluff into the air and watched it fill in and reform once more. Below, the normally bright green grass was more vibrant today, glittering like emeralds. The sun, in all its golden brilliance, illuminated the sky, so it too seemed to be made of rare gems.

I loved patrolling this area of Heaven. Rarely anyone came out this far, and there was a special peace and beauty that lived here. It was difficult to put into words. This section was like a private reading nook. More than once, I'd brought one of the great books of history out to this location and let myself relax in the soft grass as I read. Here, the quiet took on another level, and the warmth of Father's love washed over me, filling me with a clear purpose.

I pulled up as I reached the end of the area and turned toward the magnificent ivory palace. To behold the Palace of Creation brought emotion to my soul. Every time I held still and stared at the tall symbol of hope, a tear would slide down my cheek as a warmth would fill and spread throughout my body. The walls glimmered like an infinite number of diamonds and pearls, and the rich blue sky made the perfect serene backdrop for the place to shine like a beacon. The gilded peaks glistened, each marked with a golden statue of one of the angel guardians assigned to protect this place.

I smiled wide as my eyes fell on the statue of myself. It was the peak just to the left of Father's. A sense of pride filled me, and my chest pushed out as I took in the magnificent sight as I had done many a day and would never grow tired of seeing.

"Hi, Maddix!" I looked over my shoulder and saw one of our newly appointed guardian angels waving. She had her week-old infant wrapped snugly in her arms.

"Do you have a name yet?" I called out.

"She has been blessed to be a guardian angel like myself when she is grown, so I'm calling her Tikshya so she will be filled with patience for her coming responsibilities."

"Wonderful choice." I gave her a salute. My hand made a fist as I laid it over my heart and smiled.

I stayed a few moments longer than I should, just staring out over the beauty and the angels hard at work in the distance. I rested my hand on the golden hilt of the sword strapped to my hip as my fingers traced the intricate lines of the finely crafted piece. The uniqueness of it symbolized my rank amongst my brothers and sisters and I took immense pride in the piece Father had created.

With a single thrust of my powerful wings, I was quickly off to finish my loop—banking to the left, the golden-colored tips of my wing disappeared amongst the white as I veered toward home. It felt amazing to stretch out my wings, pushing myself and rejuvenating my senses.

If there was wind here, I imagined it would blow in my face, but this was a place of perfection. The wind never stirred, the temperature was always the same mix of not too hot and not too cool, and the lands were always bright with a kaleidoscope of colors that shimmered no matter the time of day. Why would anyone ever want to leave this place?

Spotting old Shilo, one of the oldest angels amongst us, I pulled up and landed beside him.

"I don't need your help. I'm not that old," Shilo said, waving his hand in my direction. Not bothering to listen to him, I bent to pick up the large basket of ripe serenity fruit he'd dropped.

"Aw, don't be like that. I would stop if it were any one of my fellow angels." I held out the large basket for Shilo to take, a wide smile on my face.

"Careful, you smile like that for too long, and it may stay that way, son," Shilo said, taking the offering.

"That's my plan."

"Really, and what is your plan for the humans and all the trouble they are stirring up on Earth," Shilo asked. "Do you think your pretty smile will keep them from turning into the miscreant creatures that they are?"

My face fell a little at the mention of the humans. I didn't have anything against them, but Father adored them like they were to be celebrated, and I didn't see why. In a very short time, they'd become famous for causing trouble and hurting one another and the other creatures that inhabited Earth. They systematically destroyed the land they lived on without a care, and worse yet, they barely listened to the angels sent to protect and guide them.

Many angels quit and were banished from Heaven for not doing their designated duties, yet I didn't blame them. Not only was it a difficult job to look after the humans when they didn't want our help and blatantly ignored us, but it seemed like they weren't held to as high of a standard as the rest of us. The situation was a nagging worry in the back of my mind. To be so conflicted about who was right when my loyalties were firmly with Father was disturbing.

The tension had reached a boiling point over Father's unconditional love for them. Those that were duty-bound to protect the humans even questioned Father, and a divide had started to brew among all the angels. Complaints and bickering had been festering on both sides of the argument from the moment Lilith had fallen from grace.

I lifted my shoulder, unsure what Shilo wanted to hear. "My goal is always the same, to make sure that all those know what it is to give wholly of oneself to others—and how good it can feel to be generous in all things. And trust me, if I can show all these stubborn, set in their ways, angels a thing or two, then I'm positive I can pull it off for Father's humans. It just might take me a bit more time." I gave Shilo a wink.

"You have always been a good one, now begone with you before anyone else passing by thinks I'm a decrepit old angel in need of help," Shilo teased, making me laugh.

"Okay, okay, I'm going, but you know if you ever need anything...."

"I know what cloud you like to perch on and the pretty little blonde that happens to sit there more and more frequently." Shilo's soft blue eyes twinkled with mischief.

I flushed hot, the smile miraculously spreading a little wider across my face. "I think that is my cue to get going. See you, Shilo. Have a great day!"

"If you're going to unite with that sweet girl, could you please make sure to do it before I wither away into nothingness," Shilo called out as I leaped into the air.

"I promise it will be sooner rather than later. Besides, it's going to be a long time before the day of your withering comes," I said back. With a thrust of my wings, I was off again, ready to have a cup of tea and a slice of homemade bread.

I guess I shouldn't be surprised that Shilo knew I'd been spending more time with Callista. It was bound to get out that I fancied her, and it seemed she felt the same way. Deciding to make a quick detour, I slipped beneath the thick clouds and stared at the opening to the River Styx. I slowed my pace as I made my way past the unusual area and watched in fascination as the human souls drifted lazily to the bank of Grace. Some of the souls had already emerged from the water, and in the customary single file march, they made their way toward the wide-sweeping arches of Heaven's entrance.

Humans were an unusual bunch indeed. They certainly didn't like to listen to the sage advice given by their designated angel. It was becoming a pandemic that the angels sent to work below would come back and beg for relocation. Why were these creatures, these humanoids, made to be so stubborn? What purpose did Father see in such a thing? Then again who was I to question Father's will?

Shaking my head in wonder, I continued on home. I spotted Callista when I was still a little way out. Her waist-length golden hair shone in the sunlight. She'd settled herself on the little bench outside my modest home, her hands kneading the material of her simple white tunic. Landing beside her, she jumped up with a start and then sighed as she recognized me.

"Hi there, sorry I didn't mean to scare you." I wrapped my arms around her, and she gripped the white leather straps of my armor. "What is it? What's wrong? Why are you shaking, Callista?"

"I'm sorry, it's not you that has me out of sorts. Have you not heard?" I smoothed back the soft blonde waves from her delicate face and focused on Callista's unique blue eyes that sparkled like the rarest turquoise gem found in Heaven.

"Heard what?"

"Lucifer, he's decided to wage war on Father."

My smile fell as my hand dropped to grip the top of my sword. "That cannot be true. Lucifer has his issues with Father, yes, but to wage war? To try and overthrow him? That's just terrible gossip, and you shouldn't be spreading that around. It will only cause unnecessary panic."

"No, Maddix, it is true. I saw him in the great hall today while I was working. Lucifer demanded that Father stop favoring the humans over the angels, that they were a lesser species and should be treated as such. He said that it was blasphemy to push our kind aside, his loyal children, and if Father continued to raise the humans on a pedestal, then it was time he stepped aside and let someone else rule."

"What was Father's reply?"

"Father said he loved all his children equally, that there was no pedestal, only equal parts of the same," Callista said. "I have never seen Lucifer so angry. He stormed out and said that Father was no longer fit to be our Father, and it was time Heaven found a new ruler, one that would look after the angels the way they were meant to be." A lone tear fell from Callista's eyes.

Wiping the tear away with my thumb, I gave her nose a reassuring kiss. "I'm sure it will all blow over. You know how Father and Lucifer can get. They rarely see eye to eye at the beginning of any argument, and yet they always find common ground in the end."

"Maddix, this was different. Father laughed at Lucifer like he was a mere child. Father said that the humans should be the one creation that Lucifer should love most, as they were made in Lucifer's ilk. You did not see the anger in Lucifer's eyes and the way he stormed out after the insult...I don't know, but Michael arrived shortly thereafter, and he and Father ushered everyone out of the palace so they could speak privately." Her fists tightened on my battle armour straps. "I can feel..." Callista stepped back and moved her hand around over her chest. "Something terrible is going to happen, I know it. And I don't want you to get caught up in it. Please, Maddix, I know you want everyone to get along, but I don't think you can fix this. Whatever Lucifer decides to do, stay out of it and let Father deal with him."

"Callista, I'm sure you are worrying for no reason. Father will forgive Lucifer like he always does, and Lucifer will calm down and see that Father isn't turning his back on us and apologize for his outburst. And although I do appreciate you warning me and if—this is a very large if—something was to happen, I must get involved. I am one of the guardians. It is my duty to protect Father, the angels, and this place. To protect you." Cupping Callista's face, I laid a soft kiss on her nose. "Do you want to come inside? Maybe a hot cup of tranquility tea will settle your nerves."

I held out my hand toward the door when abruptly, the world around me shifted as an ear-piercing roar, not of this plain, echoed in the distance. The terrifying sound made the hair on my arms stand on end. Releasing Callista, I reached for my sword as my eyes searched for what could've caused the resonance of terror. The terrifying sound wailed again, along with a deep rumble of thunder, booming in anger. The rich blue sky rippled as if a pebble had been tossed into the water, and a strange vibration shook the surrounding trees and leaves that had never felt the wind. The noise of them rubbing together was unbearably loud. It was as if an earthly storm was rolling in on the horizon like the humans had found a way to touch Heaven before their souls had arrived.

"This is impossible," I said.

A blanket of blood red and fiery orange slowly consumed the once bright blue sky in the distance. I took another step away from Callista as I, like so many, watched to see what it was that could do such a thing. In all my years, I'd never known anything that could change the sky other than Father himself.

Another roar, louder this time, sounded in the direction of the golden gates. The piercing sound sent shivers racing all over my body. Whatever it was, it was big, and it was powerful. The ground trembled slightly underfoot, and I looked down at the perfect green grass. The little blades were shaking violently—none of this made sense. There was nothing even on Earth with the humans that could do such a thing.

Nothing was strong enough to disturb Heaven. The palace's normal shimmer changed, and the energy it was casting off made me rub my chest. It was a warning. What was coming was real, and it was dangerous.

"It's him," Callista whispered as she held on to my arm. "Look!" She pointed toward the holy gates.

My eyes swung in the direction of the tall golden gates, and my mouth fell open in bewilderment. A massive black snout from a beast I had not seen before pushed through the clouds. The head was larger than I could even begin to describe. The front legs and body were next, and my eyes widened as a mammoth creature that was black as the furthest reaches of Hell was exposed. A great dragon the likes of which I'd never seen emerged from the Heavenly white and parted them like it was the Red Sea. It was unimaginably large, and it hurt the eyes to stare at it directly. As the tail fully emerged from the clouds, the full length and breadth of the beast were displayed. This thing was not of the human realm, it was not of this plain, and I'd never heard of such a creature lurking in the depths of Hell. No, this creature was made from a darkness that wanted to consume all in its path.

Its large red eyes sent an unfamiliar emotion straight to my gut. I looked down at my stomach and back up at the beast. Was this fear I felt? I'd never known fear, and yet this creature, this blackened beast from the underworld that had burst through the serene white clouds, was most certainly causing this reaction.

Human souls scattered to the winds as the dragon knocked them asunder, their ghostly bodies disappearing, in the unsafe space between the River Styx and the safety of Heaven. The gates that normally looked impenetrable seemed flimsy in comparison to the enormity of the creature. Wings blacker than the Hell realm itself and larger than anything I'd ever witnessed opened wide as it finally dropped with a boom to stand on the clouds. Smoke swirled into the air around the beast as the normal mists evaporated under its dark touch. The claws of the great creature pawed restlessly at the clouds. I watched in disbelief as the clouds the creature touched did not reform but remained blackened and charred. If it could destroy the land it stood on, what would it do to our home if it made it through the gates?

Suddenly, there he was, my brother upon the back of the beast that threatened our home. He stood like a tiny flea between the wings of the dragon, and my heart sank. There would be no coming back from this. Whatever this was, Lucifer would most certainly be cast out of home.

Smaller creatures from the same hellish plain followed in the beast's wake, tainting everything as they dotted the sky. Fire replaced the smoke that rose in streams from the dragon's nose in funnels so high I couldn't see where they stopped, but the immense heat could be felt even from this great distance.

"No, this cannot be happening. My eyes must be playing tricks," I said, and yet the pounding of my heart and the blood coursing through my veins told me I was indeed seeing the impossible.

"This is no trick, Maddix. I see it too."

My wings spread open, and I took a step to leap into the air, but Callista squeezed my arm hard. "Please, Maddix, don't go, don't get involved."

"Callista, I have to go, I'm an archangel, and those are my brothers and sisters," I said as the great dragon roared again. Lucifer's voice could be heard in the distance as he yelled at those that manned the gates to open them or die. Angels of every age and rank gathered to witness the unbelievable sight.

The guards at the gate drew their weapons in defiance, just as the dragon reared. Standing at its full height, I gasped at the sheer size of the beast—the front legs clawed the air with long talons as the tail lashed from side to side.

The large pillars of flame rescinded from the sky toward the dragon's head, and all I could think was to scream, "Look out!"

The beast brought its feet down, and with such force as it roared that I had to catch Callista from falling as the ground quaked. A fiery breath flowed from the dragon's mouth and covered the golden arches until they could no longer be seen.

Like we'd all been transported into the middle of an earthquake, the ground shook and vibrated as the power of the gates and the beast collided with a *Boom*. I stumbled where I stood but held Callista to me. Hellfire that didn't penetrate at first began to seep under the gate and then unbelievably poured between the bars. The deadly fire trundled out of the dragon like tall waves in the ocean, and I watched in horror as the golden gates that stood tall as a symbol of peace and protection for many generations erupted into flames. The holy metal groaned like someone was screaming as they warped and bent away from the onslaught.

The dragon violently smashed its head against that which should never have been penetrable. With each powerful blow, I stumbled again, bumping into Callista and knocking her to the ground.

"I'm so sorry," I said as I helped her to her feet once more. "Get inside my house, hide and stay there."

But she didn't hear me. Her eyes were fixed on the creature at the gates. Like a massive battering ram and one last Heaven-shattering blow, the dragon crashed its wide head into the gates and blew them wide open, the sound so loud that it was like the sky itself split open to swallow all of Heaven.

If I hadn't seen it with my own eyes, I'd never believed such a story. It was impossible, unfathomable, and it had only just begun.

One deadly clawed step after the other, the dragon marched further into the plain of light and tarnishing the tranquility where it should never have been. All that followed in its wake were granted access to the holy sanctuary. Head low, it sucked in the streams of fire and opened its mouth. The fire billowed in a deadly ball before bowling over everything and everyone in its path. Lucifer didn't seem to care that the creature he rode was taking out those he claimed he wanted to protect.

The handful of guards that fearlessly manned the gate now turned to flee, but the fire was faster. I cringed as their high-pitched screams reached my ears. My mouth fell open in shock as the once-beloved family members fell from the sky as blacked lumps of undefinable masses, then burst into ash. What was left of their bodies slipped through the clouds and disappeared to rain on the Earth below, and a flurry of white feathers scattered around the great beast and Lucifer, like slow falling snow.

The ground beneath my feet groaned, and I would have sworn I heard a crack in Heaven's foundation as the beast's final leg stepped over the threshold. The deafening triumphant growl sent another shot of fear down my spine. Michael and the army of warrior angels rose from the palace in single file, their stunning white Pegasus's leading the charge as the dragon headed straight for the ivory palace.

"Callista, please go into the house and remain there until this has passed. Do not come out until either myself or Father says it is alright."

"I beg of you, Maddix, do not go. I fear I will never see you again. You know I sense these things." Her voice trembled as tears slipped down her cheeks. "I love you. I don't want to lose you."

I stared down into the stunning blue eyes that had stolen my heart the moment I'd seen them. No matter what my heart said, I couldn't let my brothers and sisters fight amongst themselves like this.

Cupping Callista's face, I captured her lips in the sweetest of kisses. Lips that I could kiss for eternity and never grow sick of moved against my own.

"I promise you that I will return, but I must go," I said and gently pried her hands away from my leather straps. "I will return to you, Callista, for I love you too."

Rising swiftly into the air, I pumped my wings hard as I aimed for the siege that was now fully underway. I had to stop my brothers and sisters. This was madness.

CHAPTER
TWO

R*IKER*

The men behind me were like angry squirrels chattering at one another. The boardroom was full of my chief executives as they argued over the most recent acquisition. My head hurt from the bickering over what the best course of action was to make the most money: dividing it up and selling off the pieces or keeping the assets. It should've been easy enough, but those who sat around my table had their own agenda—one they didn't speak about out loud and would deny if ever asked. I, on the other hand, did not play fair, and I knew exactly what each desired. It gave me great insight into which strings I should pull on to get my little human marionettes to dance to my tune with the perfect accord.

The stiff brandy deliciously burned my throat as the dark drink lingered on my lips like a kiss. Blocking out the droning sound of the men arguing, becoming bored with the debate, I stared out the large windows to the car lights far below.

I owned this building, as I owned most of the others that surrounded it, but this one was my biggest accomplishment yet. It was the largest in the city and stood out as a black diamond, a crown jewel of sorts. The other buildings could not compare to the shimmering beauty or highly sought-after location. The rent that I charged per floor was way more than what the market demanded, and yet my mere presence in this place had people clamoring to say their company was here. Their need to be the best, the drive to have it all flowed through every piece of furniture, fixture, and wall in this place. The energy was intoxicating to these mammals, these humans. Many went bankrupt trying to keep up with the astronomical rent.

Did I care? No.

My eyes scanned over lady liberty in the distance, the setting sun allowing the torch to be seen. The humans fawned all over it like it was Father himself. It was a symbol of hope, prosperity, and guidance—blah, blah, blah, puke. The idea was preposterous and a most hilarious construct as far as I was concerned. What a joke. Humans wouldn't know how to unite if it bit them in the ass. They were pathetic, strange, and highly disappointing creatures of weak bodies and minds. They were vertical, hairless cats with no tails. I smirked as the image of humans naked, running around came to mind. I mean, really, temperamental cats with no fur, what was the point, Father?

The flame in the torch of the ridiculous statue's hand glowed brighter as the sun dipped a little lower, and as much as I thought the piece of construction was for those with a simplistic mind, I found myself staring. Despite the fact it was not yet dark, the moon was already out, and the reflection was dancing on the water. This view was one of the few things I truly enjoyed about being on Earth—well, I enjoyed that it didn't cost money or power to enjoy, that is.

A hand slapped on the table as the conversation took a turn and became more heated. Not that I cared, it was all the better for me if they constantly stayed at each other's throats. Greed was best nurtured amongst those with dissonance.

"Riker, what do you think?" George's voice asked, and I sighed before turning around to address the room.

Neven, the closest thing I had to a best friend, sat off to the side in the more comfortable chairs. He was the image of relaxed, and yet the zoned-out look and absentminded swirling of his drink told me he was already checked out of the meeting.

"I think this is a waste of my valuable time." I almost snickered as their mouths dropped in perfect unified symmetry.

Well, at least you can all agree on one thing.

"But...but..." George licked his lips and stared around the room for one of the others to speak up.

I didn't need to reach out and touch their minds to know what they were thinking.

"This is what we will do," I said, cutting George off before he could begin a boring rant.

"The company acquired is a broadcast and media company," I paused for dramatic effect. "We have been wanting to find a way to spend less and advertise more, so although in the short-term we can gain an extra ten million if we pieced it off and sold now. We stand a chance at saving hundreds of millions by bringing Marabellum Communications into the fold." I gripped the back of the large black leather chair at the head of the table. "Marabellum has a radio, online, and television division, and unless you are all fine with paying exuberant fees to create our media marketing campaigns, I'd suggest you all run along and find the best ways to put these assets to use."

"May I make a suggestion?" Neven spoke up, and all heads turned in his direction. "The company already broadcasts on a number of major markets. Why not pursue a few more popular shows and sell more expensive advertisements? If you could land something as popular as the Super Bowl, for example, it would be beneficial to all our divisions."

"That's brilliant!" George's eyes lit up as the greed that flowed through his veins pumped wildly through his heart with a deep rhythmical sound that called to me. George's lip curled up as his excitement built. "You three are with me, and we will take on the television division." He pointed to the three closest to him and jumped up like a kid at Christmas to run and get started. Or at least it was what I assumed kids looked like at Christmas, another moronic human creation. I mean, really, who came up with a fat man in a red suit delivering gifts for free? For free! I shook my head at the notion.

It really was quite sad how easily humans could be manipulated and persuaded with the dangling of money and power under their noses. I watched as the rest began to pair up and take off, each with their own simmering and greed-filled agenda. It was like watching a corporate version of Survivor as the remaining people chose their favorites to play in their sandbox. I tapped my chin as I watched the chaotic humans argue and wondered who would be voted off the island this time. There was always one that was left out.

Once the last of the hairless cats scampered out, I sat down at the computer to go over the latest fiscal quarter. To anyone else, it may have been the most boring read in the universe, but not to me.

Neven rose from the leather chair he'd been lounging in and strolled across the room, a glass of whiskey dangling between his fingertips. "You want to go to Dai's fight club tonight or maybe hit up Triel's new restaurant, Ekron? Just to do something different."

"No, and no, not tonight. Wait a minute, Triel? Why in the name of Hell would you want to go to Gluttony's new place? Although you know I love Vegas, but I have zero interest in seeing that gloomy fucker."

Neven shrugged. "The food is supposed to be awesome, and I find him odd but highly interesting."

I lifted my brow at Neven. Not that I cared who or what my demon friend fucked, but even he should have limits. Gluttony was not the demon you ever wanted to get into bed with, in any context.

"Would it do me any good if I said stay away from him?"

"I'm not interested in a relationship with him. I just find him fascinating. Once, I saw him order a demon to pluck out a human's eyes while the demon fucked its mouth. What can I say? It was hot."

"I'll take your word for it, but know that if you go, you may not return." I turned my eyes back to the computer screen and smirked as I scrolled to the line that showed the total growth over the last quarter. We were up almost fifteen percent across all divisions of the company.

"Fine, I guess I will find something else to do," Neven grumbled as he pouted like a human child, which considering his substantial age, was impressive.

"Like Skye," I countered, and Neven laughed.

"Yeah, I would, but she's still visiting Asmodeus's palace. Not the best idea for her to hang around the demon of Lust's place, but she insisted on going. He does have great orgies, but last time I went, I was gone for months, and my cock wouldn't stand straight for a whole month when I got back." Neven looked down at his crotch and patted the front of his pants. "I thought the thing was broken."

"That was a little too much information."

A soft rap at the door had both of our heads turning in that direction. Shilo stood just outside the door, his back straight, his face void of all emotion. He was the constant professional. I had no idea why Shilo wouldn't stop with the old formalities. We were no longer in Heaven, and I was no longer the angel that I'd once been.

"Shilo, is everything alright?"

"Yes, Master, all is fine. I've come to see when you'd like me to have the car readied?'

I peeked at the time and then at the screen. I wanted a solid hour to go over the latest reports first, my little colorful graphs of joy. "Give me an hour, and I will be ready to head out."

"Very good Master, I will see to it. Neven, will you be attending the residence this evening?"

"No, I'm heading out, but thanks for the invite. We all know Riker wouldn't have bothered to invite me over."

I smiled as Shilo answered the teasing jest. "Master works very hard and diligently to provide us with a level of comfort that I'm sure you have grown accustomed to, Neven. Maybe you should appreciate that he considers you a friend at all."

Neven opened his mouth and then closed it again, not daring to argue with the much older angel. Fallen or not, Shilo could still hold his own if needed.

Neven tipped back the rest of the whiskey, the glass making a thud as he placed it on the corner of the desk. "See you later Riker. I'm out."

I watched my friend leave along with Shilo close on his heels. Pulling up my sleeve, I stared at the symbol of greed, the brand a constant reminder of my traitorous Father and my fall from grace to this armpit of the universe called Earth. I'd used to see it as a stain on what I'd become, but no longer. Maddix was dead, and Riker was all I craved to be now. The joke was on Him because I not only embraced my role as one of the seven deadliest sins—I mother fucking owned it.

THREE

M INETTA stood away from her desk and stretched, raising her arms above her head as she tilted from side to side. She adored her job, but the long shifts at the computer taking calls took its toll on her body. Yoga was a must for her to stay limber, so she twisted from side to side, slowly taking in her fellow coworkers and the space that surrounded all of them. She had no idea why they would paint this place such a drab grey with matching cubicle areas. It seemed like they wanted everyone to be depressed all the time. Minetta bent over at the waist and let her arms hang forward. Her fingers brushed over her toes as her back eventually relaxed enough that she could grab the tips of her shoes.

"That is one nice ass," Jared's voice called out.

She peeked around her leg, and sure enough, he was standing on the raised walkway with one of the other guys that worked in the building. They leaned on the railing as they openly gawked at her. Jared gave her a wink as he stuck his tongue out, waving it up and down suggestively.

Ugh, gross.

She continued to exercise, ignoring their comments, and rolled her shoulders before taking her seat once more.

"Stay bent over like that for too long, and you might find you get a juicy surprise from behind," Jared said.

"Hey asshole, take your sexist comments and shove them up your ass before I have you written up for inappropriate workplace behavior," Penny yelled, holding up her cell phone, the threat made clear.

Minetta wanted to shrink down in her seat and disappear. She hated confrontation, and here she was smack dab in the middle of it. "It's okay, Penny," she whispered.

"No, it most certainly is not! He's a fucking pig." She made oinking noises at the guys, and Minetta wanted to crawl under her desk as the entire call center quieted with the show. Penny placed her hands on her hips, fuming across the narrow aisle from her cubicle. Penny was only a year older than her, but her friend was like a mother hen in the office, and she took her role seriously. Rude co-workers, unfair pay, even the quantity of unhealthy snacks in the cafeteria, Penny was ready to Mother hen the hell out of those situations and more.

"Why don't you loosen that knot on your head, and maybe you'll actually get a guy to be interested in you," Jared said but luckily sauntered away before the fight could escalate further.

Penny only ever wore her hair one way at work, and that was in a high ballet-style bun. Her hair was beautiful, so Minetta had no idea why she didn't let it down once in a while. "Can you believe the nerve of that prick? Minny, you really need to stand up for yourself. You have enough ammunition to have that dirtbag fired. I don't get why you let him speak to you like that."

She rubbed her face and sighed. "I know, but I just don't want to cause trouble. You know me, Penny, I hate when there is a mix-up with the lunch order, let alone something like this."

Penny opened her mouth to most likely continue berating her for not being tougher when her headset rang with a call.

She hit the talk button. "Nine one one, what's your emergency?"

"You have to save me!" The man's voice yelled into the phone, startling her. Even after working here for the last few years, she never got over the initial burst of adrenaline that accompanied the fear in a caller's voice.

There was a crackle of a bad connection, and it sounded like he was moving. She focused on the sound a little harder, and it was definitely the soft thud of feet, but the weird noise accompanying was the sound of something nylon, a windbreaker maybe. She'd gotten way too good at learning different sounds through the phone. She knew how to differentiate types of clothing, different screams, and even different breath sounds. Like an elaborate painting, she could picture them in her mind.

"Okay, Sir, can you tell me your name and what is happening?" Minetta said, her fingers poised to take down the information.

"It's after me...I can't shake it. Oh my god! I'm going to die, please, please save me," he blurted out, his voice high and hysterical.

"Sir, I can only help you if you tell me where you are?"

"Central Park. Aahh, no, how did it get over there. Shit!" His breathing was loud in her ear, the steady panting of his lungs working hard as he ran.

"Okay, Central Park, that is a good start. Now, what is after you, Sir?"

"You won't believe me." He sounded close to tears, his voice changing again, adding a little gasp.

"It's not my job to judge you, Sir. I'm here to help. What is after you?"

"Please just send help."

Minetta stared at her multiple screens and typed in the call as she muted herself. She glanced at the board, and N-657 was the closest car. She quickly radioed them and relayed the little bit of information she had before switching back to the unknown man.

"Sir, help has been dispatched to your location. What is your name?"

"My name's Sam. No, no, no, how can there be more of them? No please, this can't be happening, please help me," he begged, his voice breaking with obvious fear.

Minetta was starting to wonder if Sam may have taken something and was having a terrible hallucination. It most certainly wasn't the first time and wouldn't be the last that she received a frantic call like this. Yet, something about this man's tone had a slightly different feel to it. She couldn't put her finger on what it was that was making the hair on the back of her neck stand on end, but she was nervous for him.

"Sam, take a breath and tell me what is after you."

There was more thumping of feet and then the distinct crunch sound of a gravelly surface. She tried again to get Sam's attention, but all she could hear was, "Oh god, oh god." There was a groan and then the rustle of leaves or bushes as they rattled loud in her ear. "Sam, are you still there?"

"Shhh, they may hear you."

Minetta lowered her voice to play along. "Sam, the officers need to be able to find you to help you. Where are you now?"

"I'm hiding in some shrubs near the center of the park. Our Father, who art in Heaven..." Sam whispered. She recognized the Lord's prayer even though she didn't attend church often. She quickly typed into the screen that the complainant may be on an unknown substance. There were too many drugs that seemed fun to try until you ended up naked and running down the street being filmed by hundreds of people. It was either that, or he could have a mental health issue. She quickly added that to the notes on her screen, but he didn't seem confrontational.

Minetta didn't doubt that Sam's fear was real. His voice was laced with terror. The question became, was his fear over a real threat or one that was attacking only his mind. The officers would handle the situation with care regardless. Still, if there was an assailant with a gun, that was a very different situation than someone in the throes of something medical.

"Sam tell me this, what is your last name?"

"Bailey." She typed in the new information, and unfortunately, there were thousands of Sam Baileys in the system. She needed more info. Maybe a family member could provide insight if he was spiraling.

"Sam, what's your birthday?"

"Umm..." There was a long pause, and she could barely hear him breathing. "555 River Road."

She started to type and then realized he'd given her an address and quickly switched screens. The address belonged to a Karen Johnson. This made no sense. "Sam, you're doing well. Just relax. The officer is only a minute out. Now can you give me your birthday this time, Sam?" She tried again.

"I can't. Oh God, I'm so sorry."

"Sam. Sam, just listen to my voice and breathe."

"Shhh, I can hear them coming," his voice shook. The wavering voice sounds came through the headset making her body involuntarily shudder. "I'm sorry. I'm sorry that I was a bad person. I'm sorry that I stole and cheated and lied and drank too much, and I'm sorry I hit that girl and ran. I swear I didn't see her. She just appeared in the middle of the street, but I was so scared I just drove away," Sam rambled rapidly. "I can hear the sirens, but they're too far. Those thing they're going to get me. I don't want to die, please."

"Sam, what girl?" she asked, completely confused now at the turn in the conversation. Minetta looked up at Penny and the rest of the dispatchers who'd gravitated to her desk and the odd call as if they could all hear the desperation in Sam's voice.

"I don't know...I didn't know her name. I just hit her and took off." Sniffling came from the line. "She was so young, but I swear I didn't mean to do it. Please, you have to believe me, please. Make them leave me alone. I didn't do it on purpose. I wouldn't."

Her hands flew across the keys, digging into the stored banks of calls looking for anything that was a hit-and-run for a young female victim. Sadly, there were over five hundred in the last year. She had no idea how to narrow this down.

As her eyes scanned back and forth over the lines of names and addresses, her hand froze on her mouse as 555 River Road was one of the addresses of a victim. She doubled clicked on the line, her eyes scanning the general occurrence.

Lizzy Johnson, six years old, ran out into the street chasing a ball. Victim was hit by speeding car doing approximately 40miles/hr. Vehicle believed to be a red, two-door was seen speeding away from the scene. No Marker. Officer Jansen performed CPR, but the young girl was pronounced DOA at the hospital.

Minetta wiped away the single tear that was traveling down her cheek. This bright young life narrowed down to a few clinical lines. She swallowed down the mixed emotions as she turned her attention back to Sam. Regardless of what had happened, at this moment, Sam was the individual in need of her help.

"Sam, are you still with me?"

"Yes." The one word was strangled and ended on a whimper and a sniffle.

A deep rumbling growl traveled through the line, and the hair stood up on her arms as her heart rate picked up. Eyes wide, she sat back in her chair, her own breath unexplainably quickening like the growl had come from inside the room. "Sam, what's happening? What's that noise?"

There was no response, just heavy breathing. "No, please!" There was a thumping sound, and then Sam's voice became distant as the rustling got really loud. "No! Ahh!"

Loud screaming full of terror filled her head-set, her hands covered her mouth. The ear-piercing shriek came again, and she grabbed the headset throwing it off. She didn't even care as they pulled free of the phone and smashed into the computer. The problem was without the headset on her, the sound of Sam's screams were louder as the call came through the speakers attached to her computer.

She looked up as those around her stood and looked down at her phone, transfixed by the terrifying sound as she was.

Panic rippled down her spine. The growling that sounded like a pack of really large dogs made her rub over the skin on her arms. She could almost see them in her mind, and they sounded huge, like wolves or worse. The snarling was loud and had a raspy rattling to it like there were thousands of whispering screams riding the growl.

She shivered, wrapping her arms around herself. The sound had her blood running ice cold. The screaming reached a hysterical crescendo as it mixed with the sound of tearing. She closed her eyes and turned her head away from her computer, but her expert listening skills couldn't block out the sound that was not clothing, and she felt like she was going to be sick.

As quick as the screaming started, it was over, and all was silent.

Hands shaking, Minetta reached for the headset and, with a great deal of effort, managed to plug it in before slipping the head piece back into place, the little microphone in front of her mouth.

"Sam? Sam, are you still there?" Silence was the only noise except for a few frogs and crickets singing in the night. "Sam, please answer me."

"Hello? This is constable Brown. Who is this?"

"Hi constable, this is nine one one operator, I.D. number three, three, three, seven, seven, seven. I was on the phone with the male party in distress. Is there any sign of a man in the vicinity?"

"No ma'am, I'm sorry, the only thing here is this phone and...." There was the sound of the constable moving around. "I see some claw marks and what may be a small clump of fur. There is no sign of a victim and no blood. I'm sorry, I think I'm too late, but I can't see any signs of a struggle that looked as if a body had been moved or dragged away. I will keep looking."

Minetta jotted down all the details of the call and then sat staring blankly at the computer screen until it transformed into little colorful flowers zipping around in its screensaver state. She wasn't going insane. She had heard the strange growls before Sam disappeared, so how could there have been no trace of him?

"Hey, girl, are you alright?" Penny asked, laying a hand on her shoulder.

"I don't know," she answered honestly. "Did you hear that? I mean, you had to of heard all that snarling and growling?"

"It was hard to hear anything else over the screaming. Come on, shifts over, and I'm going your way tonight. I'll drop you off at home. Seems like a good night not to be roaming around alone in the dark or riding a bus with a bunch of strangers."

"Yeah, thanks," she said, but her mind was still in Central Park with Sam and his mysterious disappearance.

Minetta grabbed her jacket and purse and paused, staring at the headset. The gut-wrenching terror in Sam's voice wouldn't leave her thoughts, and an odd image of massive midnight black dogs with red eyes popped into her mind. It was the way he begged her to forgive him like she alone could have given him the forgiveness he sought. She closed her eyes and shook her head to shake the strange visual.

"Let's go. This elevator is not going to hold on forever, girl!" Penny said.

"Coming!" She flicked off the screen and shivered as the sensation of being watched washed over her.

MINETTA

"Thanks for the lift," she said, getting out of Penny's car, waving. Her friend waited until the door was unlocked and the lights were on before she drove away.

As soon as she stepped inside the house, she froze. The lights to the basement were on, and she could hear the television blaring the Thursday night football game.

"Aw, come on! That was a foul. Any idiot with half a brain could see that." James's voice wafted up to her from the lower level. She sighed and proceeded to hang up her coat before making her way down the stairs. James was her boyfriend, or at least that is what she assumed they were.

They'd dated off and on throughout high school, but he had left her a few times to 'explore his options.' She didn't know why she kept letting him back into her life. Every time she thought about it and asked herself why, she couldn't come up with a logical answer. Maybe it was because he was familiar, and she knew what she was getting into with him. There was also the fact that her father had always liked him because he played the quarterback in high school. James was great at making parents fawn all over him with his charm and good 'ole boy smile while he talked about football and other things she had zero interest in.

At the thought of her dad, her heart felt heavy in her chest. The dull ache that had become an old friend since he'd passed had her rubbing at her heart. She'd thought with time, it would've gotten easier, and in some ways, it had, but most of the time, the thought of him made her long for her childhood and the moments she never got to have.

"James, what are you doing here," she asked as her feet touched the soft carpet of her newly finished basement.

She'd decided on a dove grey for the walls, but the carpet and trim was a color called off-white, snowball. The cushions and pictures on the wall added a splash of yellow and turquoise. It was the only room in the house she'd decorated to feel like her. It was supposed to be her she-shed, but James had taken it over for himself.

His feet were on her new coffee table, and she could see wet rings from his beer bottles littering the top. He was never going to wipe those up. She had the biggest urge to throw him out on his ass, but she knew she wouldn't. She was weak, and he knew it.

"What? Is that any way to greet your man," he asked, never taking his eyes from the television screen. The men on the screen ran around the field, their bright red and blue uniforms clashing as someone was tackled to the ground. "Woo! That's it, boys, take them down."

"I'm serious. How did you even get into my home? And where is Toby?" She looked around, assuming her dog would be down here with James but didn't see him.

"Babe, re-fuck-ing-lax, I had a key made. I mean, I'm always over here fixing something for you, Figured it was time I had my own key.

And that stupid mutt of yours is locked in the spare bedroom. I hate that thing. You really should get rid of it."

Minetta's mouth dropped open, not even sure what to say first as her mind fritzed. Before she could comment, James belched, the stench instantly hitting her. She waved her hand in front of her nose, wanting to gag.

"Here, can you get me another beer since you're up? Oh, and I ordered pizza. It should be here shortly. Good thing you got home when you did. I realized I forgot to bring my wallet."

Minetta snatched the bottle out of James's hand, and as soon as her back was turned, he cracked her hard on the ass. "Ouch! James, don't do that."

"Come on, babe, it was just a love tap. Lighten up, for fuck's sake. You're always such a pill."

Unable to deal with him right then, she marched up the stairs and put the empty beer on the counter. He could get his own beer if he wanted it. She was going to find her dog. Other than Penny, Toby was her best friend, and she hated that James treated him like a pest.

Her home was a simple two-level, two-bedroom, and bath-style house. She had exactly two plates, two bowls and two sets of cutlery. Penny always joked that she had a thing for *Jacob Two Two*. The colors upstairs were still the same bland neutral from when she moved in, not really caring if it was done up fancy or not. She had the odd picture and plant placed around the home, but nothing matched, and she was fine with that. It was completely unique and one of a kind. She pushed open the spare bedroom door, and Toby's large tail thumped happily on the twin bed that he dwarfed.

"Hey there handsome, was James mean to you," she cooed, and his tail wagged a little harder as his overly large body slid lazily off the bed to wander over. He was an English Mastiff, but even for his breed, he was massive. Reaching the mid-two hundreds in weight and adding in his height, he could have been classified as a small pony. She bent over and gave his large soft ears a rub as she kissed his sweet face. "Let's go for a walk." At the mention of his favorite word other than treat or bed, he padded noisily to the front just as the doorbell rang.

Annoyed all over again, she grabbed her purse and opened the front door only to have the pizza guy jump backward off the low landing as Toby let out a single woof. The sound was deep, and she laughed in her head as she figured it would look like the bark pushed the guy backward. She smirked a little. Toby wouldn't hurt a flea, but he sure as hell looked terrifying.

"How much is it?"

"Um, forty-four, ninety-one." The guy leaned in, holding the overly large pizza out.

"What the heck did he order," she grumbled to herself as she dug around for the money. "Stay," she said to Toby. She didn't need this guy to sprint away with the food. "Here's a fifty. Keep the change." She made the exchange, and the entire time the guy kept his eyes glued on Toby. "Your pizza is on the counter!" she yelled down the stairs.

"What about my damn beer?"

She bit her tongue to keep the sarcastic retort to herself. "Sorry, Toby needs to go out. You'll have to get it yourself." She could hear James swearing as she closed the front door. "Don't look at me like that. I know I'm a damn pushover, and I should dump his ignorant, selfish and lazy ass," she said to Toby's upturned face. He nudged at her hand with his head. "I will. I just need to get the nerve up. Come on, let's get that walk in."

The entire walk, all she could think about was Sam and what had happened to him. Could she have done more to get help to him sooner? Had it all been a prank meant to scare an operator? That happened more than people thought. People really could do the stupidest things, especially when alcohol or drugs were involved. Unfortunately, no new epiphanies came to her on the stroll.

The television was still blaring when she got back home, and she rolled her eyes, just wanting to get a quick bite to eat and some sleep. She marched down the stairs and just caught the tail end of James's conversation.

"I miss you, love you too."

She stopped dead in her tracks and stared at his smiling face. He was smiling like she hadn't seen him do in a long time. Even though she knew she didn't love him anymore, the idea of him cheating and being so blatant about it in her home hurt. He glanced over at her, and his face paled.

"Who was that," Minetta asked, crossing her arms over her chest.

"My mother, she said to say Hi and that she hates not seeing us more." He patted the couch cushion beside himself. "Come here, babe."

She nibbled her lip, unable to decide if he was telling the truth or lying to her again. She'd never known him to talk to his mother so sweetly, but... "I just came down to tell you I'm going to bed."

"What? It's early, and I thought I'd at least get a blowjob out of tonight. I did fix that tap in your bathroom like a week ago and haven't gotten a thanks." That was totally a lie. She'd made a delicious meal and bought him a case of beer as well as gave him a dreaded blowjob. She actually enjoyed sex and blowjobs, but it felt like work with him. Like she was prostituting herself out to have some help around her house. It made the entire encounter unpleasant.

"Are you joking right now," she asked, a rare moment of anger creeping into her voice.

"What do you mean?" James stood and crossed his arms over his chest.

She mimicked his pose. "Let's see. You make a key for my house without my permission. You stick my dog in a locked room and tell me I should get rid of him. Then you proceed to order pizza that I end up paying for, and I'll bet there isn't even a piece left for me."

He shrugged. "I was hungry. You know how I get when I'm hungry and don't eat."

"Right, well, that doesn't explain you swearing at me because I didn't serve you a beer like I'm your maid, and now I walk in on you and the girl you have on the side, on the phone, in my home. My home. You didn't even have the decency to go outside, or I don't know, go home to your place."

"Babe, come on, I swear that was my mother, and I only swore because the game was pissing me off. I was losing money on the game. I didn't mean to take it out on you."

"You always have an answer for everything."

He walked toward her, his face pulling down in the same stupid fake frown he had since they were teens. "Babe, don't be like that. You know I love you, and I'm sorry I was so distracted and rude when you got home."

He massaged her shoulders as he leaned in and kissed her forehead. She could feel her resolve begin to weaken. "You know you're the only woman I want. I mean, feel this." He grabbed her hand and laid it over the distinct bulge in his pants.

James was still just as good-looking as when they were teens. She had been a freshman and he a junior when they met. Of course, he was the popular jock, and as the resident nerdy girl, they made the perfect cliché. It had made her feel special to be dating the hot football god of the school. His shock blonde hair was perfectly styled and didn't have a spot of grey in it for being thirty years old. His bright blue eyes were still the sexiest she'd ever seen, and his tall body was fit in all the right places—yet she didn't feel anything anymore. There was no pull of excitement, and the once fluttery sensation she'd get whenever he looked her way had flown away. When she tried to picture her future, she couldn't imagine it with this man. He'd become a stranger with a face she recognized.

She pulled away from what felt like a stranger's dick and gave him a weak smile. "I'm sorry, I'm really tired. It was a long day."

"Fine, I'll just use my hand again, just like last time and the time before that. I don't know why I stick around," James mumbled as she made her way up the stairs.

She paused, her foot hovering over the next stair as she tried to will herself into telling James to get out of her home. Shaking her head instead, she made her way to the bathroom. Why was she always so weak when it came to him? She'd become one of the girls that called in needing help, and the anger burning in her chest was directed at herself.

The image staring back at her from the mirror over the sink looked dull with dark circles under her eyes. Her mother would have said her eyes looked like two piss holes in the snow. The thought made her smile a little as she turned on the cool water and splashed some of it onto her face.

Why couldn't she simply say what she wanted from people? Why couldn't she do something for herself for a change?

Gripping the edge of the sink, she sucked in a deep breath as she made up her mind that from now on, she was going to be more selfish.

FIVE

RIKER

"Oh my God, yes!" the girl I was fucking screamed and then covered her mouth, knowing the drill. I smacked her ass hard as punishment for the noise, and instead of accepting it as what it was, she groaned and came all over my dick. I pulled out to leave her to her writhing pleasure and moved on to the next ass sticking in the air.

I didn't bother to look at their faces, couldn't tell you their names, race, or fuck if they were even actually women. It didn't really matter. It was a hole to use when my dick got hard. It was an interesting and annoying feature of being on Earth for so long. The thing had a mind of its own and needed to be tamed. I'd tried beating it down with whatever was at arms reach in the beginning, completely horrified I couldn't control the stupid bodily reaction, but that only seemed to make it worse. In fact, it seemed to like being smacked—fucking weird.

The issue was I was busy, so spending what humans called "quality time" with someone was a waste of mine. Being a fallen angel did have an interesting perk that both women and men seemed to fawn over and made finding suitable holes as easy as ordering my espresso—I could fuck for hours and work at the same time. It was a challenge now to see how many women I could service in the time it took me to finish my reports. Sex, money, and a bit of gamesmanship, it really didn't get much better than that.

Once a week, a bed was brought into my office for the occasion, and the lines of women had gotten so long I invited Neven to join in the amusement. He was currently facing me, his own lineup of girls groaning and whimpering as he worked. Being only demon-born, he didn't have quite the same stamina, and I could see the sweat trickling down his chest as his hips thrust fast into the braying woman with the strange dangling tag around her neck.

"Hey, shut that one up," I bit out, and Neven reached forward, grabbing the woman by the hair. He yanked her up enough to clamp a hand around her gaping mouth as her eyes rolled back into her head with pleasure. "What is around her neck?"

"Oh, you like?" Neven held up the old chain with the large tag that seemed to be name identification.

"I guess. What is it for?"

Neven smiled wide as he dropped the chain and wrapped his hand in the woman's hair, riding her hard. "The ones I really like and want to come back, they get a name tag. This one is Bianca."

"They're human. What does it matter if they come back?"

"Think about it. We're always having to train them when they are new. It's tiresome. This way, the ones that are a good fuck and already know what I like and what is acceptable have the first chance to come back."

"Oddly, I find that thought process interesting. I may have to come up with my own labeling system."

My attention turned back to the tablet and the colorful pie charts.

"Shilo, can you lower the tablet a little but move the page up? I'm having trouble seeing the final projections."

"Of course, Sir," Shilo said and dutifully did as he was asked. Shilo had been one of the many unfortunate angels to somehow end up on the wrong side of the attack on Heaven and to walk the Earth forever, never aging, never able to go back to Heaven, visit Hell, or able to die. A permanent state of fucked is what I called it. I at least had my palace in Hell that I could go to get away from the hairless cats when I was tired of their company.

My pace picked up as the moaning reached the typical high-pitched wails of ecstasy. I hated that I couldn't use all my strength with humans. They were too weak to handle it, but it was a minor annoyance.

"You...are...the...fucking...best," the girl screamed.

"Shut up, I'm trying to work here, or I move on," I ordered.

"No, no, I'll be goo...ahhh, fuck I'm coming again!" Not only was this one a talker, but she was also a squirter, the clear liquid gushing out on my expensive duvet and then onto my one-of-a-kind rug.

Annoyed, I pulled out and moved on. "Shilo, make sure this one doesn't come back." Neven's idea was sounding better by the minute.

"Of course, Sir."

"No, please, don't cut me off. Please! I need you," the nameless girl I'd forget before she was out of the room wailed. She sounded like a wild animal as she was dragged away from the group.

The one named Bianca that Neven was working on gave another muffled cry as she came and went limp in his arms. Neven gave her an unceremonious shove to the floor for the guards to cart away as he moved on to the next in line.

"What do you think of the projections," I asked him.

"Honestly, they look a little low. There should be at least another three to five percent growth across the board," Neven said and then gave a small groan as he slipped into the next woman. Neven actually enjoyed sex more like a human would. I assumed it had to do with his lack of divine blood.

"I was thinking the same thing. Shilo, who do we have going over all of the stats and projections?"

"You have a team of eight individuals, Sir, but the manager of the department is Nikolas Novak."

The girl waiting waved her ass back and forth like a red flag to a bull, hoping to gain my attention. I was tempted to throw her out, but the fact she'd been quiet this whole time allowed for forgiveness. My dick slid into the third girl in the line just as the phone rang. The tablet showed that it was Skye calling, and I groaned in annoyance.

"Book a meeting with this Novak. I want to speak to him personally."

"Very well, Sir," Shilo said as I hit talk on the call.

The girl I had my dick in gave a long-drawn-out moan like a cow giving birth as she came. Skye lifted one delicate eyebrow at me.

"At it again, I hear."

"Well, it is Wednesday," I said as if that was all the answer I needed.

"Ri, you do know that Hump Day is just a saying about the middle of the week and not an actual thing, right," Skye asked, and I paused in my movements as I contemplated the information.

I shrugged, not really caring. "Whatever, it allows me to schedule everyone wanting to be serviced at one time. Much more efficient, and I get more accomplished."

"Such a sweet talker you are."

"I'm sensing sarcasm coming from that devilish mouth of yours, Skye. You know how I'm unfond of the bitch sarcasm."

"Hey Skye," Neven called out. Shilo turned the tablet around so Skye could see her brother.

"What the hell? I go away for a few days, and you find a harem to fuck?"

Anyone who didn't know the twins would have thought she was angry, but in reality, she was probably dipping a pair of fingers into herself with the visual.

"Riker is sharing. Should I be scared," Neven asked, flashing me a teasing smile.

"Who is that?" the girl I was fucking had the audacity to ask.

"I'm sorry, did you ask me something?" I glared at the girl.

"Yeah, is that your girlfriend or something?" She looked over her shoulder at me, and I could feel the seed of jealousy growing inside of her as clearly as I could feel her walls around my cock.

I pulled out of her because I had no time for jealousy. Fucking Envy was prospering in this city. I shouldn't be annoyed. Leviathan was like a little brother, but I was a greedy fucker, and I loved having my sin spread faster than a hooker's legs. I waved one of the guards over. "Blacklist this one and send in the next six."

The guard grabbed the girl around the waist, hoisting her over his shoulder.

"Put me down! I only got to come once," she cried out, smacking the guard's back. Unbeknownst to her, the guard was also a demon. If she continued to be a pest, I'd allow him to take her for a ride, which was a trip that had only a one-way ticket option available.

"You shoulda thought of that before you opened your big fuckin' mouth," the guard said, and I made a quick mental note to give the guy a bonus for his efforts.

"One moment." I held my finger up to Skye. She crossed her arms and rolled her eyes at me. She was one of the very few that could act that way and get away with it. She was my best friend, well, her and Neven. I got the biggest kick out of her. She was like a miniature supermodel, coming in at five feet tall with black curly hair and steel grey eyes. But because she was a demon, she had the strength of twenty human men. On more than one occasion, I'd watched her pitch a guy across a room for pissing her off. Neven was the gentler of the two personalities, and the differences didn't stop there. Neven stood a little taller than me at six feet five inches. His midnight black hair and steel grey eyes mixed with his perfect angular face had girls fanning themselves when he walked into a room. He was fit, but he had more of a swimmer's build like myself. With his trim waist and wide shoulders, he differed from some of our guards, who had more bulk.

Since my fall, Shilo had been with me, and the two demons had been with me almost as long. They also happened to be the only other two beings I considered a friend. My brothers and sisters, the rest of the Fallen were more like ice cream flavors, some were better than others, but Sloth I could do without though. I hated that demon. He'd always been a lazy pain-in-the-ass angel, but now on Earth, he'd become more useless than tits on a bull.

I looked over to the six girls that had just walked in. "Any of you been here before?" They all shook their heads no, their stupid giggles already irritating me. "Fine, here is the deal. I fuck you until you come. If you're lucky, twice. You kneel on the bed with your ass in the air and don't speak, don't ask me questions, and for the love of money, do your best not to make a mess on my rug." They nodded in unison, and I turned back to Skye. "Sorry about that. A bunch of new ones just arrived."

"More for me as well." Neven smiled wide. "My stamina is getting better. I'm up to thirty so far."

"Fifty-three and counting," I smirked as his face fell.

"You are one of a kind Ri, you really are, and I'm not sure if I'm jealous of you or happy for you," Skye said and tapped her chin as she pretended to think about it. I knew she was jealous. She'd always been jealous of the amount of sex I got and didn't share with her. It was fun lording it over her head.

"Did you have a reason for interrupting my work, or did you simply decide today was a good day to annoy me?" I positioned myself once more at the front of the line of wiggling asses and got to work. Shilo, the ever-perfect shadow, moved with me and held the tablet up once more for me to read.

"I thought you should know that Michael is sniffing around," Skye said, with a shrug of her shoulders. Like dropping that bomb on me was no big deal.

"Why do you think I would give a fuck about what that pompous, arrogant, good for nothing, white-winged, ass wipe does with his time?"

Skye let out a sharp bark of a laugh. "Well, he has been charged with making sure the apocalypse doesn't happen. I'm just sayin' if he's asking questions about you, it can't be a good thing," Skye said, picking at her blood-red nails.

"True enough. But, if he thinks I'm going to help him, he has another thing coming. That fucker turned his back on me and tossed my ass out when all I was trying to do was help." Distracted by the annoying topic, I hadn't noticed that my thrusting had become too hard for the mere human woman until she went flying off the other side of the bed. She screamed as she soared past Neven, who watched her naked ass sail by and hit the floor hard.

At first glance, you'd think she was injured with the limp way she was sprawled out, but the look on her face said quite the opposite.

"What was that," Skye asked as she peered at the screen as if a different angle would give her a better look.

"Oh my god, that was the best. Can I come back again," the unknown woman asked as she slowly sat up. Her hair was the perfect picture of just fucked as it stood out in every direction, and her once pristine makeup was smeared down her face from sweat.

"Since I said no questions, and you cannot follow orders, the answer is no, now get out. Actually, all of you get out. I'm annoyed now."

"Oh shit, give me a minute," Neven groaned and picked up his pace until he grunted. He flopped forward on the bed and pushed the used girl off the side. "Thank Lucifer, I didn't think I could last another six," Neven panted hard.

"But you're still hard," one of the other girls standing in the door said to me. She pointed to the substantial cock standing at attention.

"Nothing my hand or a little demon ass can't handle. Now go." The girl screwed up her face at the mention of a demon but didn't question and quickly jogged out the door.

"I hope you didn't mean my little demon ass?" Skye said sarcastically.

"You didn't seem to mind the last time I split that pussy open, but no, I was planning on using your brother since he's already here and ready."

"No, I'm not," Neven mumbled, his face planted firmly in the hoard of pillows.

"I was desperate, and it had been a while," Skye said. "It had nothing to do with your performance." Skye's lip curled up, her dark eyes glinting, which told me she was most certainly lying.

"Well, I guess I just won't fuck you anymore or give you screaming orgasms that make you pass out. Such a shame. Then again, Neven's ass is much tighter than your well-used pussy," I snarked back and watched her face fall.

I knew Skye had a thing for me. All demons were drawn to us Fallen. It was the order of things. Skye had taken to calling herself my fuck buddy, which apparently was a step up from a friend. I didn't care to be honest. She could call me whatever she wanted. It wouldn't change the fact she would never be anything more than just my friend.

"I called you to warn you about Michael, and this is the thanks I get?"

"Sir, I apologize for the interruption, but you have a meeting in five minutes about the merger of the telecommunications company," Shilo said.

I startled and blinked as I focused on his reserved face. I'd almost forgotten he was still holding the tablet he'd been so quiet and still. "Thank you Shilo. Well, I guess that is my cue to get going. Thanks for the warning, Skye. Are you going to Dai's fight club later?"

"Yeah, I got money down on a few matches. Might as well show up and give them my special brand of encouragement." A devious gleam flashed in her eyes as the tablet beeped for the next meeting.

"Call coming in. I'll see you there." I hung up before she could delay me any further. "Neven, get over her and spread your cheeks," I ordered, making him groan. "Are you complaining?"

"No, I just need another minute. You're a fucking beast."

I sighed and let my friend take the time he needed to prepare as I answered the call. It was his choice, and he'd only get fucked harder the longer he took.

"Good afternoon, gentlemen. Have you made a decision?"

CHAPTER
SIX

MINETTA sat in the lunchroom at work and held her head in her hands. She had to find a way to end things with James. When he'd finally come to bed, he'd rubbed his hands all over her body. The insistent touching woke her up even though she'd been sound asleep. She held herself perfectly still, hoping he'd take the hint and leave her alone. In the end, he acted like a rowdy teen as he practically dry-humped her ass until she rolled over. Unsurprisingly she gave in, figuring that would be the fastest way to get back to sleep. She hated herself for giving in. She hated that she didn't kick him out and demand her key back, and she hated that she was so weak. She was being emotionally abused, she knew it, and yet...

"Rough shift or rough night," Penny asked as she sat down across from her.

"Honestly, both." She lifted her head to stare at her friend. She loved how Penny's nose would crinkle just a little as she thought. Her pale skin was perfect like she was made of porcelain, and she'd shamefully been caught staring more than once at Penny's flawlessness. It seemed unnatural not to have a single blemish, a pimple, or a freckle.

"I keep telling you to leave that jerkwad. Do you want me to kick him out? Because I'll do it. I'll beat his ass all the way to curb so hard that he will never come sniffing around you again." Penny's hand clenched on the table, and Minetta had no doubt that Penny would follow through with the threat.

Minetta smiled, a small laugh escaping her throat as she pictured that in her mind. "I might have to take you up on that. I wish they had classes for learning how to become a badass or at the very least a step up from the spineless shmuck I've turned into."

Penny popped a grape into her mouth from her lunch bag and snickered. "Girl, I don't think there is a course to fix what's wrong with you, but you're no schmuck."

"Rude," she gasped and then laughed hard. "It's funny because it's so true, ugh I'm too nice. Who knew that being nice was an issue?"

"Right? I have an idea. I know. Why don't we get some dinner after work?" Penny's face lit up with the idea, but Minetta internally groaned.

"I don't know if I'm up for that."

"You're not up for a meal at a simple restaurant with a friend to have a few laughs?" Penny bit into her sandwich and gave her the death stare. The one that she gave anyone who dared to try and argue with her.

"You win. I need to go home and take care of Toby, but I can meet you after that." Minetta stood and tossed the rest of her uneaten food into her lunch bag.

"Done deal. I'll text you the location later. Did you want me to pick you up?"

"Nah, that's okay. You live across town, but I may take you up on a drive home? I'm not a fan of the late buses nor the walk to my house from the stop."

"You got it, Minny," Penny said and grinned wide.

The rest of the day had run smoothly enough. She didn't even have to deal with Jared and his asshole behavior. Small miracles.

But her luck couldn't last forever. It was raining when she stepped outside, and of course, she'd forgotten her jacket in the office. She stared up at the bland gray building and the floor she worked from outside and decided just to make a run for the bus. As she ran, her feet sloshed into puddles. Her socks and shoes filled with water, making her cringe. She danced from foot to foot, the cool rain already chilling her as she waited for the light to change. The walk sign flashed on, and she started to jog across the street.

Loud screeching had her swinging her head to the right. She sucked in a breath, paralyzed in her spot as a car barrelled toward her. Everything slowed down in her mind, the spray of water rising into the air as the car spun out of control, the look of horror on the driver's face, but it was her dog, Toby that made her heart ache. She hadn't made arrangements for him if she died. Would Penny remember to go and check on him? Panic filled her in that second as she braced for the car to crash into her.

Arms came out of nowhere and wrapped around her waist, pulling her out of the way at the last moment. She blinked, and just like that, everything was moving at full speed. The car's wheels squealed as it continued to spin past her like a child's toy as it hydroplaned on the water. The bumper had come so close that she could feel it brush against her dress pants.

The car stopped harmlessly up against a mailbox with a soft thud. She turned around to see the owner of the arms that had saved her life and stared up into the most piercing Nordic blue eyes. The man had to be a model. He had wide shoulders that felt muscled under her hands, and his tall height made her feel small, which was not unusual for her and her average height. His cheekbones were perfectly symmetrical and high. Any woman would kill to have them. Mix that with the arching eyebrows, flawless skin, and little dimple on his chin, and he looked as close to Heaven on Earth as one could get.

"Oh, thank the lord, I thought I was going to hit you for sure. Are you alright," the woman asked, running up to her. Her savior stepped back, and she wanted to reach out and yell, no, don't go. There was something very alluring about him.

"I'm fine, thanks to this man, but thank you. Are you okay?" she asked, her eyes roaming over the woman, assessing if she had any injuries.

"Just my pride. I really am sorry." The sound of a siren blared briefly as the police car pulled through the intersection and then blocked off the lane the lady's car was in to prevent a larger issue. "Oh, I better go, but I'm so happy you're alright."

Minetta turned back to the man that had just saved her. "Thank you. You saved my life. I don't even know how to repay you," she managed to stutter out.

His shoulder-length, honey-colored hair blew across his face, making him look even sexier, and her heart fluttered. She swallowed hard as she realized that he still had a hand on her waist. His body was much closer than appropriate for someone she'd just met, yet she found herself not caring.

His eyes flicked down, and she suddenly realized that the continuous downpour had made her white work blouse see-through, showing her lace bra underneath. Minetta wrapped her arms around her body and took a small step back from the stranger, his hand falling away. As it did, she took a deep breath like it was his hand that was creating the unusual connection between them, which of course, was crazy.

"It was my pleasure. The names Michael," he said and held out his hand for her to shake.

She unfolded one of her arms to reciprocate the gesture. "I...I guess I better get going. I'm getting wet." Oh god, could she have sounded any lamer? She thought, resisting the urge to smack her forehead.

"I can see that," he said, the corner of his mouth pulling up. "Here, take this." Michael pulled the long coat he was wearing off and offered it to her. Normally she wouldn't have accepted, but she was shivering from head to toe. "Where were you heading?"

"The bus around the corner."

He smiled wide like he was amused. "And where was the bus taking you?"

A flush crept up her neck, making her hot all over. "Home, I was heading home from work." For whatever reason, she felt compelled to continue to act ridiculous as she pointed across the road to the building she'd just left.

"Would you prefer a ride home?"

She gave him a small smile. "Thanks, but I better not."

She licked her lips as Michael's shirt began to cling to his body because of the heavy rain still falling, showing off that indeed her hands had felt the hard plains of chiseled muscle.

"Would it help if I told you I simply wanted to be nice, but now I kind of want my coat back?" He bit his bottom lip, and she stared in awe. That face was made for high-end fashion.

"Okay, sure, thank you. I guess I can accept. I mean, you did save my life, so you can't be a serial killer." She was losing her mind. It was the only explanation for what she'd just said.

Michael laughed, and she internally groaned. It was like she had verbal diarrhea. "I'm parked over here." He pointed to the black Lexus, and she fell into step beside him. He opened the door for her, and she slipped into the passenger seat. The fresh scent of new-car invaded her senses.

Michael slid into the seat in a single fluid motion. He was so graceful. He reached forward and turned the heat on high, and she sighed as the warmth blasted out. "So, where am I heading?" he asked as they pulled out on the main street.

"Not far. Do you know where Avarice street is?"

Michael let out a short burst of laughter, and she stared at the side of his amused face wondering what she'd said that was so funny. "I actually know exactly where he is."

"He?"

"Sorry, I meant 'it.' I know where *it* is, not he." The teasing look in his eyes made her wonder if he really did. "So, do I get the honor of knowing your name? I mean, it seems only fair since you know mine."

She flushed again and didn't need the blasting hot air anymore. "I'm sorry, I'll blame the near-death experience on my bad manners. My name is Minetta, but my friends call me Minny."

"Minetta," he said, and she almost turned into a puddle on n his car. "I like your name. It's beautiful."

"Thanks." She stared out the window, so she didn't creep him out by staring at the side of his face the entire drive.

"Do you live around here?" she asked, breaking the silence.

"I tend to move around a lot. My job doesn't allow me to settle in one location for very long."

"That must be difficult. Do you mind if I ask you what you do?" She was curious about this man. There was something unusual about him that drew her in and coated her like a warm bath, yet gooseflesh covered her skin making her feel itchy at the same time. It was very conflicting.

"I'm in the negotiations field."

"Really? Wow, I would've sworn you were a model or maybe a

movie star, and I just can't stop saying stupid things, so I'm going to be quiet now." She stared down at her hands, holding her small purse in her lap.

"No, please, I love your honesty. It's genuinely refreshing. But, to answer your question, it can be difficult, especially when the people you're negotiating with are stubborn and difficult. I have had to deal with the same people multiple times. And let me tell you, they are a piece of work."

"I know those types, frustrating indeed. So how long are you in New York for," she asked, surprising herself with her own boldness.

"I'm not sure yet. It's going to depend on a great many things." He glanced over and gave her a smile. "Do you have any plans for the evening?"

"Yes, I'm going out with my girlfriend for dinner. She thinks I don't get out enough and that my social life is deader than an orgy night at a convent." This time, she did smack herself in the forehead because she couldn't come off any worse than she already was. Maybe Penny was right, after all. Maybe she really did have something clinical and unexplainable wrong with her.

Michael laughed hard, the sound so sweet it was like a choir of singing cherubs in his car. She shivered again as the sound made her heart skip a beat in her chest. She couldn't help laughing along with him as tears trickled down his cheeks. She stared at the tears that seemed to sparkle before he wiped them away.

"You are very amusing, Minny. I think this is you," Michael said, and she looked around, not even realizing that they had come to a stop. How had she missed the rest of the drive? Had her brain been in a fog for twenty minutes?

"Thanks again." Minetta pushed open the door and took the coat off, quickly folding it to lay on the seat. She leaned in the car and forced herself to at least ask, "Did you want to have coffee sometime? Hopefully, when it's not raining, or I don't need saving?"

"You don't need saving Minetta. You never have." He reached out and ran his thumb over her cheek. "I'd be delighted to spend more time with you. Here, put your number in my phone." She blinked and sucked in a breath like she was a dolphin coming up for air. His comment should've come off strange like he'd known her longer than a few minutes, yet for the life of her, she couldn't figure out why she should be concerned. It was there on the edge of her thoughts but then would slip away again.

She looked at Micheal and then blushed as he unlocked his phone and handed it to her. She tapped her number in and saved it before handing it back.

"Minny?"

"Like I said, it's what my friends call me."

"Is that what we are," he asked, his voice caught between teasing and panty-dropping sexy as hell.

"I'm not sure yet, but I'd like to find out," she said and then closed the door. She had absolutely no idea where her small burst of confidence was coming from, but she was going to ride it. She walked to the door and then waved.

Maybe her luck was turning around.

CHAPTER
SEVEN

MINETTA had never been to this part of the city. It had an old gritty edge with rugged architecture, narrow alleys, and poorly lit streets. She'd got off the bus one stop too early, so she found herself jogging down the sidewalk for the second time today. A few people were standing around outside the different establishments, but for the most part, the street was quiet. The gold and green sign announced she'd reached her destination, and just as she placed her hand on the handle, a tingling stirred in her gut.

It was an odd sensation. She stared around the mostly quiet road for the sensation that was steadily increasing. The hair on the nape of her neck stood as if she'd come into contact with something charged with electricity. She took a moment to look up at the night sky, worried she was about to get hit by lightning. That would be her luck. Meet the hot guy and die before she got to see him again.

But all that was above her was perfectly clear, and millions of little stars shone in the distance. A revving reached her ears, and she looked down the street as an expensive car crested the hill. The bright glaring bulbs of the headlights blinded her, and she had to put her arm over her face to ward off the insufferable brightness.

The strange tingling turned into a thrumming, a heat that pulsed in her veins. She let go of the pub's door handle and stared at her hand, but the sensation remained. She looked at the car again that looked like something from a sci-fi movie, as it pulled over to the curb a block or so away.

It seemed strange that such an expensive vehicle would come to this part of the city, but it really wasn't any of her business. She shook off the strange feeling and yanked open the door before she made herself any later. She instantly fell in love with the unusual décor and the mismatched tables and booths. It was like the place had started fifty different renovations but stopped before any were completed. She stared at the green glass chandeliers as she trotted over to Penny's booth.

"I'm sorry, I know I'm running late," Minny said as she scooted into the green leather booth across from Penny.

"No worries," Penny said, her mouth stuffed full of nachos. Penny laughed as she stared at the full cheeks protruding like a chipmunk.

"This is a super cute Irish Pub," Minny said, looking around. You could tell that this place had been here a very long time. There was a feeling in the air like the walls had ghosts and could talk if asked. Black and white images hung framed behind the bar, each one a famous gangster from history only added to the mystique. You could still smell stale smoke even though small no-smoking signs were hung all over the walls.

"How did you find this place?"

Penny took a swig of her pint before answering. "It came up on one of my phone apps as a must-try for a taste of old New York and thought, why not?"

"How's the food," Minny asked, reaching over and taking a nacho to try. They were perfectly salted and surprisingly well seasoned, and they hadn't been stingy with the salsa, cheese, or ground beef.

"Great so far," Penny answered and then cocked her head and stared. For a brief moment, Minetta would've said Penny looked like a bird and not a person.

"There is something different about you." Penny waved a finger in front of her face. "You seem brighter, happier, more like the old you before you let that piece of mooching, cheating, dog shit back into your orbit."

At the mention of James, her mood fell. "I know he is all those things. I just don't know how to end it, and I know this is going to sound silly, but my dad loved him. He had this dream that I'd end up marrying a football star. It's like by kicking James out, I'm kicking the last bit of what my dad loved and knew out of my house."

"Minny, I know you miss your dad, but tell me honestly, do you really think he would want you to live your life with a man that treated you so terribly? Besides, James didn't make it as a football star. He can barely hold down a job, any job. And don't forget you still have Toby."

She swiped another nacho and popped it into her mouth. "I know you're right."

"Then you need to woman up and kick him to the curb, and the sooner, the better. It's way creepy he made a key for your house without asking you. Next thing you know, he's going to move his baby mama on the side in when you're at work and kick you out, claiming it's his house."

"That's oddly specific." Minny raised a brow at Penny, who shrugged.

"Meh, I call it like I see it, and that boy is nothing but a walking penis of pain. If it were me, I'd be changing the locks as soon as possible." Penny waved a chip over the large plate, and she was tempted to steal it. "I'd rather cuddle a cactus."

"Okay, enough about James, please. I don't want to think about him or the problem I have with trying to get rid of him for good."

"I may know a few people who can help you in that department if you want?" Minetta's mouth fell open, and Penny laughed hard. "You should see your face."

"Hey, you wanting anything," the bartender called out from the bar, his thick Irish droll making her smile along with the tattoos that sleeved both muscular forearms. She had a thing for accents and tattoos. Apparently, just because she was the ultimate good girl, she still fell into the trap of loving the bad boy.

"I'll take a pint of your best, and I'll need a menu, please." She smiled as he gave her a wink and sauntered away.

"He likes you, and that man would not be a bad way to get yourself on a new horse. Do you want me to set that up?" Penny teased.

"No, geez. I can talk to a guy on my own, you know. Besides, I kinda already met someone, sorta anyway." The stupid smile wouldn't leave her face.

"I knew it," Penny yelled, causing the few seated in the pub to turn their way. "What's he like? How did you meet him? Tell me everything!" Penny gave a little squeal that made her laugh.

The bartender picked that moment to bring the pint over along with a menu.

"Thank you," she said. He lingered, and figuring he wanted her order, she opened the menu and picked the first burger she saw.

"Good choice," he said but continued to stand at the table, staring at her rather than taking down what she wanted. Minetta squirmed under the heated stare, but Penny came to her rescue, thankfully.

"Uh, hello." She waved, and the bartender finally looked Penny's way. "I'd like two pounds of your hottest wings and an order of your firehouse fries." He nodded, taking the hint this time, and walked away.

"So, give me the details. Who is this guy?" Penny practically bounced on her side of the booth.

"He actually saved me from getting hit by a car. It was kind of crazy, and then he offered me a ride home."

Penny cocked her eyebrow at me. "He just swooped in and saved you, some random stranger, and you let this person drive you home? I'm starting to understand why James is still around."

"Hey, if this is going to turn into a bash Minny night, I'm out." She crossed her arms over her chest.

Penny sighed but nodded. "I'm sorry. Please continue. What does he look like?"

Minetta stared at the wall behind Penny as she dug into the memory of the stranger from earlier. She rambled on and on, and the more she said, the more Penny looked worried and not pleased. "What is it? What's wrong?"

"Nothing, he just sounds too flawless, you know? You can never trust the ones that look too perfect. Did you get a name of this way too sexy, life-saving stranger?"

"Yeah, his name is Michael."

Penny spat her beer out on the table, choking. Jumping up, Minetta dashed around to help her friend by patting her back. "Are you okay?"

Penny nodded and stood from the booth. "Just swallowed too much too quickly. It went down the wrong way. I'll be right back."

Minetta stared after her friend's retreating form as she made her way to the restroom. She thought that Penny would be happy for her, but she was getting a distinct impression that Penny was most certainly not.

EIGHT

R IKER

I pulled the Valkyrie into the VIP parking outside Dai's underground fight club. The sign above the door proudly announced *Fallen Patience Massage Parlor*. I sneered at the name—Dai was one of the few Fallen I had time for because she'd been as much of a victim as I'd been that day. Besides, Dai had ambition and built not one but many very profitable fight clubs. I should know. I gave her the start-up capital and kept a stake in the game as part of the contract.

Opening the car door, the demon waiting to take the vehicle to underground parking ran over and bowed deeply at the waist. "Firrr selgrith ogdrikos mulgrumon drag'drimuus?"

To any human, it would've sounded like the man was speaking jibberish, but I was very well versed in all the demon dialects. I'd made it a point to learn each one when I was first tossed from Father's glittery perfect home. Well, it wasn't perfect. That was the best-kept lie of all. It was his way or no way, and don't you dare have a mind of your own unless you're human, then it was completely fine to act like a savage and still be loved.

My jaw twitched with anger, but I kept my cool. I wasn't letting old resentments ruin my night.

The demon offered to clean my car, so I slipped him a hundred to do the job. Why not have it detailed while I was inside? Best case scenario, I got a clean car. At worst, he scratched my baby, and I got to kill this demon in a horrific fashion and take back my money.

I rounded the front of the car, buttoning up my tailor-made suit, and stopped in my tracks. I looked over my shoulder and then lifted my nose and sniffed the air trying to gauge the cause for the tingling sensation that was rapidly spreading all over my body. My eyes scanned the empty and darkened street. The only movement had been a random human walking into a pub, but that couldn't be the cause. I turned in a circle and looked up to the sky.

This had to have something to do with Michael's sudden and unexpected appearance. The archangel never bothered to come down off his fluffy white horse unless he was planning on trying to fuck some more shit up for the Fallen. Why he and Father couldn't just leave us alone was beyond me. There had been a great many times over the years since my fall that I felt like a bug in a jar, always poised for their amusement. Like having to live down here wasn't punishment enough. No, they had to poke at us with a stick, too.

Fuckers.

I was having none of it.

I marched to the message parlor's front entrance and pulled open the door. The petite demon behind the counter bowed and then pressed a button to grant me access to the lower level where the real fun was. There was another demon waiting for me at the elevator. Once inside, the demon used the special key to activate the lift. The mind-numb-

ingly instrumental music made me want to rip my ear drums out before
they bled from boredom.

The antique lift rattled as it came to a halt, and the doors slid open.
The pounding heavy metal music was a stark contrast to the tinkling
elevator music, and the rush of greed floating in the air invaded my
body. I could hear the cheering before I stepped out of the lift and the
distinct sound of bones breaking, followed by more cheers. Demon
Cheering 101, there is no 'oohing and awing' at a demon fight club. The
bloodier and more horrific the fight and demise were, the happier the
audience was.

This place was like an all-you-can-eat buffet for me, and my skin
sang with the pulse of insatiable greediness wafting off everyone. I also
knew this was partially why Dai, otherwise known as Wrath, had
chosen fight clubs as an establishment to own. The greed was so thick
in the air I could almost see the slithering golden strands wrapping
their way around those that cheered and continued to bet their lives
away. Each one of those down by the cage dreamed of a big payday.
They all craved to have more, be the best, hold power, and be as
worshipped as a Fallen. The only other place I could find this much
energy was when I visited the stock exchange floor. You could never
find more greedy people than those that worked there. I smiled at the
memory of the last time I paid them a visit. I would've stayed in the
middle of the floor forever if they hadn't closed and gone home for the
day. I had to be careful not to go there too often. It was easy to get
caught up in the surge of the power like a drug.

The fight club was the place to be for demons that lived topside.
There were a few establishments across the city that demons owned
that served the community, but for the most part, if you were a demon,
you came here every night. Dai had done an amazing job building the
underground rings and an even better job at promoting them. I stood at

the mouth of the entrance as the strobe lights flashed in time to the music. Those standing around lifted their hands in the air, waving demon money so that they could place their bets. Demon money was known as verok. It was made of black rectangular pieces of rock that could be used for many things, but the most popular use of the money was for favors.

To have favors owed by any demon, especially higher-level demons, was important in Hell. You either were the toughest motherfucker born, or you learned to surround yourself with those that could protect you. It was similar to a max security human prison on steroids. To not do so was certain death in the lower plains, survival of the fittest at its most crude. One thing you didn't want to become was a demon's fuck toy.

A loud roar ripped from the Gorgon demon in the cage. The large-scale covered demon was one of Dai's most popular demons. Long streams of saliva dripped from the double-headed beast as it held the smaller demon up against the bars of the cage.

"Kill him! Kill him! Kill him," those that were standing around the cage chanted.

Another roar and the large tentacled arms gripped its opponent like a python. Luckily, I was standing far enough away that when the head popped off the lesser demon's body, I didn't get hit with any of the green tendrilled gore or black blood. Those that had gathered jumped up and down as the splatter rained down on them. Small fights broke out amongst the demons that had lost their verok while others cheered and hissed to keep others from stealing what they'd won.

I stared at the glob of green demon guts that had landed at my feet and stepped over the mess, making sure it didn't touch my new shoes. The main bar and VIP area sat to the left of the hexagon arena. It was raised and gave the best view in the house. I wandered in that direction. Pausing at the bar, I leaned against one of the silver skulls that made up the long decorative piece and gave the waitress a wink. The leggy demon scampered over on her four legs, her long teal braids bouncing as she came.

"Well, hello handsome, what can I get for you this evening? Two pussies, perhaps," the pretty Shexta demon asked. The Shexta were known for their wild multiple donor sex parties. The double clenching pussies allowed for a number of interesting positions and partner varieties. But, their pussies had a drugging effect that tended to keep the donors working for months at pumping their seed into a Shexta until she was pregnant. Many had awoken months later, their cocks raw and their memories nothing but a blur. With a Shexta, you always found yourself an unwitting baby daddy when the discarded babe was dropped at your door. For this reason alone, I made sure that I never fell into the trap of that temptation no matter how much others raved about how amazing the sex was. The last thing I wanted was offspring —demon, human, angel, or otherwise.

"I'll take a martini, shaken, not stirred, and extra dirty."

"Oh, I can make it as dirty as you like," she smiled, a hint of fang showing.

"Back off, Gina, this one is mine for the night," Skye appeared beside me, her hand not wasting any time before giving my ass a squeeze.

"Does this mean I'm forgiven for my lack of civility," I drawled, my eyes openly roaming over her body.

"I don't know. Are you planning on fucking me tonight?"

Skye looked good in her blood-red outfit. The dress was skin-tight and short enough to provide easy access for later. Her thigh-high boots matched and provided an extra four inches to her height. Her long black hair was knotted up in some high-Hell fashion that all the female demons were doing at the moment, while the black make-up made her grey eyes pop.

"Possibly. What do you have under that dress?" In typical Skye fashion, she simply sat one leather-clad foot up on the bar, the dress rising and giving me a perfectly unobstructed view of what lay beneath. She flicked the silver ring that was a new edition to the tip of her clit and let out a little moan. "Intriguing indeed."

"Skye, for Hell's sake, give the man enough time to get a drink in before you start with that shit." Neven rolled his eyes as he wandered over to join us. I held out my fist for Neven to hit.

"Your sister has a one-track mind."

"Trust me, she is not in need of servicing. She made me fuck her six times when I got home from work. I'm surprised I made it here at all after the extra fucking-workout," Neven said and leaned against the bar like he was indeed worn out.

I laughed hard at the image of Neven hiding from his sister. "What was the special occasion?"

"She said it was to honor the gift of Asmodeus or some shit. She is a sex addict. That's all there is to it." Neven crossed his arms to glare at his sister.

"I didn't hear you complaining while you were stuffing your cock into my mouth." Skye pulled her boot off the bar and smoothed down the leather until it was wrinkle-free once more.

"Here you go," the bartender, Gina slid the obscenely large drink across the bar. It had extra olives, which made me smile. There was something stuck to the bottom of the glass, and when I pulled it off, it had Gina's name and number. She gave me a wink and licked her lips before heading off to tend to another patron.

I held out the napkin to Neven. "In case you're interested."

"Hell to the fuck no," Neven said, crumpling the napkin and tossing it away.

"VIP?" I nodded toward the plush area, and the still quarreling siblings followed. The demon blocking the entrance bowed deeply before stepping aside to let me pass. The long chains that hung on its body jingled with the movement.

"Mammon." Its voice was rough, like it swallowed a handful of razor blades.

Not bothering to acknowledge the demon, I walked past and looked for the booth with the best view. A number of demons that I didn't recognize were in the booth I wanted, but as soon as I glared in their direction, they bolted, leaving the booth unoccupied.

The next round was about to start, and the cage was quickly getting slippery with guts and gore, which would only add to the excitement. I sat, taking in the next opponents as they made their way into the cage. Skye continued to stand and stared down at me, her face looking ridiculous as she pushed her lips out in a typical fake human pout.

"Fine, take a seat," I said, and she immediately found her place on my lap. She snaked her arm around my neck while her hand wasted no time in undoing my pants.

"Do you have a recommendation?" I asked, and Skye paused in her action to look at the stage. She had an uncanny ability to pick the winner.

"I'd take the Jorkoran over the Sarzitkur. I've seen it fight before, and it is sneakily good for its smaller size."

I nodded, but as the fight began, I couldn't see well around her body. Sighing, I plucked her off my lap to place her on the floor between my legs. "You were making a better door than a window. If you want my dick, suck it from down there."

"You're an asshole Ri."

"And yet you keep coming back," I said, and she rolled her eyes but got on her knees.

"You betting tonight," Neven asked.

I scoffed and rolled my eyes at my friend. "You know I don't bet. I don't need luck to make money."

"It's not all about the winning. It's about the thrill of the gamble."

"Don't talk foolish, I don't gamble with my money."

"Whatever man." Neven held his hand up and called over the bookie and handed him a thick stack of the verok to be placed on the demon that Skye recommended.

I rolled out my shoulders and got comfortable as Skye continued to work over my cock. "Hey, Neven, any word on what Michael may be after this time?" Neven had the most reliable sources and was the most cunning at gathering useful information of anyone I'd ever come across. It could be the fact that he was half Imp, or it could be that he was a genius when it came to computers and all that interweb stuff. Either way, if anyone were going to find out what Michael, the all great and mighty pickle up my ass, was up to, it would be him.

"No, I haven't had time to put out any real inquiries. I've been a bit preoccupied today. My ass is still sensitive, by the way."

"Are you complaining?"

"Not at all. You can go harder next time," Neven smiled, his handsome face shifting just enough that he could pass for a man or a woman depending on the light. "As far as Michael is concerned, anything with him always gives me the willies."

"The willies?" I raised an eyebrow at the word. "Ouch! Skye, don't bite."

"But you taste like candy," her raspy voice laced with lust. "I want to swallow you whole as you come in my throat."

"Okay, you seriously need to lay off your visits to Lust's palace. You always turn into such a whore after you pay that place a visit."

"Oh please, I was always a whore, and the parties are fucking awesome. I wish you'd come with me sometime."

I stared at Skye to see if it would register that she'd insulted herself, but as the seconds ticked by, she resumed bobbing her head on my cock. I realized she didn't see it that way. I mean, I had my Wednesday, but for her, if her eyes were open, it was enough of a reason to fuck whoever was in arms reach.

"Do you think He." Neven pointed toward the sky mean my Father. "Didn't give Lust a body on purpose? You know for choosing Lucifer's side?"

"Who knows, but it's certainly possible. I wouldn't put it past Him. I can't imagine not having a consistent body. No wonder he's a bitter prick. I mean he always was an arrogant jerk, but he's been unbearable since our fall."

I turned my attention back to Neven as he typed away on his multiple phones. "Ri man, Michael's mission is like deep undercover. Everyone is coming back with crickets. I know he can't be here to put his feet up and take a load off, but none of my usual sources know why he has suddenly shown up, or why he is asking about you."

I sipped my perfect martini, the flavors intoxicating on my pallet. The fighters in the cage were rolling around in the dirt, but I couldn't concentrate on what they were doing. My mind kept playing over all the possibilities of why I was being sought out. A small moan left my lips as Skye's talented tongue indeed lapped at my shaft like I was her favorite treat.

As Skye predicted, the bright blue Jorkoran pinned the other demon, and even though this match didn't end in a head popping off, the opponent was going to need at least a week to heal from the deep lacerations. Neven smiled as the verok holder came to pay Neven his winnings.

"I do have one theory," Neven said, rubbing his chin once he got resettled.

"About Michael?" I moaned again. Skye looked up at me from under her midnight black eyelashes and smiled.

"The prophecy about how an apocalypse is to happen and the Fallen are the keys to stopping it or opening the gateways. Maybe he is trying to stop that. I mean, Lucifer has been hard at work to make sure he can take over Earth."

"Maybe, with Michael, you never know. He seems to be the only one that can get away with pissing Father off or disobeying his orders and still sitting on his pretty pedestal." I laid my head back against the booth cushion and relaxed into what Skye was doing. "I do know that I'm not helping him. Even if he were to get down and suck my cock as he begged for my forgiveness, I wouldn't help my so-called brother."

Just then, Skye did a particularly talented maneuver, and my afore-mentioned cock exploded in her mouth. I groaned while she continued to suck every last drop that I offered. She plopped herself down on the booth seat, wiping some excess liquid off her chin. She proceeded to stick her fingers in her mouth and lick up every bit.

"That was delicious, so are you going to invite me over tonight or what?"

I looked into her eager eyes and really wanted to say no. I had a million things on my agenda tomorrow, but I was having a rare moment of generousness and nodded my head yes. She smiled seduc-tively and then jumped up to presumably go and get her own drink that wasn't me.

"You do know she is getting attached, right?" I looked over my shoulder at Skye and then at Neven and lifted my shoulders, not really caring. "You did make her night, though," Neven said.

"I can make it two if you'd like to join again. I'm going to be up all night anyway."

Neven squirmed, his ass shifting from side to side. "I really shouldn't. I've been trying not to be so needy. It's hard trying to be a good demon."

I looked at his serious face and laughed. "Is that what you really want?" Neven shook his head no, his eyes flashing green as his half-demon side made an appearance. I leaned in and whispered in his ear. "You know you can't resist me, and I always get what I want."

Neven shivered and nodded slowly.

Tonight was shaping up to be not as boring as I thought after all.

CHAPTER
NINE

MINETTA jumped with the loud beeping noise. Penny hadn't been at work yesterday, which made the whole strange dinner with Penny continue to dance around in her mind. She sent Penny a text and got an 'all is well, see you next week' with a smiling emoji, but it had still taken her forever to fall asleep. Penny seemed fine when she came back from the washroom, but there was something about Penny's initial reaction that nagged in the back of her mind. On the bright side, this was James's hang-out-with-the-boys weekend, and he left a day early. So that blissfully meant she didn't have to deal with him or that situation for now.

She leaned up on her arms and looked down to see Toby. His big furry body was the reason why her legs were going numb. His entire body was draped over her lower limbs, and he didn't seem like he had any intention of moving. With a great deal of effort, she got the first one out from underneath him and then pulled her second leg free. He was such a cute mammoth.

A deep rumbling groan was his answer to her movement as he rolled onto his back. "Don't you complain to me, Mister. You could've moved, you know."

She quickly showered and checked the temperature for the day. It was supposed to be hot with no chance of showers, a perfect Friday for a fundraiser. There was an annual triathlon taking place downtown, and since they'd agreed to donate a large sum of the profits to the food bank she volunteered at, it only made sense that she worked for it too. Her boss hadn't been thrilled to give her a day off so she could volunteer, but since she rarely took time off, he couldn't find a reason to argue.

She rummaged around in her closet and finally decided on a pair of cut-off white shorts and the T-shirt the volunteers were supposed to wear.

Toby followed her downstairs, and she gave him his usual breakfast while she prepared her green tea and oatmeal with fruit. The latest Doja Cat song came on the radio, and she hummed along to it. Toby let out a woof and twisted his head, looking at her. "What? Is my humming that terrible too?" She laughed.

"Come on, you. I got permission to take your overgrown butt with me," she teased and held up Toby's leash. Grabbing her miniature backpack and her sidekick, she opened the door and swore. "Shit!"

Her heart hammered as she stared into Penny's face, her hand raised poised to knock. "Holy hell, Penny, you just scared the bejesus out of me."

Penny laughed, her bright blue eyes smiling. "I'm pretty certain there is no holy in Hell, but I get the saying. I didn't mean to scare you. Are you off somewhere?"

She pointed to the logo on the shirt with the word volunteer splashed across it. "I thought I told you about it?"

"You probably did, you know me, always forgetting stuff. Well, did you want to play hooky from the race and hang with me instead? I felt bad for my behavior the other night and thought I could make up for it. I wasn't on the schedule today, and when I called work to see about us having lunch, they said you didn't come in."

"Oh, that's really sweet, but you didn't have to drive all the way over here to see if I was okay. I'd scheduled the day off awhile ago but forgot to mention it."

Penny held up a plastic bag. "I got chicken soup. Hey, why don't we go to the beach or go shopping? Heck, we could even rent a cabin for the night, and Toby here could come as well," Penny said and smiled wide.

She lifted an eyebrow at Penny. "I appreciate the offer, but I'm looking forward to helping out today. Besides, there's no need to apologize." She lifted a shoulder and let it drop. "Girl, we are all prone to having strange days."

"Oh, okay." Penny looked around and then down at her feet, and she immediately felt guilty. "Do you think they would want another volunteer? I don't have anything else going on and would still like to hang out."

Her mood lifted, and she smiled wide at her friend. "Yes, I think they would be more than happy to have an extra pair of hands." She'd met Penny not long after she moved to New York, and they'd become fast friends, which was a good thing because she'd lost all of hers years prior. That happens when you spend all your time at a hospital instead of going to the movies or getting drunk at parties. You quickly become a non-factor. Her mother said they were never really her friends in the first place, but it was still a difficult time, and Penny had been exactly what she needed.

"Here, let me put the soup in the fridge, and we can get going," she said, taking the bag from Penny and heading toward the kitchen.

Stepping out into the sun, she locked the door, and the two of them made their way down the street. A man passed and stared at her and then at Penny. She thought that he was being flirty, but a girl walking in the same direction on the opposite side of the street kept looking over.

"Is it just me, or is everyone staring at us today?" she asked as a car slowed, and the passenger glared at her. What was everyone's problem?

"What? Oh, no, I hadn't really noticed. I mean, it is the city. You tend to get odd things happening on the regular."

"This is true," she said as they reached the bus stop.

The bus driver had been reluctant to let a dog the size of a pony on her bus, but when Toby licked her hand and laid his head on her lap, she laughed and agreed. Toby had that effect on most people. He was a suck magnet.

As they neared the location of the race, it was easy to tell something big was happening. Balloons in bright blue and green lined the route and created a massive arch over the finish line. One of the local radio stations had agreed to play music, and you could hear the upbeat tunes before they exited at their stop. There were long lines of people waiting all over the place to either get signed up, grab a free T-shirt, or purchase memorabilia.

A warm fuzziness enveloped her as she walked toward the ever-growing crowd. "Isn't this great?" Minetta looked over at Penny, but she was staring around like she was looking for the Boogeyman to jump out at her. "Are you alright? You're looking a little tense?"

A smile that didn't reach Penny's eyes spread across her face. "Just amazed is all. This is a lot of people."

"Are you nervous of crowds?"

"No, nothing like that." Penny looked over her shoulder, and Minetta followed her stare but didn't see anything out of the ordinary.

"If you've changed your mind about volunteering, it's completely fine. I'll understand if you're not comfortable?"

"I'm good, I swear. I'm just odd. I have odd moments." Penny made a weird face, and Minetta laughed hard.

"You really are, but you're also the best friend anyone could ask for. Thanks for coming. It means a lot." Minny grabbed Penny's hand and gave it a squeeze. Penny stared at her, a shimmer of a tear in her eye. "Oh, don't go getting all emotional on me. This is a fun day. We're here to raise some money, eat junk food from those food trucks, and I know you're going to love ogling the guys in their shorts with no shirts." Minetta smiled and wrapped her arm around her friend's shoulder as she led her toward the volunteer entrance.

There was definitely something bothering Penny, but that was fine if she wasn't ready to share. She'd be here whenever she was. She realized that she didn't really know much about Penny's past, especially when it came to her family or friends before she moved here from Oregon. Maybe it was the name Michael that had given her pause, maybe something had happened to her, and that had been the guy's name. Goodness, if she triggered her friend accidentally, she'd feel terrible.

Minetta hated the idea of someone hurting her friend. In fact, if that was the case and someone had, she would be livid. She didn't care about herself but no one messed with her friends and family.

Toby nudged her hand, and she looked down at him and smiled. Or dog—never mess with a girl's dog.

CHAPTER
TEN

R^{IKER} I yawned as I pulled the Valkyrie into the underground parking of the office building. The triathlon's finish line was right outside the office doors. I'd been wise enough to open the thousand-plus spots for competitors to park—for a ridiculous amount of money, of course.

"Sir," the valet said as I got out of the shining silver vehicle and stretched. It had been a late and very fun night indeed, but I'd only got an hour's sleep and was paying the price now. I never had this issue in Heaven or even Hell, but here on Earth, we Fallen had reduced powers, and we actually had to eat and sleep on a regular basis. Seriously, it was almost annoying as my dick standing on its own accord.

Reaching in the car, I grabbed the duffel bag and then let the valet take the car to my special spot. I'd had one spot made for myself that was three times as wide as a normal one and had a protective median round the spot's edge. I wasn't taking any chances that my beautiful baby would get scratched by some reckless minivan driver.

The street was already thriving with activity. One thing I never understood was why all the sins didn't park themselves among the throngs of humans and wait to soak up all their sin's energy. I mean, look at this whole event. Spectators were sitting in the stupid-looking fold-up chairs with armfuls of food and beer, already drunk, and the triathlon hadn't even begun.

There were couples unsuccessfully hiding in alleys fucking against walls while others took advantage of the large group and loud noise to fight with one another. Every single sin was proudly on display. I puffed out my chest as I took in all our hard work. Our presence alone was addictive and influential to the hairless cats without tails.

It was a ten-minute walk to get to the starting area for the swim, the first event of the three. Shilo arrived early to ensure I didn't have to wait in line. "Sir, these are for you," he said and held out the blue-colored sticker as I approached him.

"Did they have my number?"

"Yes, Sir, I ensured that you would have your favorite number, 666," Shilo said. "May I take your bag, Sir?"

"Sure." I peeled the sticker from its paper backing and pressed it against my Jammer swim shorts, and then turned to head to the starting line. "Shilo?" I turned back to look at the old fallen angel. "Thanks."

The corners of his mouth turned up slightly as he bowed his head. "It is my pleasure, Sir."

The sand was already hot as it squished between my toes, relaxing me. I made sure to stand at the front of the line and ignored the annoying humans. There was the odd demon kicking about, but I was surrounded by the insects that Father loved for the most part. It was fun to beat them in their little competitions. Besides, I knew it would be a small pinprick in my Father's side that I purposely set out to make his precious humans look stupid and prove that they truly were the inferior species.

"Hi," a female voice said, and I looked to see who had dared to speak to me. A girl with colorful pigtails and a matching outfit stood beside me. "Such a beautiful day for a triathlon. I try to do at least two a month, how about you?"

"I suppose it is, and no, I don't have the time," I said flatly and turned my eyes back toward the dark blue water.

"Um, did you want to maybe..." She started, and I cut her off.

"No, I don't, but if you require servicing, you can make arrangements for one of my Wednesdays."

"Your Wednesdays?" she asked, and I sighed, annoyed and wished the stupid race would start already.

"Please, you must have heard about my Wednesdays? I mean, that is why you're talking to me, right?"

"I don't...."

I cut her off again. "It's fine. You don't have to admit it. Wednesdays are where I fuck all of you horny women who need desperate need of servicing for a short time. Understandable considering that the men you'd normally get to choose from are pathetic and unrememberable in any fashion. You can call and make arrangements at my front desk. Just ask for the Wednesday special. You know it's quite rude of you to approach me out in public. You have some nerve."

"You fucking pig!" She marched away, and I stared after her.

See, this is why humans made no sense. I'd clearly heard her mind, and she wanted to fuck me, so I offered her an opportunity of a lifetime, and she storms off like I'd insulted her?

Forgetting the odd woman, I turned my attention to the announcer.

"Hello everyone! What a great day to raise money for two amazing causes that will significantly impact our community for the better." I rolled my eyes at the dramatic and so untrue statement. Nothing would make this place better. "When you are done with the race, be sure to pick up your prize. Without any further ado, on your marks, get set...Go!"

The little ribbon that had been my only barrier fluttered to the ground as the sea of humanity surged forward.

I sprinted down the short distance to the water's edge and dove in —there was this blissful moment where all was quiet, where I was weightless, and my mind flashed to another time.

I flew across the now dull grass toward the war that had erupted before my eyes. How could the day go from being perfect and serene, the way it should be, to this mad chaos? Angel on angel, brother on brother, and friend against friend, the sea of angels divided with many caught in between. Swords raised, and the two sides clashed, the sound like a thunderous Boom as they collided.

The fiery sky spread like a blanket across everything, making the ivory palace look like it was bleeding. White feathers floated to the ground around those maimed or dying—bright red blood sprayed in all directions as limbs fell to the ground below and painted their once beautiful home.

The wails of pain were loud in my ears as I neared the battle. My wings pushed hard and fast as I streaked across the ground and saw my shadow for the first time. I didn't have time to contemplate it as I pulled my golden sword that glowed among the darkness spreading over everything.

The mighty dragon roared, sending vibrations through my chest. The sound rippled from the ferocious beast a moment before the Hellfire poured out of its mouth. The blaze charred everything living or not living in its path, turning it to grey ash.

Lucifer rose from the back of the great beast, his black leather armor dark *against his pale skin. As Lucifer pulled his deadly sword, a sharp ring rang out that was louder than the screams and clanging of metal. Lucifer paused as Michael approached. They stared at each other—brothers once united were no longer.*

I jerked as the unbelievably loud sound of hundreds of people filing into the water brought me back to the now. I hadn't thought about that day in a long time. I shook it off and rose to the surface, my arms slicing through the cool waves until I was well beyond the pack. I could sense the creatures that lived in the water, keeping their distance from the loud chaos even though they were still curious.

I'd felt like that at one time with humans, and then I was forced to roll around in their pigpen with the insubordinate swine, and everything changed.

MINETTA

"Those can sit over there." Minetta pointed to the shady area where they were placing the extra refreshments. Penny was a lot stronger than she looked. She was easily carrying four cases at once. It would have taken her twice as long to accomplish the same amount.

"So, what do you call this...event again?" Penny said as she smoothed back the little wisps of hair that had rejected being placed in the bun.

"It's called a triathlon because they do three events. The open water swim is first, then the cycling and finally the run."

"And where exactly are we located along that route?"

"We are at the halfway mark of the run." Minetta looked around for the cups. They had to be here somewhere. She could see the bobbing shirts of the runners heading down the street. She looked around again for the boxes of cups, but they were nowhere in sight. How could she have forgotten the cups?

"Have you seen cups?"

"No, did you want to head back and get them? I can man the station." Minetta glanced up at the nearing runners.

"That's okay. Let me take a look under the table one more time. Maybe I missed a box." She lifted the blowing fabric out of the way and knelt down, looking for the elusive paper cups. She paused—her hand in the box as the same strange hum and tingling from the other night raced over her body. Her chest rose and fell faster as the feeling spread and became a constant pulse under her skin.

Minetta could hear the runners getting closer, but she couldn't focus on what she'd been doing. Sneakers pulled up alongside the table. The strange sensation was so strong she wondered if she was in the middle of a medical episode. Toby began to whine, and she started to back up to see what was wrong. But she smacked into Penny's legs Penny seemed to hit her back under the table with her knee. At least that was what it felt like since there was enough force that she crashed into the boxes. Rolling forward, she fell out the other side of the table in an embarrassing heap at the runner's feet.

Toby rushed around the table and nudged her, whining furiously, before putting himself between her and the stranger. Minetta stared at the expensive black sneakers and then slowly up at the person that was glaring down at her. He lifted the sunglasses covering his eyes, and she let out a little gasp as their stare met. She was suddenly tumbling forward into pits of beautiful amber. Other runners began to arrive around her, but all she could focus on was him.

His face was chiseled, but not the way Michael's had been. His was rugged, with a dusting of a five o'clock shadow. His hair looked perfectly unstyled, the extraordinary blond color that had streaks of gold in it would've looked messy on anyone else, but it looked sexy as hell on him. She fought not to fidget in place as his eyes roamed over her face and then lower to her body before meeting her gaze once more as she rose to her feet.

Penny was talking to her, her hands waving in the air. She should see what she wanted...but those eyes were like dark honey on golden toast or maybe like amber diamonds on a sunny day. They were intoxicating and... She was staring. Her eyes went wide, a hot flush racing through her body that had nothing to do with the bright sun in the sky.

Clearing her throat, she said, "Would you like a drink?" She snatched a bottle and held it out to the stranger, almost hitting him in the chest with her closed fist. "We have orange and... blue, whatever blue is, but we don't have cups. If you wanted a cup, then I can't help you. Did you want a cup?"

The man's features looked shocked. His eyes were a little wide as his mouth hung open. "Callista," he whispered, his brows furrowing together in what could only be confusion.

"I'm sorry, I don't know who that is. My name is Minetta."

His face darkened, his features morphing as he glared at her with annoyance. His dark stare turned on her dog that was still pushing at her with his big head, the whining persistent. "Quiet!" the man ordered, and Toby instantly stopped. She looked down at Toby, and a small ball of pissed off began to burn in her gut. No one talked to her dog like that. He put his hands on his hips, and he seemed to tower over her with that angry stare. "What kind of trickery is this?"

"Trickery?"

"You're human, but why are you wearing her face?"

Her eyes grew wide, and it was her turn to look shocked. What the hell kind of question was that? Before her brain could come up with a good comeback, he spoke again.

"And why is there no greed in you? Better question, why don't you want me? You should want me. Everyone wants me, but not you. This is very peculiar."

Minny's mouth dropped open. Something was becoming very clear—she was a magnet for crazy and assholes. "I really hope that isn't your usual pick-up line because it sucks."

Turning, she marched around the table, Toby sticking to her side like glue. Penny had stepped away from the table, her eyes staring at her feet, and she had to wonder if this jerk said something mean to her friend.

"Did you do something to her," she asked, her hands balled into fists. She cocked her hip as she glared at the overly rude man. It didn't matter how good-looking he was. She'd delt with enough jerks for a thousand lifetimes.

He looked between her and Penny. "To the Erinyes, why would I care what it does?"

"I don't know what that means. Is it an insult? You really don't make much sense. Do you want a drink or not? If not, can you kindly move along? You're standing in the way of others." She pointed to the gathering group of people that were jogging in place as they waited.

The stranger's mouth fell open, and she knew by his look he was gearing himself up for another rude remark.

"Penny, can you take over? I'm going to go get those cups after all." Looking back at the ignoramus, she shot him a little sneer. "You were in the lead, but it looks like you're going to be middle of the pack at best. I guess better luck next time. Maybe you should move along before you're dead last." She marched away, not even sure why she'd been so uncharacteristically rude. But one thing was for certain, it had felt right to tell that tall, delicious drink of water off. In fact, it had felt so good that when James got back from his boys' vacay, she would do the same to him.

She was done with letting men treat her like crap. No, she was done letting people, in general, treat her like crap.

This was the new her, and she liked this version of her so much better already.

CHAPTER

ELEVEN

RIKER

I ran down the street faster than I should. I was getting stares as I raced by all of the much slower humans. My feet hit the ground harder as I replayed every word that girl said to me. She'd been rude and sarcastic and completely insufferable. How dare she speak to me that way. Almost everyone knew who I was, and those who didn't, felt my draw, felt my presence as their superior, and craved to have my attention in some manner. Greedily, I wanted all their affections even though I couldn't stand the pathetic creatures. It was the constant torturous conundrum I'd been forced to endure.

I mean, the girl looked at me like she was interested, but her mind seemed blank or impenetrable, which was impossible. All humans' minds could be penetrated. I rubbed at the spot in my chest that still held remnants of the tingling sensation. It had started about a half-mile out from the water station and had become stronger with every stride. It had been driving me crazy, and I was sure that Michael was lurking in the shadows of one of the buildings.

And why did she have Callista's face? That was a face that had haunted my dreams for years after my fall. Was this some new form of torture that the golden bunch up on high decided to use against me? I could picture all of them looking so smug as they sat around and watched the cat and mouse game.

I ran past the final human just before the finish line and raised my hands in the air to the clapping and cheers that accompanied my win.

Last, ha! I'd never been last. I barely have to put in an effort to beat these hairless cats. I could've completed the race ten times before another competitor even sniffed at the finish line, but that wasn't the point. I wanted to show Father that his human creations were inferior as much as possible. I marched up to the small podium they'd created for the three finalists and took the top step waiting for my medal to be presented. The human announcer from earlier ran over with it dangling from his hand, and I snatched it, placing it around my neck before waving to the crowd's applause. A girl in the front row lifted her top to show off her tits, but I just jumped off the little platform, not waiting for the others to get their medals, and went on the hunt for Shilo.

I found him in the exact location I'd asked him to be and breathed a little sigh of relief that at least some things were reliable.

"Shilo, let's go," I said, and he fell into step with me as we continued toward my car.

"Sir, did something happen?" Shilo glanced at me.

"Why?" I glared at the old angel and sighed, taking a deep breath to calm myself as he took a step back. This was crazy. Why was I allowing one stupid human girl to bother me like this? Her comments were nothing to me, yet I was about to do something even more confusing. "Shilo, I need you to find someone."

"Of course, Sir. Who would you like me to find?"

"It's a human girl. Her name is Minetta."

"Minetta what," Shilo asked.

I just stared at him, blinking as my brain screeched to a grinding halt. I didn't know her last name.

"I...I don't know. It's an odd name. There can't be too many in the city," I said, waving my hand dismissively.

"I will do my best, Sir. You finished with an amazing time, and you will be early for your board meeting."

"Excellent." I pushed the image of the raven-haired beauty from my mind as I focused on the meeting I was heading to next—annoying humans.

MINETTA

"Do you believe that guy?" Minetta asked again. She paced back and forth in front of the table. "So rude, so unbelievably...rude."

"So, you keep saying." Penny sat on the water table, her legs dangling over the edge as she sipped on one of the orange drinks.

Minetta focused her attention on her friend, who had barely said a word since the encounter with the assholio. She stared at Penny's features, and she seemed annoyed, but if anyone had a reason to be annoyed it was not Penny.

"What is your problem? You have been strange all day, and now you're barely speaking to me? I finally stand up for myself, like you have kept encouraging me to do, and you act like I've committed a cardinal sin."

Penny laughed a sharp bark before she rubbed her face. "I'm sorry, but you're right he was being a real jerk," Penny whispered. "At least you never have to see him again. I mean, why would you want to see him again? In fact, it would be wise to avoid all contact from now on. He would most likely be even more of a pill."

She nibbled on her bottom lip. "You're right. I don't have to see him again. Thank God for that." Again, Penny erupted in laughter like she'd just said the most hysterical thing. Minetta shook her head at her friend, not even bothering to question the strange behavior, and then turned toward the sound of feet. The last of the runners were limping toward them, and she cheered and clapped before she grabbed a bottle to take to the stranger.

"You've got this!" She smiled wide at a woman who was in obvious pain and yet was still pushing on.

"Thank you," the woman said and took a big swig of the drink before jogging off. "I didn't think I'd make it," she said and took a few deep breaths. Despite the achievement, the woman's eyes seemed sad.

Minetta felt compelled to reach out and touch the woman's arm. "Are you okay?"

The woman nodded, but tears trailed down her cheeks. "I was supposed to do this with my daughter, but she's in the hospital fighting cancer. It's not right to be a parent and see your child suffer like that."

Minny offered the woman a warm smile. "You're out here for her?"

"She insisted that I still come to the race. It just didn't feel right, but I couldn't tell her no." The woman looked down again.

"I have an idea." Ducking under the table, she grabbed her small pack and pulled out her phone. "Turn so the camera can pick up the finish line in the background." The woman nodded and got into position and smiled wide, holding up the bottle. "Good, now give me a crazy face." A few shots later, the woman was laughing. "Perfect, what's your number so you can share these with her and she can feel like she was here with you."

The woman relayed the number, and Minny sent the photos. "Thank you, that was really kind. I don't know what to say."

"No need to say anything. I hope your daughter gets well soon."

With a little nod and sniffle, the woman shoved off and made the final dash for the finish line.

"You really are a good person Minny, don't ever lose that," Penny said from her perch on the table.

She looked at her friend's serious face and gave her the same reassuring smile she offered the runner. "Why would I?"

"No reason, I just never want you to change. It's easy to do in this world."

"Yeah, I guess it is." She figured if she were going to change that much, she would've already done it by now with the shit she'd been dealt. "Did you want to come over? I can order pizza, or there is a great new Thai place that delivers," Minny asked as she grabbed the empty boxes from under the table to clean up.

"I'd like that. We could still do the beach tomorrow if you want?"

"I would, but I'm working myself up to breaking things off with James, and I need some mental headspace to do that. I hope you understand."

What she didn't tell Penny was that she was planning on visiting her mom for a couple of days and calling in sick to work. The encounter with the woman reminded her that it had been too long since she'd been home. The thought of her mom had her mood souring once more. She'd already been through her dad's long agonizing illness, and now it looked like her mother was going to suffer the same fate, just with a disease by a different name.

"Hey girl, come here." Penny wrapped her in a hug, and she gripped her friend tight. "If you change your mind, you know where to find me."

Minetta stepped back and wiped at the wet spot she'd left on Penny's orange tank top. "Thanks, but I think this is a task I need to do alone." Toby head-butted her leg, and she reached down to pet his head.

They quickly got everything packed up and put it into a pile for the clean-up crew to come to gather. As they made their way down the street, the hair stood up at the nape of her neck, and she paused and looked around. It was similar to the sensation she'd had at work that one night. There were still a number of people walking around, but no one seemed out of place or dangerous.

"What is it? What's wrong?" Penny asked, coming to stand beside her.

She shook her head. "Nothing, I'm just losing it. Come on. I'm starving."

CHAPTER

TWELVE

MINETTA stared at the ceiling and recounted the little stars still present from the little girl who used to live here. She hadn't bothered to remove them even though James did nothing but complain about how they kept him awake at night. It was an idiotic statement. They barely gave off enough light to light up the ceiling around them, let alone shine in his eyes. It was just another way to put her down. She'd always found the star stickers had this odd, soothing ability when she was trying to sleep, but they were not helping tonight.

Giving up, she tossed the cover off and left Toby sleeping soundly. She stared at her dog, who was softly snoring on the other side of the bed like he didn't have a care in the world. If only she could say the same. The only thing aside from actual sleeping meds that might help was a hot cup of camomile tea.

Her mind kept racing as she replayed the day over and over again. Why was she still thinking about the insolent, amber-eyed man? She must really have a thing for the worst possible members of the male species. Not that she'd dated much, but if James was any indication and now her fascination with the jerk from earlier...it didn't really say much for her state of mind.

The bedroom door did its usual squeak that reminded her of every horror movie with a scene where the character is mysteriously woken in the night by the sound, the eeriness of the old hinge always making her shiver. As much as she didn't want James around, she couldn't deny she missed having a man in the house when he wasn't there. Maybe she should get like ten more dogs. Toby would like the company, and not many would feel confident breaking into a house with an entire pack waiting for them.

The board that always groaned in the hall did so as she stepped on it, and she sucked in a shaky breath as her mind began to play tricks on her. The stairs were not much better, each one announcing the age of the house in its own unique manner.

"You are totally fine. You're being silly," she said out loud. Resolving herself to her task, she marched onward. As she reached the ground floor, she shivered. The house felt cold, like really cold, which was odd considering how hot it was outside, and she didn't have any air conditioning. She wrapped her arms around herself and rubbed at the goosebumps that were rising all over her body. Chalking it up to the fact that she was scantily clad and was overtired, she headed toward the light switch in the kitchen. She really wished that the person who'd built this house had put a switch at the bottom of the stairs.

Her teeth were practically chattering by the time she reached the opposite side of the kitchen and smacked at the light switch. It clicked, but the thing wouldn't turn on.

"What the heck is going on?" No matter how many times she hit the little switch, nothing happened. "Great, just great."

This was an old house, but she doubted that the two long fluorescent bulbs both decided to blow at the same time. She wandered over to the lamp in the living room and hit the switch, hoping that it wasn't what she thought it was. It as well stayed dark.

"Okay, this is not funny," she mumbled.

She could try the hallway one, but at this point, either the power was out in the area, or she had a bigger issue with her electricity, like a flipped breaker which meant a trip to the basement in the dark. That was so not happening, and her mind was conjuring up the worst. God, she was cold, she thought as she stumbled her way over to her reading chair and banged her knee on the coffee table.

"Ouch!" She groaned as the pain lanced down her leg. Finally making it across to the chair, she grabbed the throw off the back and pulled the pretty piece her mother had made around her shoulders. It was the last thing her mother had made before her hands had become too riddled with arthritis, and her memory of how to make one of the beautiful blankets was lost in the far reaches of her mind.

Minetta leaned against the large bay window and looked up and down the street. The light right in front of her house was out, but the rest were on. She didn't know much about how the grid worked, but she was pretty certain that if the rest of the street was on, then the one was simply burnt out. Her street was usually quiet this time of night, she lived on the outskirts of the city, and the area was full of families with small children. They would all be tucked away sound asleep by now.

A hiss-like noise caught her attention. She stood straighter, listening for the odd sound again. She gave a start and jumped around as a shadow moved in the reflection of the glass. Her pulse pounded loudly in her ears as her eyes searched the darkness. Out of the corner of her eye, she could have sworn she saw movement by the front door and stared hard at the spot over the little half wall. Her heart picked up pace and pounded hard in her chest until it was all she could hear. There was a golf ball-sized lump in her dry throat, and as she swallowed hard, the movement was almost as loud as her heart.

Why was the darn house so cold? She shook again, and a small puff of steam rose from her mouth into the air. She laid her hand on the glass, and it too was freezing. Had it turned that cold outside overnight? Somewhere in her mind, she knew that unless it was winter and she had no electricity, there was no possible way this could be happening.

This had to be just her imagination playing tricks on her. Her own fear was creating the impossible. That was the only logical explanation. Nothing else moved, and annoyed with herself now, she rubbed at her eyes and headed for the door that led to the basement. It had to be a breaker, that's why the house was cold, and if that was the case, she had no choice but to go down there.

Dammit, she really didn't want to do this, but she was being silly over nothing. As her hand reached for the basement door handle, the house took that moment to shake as the pipes forced air through them. It sounded like a miniature earthquake ripping through the home as the floor and walls shook. She jumped back from the door as the handle rattled back and forth like something was trying to get out. All she could picture was a serial killer on the other side.

She bit her lip as she stared at the handle that settled after the pipes quieted, but her nerves were frayed. Her body trembled all over, and no matter how much she told herself she was being ridiculous, she couldn't stop the freaked-out sensation from traveling from the top of her head to the tips of her toes.

She looked around the darkened space, the once small rooms feeling huge and the front door very far away.

Something moved again, and this time she did jump back and stare at the living room. Someone was watching her. She could feel it, and her senses went from denial to overload with a single breath.

A sweat broke out all over her body, the moisture forming beads on her forehead and down her back. She couldn't see what it was and turned her head to the left to allow her peripheral vision to help her out. It was telling her something was there, the slow rise and fall like something was breathing. It looked like nothing more than part of the shadows, but shadows didn't move like that, and they didn't look like a large lump in the middle of her floor. If this was James home early trying to scare her, she might actually kill him.

"Who's there?" she called out, but the only sound was the same soft hiss as earlier. Her adrenaline spiked, and her mind screamed to run.

Hands shaking violently, she reached out, never taking her eyes off the spot, and fumbled for the knife she always left laying on the cutting board. Her eyes tried to make sense of the dark shape that seemed to be moving or growing. She blinked a number of times as if that would clear her vision.

She watched in horror as the thing shifted again, and this time it wasn't her mind playing tricks on her. There was a glint, a quick flash in the dark, and she realized she was staring into a set of eyes, and it most certainly wasn't James.

A blood-curling scream bubbled in her throat but was lodged there as she stared, keeping her feet rooted to the floor. She couldn't tell what the hell it was, but whatever it was began to rise from the middle of her living room like a great black blob slowly taking shape.

"This is not real. This is not real. Your mind is playing tricks. Tell it to go away," she mumbled. "Go away!" she yelled. The words had sounded fiercer in her head. But, saying it out loud didn't help. In fact, it only enforced the fact she was indeed awake, and the thing was still there.

It was in that moment, as it stretched to its full height, she realized it had been on all fours. Had it been following her? Had it been hiding in her house this whole time? Oh my god, had it been in the living room with her? Panic clawed at her throat, her pulse pounding frantically.

The animal or large man had something sticking out of the top of its head. She closed her eyes for a moment and shook her head back and forth. But, as she opened her eyes, they went wide as she stared at what looked like twisted antlers and glowing eyes.

"Go away, I'm warning you, I have a weapon," she said, her voice shaking. She pulled the stupidly small knife up in front of her, the blade waving back and forth as her arm shook violently. The lanky creature moved toward her, the sound of something scraping scratched along her floor. She'd never been angrier that James hadn't fixed her back door because it would be nice to have a backdoor that could open right about now. She was going to call someone, but no, James insisted it was a waste of money, and he could take care of it. That was months ago.

Her mind picked that moment to remember the call from Sam. The terror had been so evident in his voice and how he'd claimed she would think he was crazy if he told her what was after him. He'd been there, and then suddenly Sam simply vanished into the night.

Is this what happened to him?

"I said stay back," she said. Yet, it was herself that backed up. She at least managed to sound a little firmer as she stared up at the massive thing in her home. She suddenly wished she still had a landline and not just a cell phone that she stupidly left beside her bed. A deep growl came from the thing that was closing the distance in the small space.

It took another lumbering step, and as it did, the soft bit of light shining in from her neighbor's backyard filtered through the window to give her a better view of what she was facing.

The scream lodged in her throat, ripped from her mouth as the knife clattered to the floor. The creature before her was no human or animal from Earth. The black pupilless eyes glowed an unearthly silver in the darkness, and the too-pale skin pulled tight over excessively lengthy limbs that matched the lanky body. Pitch black claws flexed terrifyingly at the end of each pale finger, each hand the size of her head. The creature had a face that was shaped like a human, but the nose was twisted and flat. The sound she'd heard earlier was more pronounced now as she watched the air vibrating out the side of its nostrils. The mouth spread almost from one sheep-like ear to the next, and as it gapped open, she could easily see a limitless number of sharp jagged teeth.

She screamed again then something rose from behind the hideous beast and flew toward her face. The movement got her once paralyzed feet moving, and she barely made it out of the way as what looked like an octopus tentacle collided with the wall. Drywall went flying, little bits sprinkling onto her head as she ducked and dove to the ground. She crawled around the island, but her pans that hung above the island banged together. The thump and vibration behind her back told her not to look up, that she didn't want to know. Terror turned into a wild animal in her chest, as real as the creature above her.

She panted hard, and going against her inner hysterical self instincts—she looked up into the eyes of the creature on her island. The thing twisted its head from side to side like it was inspecting her as it stared down at her. That strange tail came for her again, and she rolled over onto her side just as that sharp blade-like tail dug into the cheap linoleum. She stared at the lodged spike-like barb that was so close to her face before she flipped onto her hands and knees and scampered away as fast as possible. Reaching the end of the island, she made a break for the front door. Adrenaline and panic seized her heart, making it hard to think about anything other than escape.

The same vicious growl that sounded more like a deep rumbling avalanche sent a streak of horror down her spine as she dashed around the hallway corner for her only escape route.

She screamed wildly as that tail snaked its way around her waist and yanked her back from her destination. It lifted her clean off the floor and squeezed her hard, reminding her of a python as she gasped to breathe.

"No! Let me go!" She beat her closed fists down on the strange appendage and kicked her legs wildly, not hitting anything. The tail swung one way, then slamming her up against the wall. She bit her lip hard, tasting the metallic flavor of blood in her mouth. The thing pulled her away from the wall again, and she got ready for a second impact when it hollered in a strange, pain-filled growl.

The thing dropped her, and she landed hard on her ass, the little bit of air in her lungs was forced out on impact. Spinning around, she stared at the creature as Toby gripped the creature's leg in his mouth. The normally gentle giant was snarling like a rabid beast. His massive mouth and sharp canines were embedded in the creature as he pulled and shook his head from side-to-side like he was trying to snap the thing like a twig. If this had been a human, the person would be down and possibly dead as the two hundred pound animal savagely yanked on like a beast as he defended her.

The creature let out a howl of pain again, and strange blackish blood seeped from the wound, traveling down its leg to pool on the floor. It clenched its fist, and she knew it was going to hurt her dog, her savior.

"No," Minetta screamed at the top of her lungs, just as her front door busted inward with an ear-splitting crack. Small bits of the door flew in her direction, and Minetta covered her head.

She slowly looked up to see what turned her door into kindling and saw Penny standing in her doorway. Her friend's eyes were glowing a bright orange, the color reminding her of fire, and her normally perfectly tame hair floated around her in a weightless dance that moved like it was alive.

"What the hell is going on here," Minetta asked aloud but not expecting an answer. She was losing her ever-loving mind. That was the only rational explanation for this insanity. If it wasn't bad enough that her mother's Alzheimers was genetic and she'd likely end up with it too, but now she had some sort of hallucination attacking her mind. What kind of disease was this?

The creature roared, the sound shaking the walls as Penny stepped into the house. How were her neighbors not hearing any of this? She peered out the open door, and all was still and quiet. Minetta scooted back on the floor as Penny stepped closer, but her eyes were focused on the creature that still had Toby swinging from its leg. A loud tearing sound echoed through her ears as Toby tore a large hole in the flesh of the beast. She turned her head and covered her mouth, trying hard not to be sick, as the blood poured out onto the floor.

Toby attacked again, but the creature swatted at him with its tail and sent him sailing across the room, where he crashed into the couch and flipped it over on top of himself. Penny made a hissing sound, her tongue literally snaking out and flicking in the air like a serpent.

Minetta felt light-headed, but she fought off the sensation of passing out. She needed to get out of there. As Penny and the creature squared off, she crawled for the couch toward Toby, her trapped protector.

"Hey buddy, you okay," she asked, only to comfort him and let him know that she was there to help. Then again Toby answering would be the least surprising thing tonight, considering the shit going down in her living room.

Toby whimpered slightly, but he licked her hand as she reached in to pet his head. She stood and grabbed the back of the couch, lifting hard to flip it into the upright position. Toby slowly stood but growled a deep sound, his lips pulling up, showing his large teeth at the creature.

She didn't want him to engage again and opted to get the heck out of there. She grabbed Toby's collar and ran like a little rabbit behind Penny or the thing that looked like Penny that suddenly pulled a flaming sword out of nowhere. Minetta shook her head.

This couldn't be real, this couldn't be real, but if it wasn't real, it sure as hell felt real.

She stopped long enough to grab her purse, a leash, and running shoes. Penny looked over at her as she was about to dash out the doorway. At that moment, she felt like it was still Penny and not some alien-like monster. Not wasting another second to find out what was going to transpire between crazy creature number one and the friend she wasn't sure was a friend any longer, she ran out the door.

She could hear screeching and loud banging as she ran, but she didn't look back.

Toby limped slightly, but he kept up with her as she sprinted down the road. This was the first time in her life she really wished she had splurged and purchased a car. Hell, even a shit box right now would do, and she vowed that it was the first thing she was going to do if she lived.

The neighborhood was still quiet, but the further she ran, the busier the street became. A few people stared at her as she ran past. Not surprising, considering she had nothing more on her body than her tank top and underwear, and the purse crossed over her body whacked her like a crop on the ass with every stride. Modesty would have to wait. She needed to get as far away as fast as she could from her house.

Toby began to pant hard and labored beside her. She looked down at her brave sidekick. "Do you need a rest, bud?" She spun in a circle, not really knowing where she was, and spotted an elementary school not far off. She slowed her pace but headed in that direction, and once she was out of sight from the street, she leaned against the wall to catch her breath while Toby flopped to the ground.

She was not much of a runner. The only time she purposely set out to do more than walk or her peaceful yoga was to complete her activity pin at work.

The adrenaline that had been fueling her was fading fast, and as it did, all of her limbs shook violently. Her head was swimming as her stomach once more threatened to empty itself on the ground. Knees giving out, she slid down the brick wall beside Toby and placed her hand on his heaving side. One thing was very certain. As the oppressive heat pressed in on her, she was certain it was the creature and not a random breaker on her electricity box that had caused the cold temperature inside her house. She laughed a little, the hysteria taking hold of her mind.

"Thank you," she whispered to Toby.

How had her life gone from mundane to having a winter, biohazard-like creature spring up in her living room and her best friend turning into some flaming sword using ninja?

The light-headedness worsened, and she leaned to the side, placing her head on Toby. Her lids fluttered, and the world went dark.

CHAPTER
THIRTEEN

RIKER

I hated coming down to this Hell hole, pun intended. Given a choice between Hell and Earth, I'd choose Earth every time. Hell had no redeeming qualities. It was dark, excessively hot, and stank of sulfur, dead humans, blood, shit, demon sweat, and something I couldn't quite put my finger on. It was disgusting.

Traveling the Ether was fine enough, relaxing, I guess. It didn't take much time, nor did it seem like it, but who really knew when Hell had no sense of time. Early on, I'd figured out how to manipulate my time so that I didn't randomly disappear for months or years on end. Businesses tended to fail when you poofed out and didn't return. Considering I didn't like to fail, there were a few...unhappy moments during those first few trips.

I stopped to stare at the River Styx tunnel that fed the Hell mouth and the supernatural sorting station. What else would you call the spot that shuffled you off to Heaven or Hell, and you didn't get a say? It really was just like recycling at a factory.

The River was something that I used to find fascinating and enjoyable once upon a time. Now when I wandered the cavern with its dark shore and stared at the ghostly human faces floating by to be sorted like cattle, I felt...nothing. I always had the strange urge to walk along the water's edge and talk to the spirits like they were on a bus tour.

And now, if you look to the left for eternity, all you lucky people on the right will roast down here with us. There is one catch, ladies and gentlemen. You must sell your soul to my Father by never committing a sin, don't ever step out of line, don't dare think for yourself, and Father forbids you to wish for something that doesn't align with His ideals. Well, if you are one of his angels, that rule holds true, but not if you are one of his precious humans.

Hypocritical old goat. Those that worshipped at his feet were sheep in another skin, and just because they didn't *Bah* didn't make them any less predictable.

I did like what Charon had done with his spot above the river. The café, like a restaurant, was the only place where demons, angels, or Fallen could sit and dine together. A neutral ground that no one controlled.

I decided to walk amongst the streets and buildings that led to my palace. The buildings were made of some Hell rock, black and plain and completely boring—no fancy amenities when you lived out in these parts. I didn't even want to remember what they did with their shit. My gold cape fluttered around me as a screeching giant wingbat flew overhead. The flying rat-like creature was similar to the small earthly bats, but this one could carry a full-size demon away if you were not careful.

I loved the new black and gold cobblestone, which replaced the dull grey path that had been here prior. It was my newest addition. A loud roar sounded, and then my name was called. I groaned before looking toward Leviathan's castle. Gnaarl, Leviathan's second in command, was waving wildly as he jumped up and down to get my attention. Gnarrl reminded me of the children that would run after us in Heaven, wanting to see our swords. I squinted and stared as I tried to decide if Leviathan had made this side of his castle identical to mine or if it was some sort of trickery. I raised my hand and waved back, not quite as enthusiastically.

Turning my head, I looked around Hell as I walked, and I tried to see it not as me but as someone arriving for the first time. There was one appeal here, and Father couldn't reach them down here. It was the one spot he couldn't reach in and pluck their wings off again for fun. Several demons clothed in an assortment of fancy dress weaved their way along the streets, and I knew with one glance that they were heading to Lust's kingdom. The rest of us Fallen steered clear of him. Although he didn't have any reason to attack us, you never knew what a Fallen would do when someone was as bitter as he was.

"Master, you have returned," Brill said as I stopped at the closed gates of my palace. The wide moat I'd had dug around the palace burned with Hellfire, the bright reddish flame dancing against the walls and adding an extra layer of protection from attack.

I never announced when I was coming. Better to see what the mice did while the cat was away. Brill let out a bark of noise—the single syllable command instantly had the gates opening.

He was the highest-ranking Molyneux in my army, and the first demon I befriended after my fall. I would now go so far as to call him friend.

I liked the Molyneux demons best. They were cunning and smarter than all the other war demons. They were also loyal, which was hard to find yet still large enough to scare other armies. Brill stood tall and proud, his eyes smartly averted from mine, but there was no weakness and no fear. He'd grown since the last time I'd visited, his muscled physique impressive even for his species. The black and gold leather that adorned his body made him more menacing, and that was before he'd pulled out the flaming Hellfire sword that he always carried on his hip.

After I arrived here from my fall, one of my first orders of business was to build a strong army, one that all except for Pride would fear. Lucifer, Satan, Pride, Diablo—he was the most feared of all the Seven to fall, but he was simply Luci to me. We were not as close as we had once been since the day of the fall, but we respected one another. Luci's big issue was his temper, which had earned him the label of tyrant, and he had terrible boundaries when it came to...everything. It would be nothing for Luci to wander in when you're in the shower and have a conversation about torture and his plans for Hell before handing you a towel and leaving like it was normal.

Before we made it halfway across the cobblestone entrance, a demon panting hard showed up at the gate.

"Halt," Brill barked out and glared at the unknown demon. "Blayaddt roova goust harr?" Brill had been working on his other demon dialects, and I was impressed at his ambition.

"Hasha Lucifer rammanna hest Mammon voidere shett," the small demon said, and I groaned. As if just thinking about him had made him summon me to him, the demon was requesting I attend Luci's castle before I left.

Brill looked at me to see what I wanted to do. "Yes, I will stop in on my way back up, but tell him I'm not staying. I have things to attend to."

The demon's eyes grew wide, its slim body shaking with obvious fear of having to relay the message back to its master, but it turned and scampered off.

Great, just fucking great.

I turned back to the shiny black and glittering gold palace that looked out of place amongst the dull grey and bleak surroundings. The glittering symbol of my sin was burning bright for all to see against the polished black on the front of my palace.

I honestly didn't know who would try to attack me down here, but it felt like it was the right thing to do, establish my authority right from the first moment. Now I dreamed of much loftier goals.

"How is everything going here," I asked Brill as we marched across the open expanse of the courtyard.

"Excellent, Master. The army grows, and if they do not learn to obey quickly enough, I destroy them." I nodded at the answer. I trusted Brill as much as I trusted just about anyone, which said a lot about the long-standing relationship we'd shared to date. Did I call him a friend? That was a tough question to answer, but if forced to answer, then I would say yes.

My black boots paused as the sound of a baby's wail reached my ears. I turned and looked to Brill, who made a little whining noise as he scrunched up his face at me. "What in Hell's name is that?"

"It may be easier if you see than if I tried to explain," Brill said as he led me toward the ever-increasing sound of chatter and crying.

"Am I going to want to know what you've been up to?"

"Master, I think you will be most pleased. I wished to be further along before you graced us with your presence, but enough has been done to show the promise of my work in honor of your great name." Brill reached out for the heavy golden door that had deeply embedded hieroglyphics of protection.

"Brill, don't kiss my ass." I looked at the demon, who looked like he was snarling but indeed was smiling.

"As you wish, Master."

"Those are new." I nodded toward the door and the unique designs.

"There had been a few issues with spies, they all died painfully in the lower chambers, but the door made the most sense to keep out any further prying eyes. I had those with power come and carve the protection along the door, and now anyone that does not wear your brand and hold honor for you will not be granted access."

"Well, now Brill, you do continue to impress me. Who was trying to spy?"

"No one in particular, just lower-level demons trying to dig up information they can use as leverage."

We walked silently the rest of the way, Brill leading me steadily along the corridor that twisted toward the wing furthest from my side of the palace. Brill pushed through the door to the final destination, and as I stepped into the cavernous space. I had to work hard to keep the shock off my face.

The room had been divided into two groups. The left side had been decorated with soft grays and orange—everything from newly birthed demonies to dwix were lined up talking and playing while guards kept watch. However, the right side of the room was for those reaching full demon status, each one in a different class, learning a different topic. I walked a little further along the massive cavern area, and as I did, the demons of all ages grew quiet. The youngest dropped to the floor as they placed their heads on the black onyx. The older group lined up like human soldiers, shoulder-to-shoulder they stood, backs straight, muscles bulging, but eyes averted to the floor.

"What exactly am I looking at?" I asked as I took in every little detail.

"We always had trouble recruiting demons that were the right blend of brain and brawn for the army. There were so few of any species that was smart enough or strong enough to make a good warrior, and those we did find had issues with loyalty and their own agendas."

"I remember clearly," I said. The tortured and distinct sounds of the demon's pain-filled screams were hard to forget.

In the beginning, it had been a real struggle to round up demons that suited what I wanted to have for my palace and army. Brill had been one of the very first that I enlisted, and as he proved to be a worthy ally, the more authority he was given. Only the very best would suffice, and the very best were few and far between in Hell.

"While you have been attending to business elsewhere, I realized that we may have been approaching the situation all wrong." Brill stopped, and he spread his beefy arms wide. "These are all my demonies."

"These are all your kids," I asked, flabbergasted.

"Yes, I found one thousand suitable incubators for my donations, and this is the beginning of the result. I am birthing our army to the specs we desire. Some have already graduated school and are now in the army, while others are still to be born. The idea is to have a steady supply forever. As more incubators are available, I will choose one or two others that can help with the cause, but they must be the best specimens and worthy of the task."

I looked Brill up and down, a whole new respect for the demon beginning to form. Not only for the idea, which I hated to admit was brilliant, and I wished I'd thought of it, but also because that many demon-mating-sessions was a new record even by my standards. Female demons were not exactly known for their willingness to participate in breeding. Brill had his chest puffed out, obviously pleased with his creation.

Placing my hands behind my back, I strode past the remainder of the line. Each one of the demons, regardless of age, sex, or even cross genetics, all acted the same. They were obedient, but more than that, I could see the intelligence burning in their eyes.

"You." I pointed to one of the oldest-looking demons. "Come here." The demon leaped from the line and ran forward. It went to its knee as soon as it was close enough and kept its eyes to the floor. This one was draped in the customary black leather and silver armor that said it was almost ready to be moved up the ranks. If it lived, then it too would wear the gold that was customary of all those representing me in my ranks.

"Master, how may I be of service? I live only to serve you." I raised my eyebrow at the demon and marveled at just how well they were trained, but it had also spoken in English. I could see a curl of a smile on Brill's face. I would've understood any tongue, but to choose the one I was most comfortable with spoke volumes. The lengths Brill was willing to go to...these warriors were exactly what I wanted.

"Brill, tell me how well are your warriors trained in all forms of war and battle tactics?"

"This group still needs a bit of work, but they are admirable. The oldest are nearing final testing, some may not survive, but that is the nature of the weaning out process. Jukur here is one of the top students to date. I have high hopes for him, and if he lives up to the standards I have set, he will become a breeder and my successor when the time comes."

"Is that so? Very high hopes for you indeed, Jukur." I tapped my chin as I contemplated my request. "Juker, I want you to steal a red ruby from Pride's castle and bring it to me. I don't care which one, but you must not be caught or seen by any demon."

"Yes, Master. Shall I leave now?"

"Yes, and make it quick. I'd like it in my hands before I leave."

The demon stood and turned, sprinting for the end of the hallway. Jukur disappeared out the door, and as he left, I turned to Brill. "You impress me, my friend, and that is not easy to do."

Brill's dog-shaped head smiled wide, his large fangs showing as his lips pulled back. "You honor me with such words, but I promise you, you will be even more impressed when the young one returns."

Stealing from Pride's castle was a fool's errand. If he was caught, he would be put to death instantly for trying to steal from Lucifer. But my brother had many, many guards and those strange fucked up angels he made flitting about, not to mention the dragon that lurked on the property. But, if the young demon could pull it off without Lucifer being the wiser, I'd wear that fucking gem around my neck and smile. Would Luci notice it was gone? Most likely not, that was more Leviathan's thing to count and fawn all over the pretty gems, but that wasn't the point. The point was not to be noticed, to become one with the shadows and those that protected his palace. If he could do that, the sky was the limit for the potential with these demonies.

I rubbed my hands together at the prospect. If I had my way, this army would march on Heaven one day and finish what Luci started. He'd been right that day. It took me a long time to understand his motives and what it cost me, but I did. The war was brewing once more, and we'd be ready this time.

CHAPTER
FOURTEEN

RIKER

I could almost feel the ruby burning a hole in my leather where it sat as I marched up the long path to Luci's palace. I couldn't wipe the smile off my face since Juker returned with the small stone in hand. Jukur didn't look like he even broke a sweat and returned faster than I could've placed a bet on his return time. When I asked which part of the castle he stole the ruby from, a curl lifted at the corner of his mouth, his eyes glittering with mischief as he said Lucifer's throne. I'd laughed at that, it might have been a smaller ruby, but it was worth a million large ones for being taken from that location.

I nodded to the guards manning Luci's gates and was tempted to pull out the gem and laugh in their faces, but instead, I said nothing. That ability to go unseen in Hell was worth its weight in gold, and I wasn't about to share that with anyone.

The grand doors to the massive palace opened before I reached them, and my step faltered as I took in Luci's appearance. He was dressed like he should be playing the part of a retro porn star. A long black fur coat was draped over his shoulder while wearing no shirt and skin-tight pants. His look was topped off with large sunglasses, a cigar in his hand, and a bottle of Hell Fire Whiskey in his other. All he needed was a mustache and a fedora on his head to complete the look. I had to work hard to contain my shock and plastered a smile on my face."Luci, it's good to see you." I nodded my head, but I refused to bow, kneel or not meet his gaze. If he wanted to kill me for it, then so be it, but to date he hadn't cared or maybe he didn't notice.

My eyes grew wide as Luci reached out and wrapped his arms around me in a hug. I had no idea what to say or do but reciprocated the act with a tentative squeeze. I couldn't even remember the last time Luci and I had shared a hug.

I looked over my shoulder and contemplated if I could make it out of the gate and Hell before he caught me. If he was hugging me there was a good chance he was planning on killing me.

"It's good to see you, Riker. You are looking well."

I raised my eyebrow at him. "Had you heard otherwise?" My suspicion was peaking, especially with the rumors that Michael had been lurking around.

Luci laughed a bark of a sound as he gripped my shoulder. "Of course not. It's just good to see you, brother."

My mouth lifted at the corner in a forced grin, again not sure what had gotten into Luci. He was many things, but a gracious and entertaining host was not on that list.

"Tell me everything. What have you been up to," Luci wrapped his arm around my shoulders, guiding me inside his palace. I had the strongest urge to try and run for fear that whatever was affecting him like this was inside the palace.

"The casino is doing well, and I assume you are still receiving your share of the profits?"

Luci waved a hand like that was boring. "Yes, I am, but I don't care about that."

I gave him a look that obviously said I didn't believe him because he continued to speak. "Okay, fine. I mean, I care a little, or I wouldn't have killed your last manager who forgot to pay me, but it's not really that important."

"You ripped his head off and pulled his spine out of his body," I said, remembering all too well having to find and train a new manager. It was no easy feat after that happened. Everyone had been too terrified to apply.

"In hindsight, it may have been a tad excessive."

"Right, well, my businesses on Earth are prospering, and our sinful influence is spreading faster than the plagues you created."

Loud club music echoed along the great hall, but the only words I could pick out were, "I like to move it" over the laughter and cheers. Someone swung by the mouth of the throne room ahead, but I kept my eyes on Luci's face, not sure I wanted to know what was going on.

We walked into the large space to the throne room, and unable to hide my shock, my mouth fell open. The room was set up like a frat party and a kink club that decided to have a baby with a family game night that was married to a carnival.

There was a plush bed in the center of the room with an assortment of ropes, chains, and demons swinging around from the ceiling. A bar stretched across one side of the room with demons ready to make drinks while others danced on the top of the dark purple surface.

Luci snapped his fingers, and a drink appeared in my hand and a bottle of whiskey in his. "Cheers," he said and clinked my glass. Taking a weary sip, I dared to take another step into the massive room and stared at the table piled high with every board game known to mankind, while a life-sized chess board was not far away.

A demon yelled as it rolled by in a giant ball like a huge rodent, and I suddenly thought something had been slipped into my drink. Arcade games were dinging with lights flashing, a pool table, with demons around it, placed bets as the balls clattered. Black sand from the shore of River Styx had been brought in and was currently being used by two naked female demons as they played a game of volleyball, and the roar of a tiger had me looking toward the throne to see it chained and laying at the base of the large glittering structure. It was gnawing on the remnants of something or someone, and I was suddenly even more impressed with Jukur.

What the actual fuck?

I looked at Luci, his body shimmying completely out of rhythm to the music as he smiled wide. I knew he was waiting for me to respond. There were moments in life that you really wished you could erase. This was one of those moments for me.

Where was the dictator, the man that would rip your head off for looking at him the wrong way? Where was the Master of the Under-world, who planned chaos and death, happily sucking souls up as readily as the Hell Fire Whiskey in his hand? Where was the blood on the floor and the stench of death as Luci sat in his throne barking out orders to torture more souls? What the hell happened to the man always expressing his displeasure over the number of souls coming to Hell over going to Heaven, and the sound of demons screaming as unspeakable things were done to their bodies. And where the fuck was the Hell Fire pit in the middle of the room that Luci liked to toss those in that pissed him off, so he could watch their flesh burn from their screaming bodies.

"So, what do you think?"

I swallowed hard and looked away from his keen stare. "Wow," I said.

It was all I could come up with before I reached over and snatched the bottle of whiskey from his hand. I subtly sniffed the contents and took a tiny sip convinced it must be laced with something as Luci stepped further into the room, his arms spread wide.

"I know it's amazing. I was thinking of adding an amusement park outside. I really want a rollercoaster that stretches all of Hell, can you imagine?"

"No, no I can't, but that would be something," I said and handed back the bottle.

"You can keep it. I have cases." Luci snapped his fingers, and a demon rushed over with two fresh bottles in her clawed hands.

"Why did you create all this," I asked as I followed Luci toward the bed. I had to wonder if he was sleeping in here.

"Why not? Just because this is Hell doesn't mean we can't have some fun, right brother?"

"Yes, I agree." I nodded enthusiastically but caught the slight change in Luci's face as he turned to look away. Was he bored? Depressed maybe? Was that even possible? I didn't dare ask. Even I had my limitations, so instead, I said, "Have you seen the other Fallen lately?"

"No, not really. You're all so busy." Luci sat down on the edge of the bed, but the shadows that crossed his face reminded me of a human mother that was experiencing empty nest syndrome. Not that I knew exactly what that looked like, but I had a pretty good idea.

Sucking in a deep breath, I wandered over to the large stack of games. I wasn't much for board games, but this was one of those rare moments that I knew it shouldn't be about me. Spotting the game I was after, I pulled out the drinking version of Jenga. Neven had shown me this game, and I had to admit I found it entertaining.

"Luci, come over here," I beckoned as I made my way to one of the random standing tables that were set up to have a drink. "When was the last time you got your dick wet," I dared to ask. If I was going to get away with a question like that, this was the day...or night. Who knew what time it was down here.

Luci scoffed and rolled his eyes. "All the time." Laying the game on the table, I stared at Luci and gave him my best 'don't lie to me' face. "Okay fine, it's been a bit," he said quietly. "But, not because I can't," he finished making me smile.

"I'd never think that. We're going to need two of your best demons and two more bottles of whiskey for this." I quickly erected the game and smiled as I remembered how it was to be set up. Neven would be impressed.

Two leggy demons swayed in our direction as Luci waved them over. I looked them up and down and decided they would do. Not my first choice, but the Ol'guth demons were accommodating and a favorite even at my casino.

"Pick a demon," I said, not caring which one I got. Once the demons were chosen, I quickly instructed them to bend over and grab their ankles.

"What are we doing?" Luci eyed the game.

"Here are the rules. We each hold a bottle in one hand and fuck these demons, but to add excitement to the game, we will play Jenga at the same time. To play the game, you pull on one of the little pieces of wood, read what it says on the piece and then do or say what's there, and you sit it on top of the tower without making it fall down. Each successful piece pulled, you take a swig of the whiskey. But, remember you can't stop fucking the girl."

"What's the goal?"

"There are three goals. The first is to get shit-faced drunk. The second is to see who can make the demon come the most before they fall over, and last and certainly the most fun, the winner gets bragging rights. Do you think your pride can take losing to me?"

Luci's nostrils flared with the challenge. "Fuck that. You're going down, brother."

"I should tell you that Leviathan would really love playing this game," I said and internally laughed my ass off as I pictured the look on Leviathan's face when Luci tried to get him to play this game. That Sin was so prim and proper that he made the word 'stately' look shabby.

This was not how I saw my trip going down here, but as the game started, I had to admit it was fun. I laughed hard as the first tile Luci pulled said he had to add the saying, 'in my pants,' to the end of everything he said. It quickly became clear that I wasn't getting back to Earth on schedule.

FIFTEEN

MINETTA sat up straight and gasped as the memories of the creature invaded her mind. The sun was shining in through her parted curtains, and she stared around her room. The only words coming to her mind were, "what the fuck?"

Toby was in his usual spot beside her on the bed, and he was softly snoring, his side rising and falling as if there wasn't a care in the world. She leaped from her bed and looked down at herself. There wasn't a mark on her except one tiny bruise that she could've gotten anywhere. Breathing fast, she grabbed her phone, not wanting to leave it behind this time, and yanked open her bedroom door. She jumped back half expecting to find the strange beast hanging out silently on the other side, but all that was in the short hallway was her bookshelf. She peered out her door and down the stairs.

"Toby, come," she said, and he lifted his head long enough to moan and then flopped it back down. "Really? You're going to make me go down there by myself after last night?" His soft snores were his only reply. "I'll remember this."

She tiptoed along the hallway and cringed with every creak that her feet made on the stairs. The sun was also shining in the living room, and the kitchen windows, and not a damn thing was out of place. She jogged across the kitchen floor and hit the light switch. The old bulbs hummed and then came on, bathing everything in the warm glow.

Her mind was racing. She couldn't have imagined all of that, could she? The knife she used to cut her morning fruit was exactly where she always left it, and her mother's throw was once more laying over the back of the chair in the living room.

"No, no, no, this is not happening. It had to be real, it had to be," she mumbled, not yet sure what freaked her out more. The fact that she possibly was losing her marbles or that if it was real, then that creature existed. Both seemed equally terrible possibilities.

Chewing on her lip, she made her way to the living room and even got down and inspected the floor, not a scratch, not a dent, not a droplet of the black blood anywhere. Shaking her head, she stood and went to the front door. It, too, looked perfectly new. She turned and stepped on something sharp.

"Ouch," she yelped as she jumped and leaned against the wall to look at the bottom of her foot. She stared at the small red sliver and then at the door. Reaching down, she picked out the piece and held it up to the light. It had happened. Anyone else would say she was crazy. Shit, she still might be losing it like her mother had, but she felt it in her soul that what she'd seen last night was real.

She needed to get out of this crazy city for a while. Maybe this was a sign, a warning of sorts. She had no idea what it could be a warning of, but it didn't matter. She didn't want to spend tonight in the house. Running up the stairs, she pulled her small traveling suitcase out from the closet and threw everything in she thought she might need to go away for a few days. She'd planned on seeing her mother anyway, so this was simply an added incentive.

Next was to get Toby ready to go, and lucky she was a crazy dog mom and had a travel bag for him. She stuffed in his favorite toys, and his bowl then grabbed the unopened bag of dog food.

She dashed into the bathroom wanting to shower, but as she looked at the tub and thought about the prospect of being naked and alone there, she nixed that idea. She scooped up the toiletries and stuffed them into her suitcase before zipping it up. The last thing to get ready was herself, so she quickly changed.

Pulling out her phone, she dialed an Uber and then whistled to get Toby to come so they could wait outside. The warm glow of the summer sun shone down on her, but it didn't seem to matter. She was still cold inside. By the time the car arrived, she had herself in a panic, but the sensation settled once she and Toby were on their way and away from the house of horrors.

"Are you sure this is where you want me to leave you?" the driver asked. She looked over her shoulder at the used car dealership and nodded.

"Yup, it's time I got myself a car, and today is the perfect day to do it."

"Alright, lady, if you need me again, here is my personal business card," the young man held out his hand, and she took the little card.

"Thanks." Picking up her luggage and Toby's leash, she walked toward the blowing red, silver, and blue fringe lining the car lot.

R IKER
I yawned as I made my way up in the elevator to the penthouse. I stared at the bags under my eyes in the mirror and rubbed at my messy hair. Either these mirrors were wonky, or I looked like a bag of shit that had been dragged through a knot hole backward.

The elevator dinged as I reached the destination and walked into the long hallway that led to my home. I stopped and fixed a vase that was out of place and fluffed the assortment of cream-colored flowers.

This penthouse was way too much for one person. Even with Shilo here, it was too much space, but that wasn't the point.

One thing visiting Hell always did, was wipe me out. I ended up with Gnarrl over at Luci's and Brill and others who wanted to let loose. That was a mistake. I ended up being dragged over to Leviathan's palace before I could escape back to Earth.

B *rother, it's good to see you. Come, you must see what I have planned for the castle." Leviathan's ever-stately demeanor was in place as he led them through one perfectly kept room to the next. A stark contrast to Luci's palace.*

"You mean manipulating your castle, so it looks like mine isn't good enough?"

"Yours is stunning, brother, but look at this." Leviathan pulled out blueprints and laid them on a massive table. I took a look and cocked my head, not sure I was seeing clearly, and then up to my brother's face.

"You are kidding, right?"

"No, why would I kid?"

"This is a carbon copy of Lucifer's palace. He will not be happy, to say the least," I said.

"Brother, you worry too much. Lucifer won't even notice. He is far too busy for such trivial things."

I wouldn't count on that, I thought but kept my latest encounter to myself.

"I wouldn't do it if I were you," I said.

"I will think on your warning," Leviathan said, but I knew he wouldn't.

Gnarrl grabbed my shoulders. "You are going to stay to party, yes?" He nodded like that would help him get the answer he wanted. "I got some Blood Rot."

"I don't think I can stay. I do have to get back."

Gnarrl jumped around, the entire place shaking. "You have to!"

I sighed as he shook me, his face terrifying and yet so happy, I couldn't say no. Gnarrl was just a young demon when we all fell, a pathetic and tiny thing at the time that was picked on by the larger demons. Leviathan took him in, and we developed a friendship of sorts over the years. He was more like a giant pet, but I was one of the few that wasn't afraid of Gnarrl and his hideousness, and I could actually understand him when he spoke.

"Fine, I'll stay a little longer."

I shook my head to get rid of the images and pushed open the penthouse door. I checked my phone, and luckily I was only gone for a week—enough time to say vacation, not enough time for anyone to worry. The sun was pouring in the massive windows that lined the entire side of the penthouse, the sun making the black and white interior feel starker as it was coated in the golden hue.

The place felt different. I couldn't put my finger on it.

My eyes scanned the large space and focused on the sparkling overhanging pool with the glass bottom that I was so proud of—it had been such a unique addition at the time. Now it was common, and I didn't do common. I looked at the décor and sighed. This place just didn't feel like home anymore. I would start looking to move and upgrade. There were still a great many things that could be improved upon with the next place.

My phone dinged with a million reminders and messages that couldn't connect with my phone in Hell, the thought was wildly funny in my tired state, and I laughed hard.

"Sir, you seem to be in a good mood. The trip must have been exactly what you needed," Shilo said, appearing from the kitchen with a coffee and a green smoothie in hand. His voice was chipper as he smiled at me. "I prepared these in case you returned."

"Shilo, you are the best. Only maybe Brill can compare to you."

"Thank you, Sir." He bowed deeply. I'd told him over and over he didn't have to bow or call me sir, but it didn't matter. The fallen angel wouldn't do things any other way.

"I'll take the green smoothie to cleanse myself. I ended up having a bit too much Blood Rot, Hell Fire whiskey, and pomegranate juice. I'm lucky I made it back at all."

"Indeed, Sir, time is unusual when that particular concoction is at work," Shilo said as if he had firsthand experience, but I highly doubted it.

Humans thought that the apple was the original forbidden fruit, but they would be wrong. Not surprisingly, humans tended to get almost everything wrong when it came to my Father. It was a pomegranate and when you mixed a Hell grown pomegranate with a drop of demon's blood, watch out. That particular combo became the world's best aphrodisiac mixed with the best party trip ever. Hell, it sparkled like a glittering disco ball. It was a really good thing that cell phones and cameras didn't work down below, or there would be some pretty interesting blackmail material.

I walked toward the bedroom, desperately needing a shower and sipping the smoothie that Shilo always managed to make taste fantastic.

"Um, Sir."

I turned to face Shilo, who was still standing by the kitchen wringing his hands together. I intuitively knew something was wrong, something I was not going to like.

"What is it, Shilo?"

The old angel cleared his throat. "I think I found the girl, it took some digging, but there were very few with the name Minetta in the system and only one with the description you gave."

"Okay, and?"

"I have since learned of the house's location, and I took a trip out to investigate and bring her to you if you desired. But it seems she has left, and I do not know if or when she will return." Shilo shifted back and forth from foot to foot.

A small and highly unusual shot of anxiety stirred in my gut. "What do you mean she has left?"

"I am not sure, Sir. Maybe a vacation, or maybe she moved. The mail is piling up at the home, and there is no sign of anyone coming or going. I'm sorry I failed you, Sir." He looked down at the ground.

"You didn't fail me, Shilo. Send me the address. I'll see what I can find out." Turning, I walked away in search of a much-needed shower and my bed. The problem was my mind was once more consumed with a raven-haired beauty with eyes like the Caribbean Sea.

CHAPTER
SIXTEEN

INETTA walked up the path to the nursing home, the same routine she'd done every day for the last eight days, but today felt harder, heavier. Taking a moment to gather herself before she walked into the overly depressing spot, she sat down on a park bench with her small purse clutched in her hand.

One thousand five hundred and eighty-five days was how many days she'd sat in a place similar to this as she held her father's hand. Terminal brain cancer, she remembered those words clearly when her parents had come home from the doctors. With aggressive radiation treatment and surgery, he might make it another two years.

· · ··

"What do you mean you only have two years? You have to see me graduate and get married. How about grandchildren? Don't you want to be here for that," she fumed, anger pushing down the fear and sadness.

"Of course I do, sweetheart. You are my pride and joy. I want to see all those things with you and for you, but this isn't something I chose," her father said calmly, his hand reaching for hers.

She jerked her hand away. This wasn't right. He was a young man, still in his prime. He hadn't even reached fifty yet. How could this be happening?

"You need to fight this! You can't die. I'm only sixteen. I can't lose you." Emotion taking control, she stormed from the room and ran outside. Legs pumping hard, she passed the chicken coop and then the couple of cows who stopped grazing long enough to watch her race past. He can't die. He can't leave her yet.

She and her father had always been close. He taught her how to ride a bike. He taught her how to throw a baseball, he took her fishing and even showed her how to milk the cows properly. Her dad was everything, her friend, and her tutor for school, but he was her dad and protected her most of all.

Tears streamed down her cheeks, and she eventually flopped under one of the apple trees, simply unable to run any longer. She wrapped her arms around her knees and buried her face to cry out the pain that was threatening to consume her. Even as she cried the millions of tears that never seemed to want to end, she couldn't make the pain go away.

"Sweetheart?"

She looked up at the sound of her father's voice. She didn't even remember the sun setting, but as she stared at her father and the stunning fiery sky in the background, she could almost picture him with wings. He was meant to be an angel. He'd always been one. Just all too soon, he would have wings for real.

Her lower lip trembled, and she wiped at the tears with the back of her arm. "I can't lose you, dad. I know that sounds selfish, but I'm too young. We have so many things that we've planned to do. You and mom were talking about us taking a trip to Montana. What about that? Or going to see Japan, you always said you wanted to go there. We've only been to two baseball parks, and we were going to see one a year and start a photo album of our adventures, and...." She stopped talking, unable to get the words out.

Her father lowered himself to the ground and mirrored her position. "We will still take that trip to Montana, but I don't think Japan is going to happen, and we will get a couple more baseball games in."

"It's not the trips or the games dad. This is not fair! Why do so many evil people get to walk around and hurt others and be mean to one another, but you have to die. Why you? I hate God! I hate..." She broke down, bawling again, and her father wrapped an arm around her shoulders, pulling her into his side.

"I know that this hurts so much right now, and I won't lie to you, there are going to be terrible days ahead, but Minetta, you are so special. You're this beautiful spark and light of warmth and kindness that this world needs. No matter what happens, no matter how soon I'm taken, I want you to remember how much I love you, and I want you always to remain this person you are right now."

"I don't know if I can do that, dad. How can I go on with my life like everything is okay, now or when you are..." she bit her lip, not wanting to say the words again.

"Because my dear, life is always going to throw you curveballs, and you are most certainly never going to expect the knuckleball coming, but it's all in how you learn to approach the next pitch."

"Really, dad? A baseball reference now?" She smiled a little as her father laughed.

"I'm still holding out hope you'll turn into a boy and make the Major Leagues," her dad teased as he nudged her shoulder.

"Dad!"

Minetta took a tissue out of her purse and wiped it under her eyes. How fast time sped up when she knew there was a limited amount of it left. What had seemed like forever in front of her was gone in a blink, and so was the man that taught her to be the best possible version of herself. She and her mom got through the worst of it together, each taking turns at the hospital so her dad would never be there alone, would never have to wonder if he was loved.

She sniffed and then blew her nose. Sucking in a ragged breath, she stood and walked to the nursing home's front door. She didn't have anyone to sit with her and help her through things this time. But, a small smile graced her lips as she remembered her dad's final words to her.

"Don't ever let life beat you down, Minetta. Sometimes it will simply throw you the cutter when you were expecting the heater down the middle. Take what the pitcher throws you and hit it out of the park. You're an all-star, my baby girl. You always have been."

CHAPTER
SEVENTEEN

R IKER

I leaned back in the leather chair and stared at the ornate solid gold frame that held an oil painting of myself. I wanted to make sure that everyone who walked into this office knew who sat in the big chair. The fire, although totally un-needed, crackled softly in the matching fireplace, casting dancing flames across the black leather furniture. I watched the flames that reminded me of Hell and zoned out on my conference call. The man on the other end of the speaker was a blowhard, and I was waiting for him to stop talking long enough to turn his offer down. I don't think he'd taken a single breath the entire twenty minutes that he'd been blathering.

"As you can see, Mr. Rhodes, this is a perfect opportunity for both our companies to make a lot of money," he finished.

"No, actually, I don't. This is a fantastic opportunity for your company to ride the lucrative tailcoats of my company, but there is nothing appealing in this deal for me."

"I don't agree. I'm sure if you look again at the numbers—"

"Let me stop you right there." I'd already reached out and touched this man's soul. I knew what he wanted. I knew the greed that lay beneath the surface of the calm, kind exterior he portrayed, and he was not the grandfatherly sort. He might have everyone else fooled, but I was the sin. I tasted it on my tongue like fresh baked goods and swirled it around in my mouth like a fine wine. His essence was strong with the desire to be powerful, to have more and I was about to exploit that.

"I do not wish to waste your time or mine, so here is the deal. If you want to do business with me, your company will be absorbed into mine, and I'll do what I wish with it. You will get a seat on the board and a raise in salary. This will increase according to my company's yearly performance, which is what I know you want desperately. But the company becomes mine, you will no longer have anything to do with it other than at the fiscal board meetings, and if I decide to sell it, you will be paid out accordingly. Now you have forty-eight hours to make up your mind, but I have somewhere else to be this evening. Make an appointment for two days from now."

With that, I pressed the end button and gathered up the folders on my desk. Although I had cameras hidden in the office, it was still better to ensure that anything I didn't want prying eyes to see was securely locked away.

My phone rang, and I thought it was the man calling me back, but Neven's name glowed on the display.

"Neven," I said in greeting, but all I got was dead air. I looked at the phone to make sure it was still connected. "Neven, are you there?"

"Yeah, I just don't want to tell you this, so I'm stalling."

"At least you're honest. Now, what's going on?" There was a dramatic sigh on the other end of the line.

"So you know how we thought that the sales projection was low?"

I stood a little straighter. "Yes, of course, what of it?"

There was the audible sound of swallowing on the other end of the line. "Neven, I'm not going to punish the messenger. Just get on with it. I have something I want to do this evening."

"The manager Nikolas Novak has been siphoning money from all the areas of the company and falsifying the projections to match what he's been taking. To date, I have found over twenty million that has been stolen," Neven said it so fast I wasn't sure that I'd heard him correctly, but the rage that burned in my gut told me that I had.

"Find him and bring him to my office. I'll be back in a couple of hours. I expect him to be here by then." I hung up the phone before I crushed it in my palm and sent a mental message to Brill that I had a job for a couple of the warriors.

I took a steadying breath to calm myself before wings decided to sprout from my back and tear my good suit.

I'd planned on taking a trip out to see if the human female Minetta had returned, so tonight, I was making sure I made it to her place. Maybe if I saw her again and told her that nothing would ever happen between us under any circumstances, I could get the vixen out of my head. I was starting to wonder if she was part siren, and if that were the case, I'd have to kill her. The hairless human was trying to lure me into her snare, but I wouldn't let that happen. She needed to be told to back off.

Shilo had already been sent home, and I had to admit I liked the quiet. No phones ringing off the hook, no one running down the hall waving papers for a deadline, no one interrupting me with a new crisis that had to be taken care of right away. I boarded the elevator as my phone rang, and I wanted to kick myself for even thinking about how blissful the quiet was.

"Skye, I wondered when I would hear from you. You have an uncanny way of knowing when I have returned from down under."

"Why is it you don't sound happy to hear from me? The last time we were together, I distinctly remember you being more than excited to see all of me." Her voice was laced with lust as she practically purred into the phone.

She was trying her best to seduce me, the Asmodeus side of her personality showing. Both her and Neven had been born from a human female, but she had been seduced and raped by a demon that was under lusts influence. After they were born, they were unwanted by their human mother, so since they were half demon, they were cast out and became victims of the Pit of Despair. If you crawled into the wrong hole with the wrong demon, it was very easy to end up tossed in the pit. I liked plucking demons from the pit when they got stuck in the swirling mass of nothingness. They were loyal and worked hard not to end up back there again. I had more than one demon working for me that I'd found there. It was kind of like finding a pool of the best fish that no one else bothered to seek out.

"I'm heading out, was there something you needed?"

Skye sighed loudly. "Welllll, I was going to see if you wanted to get together, but obviously that isn't going to happen," she said. I heard the annoyance in her voice, and I picked up on a thread of jealousy.

I rubbed my face. Neven was right. Skye was more attached than I ever intended for her to become. "I thought you were going shopping in Europe for a few days?"

"I already did."

"You could always visit Hell again. I know a number of demons that would be happy to make sure you're never in need of sex," I said, hoping she'd take the hint. I didn't want a relationship. I didn't even want a regular sexual partner. There was a reason I lived the way I did. The friendship between Skye, Neven, and myself had started a long time ago, and I should have never let it turn into something more. That was my mistake. I didn't make them often, but allowing her to call us fuck friends, to put a label on us, was most certainly up there.

"You know I don't like going there often. It does nothing for my complexion and doesn't have the same food choices. Humans have a flare for cooking, and the demons in Hell could learn a thing or two from them." She was moving around, and then I heard the sound of water as a shower was flicked on. "I could send you a photo of the naughty things I'm going to be doing in the shower very soon. There are some very interesting positions I've wanted to try."

"As I mentioned, I have a prior engagement."

There was a dramatic sigh. "What are you doing tonight that makes it hard for us to get together later?" she asked, her voice dripping with irritation.

The tone prickled my anger. She was a demon and lucky that I paid her any attention at all. The decades of friendship would mean nothing to me if she continued to press.

"Skye, remember who you are speaking to in that tone. Maybe I have made a mistake allowing you to run amuck with whatever you want and treat me like I'm some toy boyfriend, but make no mistake, I am not."

"No, I, umm..." she stammered.

"Would you like me to send you back to the hole you were pulled from?" I could hear a heavy swallow and her breathing pick up through the line. I wouldn't really put her back in the Pit of Despair unless she forced me to do it.

"Whatever, Ri, you're so bloody fickle sometimes."

I rolled my eyes. "I have to go."

I hung up the phone and stuffed the thing in my pocket as I marched toward the Valkyrie.

The drive to Minetta's home didn't take very long. It helped that traffic was light with vacationers out of the city, and the area she lived in was a less wealthy part of town. I didn't take vacations, not in the way that humans did. The laying around on a hot beach with fake coconut smelling oil coating their skin reminded me of pigs getting ready to be placed on a spit. Going to Hell was still work. It had its partying moments, but that wasn't why I went.

I sat in the car for a long time, wondering why I was even here. My finger tapped on the top of the steering wheel as I thought. Had I not just been thinking that I didn't want a relationship, and I certainly didn't want one with a human? What kind of life would that be even if I did want one? A mere fifty years would be the best that we'd get.

I started the car getting ready to drive away, but a shadow moved around inside the dimly lit home, and I couldn't drive away without speaking to her at least once more. Even if it was to confirm what I already knew, which was I didn't want anything from her and for her to stay away from me.

Pushing open the door of the car, I stepped out into the humid night and marched for the beige shoebox home with the blood-red door. I pounded on the wood surface and did so again when she didn't move fast enough.

"What?" A man glared at me as he pulled open the door. I stared at the male human, my eyes traveling up and down his body. This human was the equivalent of a flea hitching a ride on a fly as it ate a pile of shit. Not exactly what I expected to find. "Who the fuck are you?" He gripped both sides of the door frame and flexed his arms like that might actually make him look intimidating.

My eyebrow rose at his words. "I'd ask you the same question. Is this the residence of Minetta Johnson?"

"And what is it to you if it is?" The human male said.

It was obvious he felt threatened as he stepped back and crossed his arms over his chest, his stance widening as if trying to warn me off from the house or the other occupant. No one kept me from anything that was mine or what I wanted, and even though this girl wasn't in either category, I still didn't take kindly to being told no.

I narrowed my eyes at the man, my ability reaching out to search his mind and soul to give me the best picture of who was before me.

"Tell me are you sleeping with her? I mean, is she really into a sloth, like you," I asked, not able to picture this selfish man with the woman I'd met.

I shouldn't care, but a thread of jealousy lanced its way through my psyche and proceeded to mount the monkey bars in the back of my mind. I didn't like this man, and I certainly didn't want him near Minetta. If I needed to remove him, I would.

"What the fuck did you just say to me, asshole? You can't come here with your fancy three-piece suit and think you can talk to me like that," the man yelled. It was a complete overreaction and spoke once more to his rising insecurity.

"Just go get Minetta, please. I need to speak to her. I don't have time for a cock comparison. It's trivial. Besides, I already know that my wallet and dick are larger," I said and straightened the sleeve on my suit jacket. My hand reacted at the first flicker of movement. The fist had been coming for my face, but I easily caught it and squeezed hard. A yell came from the pathetic human as the bones loudly crunched.

He began to crumple to his knees, but I kept him upright enough to push him back so I could step inside the home. I was done with trying to do the civilized thing and reached out with my mind to search the home, but only found this swamp thing of a man to be here.

"Where is Minetta?" I felt the distinct touch of his mind as my ability seeped deeper into the dark recesses of his brain to pull the answers I sought forward.

He grabbed his head with his free hand as he fought the pain of my abrupt intrusion. It would do no good, though, and his mouth began to spew the answers like a geyser.

"Minetta went to visit her mother."

"And where does her mother live?" I asked.

"Maryland, she went back home to Maryland," the man whimpered as my fist tightened slightly.

"And when is she due to return?"

"I don't know," the man said. I looked around the small space and spotted a couple of packing boxes.

"Is she moving?" I really didn't want the answer to be yes. For whatever reason, I was fascinated with the girl, and the thought of her leaving for good did not sit well in my stomach.

"I don't think so, but I don't know for sure." The man let go of his head as I released the power over his mind and then let go of his hand, and he sank to the floor. I could've been more subtle, to the point that he wouldn't even have noticed my influence, but this was more efficient, and I liked seeing him in pain.

"What are the boxes for then?" I nodded to the three average boxes sitting in the narrow hallway.

"The bitch kicked me out. After all I've done for her over the years, she kicks me to the curb. She knows I don't have a job right now. It was a bitch move, and I should've left her uptight ass long ago."

My lip curled up as I reached out and grabbed the man by the neck. Pulling him to his feet, I slammed him against the wall. His eyes went wide as I proceeded to lift his feet off the floor. Fear danced in his blue eyes as I felt my eyes flash with power and knew that they were glowing slightly. It was rare that my anger would make me show even a modicum of my true self to a human, but this man was pushing the right buttons.

"What the fuck," the man whispered as he stared into my glowing orbs.

"Does Minetta know you have a 'girl on the side' that's carrying your child, James?" I snarled, my voice deepening with the building rage. "Does she know you've been stealing from her for years and planned on leaving her once you used her connections to get a job where she works? Does she know you made friends with some men there and planned on getting her fired so you wouldn't have to work with her? And does she know that you never loved her although you claimed that you did? My guess is that she doesn't know any of that, and she never will." Pulling James back, I slammed him against the wall again because it felt good to do so.

"You'll not pursue a job at her work. You can cancel that interview that's set. You will not get her fired, and you will never darken her door again." A trickle of true terror traveled through James's body as the stench of fear wafted off of him like a spoiled cologne. "I'm pretty sure she's not the one who is the bitch in this situation. If anything, I'd say she wisened up."

I let go of his neck, and he dropped to his feet, but I placed my hand on the wall beside his head, making sure he still felt as trapped as he was.

"Do not mess with me, James. I will hunt you down like the stuck pig you are, and I will hang you over an open spit of Hellfire for all eternity. Now get your shit and be gone. Do not bother Minetta again, or I will return."

James's eyes were wide. Every muscle coiled to bolt the first moment I allowed him. I leaned in close to his ear. "You should know, I'm not a very nice person when people don't listen to me, and I actually kind of like it when they don't. This is where you leave while you still have two functioning legs and the junior one in the middle because I'm tempted to rip off all three." I stepped back from James and felt my eyes return to normal. "I meant go, now," I said quietly. James acted like I'd shot him out of a cannon as he dove toward the boxes.

Arms shaking, James stacked them on top of one another and bolted out the door. Bending, I grabbed the sneakers that were obviously his and threw them out the door after him. One hit him in the back of the head the other one hit the middle of the back as he loaded his vehicle.

Smiling, I slammed the door. Now that the trash had been taken out, it was time to learn more about my mysterious little raven beauty.

CHAPTER
EIGHTEEN

R IKER

I really had started out trying to be nice, but my patience quickly evaporated as the words, 'the money is gone,' came out of Nikolas's mouth.

"What do you mean the money is gone?"

"Please don't kill me," Nikolas begged as he knelt before Brill and the two young warriors that he'd brought with him.

The reaction Nikolas had when Brill walked into the room and showed his real face and not the human illusion demons created when here on Earth had me laughing so hard that my sides hurt. It had almost been enough for me to let the man go knowing that his nightmares would stalk him as punishment, but that was not my way. You didn't get to steal from me and live.

"I have to tell you, Nikolas, you're not off to a very good start." I rose to my feet, and he grabbed at my legs, the desperation evident in his eyes. "Where has the money gone, Nikolas?"

"I don't know. I...I...was going to put it back, I swear. I stole it to invest, and I was going to take the interest and pay back what I'd taken, but it disappeared out of the account."

"So, you wanted to get rich off my money and my hard work, and then before you could put the money back, it gets stolen from you?"

His eyes looked extra large behind the thick glasses he was wearing, making him look like a bug. Nikolas nodded furiously as tears streamed down his cheeks. Annoyed, I snapped my fingers, and the two warriors each grabbed an arm and pried his fingers away from my pants. The one warrior tossed the much smaller man over his shoulder as Nikolas screamed hysterically, squirming like a worm on a line.

"Last time Nikolas, where did my money go?"

"I don't know. I don't know who would've known that I'd taken it in the first place. Maybe someone in the office, or someone at the bank that I transferred it to, I swear I don't know."

The warrior slammed Nikolas down on the metal slab table with a bang. Nikolas's face contorted with pain and made a stupid-looking duck face as all the air was driven from his lungs.

The man coughed and cried as the warriors strapped him down, his arms secured above his head while his feet were cinched to the bottom corners of the table.

"Please, please, please, you didn't need the money. I meant no harm. I borrowed it. I swear I didn't plan to steal it."

Marching over to the table, I leaned over the man, my eyes glowing bright with anger. "Whether I need the money or not is not the point. It was mine, I'd earned it, and you took it. That is a cardinal sin to me."

"I'm sorry, I'm so sorry," Nikolas blubbered.

"Do you like hot pokers Nicolas," I asked as I stared into the man's eyes. He seemed hypnotized by the swirling color, his eyes zoning out.

"I...I...please don't do this," he cried, but his tears had no effect on me.

Leaning closer to his ear I smirked as I whispered, "because you're going to learn just how hot hell is, inside and out." Nikolas whimpered. Pushing myself upright, I smoothed out the front of my shirt. "Greed is a terrible thing when it consumes you, Nikolas. I should know." I smiled at him, my power still churning, so I knew my eyes were still glowing an unearthly gold color.

"I'll pay you back," he said as I made my way toward the exit.

Pausing, I turned back to face the man that had already purchased his one-way ticket to Hell.

"Yes, you will, Nikolas, in this life and the next. Do you know what catches a high price on the market?" The man didn't say anything other than softly begging me not to do this. "Organs do, and Brill here, well he's a professional when it comes to extracting organs, aren't you Brill?"

"Yes, Master, I am," Brill said and licked his lips, making Nikolas scream wildly once more as he pulled foolishly on the bindings.

"Take anything you can fetch a price for in Hell and dispose of the rest." I started to walk away and stopped to turn back. "One more thing, when his soul arrives in Hell, find something delightfully terrible to torture him with. You see, Nikolas, you'll never escape your mistake, even in death. No one steals from me and lives to tell the tale."

The screams started before the door was closed. I glanced at the time and groaned, two hours until my meeting, and then I had a flight to catch. I guess I wouldn't be getting any sleep again. Killing humans was such an annoying waste of time.

CHAPTER
NINETEEN

MINETTA needed to get back to work before they fired her. She also needed to get back to the house, where she was pretty sure she had her first delusion. It was a very real sign of early on-set dementia. Or she really did see a creature from god-only-knew-where in her house, and her friend lit up like a living breathing fire entity. Either option was not sitting well with her.

Minetta walked the last of the boxes from the farmhouse to the moving truck and then pulled the door closed. Turning, she leaned against the truck to stare at the home she'd grown up in. The tire swing, although weathered, still gently swayed in the breeze, and she could still picture the animals that she'd tended to each day. The rabbits and horses had been her favorite. Her one regret was being too scared to let her dad teach her how to ride. She'd brush the horses for hours, but the thought of getting on one had her sweating bullets and pulling back like she was the one on a tie chain.

She had no idea who the new owners were, but the key in her hand was the last goodbye to that part of her life with her parents.

Ninety-eight days from the day her dad had passed was all it took until her mom was diagnosed with a disease that had slowly stolen pieces of her mother, leaving in its wake a sweet stranger. She wrapped her arms around herself. This was a lot harder than she'd imagined it would be. Other than short visits to her mom, staying away from the farm for the last couple of years had allowed her to block out what her mother's turn for the worse really meant.

With her head held high, she made the last trip she'd ever make to the front door. "I love you, mom, I love you, dad. I miss you both every day." She laid her lips on the key and put it in the mailbox like she'd been instructed. She rested her hand against the door and smiled as a memory of her and her parents smiling and laughing as they sat outside under the sun came to her. That was how she wanted to remember this place, not the sad and empty building it was now.

Wandering back to the moving van, she hopped in the front and headed toward the hospital to see her mom before returning to New York.

"You ready to get going, bud," she said to Toby, who was snoozing with his head hanging out the window.

Her hands found his soft ears and began to scratch him the way he liked, and he woke and sleepily glanced at her. "Yeah, I'm about that excited too."

R IKER
     I stood and rolled out my shoulders as the plane came to a
     stop. It wasn't a long flight, but I preferred to use my own
wings rather than these terribly loud and annoying metal tubes. I gave
Shilo's shoulder a squeeze, and his eyes fluttered open.

"Oh Sir, I'm so sorry, have we arrived?"

"We have, not long ago. They are just bringing the vehicle over
now," I said as I watched the Lamborghini slowly pull up.

"Smashing, another sports car." Shilo groaned.

"I'm sensing you do not enjoy my driving."

"I would never say that, Sir." The hint of a smile ghosted his
features before his face grew serious.

"Of course, you wouldn't. But you don't enjoy it, do you?" Shilo
looked to the floor of the plane. "I'm not angry. I'm just wondering
why?"

"Sir, does the term bat out of hell mean anything to you?"

"I do not drive like how those pesky creatures fly. Do I?" I said as we
reached the tarmac.

"I have only tossed my cookies once since I was banished, Sir, and it
was while you were driving. That should tell you all you need to know."

I crossed my arms and sighed. "Fine, you drive. I'll navigate." I
marched around to the passenger side of the car and slipped in. Shilo
stood still, eyes wide as he stared at me. "Well, come on, we don't have
all day."

Shilo slowly wandered over to the car and jumped into the driver's
seat, running his hand over the steering wheel. "Thank you, Sir."

"Would you please call me Riker or Ri or really anything other than
Sir?"

Shilo's face swung to look at me, his old eyes full of a childish
exuberance, and stared back. "I'm sorry, Sir, fire me if you must, but I

cannot refer to you so informally, not anymore, not since that day and you took me in. I was broken, and I was beyond myself. You will forever be my Sir."

I sighed and gripped my friend's shoulder. "Fine," I said to the man I'd known since I learned how to talk. "Let's get going. The jet is going to refuel while we are gone."

The drive from the airport to the country property was relaxing. It was the first time that I'd let anyone else drive me anywhere in a very long time. I'd left the windows down, and the wind was blowing my hair back while the sun warmed my skin. Shilo turned onto a dirt road that shook the fancy car violently.

Shilo slowed and pulled onto the driveway. I looked around, and even though the place was simple and small compared to anything else I'd ever owned, it felt welcoming and warm. A dull ache formed in my chest, and I rubbed at the spot as I stared up at the weathered farmhouse.

Stepping out of the car, I listened for any sign of Minetta, but the place was quiet. Drawn to the swing, I wandered over to the large tire. Closing my eyes, I reached out and touched the rope. I sucked in a sharp breath as the image of a young girl laughing, her black hair flowing as she leaned back and yelled faster, flowed through me as if it was my own memory. A man pushed the tire, and she giggled, her blue eyes shining in the sun.

I jerked away from the tire and stared at my hand. I didn't know why but something wet ran down my cheek. I tentatively touched the moisture and stared at it. Was I crying? I never cried. Why would this happen? I gave the tire a long dirty stare like it had special powers as I walked away and met Shilo on the creaky old porch.

"Is she here?"

"I'm sorry, Sir, everything is gone," Shilo said. Shilo peered in the window, his hands shading the side of his eyes as he looked around.

"Shilo, tell me something. Am I chasing my tail, and if I am, why am I doing so?"

"What do you mean, Sir? I was unaware you had sprouted a tail. Is this a recent occurrence from your trip to Hell?"

I glanced over at Shilo and laughed.

"I'm sensing sarcasm." Shilo didn't confirm or deny, but the little lift of his brow confirmed my suspicion. "No Shilo, it means that I am chasing myself in circles. I don't chase things. I make things happen, or people chase me. I don't chase business deals or anything else, yet here I am, standing on this practically unknown girl's porch, and she is gone. My second attempt to contact her, and she's gone. My question is, why?"

"Why is she gone, Sir?"

"Really, Shilo?" I sighed. "Why am I chasing her in the first place?" I marched away and leaned against one of the covered porch's pillars. "Why am I even here? Does this place look like somewhere I would purposely visit?"

"May I be frank, Sir?" Shilo leaned his hands on the railing near me. The way the sun shone on his face, I could picture him as he once was, in his long white robes with wings that had a few grey tips from age. He'd always been a good angel, and what did that get him? He'd been tossed away like garbage even after centuries of loving and worshiping at my Father's feet, just as I had been. Shilo hadn't deserved that. None of the Fallen had.

"Yes, of course, I prefer if you were honest."

"I think we are here because you like her."

I looked at Shilo, my brow furrowing at the crazy notion. "That's ridiculous. I don't like humans. Especially not to..."

"Date?"

"I guess that's the word. Date, pursue, have relations. They are...not my taste, and besides, I don't date. I fuck, I have fun, I party, and I control, but I don't date." I crossed my arms over my chest and looked out over the lawn and the car that looked totally out of place.

"Then tell me, Sir, what is your taste?" Shilo raised an eyebrow at me, and I opened my mouth and closed it again. "Do you even know? At the risk of insulting you, I am not sure you have given yourself a chance to know what or who you would like on this Earth."

"Why would I?"

Shilo sighed and turned to stare at me. "Sir, I wish only for you to find true happiness. As you mentioned, the wealth is fun, but does it bring you peace?"

I couldn't answer that and looked away instead. "Come on. We might as well go. There's no point wasting more time on this fool's errand."

"Sir."

"Shilo, I don't want to hear any more of this liking a human nonsense. She fascinates me because I didn't feel greed in her heart. I just wanted to know why." I rationalized, but I didn't know who I was trying to convince, myself or Shilo.

Shilo sighed but nodded. "Alright, Sir. Then we shall not speak of this place or the young female Minetta."

I nodded in agreement. "That's right. We won't."

"May I make one suggestion before we go, Sir?" Shilo said, and I stopped on the flaking wooden steps to stare at him. "Just in case you see her, maybe a quick walk around here to learn a little about who this girl is would be wise. There could be valuable information as to why she has this unusual effect on you."

I rubbed my chin as I pondered Shilo's logic. "Alright, better to be armed with knowledge." I marched back up the stairs and grabbed the doorknob.

CHAPTER

TWENTY

MINETTA sat down at her desk and stared over where Penny would normally sit. Minetta had put in for a shift change while she was away. She wasn't sure if what she'd seen at the house was real, but she had no intentions of putting herself in Penny's orbit until it was sorted. It was a tough call to make, and she was pretty sure that Penny's feelings would be hurt, but what could she say?

Hey just need some time away from you until I figure out if you are some fire creature that I think saved my life, but you could've been there to kill me, so until I figure it out, I'm gonna need a breather? It's either that or I imagined the whole thing, and now I feel totally awkward for avoiding you. I hope you understand?

Penny was her only real friend, the person she would text or call when something weird would happen or if she had a bad fight with James. Even when she'd visit her mom and had a tough visit, it was Penny who had always been there to talk to and pick her up. While away, she'd ignored all fifty texts and the phone messages that had filled her mailbox.

Maybe she hadn't made the right call.

The programs she used had barely fired up when her first call came in. "Nine, one, one, what's your emergency?"

"Hi, I wanted to complain about a fire truck blocking the road. I can't get down my street to my home. I mean, I know they have a job to do, but do they really have to take up the entire road?"

"Where are you located, ma'am?"

"Five, five, five, Lord Duffy Drive."

She pulled the area up on the screen, and there was a major house fire in progress. The entire road was closed as the fire had already spread to another townhouse.

"Ma'am, I'm sorry, but there is an ongoing fire at that location. You won't be able to pass through until it is safe."

"Well, that's not good enough. I have frozen food in my car, and I need to get it in the freezer, or I will be charging the city."

Her line flashed with another caller. "Ma'am, I'm really sorry that this has inconvenienced you, but your concern is not a nine, one, one emergency. I'm going to have to let you go."

"I want to speak to your supervisor!"

Of course, you do.

"One moment." She transferred the call to her supervisor's office and answered the next caller.

"Nine, one, one. What's your emergency?"

"Ah yes, Hi. I just had my car impounded, and I want to know how I get it back?"

She shook her head and rubbed her eyes. "I'm sorry, Sir, this is not an emergency question or situation. I would call the company that impounded your vehicle to get the answers you're looking for." She hung up and hit the button for the next caller.

"Nine, one, one. What's your emergency?"

"Um, yeah, Hi, I need some help."

"Okay, Sir, what do you need help with?"

There was a long pause, and she could hear a female voice in the background encouraging him to answer the question. "I have a summer sausage in me," the man groaned as her fingers stopped typing.

"I'm sorry, did you just say you have a..."

"Yeah, I did, and it hurts. It went all the way in. My ass literally ate the sausage."

"So, there is a large sausage in your backside?" One of the other call-takers burst out laughing, and Minetta had to cover her mouth not to follow suit.

"Yeah, my wife bought it cause it was the size of my forearm. Said it would feel good, and it would be fine since it had a string. But it just shot up in there so fast, and it sucked the string in, right off my finger. I need to get it out, it was spicy, and it's starting to burn." She bit her hand not to laugh.

"I will dispatch an ambulance to your location, Sir. What is your address?"

"No, I can't have them showing up here. I don't want my neighbors to know. Can't you just help me?"

"I'm sorry, Sir. How would you like me to assist you in getting the sausage out of your backside?" She had to bite her lip to keep a straight face.

"Don't you have like instructions or something?"

"I'm sorry, Sir. They don't train us for this particular issue." She covered her mouth as more people overhearing her conversation began to laugh in the office. She typed in 'a foreign object stuck in the rectum, possibly a sausage' on her screen and really wanted to see the paramedics' faces when they saw the call. Sadly, this was not her first unique item stuck in a rectum call. "Sir, you're either going to need to make your way to a hospital, or you're going to have to have an ambulance come and get you. So please, what is the address?"

A loud noise started up, and she gasped as she realized it was a vacuum. "Sir, what are you doing?"

"My wife said we should try the vacuum. Ahhh, shit, that hurts. It's moving. Can you grab it? That's it, grab that sausage, babe. Fuck, pull it harder."

"Sir, please don't tell me your wife has a vacuum up your rectum," she asked, her voice cracking. She had to it the mute button as she couldn't hold back the laughter any longer. She gripped her stomach as tears poured down her cheeks.

"It's moving. Fuck, yes, yes it's still coming, can you see it?" The man sighed loudly into her ear, and she wasn't sure if it was from relief or pleasure. "Crisis averted, it's out," the man said. "Thank you, but I don't need an ambulance."

"I would recommend getting checked out to be safe, Sir."

"I'm good now, just a little warm."

"Have a good day, Sir." She hung up the phone and had to grip the edge of her desk as she released the laughs she had struggled to keep in check. Yes, it was going to be one of those days.

She hadn't been wrong. By the time work was done, she was officially worried about humanity and its sanity as a whole. We are all in a lot of trouble if the people that called in were any indication of who was going to be voting and running the country in the future. She picked up her phone to text Penny and tell her about the sausage guy, but her fingers stilled as she stared at the fifty unread message bubble.

Instead, she flicked off the computer just as her cell dinged with a text.

Why hello there beautiful? I was wondering about that coffee?

She stared at the text and the unknown name and was drawing a blank on who this could be. She didn't bother to answer it, figuring it was most likely a scammer or wrong number. Her phone dinged again, and groaning, she opened the message.

Please don't tell me you've forgotten me already? How many guys do you have saving you from out-of-control vehicles?

Her heart pounded a little faster as recognition set in. Michael. A smile slowly spread across her face. When she hadn't heard from him, she'd assumed she'd scared him off.

I try only to need rescuing once a month. It takes too much to remember any more shining white knight's names than twelve in a year.

LOL! So about that coffee, would you be interested?

She chewed her lip. She'd just broken up with James after basically being together with him for nine years. Off and on, but still. On the other hand, she needed to get out there. Besides, how many times did someone like this man walk into a girl's life?

Okay, I can do coffee, when and where?

How about right now? I happen to be in the area for work and could meet you at Café Salvation, around the corner from your work.

She'd only been there once because the prices were out of this world, but she could splurge his one time.

Okay, I'm still in my work clothes, though.

As long as they are not sopping wet again, I'm in. Although you looked very delectable in that wet T-shirt contest look you had going on. It was very distracting.

Heat rose up her neck, and she took a deep breath, the smile once more breaking out across her face.

Sorry, that was a one-time deal.

Too bad, I was really hoping for an encore performance at some point.

LOL!

I'm sorry that was probably too forward. Did I scare you off?

Nope, I'll see you in five.

The elevator couldn't move fast enough. The doors opened, and some of the next shift was arriving for work. Penny stood amongst them. She locked eyes with Penny as they passed one another. She seemed to be her normal smiley self, her hair in the perfect bun. It only made her feel crazier.

"Hey girl, I'd stop and chat, but I'm running late. See you later, Minny. We need to catch up." Penny smiled as the doors closed. Minetta stared at the doors until they opened again, and more people filed out. She'd expected to feel instant fear the next time she saw Penny, but instead, she felt...normal. What the hell was wrong with her?

Pushing Penny out of her mind, she pushed her way out the front doors and made her way around the corner.

It's just coffee, don't be weird.

She told herself as she pulled open the door to the busy, hip location where the music was too loud and the people more so. The smell was delightful, and she took a deep breath of the rich coffee scent that married perfectly with the hum of espresso machines hard at work. A few girls were leaning up against the island where you could doctor your beverage, but their drinks were untouched as they stared across the room.

Following their gaze, she found Michael sitting in the corner looking at his phone. His eyes lifted from the phone as if feeling her gaze and smiled wide, making her pulse race. She raised her hand in a dorky wave and then turned to face the front of the café as the line moved up.

So much for not acting weird.

"I've got it," he said, from right behind her, making her jump.

"If anything, I've got it. I need to repay you for your kindness."

"Nonsense. Now let's see. You strike me as a chocolate, chai tea, latte, half sweetener but two cream kind of girl."

Her mouth fell open as he said exactly what she was thinking of getting. "How did you do that?"

"I'm in negotiations, remember? I'm good at reading people. Your eyes were lingering on today's special." Michael gave her a wink and then leaned over to give the barista their orders. "Tell me about yourself, Minny. What do you like to do for fun," Michael asked as they made their way over to the table he'd occupied earlier. It was shocking that no one had taken it in his absence.

"I'm not terribly exciting, I'm afraid. I like yoga and books. I love to take my dog for walks. Oh, and I help out as a volunteer at all sorts of events."

"Like this one?" Michael turned his phone around, and it showed a picture of the fundraiser she'd volunteered at not too long ago.

"Yes, I was there, actually."

"It was really nice of Avidity Enterprises to donate such a large amount of money to the cause."

"Really? I didn't know. I actually don't even know what company that is." She sipped the hot drink and moaned a little. There was a reason this was the most expensive and most popular café around.

"It's that new tall black building with all the silver and reflective black glass," Michael said and then sipped his cappuccino.

"I know the building, just nothing about the company."

"Neither do I really, but they handed over two hundred thousand for the food bank." She choked on the sip of her latte.

"Are you serious? That's incredible. That will feed so many people." She smiled wide, thinking of all the families they could help with that kind of donation.

"I know, which is why it makes it so terrible that no one has recognized the company for their generosity. Things like that can make a company not want to do it again in the future. You know they could feel like it wasn't appreciated."

"I hadn't thought about that. Oh my." Her face fell as she thought about such a generous donation not coming in again because someone had forgotten to thank the company.

"Anyway, enough about that, tell me more about yourself." Michael sat back and seemed to hang on her every word. Whether he really wanted to or was just being polite, she couldn't tell, but it was nice to have a conversation with a man that didn't treat her like a personal maid.

"I grew up in a small town in the country but always wanted to come to the big city and fell in love with my job, and here we are."

Michael's phone dinged, and he looked at his watch. "Shoot, I have to get going. I have a late meeting tonight. I would love to pick this up where we left off, but how about over dinner? I have another meeting tomorrow, but how about Thursday evening?" He smiled again, and she was sure she heard every woman and some of the men sigh.

"I would like that."

He walked her outside, but before he left, he took her hand in his and kissed the back of it. "I'm looking forward to Thursday, Minny. You don't mind if I call you that do you?"

"No, feel free, all my friends...." She stopped herself from repeating it again like a broken record. "Yes, you can call me Minny."

He wandered down the street, his business casual outfit hugging his ass and shoulders, giving her one hell of an amazing view.

"Oh shit, dinner," she mumbled. "I need something to wear."

Great, now she had two errands to run when she was done with work tomorrow.

CHAPTER

TWENTY-ONE

MINETTA Work ended much like the day before—she saw Penny again, and exactly like the day before, she acted like nothing was weird between them. Minetta was really starting to wonder if the entire creature situation had been lack of sleep, maybe a little heat stroke, or even stress over the whole James thing. She was actually pleasantly surprised he had not tried to beg her to come back like every other time they split. She hadn't been up for that argument.

She made her way down the street to pick up her order of chocolate flowers and fresh fruit shish kebobs. The arrangement was stunning, exactly what would make a great thank you gift. She whistled as she walked the rest of the way to the tall black building that Michael had mentioned. The doors automatically spun, granting her entrance without having to stop. The lobby was the largest she'd ever seen, and the way the building had been designed, you could stand in the middle and look up to see the sky out the massive panes of glass at the top. It was like the building was cored out in the center like an apple.

Everything was decorated in black and gold with sand-colored accents—she'd never seen anything so lavish. She suddenly felt very out of place in her basic work pants and cotton uniform shirt as women and men passed by in more expensive outfits than she could ever afford.

Minetta made her way over to the reception area, and all those that were working looked like the 911 call center did on a crazy day.

"Can I help you?" a girl behind the counter asked as she pushed buttons on the large phone and clicked the mouse at the same time.

"Yes, I wanted to drop this off...."

"Oh wait, what day is it?" She looked at her screen. "It's Wednesday. I'm sorry, just take elevator six to the top floor. Everyone else is up there."

"The top floor, but I...."

"I'm sorry it's that way." She pointed behind her. "I need to get this line. Avidity Enterprises, how may I direct your call?"

Deciding to just go with it, she walked to elevator six and pressed the button for the top floor. Seemed appropriate that those who ran this place would have their offices at the top.

She grabbed the railing around the interior of the elevator as her stomach flipped with the sudden lurch as the lift shot up like a bullet. If she thought the start had been bad, the stop was worse. She felt like crawling out of the elevator as her legs shook and her stomach rolled.

Minetta looked out the elevator and to the right. There was a wall of windows that looked out over the city, but to the left sat another elaborate desk. She made her way over, but there was no one sitting behind the desk. She could hear talking and decided to follow the sound. She turned the corner at the end of the hallway and almost ran into a girl leaning against the wall.

"Oh, I'm sorry," she said.

"You here to see Mr. Rhodes too?"

"I think so. This is for him." She held up the basket.

"Just tell whoever is at the front of the line that you're here to drop that off." She pointed to the front of the very long line of women. "That way, they won't get angry."

"Thanks." That was an odd comment but shrugging it off she continued on her mission. Minetta glanced at the women as she walked along the long line. Not one of them smiled or said Hi back. They all seemed more like they would prefer to slit her throat and had to wonder what their problem was. She held the basket up like a shield and stayed as far away as possible. She had no idea what was happening but figured it had to do with a job.

Reaching the front of the line, she smiled at the girl at the front. "Hi, I'm just delivering this," she said, remembering the other girl's warning.

The pretty blonde nodded and stepped aside. As soon as she stepped over the threshold, she knew something was off. The room was similar to a sitting area with a bar space, four leather chairs that filled the center of the room, surrounding a large coffee table in the middle, but that wasn't what had her attention. Two large guards stood like statues outside of an almost closed door, but the sounds still carried, and she would have sworn someone was having sex. And not just sex, but hot sex that had someone moaning loud.

A strange little tingling sensation took over her body, so she rubbed at her arms. But not even the sensation could've prepared her for the sight that greeted her eyes as the door to the slightly ajar office opened wide.

"Next!" a man's voice yelled.

Four women holding onto their pile of clothes wandered out, but there was still another bent over a desk while a man was taking her from behind. The basket fell from her hands, and the man turned his head to look at her.

It was him. The man with the amber eyes. Their eyes locked as the strange tingling sensation erupted in her chest, making her heart beat hard. She stood there a moment longer than appropriate, and her mind scrambled as she tried to make sense of what was happening.

Her brain kicked into gear and with it the mortification as she sprinted for the door, basket forgotten. She raced past the long line of women who stared at her jackrabbit exit. Her finger pressed the elevator button, wishing this place wasn't so bloody tall, so she could've just taken the stairs.

"Minetta!" She heard her name called. She had no idea how this man found out her name, but thankfully the elevator doors opened, and she jumped inside, the button making clicking noises as she pressed it again and again for the ground floor. At that moment, she was thankful that the elevator was like a rocket. Stepping out of the small space, she marched out the front doors. Anger, humiliation, and an emotion that made no sense at all burned in her gut. Now, it made total sense that she'd laid in bed over the last week and fantasized about him because she couldn't pick a good man if he were the only one in the room.

Why was she a magnet for assholes?

Why don't you want me? You should want me.

His words replayed over in her mind.

Hell to the no Mr. Rhodes, she most certainly didn't want him.

RIKER

"Minetta!" I yelled, but between the compromising position I'd been in, and the line of girls that quickly blocked my way as they pawed at my body, I'd been unable to reach her before she slipped into the elevator. The look in her eyes...why should it bother me?

"Shit," I growled. "Everyone out now," I yelled.

The girls ran for the door, the guards growling and picking up those that were stubborn. As they scurried along the hallway, they reminded me of a rat infestation fleeing an exterminator.

How had this happened? And worse, why did it bother me that she saw me like that? Annoyed, I stomped my way over to what Minetta had dropped. Bending, I picked up the large fruit basket and what looked like broken chocolate flowers from the floor. Ripping the little card off the plastic, I flipped it open.

Thank you.

Your kindness and generosity are so appreciated. I know thousands will be affected positively by your donation, and I just wanted to tell you how much it means to all of us who volunteer at the Food Bank but especially me.

Please accept this token of our thanks.

Minetta

"What fucking donation?"

"The one I gave."

My spine straightened, a snarl on my lips as I stood to face Michael. My brother leaned against the door, looking as smug as I'd ever seen him. His arms were crossed over his chest, a smile on his lips, challenging me.

"I wondered when you would show up. I'd heard rumors of you sniffing around."

"Ah, the proverbial grapevine," Michael drawled, and all I could picture was ripping his head from his body.

"You're like a cockroach, Michael. You kicked my ass out of Heaven, yet you can't seem to stay away." I tossed the basket on the table and went in search of something strong to drink.

"What can I say? I miss you."

"Well, maybe you should've thought of that before you betrayed me." I glared over my shoulder at him as I poured the well-aged brandy. "Especially since I didn't do anything wrong."

"That is a debate for another night, I have somewhere to be, but I wanted to come by and say Hi. Let you know I'm in town for a little bit."

"You are so full of it. You don't do anything without an agenda. So tell me, brother, what do you want from me, and what does it have to do with that girl?" I leaned against the small bar in the corner, my eyes shooting daggers as they stared at Michael.

"I don't want anything from you, brother. I simply wanted to know how you were doing. As for the girl...." Michael shrugged. "She seems interesting, really a one of a kind. She makes me laugh, and well... I plan to take her out to dinner tomorrow and then see where the night leads us. I'm sure I don't have to tell you what I mean." Michael smiled, his perfectly white teeth showing.

My hand froze as the glass touched my lips. "What exactly do you mean you're interested in her? When it comes to you, that could range from friendship all the way to she needs to die. That's a lot of wiggle room."

"Oh stop, I mean it exactly the way it sounds, brother." Michael gave me a wink. "As for the donation, that was just me being nice. I wanted to give back, and this way, everyone thinks your company is extremely generous, and you didn't have to hand over a single dime. What great advertising, it's a win-win for both of us."

"My company already is the best."

"Maybe, but now people that have never heard of you will know the company name."

"My company doesn't need your brand of help, and I don't want you seeing Minetta," I said and then mentally kicked myself for my loose tongue. Rule number one with Michael, don't let him know he's getting to you. But the thought of his hands running down her body, his lips touching hers, was enough to make a sin want to kill.

"Why do you care about this simple girl anyway? I thought you hated all humans and anything to do with them, except their money, of course," Michael twisted his head like he was some fucking bird analyzing me. I hated the look. I hated his face. I hated everything about him.

"I do hate them."

"Well, then there we have it. There shouldn't be a problem. I will wine her, dine her, and see where the night leads. She does look like she would be quite the hellcat in bed. Don't you think? It's always the quiet ones you have to watch out for."

I was back to wanting to rip Michael's face off. How dare he step foot in my building, but now he was threatening to fuck my girl. Mine! Not his, not anyone else's, mine.

"You stay away from Minetta!" I pointed my finger at my brother as I took a threatening step in his direction.

"The gentleman doth protest too much, methinks."

"Don't you quote that shit to me, you white-winged prick. You stay away from Minetta. I mean it, she doesn't need the likes of you screwing with her head. We both know you're not actually interested. If you're sniffing around her, then you plan on hurting her or using her as a pawn in one of your games."

"So, your version of screwing with her head would be acceptable? Fucking thousands of girls before her eyes and, in the end, throwing her away like yesterday's trash would be considered okay? That emotional and brain fuck is fine? Interesting brother. How you blur the line of what is right and wrong for yourself is intriguing, to say the least."

"I don't care what you think of me, but I'm warning you, you stay away from her." Michael raised his hands and made a mocking face like he was scared. "I guess I've been told then by the big bad Mammon. Too bad I don't answer to you and am free to do what I want. Besides, do you really think she will want anything to do with you after what she saw? Be real, brother. That one is never going to want someone like you. I win again. See you around. I have to plan the big night, and I want to make sure it's one she'll never forget."

Michael sauntered out, and I couldn't stop my chest from heaving with a potent mix of mad fury, jealousy, and the need to have Minetta for my own. Micheal thought he'd won. He did this. He somehow knew I was interested in the girl and then manipulated it so that I wouldn't have a chance.

"Not exactly Heavenly," I yelled toward the ceiling. "You fucking hypocritical angel!"

Michael didn't take a shit or wipe his angelic ass without running it past my Father, so if he was here fucking with me, it was with my Father's blessing. That's a fantastic family dynamic right there.

It didn't matter, Michael may have won round one, but if he thought I would give up that easily, he didn't know me as well as he thought. I don't lose. I never lose. The girl would be mine.

TWENTY-TWO

Minetta walked out of the mall with her shopping bag. She purchased a simple black dress and a few new shirts and pants for work.

As she walked down the street toward the parking garage, she looked at the time and knew she needed to get home to Toby. She stopped walking, her eyes staring at the old building across the way. Jogging across the crosswalk, she ran up the front steps, unable to help herself. It was like the building was holding all the secrets, and the answers she wanted were inside.

Sprinting up the stairs, she pulled open the large doors and stepped into the library.

"Oh my," she whispered as she stared at the countless rows. There was a little kiosk-type area, and she made her way over to the computer.

Her fingers sat on the keyboard as she thought about what to type. Finally, the words demons, mythical creatures, folklore, and dementia were her search words. The sound of the mouse clicking on search echoed in her ears.

What was she doing? This was crazy. She's lost count of how many times she'd either said those words or thought them over the last couple of weeks. The little spinning wheel stopped, and there they were, hundreds of different choices.

"Oh boy." She quickly jotted down the aisle and rows and was off. She got turned around twice but, in the end, found what she wanted in the furthest back corner of the second level. She ran her finger across the spines, her eyes taking in all the titles on a topic that she'd never even thought about until a couple of weeks ago.

Demons, Devils and the Differences Between Them

How to know if you are being hunted by a Demon

From the beginning until now. A complete breakdown of human history and the angels and demons that walk among us.

There were way too many to choose from, so she stepped back and stared a little dumbfounded. She was short on time, so she decided that she'd just start at the beginning of the aisle, and if they didn't have what she was looking for, she'd return them and simply continue to work her way through them all. Reaching up on her tiptoes, she was barely able to reach the start of the section. Her hand wrapped around the first spine, and as she pulled it down, a sound came from behind her.

Jumping, she spun, book in hand, but no one was there. Her heart was pounding hard as she bent to look through the shelving at the next row. Nothing moved as her eyes scanned the space. Then she peeked around the corner of the long shelf. The narrow aisle way was shadowed but empty. The dark was just the dark.

Shaking her head, she grabbed the next two books that were more like encyclopedias, they were so large. The strange sound happened again, and the hair stood up on the nape of her neck as a shiver raced up her spine. She didn't move. She barely took a breath as she listened for the noise that sounded like the raptors made in the Jurassic Park film.

If there was a fucking dinosaur in the library she really didn't want to know, that would be it. She'd throw in the white towel on her sanity. Licking her lips, she looked up at the large old lights that hummed and dimmed for a moment. "Nope, I'm done," she said and took off.

It's just an old building, nothing more.

She told herself as she jogged down to the lower level, where she took a deep breath as the fear that had kindled upstairs vanished. Making her final stop, she found the medical section and grabbed the book, *Diseases of the Mind*, from the shelf. Adding it to her stack, she made her way to the front counter.

"This is an interesting combination," the woman behind the counter said as she placed the load down. The woman looked exactly the way you'd picture a librarian. Grayed hair pulled up into a slick bun on her head that reminded her of Penny—glasses with a little chain that wrapped around her neck and a simple dress with a warm-looking cardigan over the top.

"Yes, I'm doing some research," she said and smiled.

"I see. Well, if you're looking for information on dark lore, then you need this book." The librarian walked over to the returned shelf and pulled out another book. "You're in luck. It was just returned."

"Is this a popular topic?" She was intrigued to know that not only had there been hundreds of books written on the topic, but people were reading about it now. Was she not the only one that experienced something strange and wanted answers?

"Oh, my goodness, yes, people have always been fascinated with the unexplainable. Other than our romance section, it is the most popular section we loan out."

"Wow, I had no idea." She pulled her library card and held it out to the librarian to scan.

"Is there something specific you were looking for?" the librarian said as she scanned the books into her computer system.

"I'm not sure yet. Have you ever heard of a creature that can make a room really cold, and look so pale that it was almost translucent with black eyes, a flat squished up face like a pug, but a lot scarier, with nails like claws? she asked and then took a breath. "Oh, and a really long tail, like a scorpion." She paused as the librarian looked at her over the top of her glasses. "It was a dream after a scary movie," she said and then cleared her throat as she realized what she must sound like to the older woman.

The librarian stared at her and blinked. For a moment, she thought the woman was going to confirm that she was indeed going nuts and needed to get the hell out of her library. But instead, she said something she hadn't expected.

"Sounds like an ice demon. They're not known in these parts, mind you. Their lore is based mostly on areas that are cold, as you can imagine. Their name slips my mind, but you will find it in this book." She tapped the one that was the newest addition to her stack.

"Really? So do you believe in all this stuff," Minetta asked, her voice a soft whisper.

The woman removed her glasses, so they dangled from the little chain around her neck. "My dear, this is a big old world with many things in it that we cannot explain—everything from life on other planets to the age-old battle of how humanity came to be. You will always have science and religion pulling in opposite directions, but I think there is value in learning about both. Why can you not have a Devil simply because you believe in science? Do you see what I'm saying?"

"I think so."

"Let me put it to you like this. Have you ever had a moment where you thought to yourself, I've done this before, or I've met this person, but can't remember where? Or, how about you felt a presence around you, maybe someone that has passed, that you loved?"

"Yes," she said and shivered as she remembered the feeling she got for weeks after her dad passed. She felt like he was always in her room at night watching over her as she wept.

"And how did you explain that away? Like, how did you decide that it was nothing?"

Minetta bit her lip and thought about all the times since her father's death she'd thought she felt him around her like he was still looking out for her.

"I guess, I just thought it was my mind playing tricks on me. When my dad passed, I wanted him back so badly that I thought my mind simply believed he was there as a coping mechanism. I missed him and figured the sensation was my way of still having him feel close." She shrugged. "That must sound absurd to you."

"Not at all, my dear, but what if he really was still watching over you? Would that make you happy or freak you out?"

Minetta leaned against the librarian's desk and didn't know how to answer the question. The idea of her father still looking out for her was what she'd always wanted, but if he really was watching out for her, then what else was out there that she couldn't explain?

"I'm not sure," she answered truthfully.

The librarian smiled and put her glasses back on. "I think you know the answers to the questions you seek."

"I do?"

"Yes, my dear, you do. The problem is you are not ready to face the reality of the answers in your heart or mind. Here you go." The woman held out a bag with the books, and she added it to her hand, holding the dress.

"Thanks."

Minetta walked out the doors feeling more confused than when she went inside. If there really were things like this supposed ice demon that couldn't be explained, then that meant she had to re-evaluate everything strange that had happened to her throughout her life.

She looked back at the building and thought she saw a shadow in the top window staring at her, but when she blinked, it was gone.

CHAPTER
TWENTY-THREE

MINETTA pulled the headphones off her head and hooked them over her monitor screen. It had been another strange day filled with people doing things to themselves or others that left her shaking her head. It didn't help that all she could think about were the books she'd stayed up reading all night. That had been a mistake.

So many different demons and devils. She hadn't even known there was a difference. She'd always thought there was one devil, the archangel that was thrown from Heaven, Lucifer. She'd ended up turning on every light in the house and had candles lit just in case as she wrapped herself in the throw her mother made for her. She sipped her tea as she curled up on the couch and began to read.

She found her ice demon alright. It was terrifying how similar the hand-sketched image was to the thing that had been in her home trying to kill her. Yes, she was coming around to the idea that the whole incident had been real. The question was, why was it after her? As she'd read, it sounded like, for the most part, despite their fierce appearance, they were actually quite docile. Like the librarian had mentioned, they preferred cool climates due to their cold nature and only attacked when threatened or if they came across an animal like a polar bear or fur seal being attacked. They would defend the animals that felt most akin to them.

She'd never been anywhere that cold, other than here in winter, and she'd certainly never hurt an animal. While she was feeling brave, she began searching for what her friend Penny might be. Yes, Penny was still her friend, but she could be one of these creatures at the same time. The thought baffled her brain, but if she was going to be open-minded, well, this was a good place to start.

It had taken most of the night, but just as the sun was rising, she found it, or her, Penny. There was an image of a male and female demon that had flaming red hair that floated around them with pale flawless skin. Their eyes were always an unusual orange, but they could charm their appearance to make themselves look human. They were fast and strong, and they carried a flaming sword as a weapon. But what caught her attention was that they had red feathered wings, the symbol of their fall from grace. Erinyes was the term used to describe the angels cast out for falling for temptation. Banned from their home, they were dragged down to Hell, where they took on their new appearance and struggled to fit in. They were not demon enough to be a demon and no longer able to go home, so they were left floundering and walking the Earth in a form of purgatory.

Minetta reached out and picked up a picture of her and Penny together. She ran her thumb over her friend in the photo, taking in her smile and her pale skin. She'd felt drawn to Penny like they'd always been friends and had finally found one another. Penny said she didn't speak to her family, that there had been a big blow-up, and she hadn't seen them for years. What had seemed like a simple conversation about family now had created so many more questions. Putting the picture back on her desk, she headed for the elevator and arrived just as the doors opened.

Penny was the only one inside, and Minetta swallowed hard as she stared at her friend's face. Their eyes locked, and as they did, she saw Penny in her home sipping coffee looking the way she did now, but she also saw her with her glowing eyes and fiery weapon.

"It's true, isn't it?"

Penny didn't make a move to get out of the elevator and didn't say a word. Her features were as serious as Minetta had ever seen.

"That's why you haven't bothered to ask why I changed shifts, checked to see if I wanted to do dinner, or hadn't responded to your messages. You knew I was avoiding you, but you've been hoping I'd just chalk it up to a moment of insanity, and everything would go back to normal. But it can't, can it? I now know the truth, so what does that mean?"

"Get in the elevator, Minny. We need to talk, and this is not the place to do it."

"If you think I'm getting in there alone with you, you're crazy," she said and stepped back.

"Minny, this is no joke. Get in the elevator."

"Thanks, but I'll pass."

"Ohhh, is this a lovers quarrel," came Jared's snide voice.

"Shut up, Jared!" Both her and Penny barked out at the same time. Any other time they would have laughed, or Penny would have given her a high five for standing up for herself, but not tonight.

"And they say men are the issue at the office. Obviously, those people never worked with a bunch of hormonal women." Jared marched off before she could make another comment.

Such a dick.

"I need to speak to you, Minny. It's important," Penny said, quieter this time. Penny held out her arm to stop the doors from closing.

"Whatever you have to say to me can wait. I have somewhere important to be tonight, and I'm not missing it for this. I've already spent too many nights wondering and worrying over whatever happened." She walked toward the stairs and heard Penny swearing from the elevator.

She'd only made it two floors down when a door opened on the next floor down, and Penny walked up the stairs at her. She swallowed the lump in her throat as she realized just how alone she was. Penny could kill her, and no one would hear her scream. She took a step backward and almost ended up on her ass on the stairs.

"Stay away from me," she said. She was scared, terrified actually, but more than that, she felt betrayed. Penny was her best friend. She thought they shared everything, but now she didn't even know who this person, this thing, really was.

"Minny, I'm not going to hurt you."

"You expect me to believe that?"

She sighed and placed her hands on her hips. "Look, can we just talk. I need to explain some things to you. You're in grave danger and—"

Minetta threw her hands up. "Stop! I don't want to hear this right now. I can't hear this right now. I'm going out tonight and looking decent for a change. That is all I want to worry about. Whether you're an Erinyes or not, whether what I saw in my home was real or not, or whatever else you have to say to me can wait."

Penny's eyes were wide with shock. Taking the opportunity, she went to jog past Penny, but she snatched her arm and held her firm. Minetta pulled back, her hip pressing painfully into the railing.

"Let go of me," she said as she stared at the hand that could snap her neck.

"Fine, we won't talk tonight, but we need to speak. It is very important." Penny released her arm, and she slumped with relief. "Minny?"

Penny called out when she reached the next landing. Minetta stared up at Penny, a sad expression on her face. "Please, don't be scared of me. It's still me, you're still my best friend, and I really am trying to protect you."

"How am I supposed to believe that, Penny? If you are what I said, then our entire relationship has been based on a lie."

"Has it? What exactly would you say if I told you what I am? I can tell you what you'd say. That Penny is fucking crazy. She is right off her rocker. She believes she is a fallen angel. Maybe I can get her some help and put her in a home. Maybe she can keep my mother company."

Minetta sucked in a breath. "How dare you bring my mother into this. What she has is real, and...and, what you did has made me question my own sanity. That is not what friends do."

"I'm sorry I said the comment about your mom, but Minny, I protected you. That is what friends do." With that, Penny pulled open the door and disappeared, leaving her and her pounding heart alone in the stairwell. Minetta turned and ran down the rest of the stairs, her feet echoing as they thumped along the concrete. She burst out into the lobby, the door banging, making everyone stare, but she didn't care.

Penny had just admitted that she was a demon, a fallen angel. What the heck did she do with that information?

MINETTA pulled her used Mini Cooper into the public parking and handed over the obscene amount of money it cost to be this close to downtown proper. The night was warm, but she'd purchased a sheer shawl to go with her dress and decided to take it just in case the restaurant was cold.

Michael had texted her the location. When she looked up the place, she almost died at the prices on the menu. When she voiced her concerns, he simply sent a laughing emoji and said, "See you tomorrow night."

To say she was happy she'd purchased the simple, yet sexy little number she was wearing was an understatement. She was terrified she was still going to be underdressed. Grabbing her little black clutch, she locked her door and made her way up the street, her new heels clicking softly. She wasn't accustomed to high heel shoes and felt completely unstable on the three inches of strappy sexiness she opted to wear.

She spotted Michael standing outside the fancy restaurant. He practically glowed under the lights. He looked handsome in his suit and the long black coat that almost touched the ground. It gave him a dangerous and dashing look. He smiled as she stepped up to him, and he pulled out a single flower from behind his back that she couldn't name.

"C'est pour toi ma ravissante beaute. Mais, aucune fleur ne pourrait se comparer a vous." Michael held out the flower for her to take and heat crept up her cheeks. She reached out and took the vibrant flower, the petals sparkling slightly in the dim light like the petals had been kissed by crystals.

"Thank you. I don't know what you said, though," she said shyly. She brought the flower to her nose, and the scent was sweet and oddly addictive.

A sudden tingling in her chest had her sucking in a sharp breath a moment before a voice spoke behind her. "He said you can't compare to a flower. I would have picked something a little less mundane, but that's me."

She knew the voice and didn't want to turn around, not after what she'd seen. She'd rather smack her head on the wall instead of speaking to him, but instead plastered a smile on her face. Minetta slowly turned to face the man she now knew as Riker Rhodes.

There he was in the flesh, just with a lot more clothes on this time, although her mind hadn't forgotten the pleasant visual of his muscles bulging and his ass flexing. His amber eyes bore holes into her, and she swallowed hard. If meeting Michael had made her heart pound this quickly, then Riker's made it want to jump out of her chest. Her body flushed so hot, she had the urge to fan herself as she stared back.

Straightening her spine, she managed to keep her wits about her, not wanting to give away just how uncomfortable she felt.

"Brother, what a surprise. How lovely it is to see you again so soon," Michael said, and her mouth dropped open.

She stared between the two men. "This man is your brother," she asked in disbelief. "Forgive me. I'm having a hard time seeing the resemblance."

"Yes, well, I'm not surprised. I am the far better-looking brother," Riker said, his tone as arrogant as the man himself. She pursed her lips and glared at him.

"That wasn't what I meant," she said.

"Do the two of you know one another," Michael asked.

"I wouldn't put it that way, more like an unfortunate brief acquaintance," she said. She refused to look back at Riker, but she could feel him staring at the side of her face and then back at Michael, making this already weird encounter feel wildly uncomfortable.

"Oh really? That must be a fascinating story. Tell me, how does a nine, one, one operator meet a high-powered executive? I hope my brother wasn't in any distress," Michael asked, and she saw Riker's lip lift up, his eyes hard as he glared at Michael.

She didn't really want Michael to know about the unfortunate situation of seeing Riker having sex. He had been the one to mention the building and the donation, but he never asked her to go. This was awkward no matter how she cut it. "No...um," she started, but Riker finished for her.

"Minetta was a volunteer at the triathlon I competed in not long ago. She was nice enough to serve me some much-needed refreshment. Isn't that right, Minetta?"

She bit her lower lip and nodded and silently prayed that Michael didn't press for any further explanation. She suddenly needed wine, lots and lots of wine. It didn't help that she liked the way her name sounded coming out of Riker's mouth. The image of him calling out her name as he pounded into her had her clearing her throat and fidgeting. She averted her gaze and took a steadying breath.

"Sorry, I'm late." Minetta's eyes rose to stare at the petite woman who suddenly appeared.

The woman linked arms with Riker, and she felt herself staring as he laid his hand on top of the woman's. She was beautiful in an adorable way. She had a round face with big grey, doe eyes that seemed to scream sweet, yet her overly revealing dress and roaming hand told a whole other story. "Darn traffic this time of night, right sweetie?" the woman said, and Minetta watched Riker carefully. She got the feeling he didn't like the pet name, but if he didn't, she couldn't tell for sure. His face was set, his lips in an unreadable line.

"Michael, it has been a long time. How are you?" the woman said.

"Come now, Skye, you don't need to pretend to like me. We both know you'd prefer I never stepped foot in this city again," Michael smiled warmly, and she felt like singing, 'which one of these doesn't belong with the others.' Seriously, she couldn't have felt any more out of place or awkward if she'd set out to do so and contemplated walking away to leave the three of them to have dinner without her.

"It may be true. We have had our differences," Skye said and laughed her voice grating. "Isn't that right, sugarplum?"

Minetta's face scrunched up, a little bit of bile rising in her throat at the terrible nickname. Okay, it really was time to get away from these two.

"We should probably get inside," she whispered to Michael.

"Yes, Minny, you are quite right. I have a fabulous idea, brother. Why don't you and Skye join us this evening? I'm so rarely in town for long periods, and we could certainly use the time to get caught up. And, all of us could get to know one another better. Wouldn't that be fun?"

Minetta's eyes went wide, the fake smile spreading across her face as she clenched her teeth from saying what she really thought of that idea. "Oh, I don't think your brother would want to sit with us," she gave a fake little laugh.

"We'd love to," Riker said smoothly.

"We would?" Skye gasped, voicing what Minetta was thinking.

"My brother is right. I don't see him nearly enough. It has placed undue stress on our relationship. Why not have a delightful meal with him and his date for one night?"

Skye's mouth fell open. "Um, maybe because it wouldn't be delightful."

Minetta stared between the three people. She could cut the tension with a knife. Why in the heck would they want to spend a single second together, let alone an entire meal?

"You don't mind if we join you for the evening, do you, Minetta?" Riker's intense eyes returned to hers, and she felt the challenge spread throughout her body.

Hooking her arm onto Michael's, she smiled wide. "Of course not. Why would I?" Riker's cheek dimpled as he smiled, lighting up his eyes. It was the first real smile she'd seen on the man.

"Well, then I guess we better get in there before they give our reservation away. Let the games begin," Michael said.

Games? She felt more like she was in the middle of a war.

How had her night gone from a wonderful date to this? Her stomach flipped as Riker followed them inside. Of all the people in all the cities... this was Murphy's Law at its finest.

TWENTY-FIVE

RIKER

It paid to have greedy acquaintances. I had placed a call to every popular restaurant in the city and offered the person handling the bookings the same thing. Five grand cash if they could confirm two names for dinner that night and if so, what time. It hadn't even been an hour, and I found where Michael had booked dinner for him and Minetta.

The moment I saw her standing outside with Michael's self-righteous face smiling at her, a flower of destiny in his hand, I knew there was no way I was letting them go home together. That fucking piece of manipulative shit wasn't getting his hands or any other body part anywhere near her. Even if I had to follow her home, Michael wouldn't get a peek of what lay beneath her dress.

I licked my lips as I approached them. Her shapely legs could be seen just above the knee, which was not near enough. She'd curled her hair, so it lay in soft waves around her face, framing it and her glittering blue eyes. She'd gone out of her way to make herself look like a walking piece of dessert, making my spark of jealousy burn a little hotter.

She had a gentle swell to her hips, and my hands itched to feel her skin. With each step, it became more and more agonizing to keep my calm façade in place. As Michael placed his hand on her lower back I almost lunged at the fucker to rip his arm right off his body. My teeth were so tightly clenched that my jaw cracked with the force.

Minetta turned as they reached the maitre'd and her subtle perfume, the low scooping neckline of the dress, had my mouth watering. I could almost taste her sweet flavor on my tongue. Her eyes flicked up to mine, the look quickly turning into a glare, and I wanted to wipe that look off her face. Kiss her stupid until she no longer cared about what she'd seen. She had to be more than an average human. No human could affect me this way...could they? No, that was a ridiculous thought. But if she wasn't human, then what was she?

"What the hell are you doing? Why did you agree to eat with them? With Michael of all people," Skye whispered only loud enough that I could hear.

"What better way to figure out what he's up to? Besides, we were going to eat here anyway. Can you honestly say you wouldn't be distracted with him in the room?"

"I guess that would've depended on where your cock was." Skye smiled at me.

"Skye, not now, not here," I whispered harshly under my breath, and her mouth pulled down into a little frown.

"When did you become a stick in the mud?" she grumbled.

"Do you want to stay? If so, then you will act accordingly. If you don't, make an excuse and go to the party you wanted us to attend instead." I suddenly felt like a parent telling a child to be good. Skye was not wrong, though. When had I become concerned with what anyone thought? Least of all humans.

"This is the best seat in the house," the maître de said, and I smiled as I stared at the horseshoe-shaped booth. Michael allowed Minetta to scoot in first. The look on her face was priceless when she looked up, and I was the one beside her in the middle, not Skye, which I'm sure was what she was expecting.

I picked up the wine menu and held up my finger to call over the closest waiter. "We'll take four bottles of your most expensive wine, two red and two white."

"Right away, Sir."

"Now, brother, that wasn't necessary. If I didn't know better, I'd think you were trying to show me up." Michael looked at me over Minetta's head, who was dutifully staring at a menu. The only problem was her eyes weren't moving, so she wasn't really reading.

I wanted to reach out and touch her mind, find out what made her tick, figure out the optimum way to best Michael at his own game, but as her eyes flicked to mine, I couldn't do it. I wanted her to trust me.

"Not at all, Michael. This simply seemed like a good reason to celebrate. It has been a very long time since we've had a drink or shared a meal together."

"Alright, good call." Michael smiled at me before turning his attention to Minetta. "Order whatever you want off the menu." Michael brushed his hand across hers and the subtle, blushing smile she gave him had a growl forming in my chest.

I couldn't stop staring at her profile. She chewed on her lip as she thought about the options, and it was the most endearing thing I'd ever seen. I wanted to be that lip, no I wanted to bite that lip.

"You're buying right, sweetie," Skye asked, and I made sure to glare at her for yet again using a pet name for me. She smirked, and I knew by the look on her face she was having fun messing with me. We were definitely having a chat later.

213

"Yes, Skye, my dear, you choose whatever you want. In fact, all of you choose whatever you want. It is on me."

Michael lifted one perfectly manicured brow at me. "Brother, I don't think that will be necessary. I'm quite certain I can take care of Minny's and my order. I'd asked her out on a date before we decided to dine together."

I sat back, opened my hands, and smiled as I gave him the best, 'I want to fuck you over,' smile I could under the fake ass one I had plastered to my face. "How about this, you can get the dessert. Next time, we will switch."

"There will be a next time?" I didn't bother to answer the question as he smirked at me. "Alright, that seems fair."

"It's okay. I'll pay for myself, but thank you," Minny spoke up.

I opened my mouth to argue with her, but the waiter arrived with the wine and began taking orders. My brother, of course, taking full advantage of my stupid moment of generosity, ordered three appetizers and capped it off by ordering the largest and most expensive entrée on the menu.

The waiter looked at Minny, and she cleared her throat. "I'll just have the house salad with a vinaigrette dressing, please."

"Are you on a diet or something?" Skye said, and Minny's cheeks pinked as she laughed nervously.

"Minetta, I promised you dinner. Please have whatever you would like," Michael whispered and reached out, placing his hand on her shoulder. I clenched the napkin in my fist, visualizing cutting my brother's hand off as his thumb rubbed over her delicate skin. Michael looked at me over the top of Minetta's head with a subtle curl of his lip and a suggestive look in his eyes. It was a challenge, and it was almost my undoing as I gripped the bench to keep from leaping over the top of her head and tackling Michael right there in the restaurant. If he kept that shit up, I might just do it and then buy the restaurant to pay for the damages.

Skye picked that moment to squeeze my thigh under the table, and my eyes swung to her. "What are you doing?" I mouthed, and she shrugged, sliding her hand a little higher. As inconspicuously as possible, I grabbed her hand and pulled it off my leg, placing it on her own. "Don't." I mouthed again, and she rolled her eyes, taking a large gulp of her wine as she slouched back into the bench.

I turned my attention back to Michael and Minny, but whatever had been decided was over because the waiter was gone. "Michael, tell me how long are you going to be in town," I asked. I knew whatever he said would be bullshit. He had a way of telling you something and yet nothing at the same time.

"It's up in the air right now. My boss can be a bit unpredictable with my work schedule."

"You don't say." I took a sip of my wine before turning my attention to Minetta or Minny as Michael called her, and I decided to try out the nickname. "And what about you, Minny, what do you do for work?"

"Minetta."

"Pardon," I asked.

"Please call me Minetta. Only my friends and family get to call me Minny, and we are neither," she said flatly.

My body flushed hot as Michael choked on his wine and grabbed a napkin as he began to cough—it served him right. The fucking male already had Minetta turned against me, but that was okay. I loved an opportunity to beat him, and the game just became more interesting.

"My apologies, Minetta, I do hope I can rectify that situation and you will consider me a friend at the very least." I paused and gave her a small smile, but she seemed completely uninterested. "What do you do work," I asked again, trying to break the awkward silence.

She lifted her shoulders, and the movement was sweet and casual, and I wanted her to do it again. "Michael already told you, I'm a nine, one, one operator."

"You're right he did. I'm sorry. I will assume you like your job?"

"I love it, actually. To be able to help people when they need you the most—it's very rewarding. I mean, it has its days that are tough and others that make you shake your head, but on the whole, it's wonderful," Minetta smiled, it was the first real smile I'd seen from her, and my pulse jumped as blood whooshed through my veins.

"Ever have anyone kill themselves on the phone with you? All that begging and crying and then screaming. That would be pretty sic," Skye asked, and Minny's smile fell. "Or have you been on the phone and there is some psycho chasing someone, and it's all Texas Chain Saw Massacre with a chain saw or maybe like a drive by with guns firing loud in your ears, but you can't do anything to help so you feel useless?"

"Um..."

"Oh, have you ever had someone pocket dial you while they're doing the nasty? I've heard of that happening. A husband accidentally called his wife while fucking someone else, and she heard the whole thing. Their all like, oh yes fuck me baby harder, oh, oh, oh," Skye said dramatically. She moved her hips back and forth on the bench and my mouth fell open with her act. "Can you imagine? I mean, that would totally end up on some blooper call somewhere, right? Or maybe start an officer orgy." She giggled and chugged what was left of her glass of wine.

"No, I can't say I've had any of those calls before, and no office orgy. Sorry to disappoint you."

"That's too bad. Can you move up in that job, or are you permanently stuck as a call taker? Just a kind of go-nowhere gig?" If looks alone could kill, Skye would've been dead on the spot as I glared at her. Unfortunately, it was not one of my abilities.

"I could become a supervisor, but I really like what I do. I don't do the job to make millions," Minetta said, and I knew she meant it. I'd never met someone that truly meant that, but she did. There was no need of any kind coming off of her. It was refreshing and alarming. I couldn't wrap my mind around how this was possible. All humans were needy and greedy and selfish creatures. I hadn't met one yet, until her. She didn't have a thread of it running through their veins.

"Yeah, I can clearly see that," Skye said. Minetta smoothed out her dress. Why the hell wasn't Michael defending her, she was his date. Why wasn't he telling Skye to back off?

"Oh, I didn't mean it offensively. I hope you didn't think I meant you looked bad? I mean, it's a cute dress for a Hundo." Skye smiled, and I suddenly wanted to smack my best friend.

"Thanks, I think. Skye, what do you do for a living," Minny asked.

"I'm a bartender at a sweet club, and I fuck people." I choked on my wine and regretted for the tenth time in less than five minutes that I'd invited Skye. It had seemed like a good idea at the time, an extra set of eyes on what Michael could be up to, and as an added benefit, her being there could hopefully make Minny jealous, but now I wasn't so sure.

"You have sex with people? Like as in you get paid for it?" Minny lowered her voice, her eyes flicking up to me. I fought the urge to squirm in my seat as Skye laughed loudly, drawing the attention of a couple nearby tables.

"No, I don't get paid for sex, although that's not a bad idea now that you mention it. I mean, I am damn good at it. I should be getting paid something."

"Then what did you mean?"

"I'm just great at it. Guys literally can't get enough once they get a taste. I mean, why do you think Ri, here, keeps me around? It's like, all night, wild-animal sex. He is a dog in bed." She lowered her voice, and I felt frozen to my seat as the horror of her words played out before my eyes. "Trust me, girl, he only has eyes for me."

"I'm finding that hard to believe considering there seems to be a great number of women that he has eyes for regularly." Minny shot me a look, and for the first time since my fall, I wanted to crawl under a table and hide in a hole. This conversation had driven right off the tracks, into a ditch, and was heading for water, and I didn't know how to get it back before I drowned.

"Oh, you mean his Wednesdays?" Skye offered, and I glared at her, warning her to shut up with my eyes.

"His Wednesdays?" Minny raised her eyebrows.

Skye leaned in a little closer and waved Minny in like it was a big secret, and as Minny did, her arm brushed up against mine. I had a twinge of guilt as pleasure raced through my body. I couldn't stop staring at her. I was starting to feel like a fucking perv as I fantasized about pushing her over onto the bench and lifting that little dress up to fuck her right here while Michael watched me take her from him.

"Yeah, he screws like every girl that signs up on Wednesdays. He feels sorry for them since they don't get serviced well at home, so we have an understanding. I swear he thinks Hump Day is a real thing."

"Can we get more wine? This bottle is almost gone." I held up the bottle and waved over the waiter. "I think we're going to need it," I said and looked over at Michael. "Do you have any special plans while you're in town," I asked, hoping to change this conversation to anything else. I would have settled for literally any other topic.

"Nope, but I'm really intrigued by this Wednesday thing. Where do you find the stamina? I can't believe you have such an active sex life, brother. Mind you, that is extreme at it's finest and we all know you love your extremes. I'd love to hear more."

I looked down at the table. "I bet you would," I mumbled. "If you'll excuse us, Skye and I, we have a couple of things to discuss." I pushed her with my hip out of the booth, and she grumbled but slid out. I directed her toward the back door of the restaurant. As soon as we were outside, I turned on her.

"What the hell are you doing?" I growled. "You're making me look like a complete asshole."

"First, you are an asshole, but that is your charm. Second, are you kidding me right now? Everyone in that place can see you acting all googly-eyed over that twerp of a human. What the hell is wrong with you?" Skye pointed toward the closed door. "That desperate puppy dog act you've got going on in there, is not like you. In fact, none of this is like you."

Skye walked a few strides away and then turned to continue her tirade. "You're breaking bread with Michael! Mi-ch-ael, the fucker who threw your ass out of Heaven, or have you forgotten?" she continued, mimicking me in a high-pitched voice. "Ohhh, Michael, it has been a very long time since we have shared a drink or broke bread together. Why don't I get on my knees and suck that glittering angel cock of yours while I'm kissing your ass?" She stuck a finger in her mouth and made a gagging noise. "Please spare me. I don't care if you want to fuck the human. I mean, you literally fuck a hundred of them a week, but she is a goody, goody, and you're making an idiot out of yourself trying to pretend to be something you're not. Nope, huh-uh, that was too much for this demon to stomach." Skye crossed her arms over her chest. "I mean, did you see the way she looked at you when I mentioned Wednesdays?"

I could almost see the smoke coming out of Skye's ears as she finished venting.

"Well, I'm so happy you have decided you're in charge of my life and my dating life to boot. I was unaware I needed a coach on how to get through a day. I guess you can think about how much non-fun I'm having without you from home. I want you to leave. No, on second thought, I'm ordering you to leave. And, Skye, don't fucking challenge me or set out to embarrass me like that again, especially in public, or it will be the last thing you ever do before I send you to scrub out the shit troughs for all eternity in Hell with a chastity belt on that pussy of yours."

Her eyes went wide like I'd threatened death. "Ri, I'm your best friend, and for you to be doing this, there has to be more going on here than what you're saying. If Michael has done something to mess with you, just tell me? I'm looking out for you." Skye placed her hands on her hips as she spoke. The thing was, Michael was indeed messing with me, just not the way Skye thought, and she'd never understand. I didn't even understand, so how could she?

"Skye, I don't need you to look out for me. I'm a grown-ass man, a fallen archangel, and a demon, a mother fucking sin—I'm pretty good at looking after myself. I have lived longer than ten of your lifetimes and am still here. Trust me when I tell you, I know what I'm doing, and it's obvious asking you to come was a mistake. Go home."

"You're unbelievable. If Michael isn't screwing with you, then the girl is," Skye said as I pulled open the back door.

"If she is, then it is my choice to let her screw with me, just like your life is your choice. Please try to remember who gave you that life. That was the whole point of me pulling you out of the Pit of Despair so that you could live your life. So go live it." I marched back inside and went to the restroom to freshen up before returning to the table.

"Did Skye decide to leave? Such a shame," Michael said as I sat back down.

"There was another event she wanted to attend, a last-minute invite, and she decided to head to that." Michael looked like he was going to question more, but his phone rang.

"I'm sorry I have to take this," Michael said and got up to take his call. I turned to look at Minny, who was nibbling on a bun.

I slid a little closer, and her body tensed as her hands stopped moving. She literally looked like she'd just frozen in place. There was an electrical charge in the air between us. She had to feel it, too, because it was impossible to ignore.

"Minny?" I whispered, my voice rough with the strain of trying to keep control of myself. When she didn't look at me, I brought my finger up, and as my finger touched the smooth skin of her chin a shock raced up my spine. The searing heat spread, my pulse pounding as those sea-blue depths locked with my own. The air vibrated around us with charged energy. I wanted her. I wanted her laid out under me, and I wanted to see her face as she came screaming my name—no nameless ass in the air routine with her. I wanted to feel her come. I wanted to bring her more pleasure than she'd ever known, and I wanted to hold her when we were done.

Suddenly, I could hear laughing and see a child on a swing, the sun was shining, and Minny was running around a yard with another—so similar was the property to the one I'd visited in Maryland. I blinked, and the image was gone.

"I'm sorry," I managed to say around the unknown emotion that was gripping my throat.

"For what," she said softly. Her lips were begging to be kissed as she looked at me from under her thick lashes. I was tempted, so tempted, but I feared I wouldn't stop if I took a taste.

"For what you saw when you dropped by and for being so rude to you at the race." I had no idea why it bothered me, but I didn't want her to see me as what I was, as what I'd been since my fall. It shouldn't bother me. I was Greed. I was Mammon, I was...I had no idea anymore as I stared into her eyes.

She started to turn her head away, but I cupped her cheek and ran my thumb across the softness of her skin, desperate to keep the connection. She was so different, so unique. My abilities reached out, and wrapped around her body. There was still no sin that I could taste making her even more alluring. None of any kind lingered on her skin, and there was not a drop of greed in her soul. It wasn't impossible, but she was pure, a pure soul, and I wanted her for myself. My greedy need to have all that was special understood what she was. She was one of a kind.

"You don't need to apologize. I barely know you. I was shocked by what I saw, but it's your life and your building. I was the one trespassing." She slid away from me, and a thread of panic swirled as our connection broke. "Can you please make my apologies to Michael? I need to get home. I'm feeling a bit under the weather. Thank you for the wine. It was quite lovely."

She stood, and I watched her leave, not sure what to do. I wanted to chase her down, to stop her and make her give me a chance. A chance at what I didn't know...be better maybe? That was ludicrous. Or was it?

"I'm gone less than five minutes, and you scared Minny off. Good work," Michael said as he sat back down.

"I didn't scare her off." At least, I didn't think I had. "Besides, aren't you going to go after her?"

"Nope, not tonight. Unlike you, I have time with her to make up for this weird evening." Michael tore a chunk off a bun and sat back smiling as he chewed on it. "I'm pretty sure she saw enough of you in action to ward you off for good. I should buy Skye a thank you gift. I couldn't have asked for a better sidekick and one I didn't even have to ask to join in and help."

"You set this up, didn't you? You knew I'd come."

"Honestly, I had no idea if you would or wouldn't crash my date, but if you didn't, I'd have an amazing time with an amazing woman and if you did... well, let's just say you're an entertaining car wreck that would take care of itself. You just didn't realize how far you'd driven off the cliff until this moment. Either way, you made me look like a superstar in her eyes." Michael sipped his wine, the cocky grin returning to

222

his face. "I mean nothing that Skye said was a lie, was it?" He lifted a shoulder and let it drop.

"What is this shit, Michael? What game are you trying to pull with me? Are you bored up there and have nothing better to do than harass me?"

"What are you talking about," Michael asked, taking a sip of wine and relaxing back into the booth. It annoyed the fuck out of me that he looked as cool as a cucumber, and I was turned inside out.

"Don't give me that." I crossed my arms and looked away from him. "Did you send this girl to hurt me? I mean, other than the raven hair, she is the spitting image of Callista. Is this another sick way to show off that I can't come home?" I said, and even though I was angry, I couldn't keep the hurt out of my voice.

"Do you really think I'd do that to you?"

"Are you really going to make me answer that? You've done more hurtful things, starting with agreeing to toss me out of home."

"This again. Can we move past it already? You had to know that what you did was going to have consequences."

"I was only trying to help," I growled, my fists clenching. "You know what, never mind. No matter what you say, I'm not going to believe that you aren't up to something even if it has nothing to do with Minetta."

"Believe whatever you want, brother, but I'm not here to torture you. Anyway, I hope you're hungry because here comes the food, and I plan on eating every bite of the meal you're purchasing." Michael smiled smugly.

"I hate you."

"I know."

CHAPTER
TWENTY-SIX

MINETTA

Note to self: the next time her gut instinct told her that it was too soon to go out on a date or do anything really... she'd listen to her gut. She couldn't believe that entire experience had happened, and that Michael and that man, that unbelievable man, were brothers?

The night had seemed so promising. The opportunity to go out on a date with a man who saved her life seemed interesting, and he was easy on the eyes—that was like a dream come true. But then Riker Rhodes had to show up, and worse, Michael invited him and that... odd woman to sit with them. It was so obvious, brothers or not, that the two of them couldn't stand to be in the same state together, let alone the same restaurant.

And there was no way she was letting Riker buy her dinner. That seemed like a slippery slope of favors to be returned. She didn't have to spend very long with him to know he didn't do anything unless he was getting something he wanted in return.

But that apology...he'd seemed genuinely sincere and upset.

"Nope, don't do it," she said aloud, shutting down the doe-eyed part of her that thought he was so interesting and not to mention hot as hell. The way he'd touched her cheek, she'd been so tempted to kiss him just once to see how his kiss would feel. She could almost feel his lips on hers. Her hand went to her mouth, a stupid smile forming.

What would it be like to be wanted by someone like him? She sighed. The earlier feeling of hope for a new start with a great guy was fading fast. Michael hadn't been much better. It was easy to see that Skye embarrassing Riker was exactly what Michael had wanted. She didn't like that any more than Riker's attitude.

Her heels clicked noisily along the sidewalk as she dug through her purse to find the car keys. She'd have to grab some drive-thru on the way home. She was ready to eat off her own arm. Minetta shivered as the wind picked up and lifted the hair lying on her neck.

"Ah-ha, there you are," someone said. Minetta looked up and screamed as a face appeared in the glass window of her car that was right behind her.

Skye grabbed her roughly and spun her around. She looked around, but the car attendant had left, leaving the gate open, and she was far enough off the road that she couldn't be easily seen.

"What the hell are you," Skye asked.

Odd, she wanted to ask the same question. "I don't know what you mean?"

"Are you part angel or lust demon? Maybe you're half siren. That would make the most sense," Skye mumbled.

"Well, that's good because you're making none." Apparently, being sarcastic wasn't the way to go. Skye gripped the front of her dress in a fist and slammed her up against the vehicle's door with a surprising amount of strength. She coughed and gasped for breath as the air was driven out of her lungs.

"You stay away from him." Skye's voice was low and had an edge to it that made her shiver.

"Who...Michael?"

"No, stupid, Riker. You stay away from him and stop putting ideas of making nice with Michael in his head."

"Look, Skye, I don't have a clue what you're talking about. If you hadn't noticed I didn't want to sit with the two of you anymore than you wanted to sit with us. Now can you please let go of me? I want to go home." Minetta tried to reason with no success.

"This isn't a joke. Riker may be a dick in your eyes, but he is a decent man. He doesn't need some little miss 'I'm better than everyone else' coming in and making trouble for him."

Minetta gave Skye a hard push and was surprised when the woman stumbled back. The look on Skye's face mirrored her own. But seriously, it was like Skye hadn't expected her to lash out. "For the last time, I don't know what you're talking about, but I do not have any plans to see Riker again."

"Maybe if I drop you off in the middle of Siberia, you'd take the hint and stay gone." Skye pointed a finger at her, and she had this urge to smack it away, but instead, she just glared at Skye, not backing down.

"Don't touch me again. Whatever it is you think I'm doing, I'm not, and I don't appreciate your accusations or attitude."

Skye took a threatening step toward her. "You think you scare me? You have no idea what I'll do to you if you keep this up," Skye growled.

"Enough, Skye, leave her alone."

"Well, if it isn't Miss Penny Wise. How are you enjoying your pathetic existence? Find a clown that will stick around, or are you still wallowing in your self-pity?"

Penny walked out of the shadows like she'd simply appeared out of thin air. She would never have seen Penny if she hadn't spoken and walked forward. She looked like her normal self, but there was an edge of power emanating from her.

"So original, Skye, and so not like you. Now scurry back to whatever rock or hole you were pulled from and leave Minny alone, or you'll have to deal with me." Penny blocked most of her view of Skye.

"You two know each other? Why doesn't this surprise me," she mumbled and crossed her arms. This night had gone from strange to worse, and somehow it had taken another step into the realm of insane. Then again, that was par for the course lately. How exactly had she walked off the trail of her normal quiet existence into this?

"She needs to stay away from Riker, she is fucking with his head, and I don't let anyone screw with him," Skye barked out.

"I'm not! I barely know him, and he's the one that keeps showing up where I am, not the other way around. Except for yesterday, but I had no idea that was his building. Like I'd want to see that," she argued. Penny looked over her shoulder at her, and she took the hint, looking away and sighed.

"Skye, that is one thing you and I actually agree on. I will talk to her. So, you can scurry off now." Penny made a shooing sign with her hands.

"If I find you sniffing around him again, I'll not be as friendly with you," Skye threatened.

The comment rubbed Minetta the wrong way, and anger flared in her chest. "Bring it." She glared at Skye. "I'm not scared of you, and you don't control me."

"Keep your pet on a shorter leash, Penny, or she may get bitten by a much nastier dog." Skye turned and marched off.

Penny stared after Skye until she was completely out of sight before turning to face her. "You seem to be attracting a slew of not-so-friendly people lately."

"I wouldn't call that thing that was in my home a person—and what the hell? Are you following me now? Your stalking is not confined to my house or at work but also on my dates?"

"I told you we need to talk." Penny's hair that had come loose from the bun was floating around her face. Had it always done that, and she just hadn't noticed?

"Oh my god, it's obvious you're not going to let this go. If I let you speak to me, will you stop following me around?"

"Honestly, probably not, but once we speak, it will all make sense." Penny looked down at her feet as she played with the small loose pebbles on the blacktop. "I need you to understand I really am your friend Minny. I don't have many friends. Well, any other than you actually, and I don't want to lose you."

Penny's face was shadowed, but it was easy to tell she felt dejected. "Fine, you win. My night was ruined anyhow. Where do you want to talk," Minetta asked.

"My place, and before you argue, I already picked up Toby."

Minutia's arms fell to her sides. "You stole my dog? Are there no lows you wouldn't stoop to?"

"I didn't steal him, I grabbed him for insurance purposes, and I like cuddling him. Come on already and stop bitching. Being a whiner doesn't suit you."

Minetta watched Penny walk around to the passenger side of the car and couldn't decide which was worse, the date she'd been on or this.

Shoulda just stayed in the restaurant and eaten because it really couldn't have gotten worse, could it?

"Nice car, by the way, it totally suits you. Love the racing stripes on the black, very sharp," Penny said as Minetta unlocked the doors and got inside.

Was it possible to go back in time and not volunteer at the

triathlon? Her entire life had been turned upside down ever since that day.

Ever since she met freaking Riker Rhodes.

CHAPTER
TWENTY-SEVEN

MINETTA

This all felt too normal. As they drove to Penny's apartment, Minetta stopped to grab burgers and ended up ordering half the menu, the two of them laughing the entire time. She could barely get the drink order out without giggling hysterically. Her make-up had started to run, so she could only imagine what the employee thought as she pulled up to the window.

Minetta caught herself looking over at Penny and trying to see what she'd missed. How do you know someone for years and not notice something this significant? Yet, even knowing the facts, she still couldn't see it.

She wanted to yell, "you're a freaking demon!" Only a few short weeks ago, she would've told anyone that tried to convince her demons were real that they were out of their ever-loving mind. She wouldn't have said it like that, but the thought would've been there. Penny was right about that.

Yet here she was sitting beside Penny with fries sticking out of her mouth, being her typical goofy self. Even as Penny sang terribly and bobbed back and forth to *Pony by Ginuwine*, she believed it to be true. Just before they arrived at Penny's apartment, Minny paused. She should be running away, screaming, or throwing Penny out of the car. At the very least, she should be terrified. So why wasn't she?

Minetta parallel parked her car in the only space left in front of Penny's building. She took a moment to look around and sighed. The city seemed the same and vastly different. The tall buildings with their lights shining, the buzz of the people milling about, and the couples holding hands as they enjoyed the evening were all normal things. But there was this underlying edge that came with the knowledge that humans were not alone, and that had her seeing the world differently. Had her eyeing everyone she passed differently.

"Penny for your thoughts?"

Penny smiled at her, and she couldn't help but return the grin, but it slowly slipped as she stared at Penny's face.

"Everything seems different, or am I just seeing everything for the first time? I feel like I just woke up from a dream or another dimension to this new reality, but it's me that has changed, isn't it?"

She watched a guy jogging by with his dog, and now, she wondered if he was a demon or something else. At this point, aliens, vampires, and hobbits could all be real and living among them. How would she know, but did she really want the answer to that question? Nope, she was definitely happy living in denial.

"Come on, let's go inside and eat this mammoth amount of food, and I will explain what I can. You know Toby will be sulking," Penny said, slipping out of the car. Grumbling, she followed Penny.

"Hey there, Mr. Granger!" Penny waved at the elderly man that lived down the hall from her. He stood next to his small fluffy white dog as he waved back. "No one else in the building will talk to him, but I like his snarky side," Penny explained.

Minetta wasn't much of an apartment fan. Even though her house wasn't much bigger, she preferred to have that separate space with a backyard. Although, if she had to choose a spot, this one was pretty nice. It was clean, and they always updated it to stay with the constantly changing trends. The lobby was nothing like Penny's decorating. Penny had a thing for the whole boho vibe and was completely obsessed with the colors red, white, and gold. Pretty much every fixture, piece of furniture, and decoration was one of the three colors.

They stepped out of the elevator into Penny's apartment hallway on the top floor. Minetta was carrying all the bags and her jingling keys as she juggled the food.

"Here, let me take some of that," Penny offered, taking three of the bags.

As soon as the door was pushed open, she was accosted by Toby. "Hey, bud! Did Penny steal you?" He licked her hand and then nudged at the bags. "Oh, you think you deserve a burger? What exactly have you done to warrant such a treat?" Toby cocked his head at her and then sat holding his paw up. She and Penny laughed hard as the goof woofed at them. "Alright, I guess we over-purchased enough for you to have one."

"Did you want to get changed out of that dress? I have some yoga stuff and a sweater that will fit you."

"Thanks, this seems a little overdressed now, although according to Skye, 'it was cheap Hundo trash.' " She mocked the sound of Skye's voice.

"Don't mind her. She's just a pissy little half-demon that gets jealous easily. And I'll tell you she has gotten too big for her britches since she's become Riker's best friend. If she didn't have him protecting her, there are a number of demons that would love to drag her down to Hell for her rude mouth. And that group would find very creative ways to fill it so she couldn't speak." Penny shivered, and she could only stare.

"Wait, so Skye is a demon too?"

Penny gave her a small smile and lifted her shoulders.

"Of course she is. I shoulda seen that coming. Let me guess Riker and Michael are as well?" She followed Penny into her bedroom and took the clothes Penny offered before being led to the bathroom.

Penny stopped outside the door and reached in to flick on the light. "Actually, they are not a demon, not really. But that is a tough one. I'll wait until you're out of the restroom to explain all that."

"Okay, thanks." Minetta closed the door to the bathroom and stared at her reflection. She had to wonder what her father would think of all this, and was he watching now and laughing or encouraging her? Turning away from the image, she pulled on the stretchy material, loving the feel of the soft workout clothes that were, of course, a vibrant red.

Walking back out to the kitchen, Minetta grabbed a burger and fries and then took her usual spot on the sofa. Crossing her legs under her, she settled with the food on her lap.

"I've been worried we'd never get back to this point. I was seriously scared you'd never want to speak to me again," Penny said as she joined her.

"Yeah, so have I, but before we can have any semblance of our friendship back, you need to tell me the truth. About everything, including how I woke up in my bed with my house looking completely normal."

Penny stuffed some food into her mouth and then set it aside. "So, how much have you figured out?"

"I know next to nothing. I borrowed some books from the library, and that was how I figured out what you are, or at least what I guessed you were. You ended up confirming it in the stairwell."

236

Minetta bit into her burger and then ripped a small piece off to toss to Toby.

"Good guess. I am an Erinyes. My fall from grace was over a man."

"Isn't it always," Minny said, and they stared at one another before another round of giggles took over.

"Good point, but in all seriousness, I fell in love with a half-demon while I was here on Earth for a job, and let's just say I made some decisions that Father didn't approve of. I was tossed out and ended up in Hell for a time when I finally decided that Earth was a better fit for me." Penny shrugged like what she'd just said was the most normal thing.

Minetta gave the other remaining burger to Toby and leaned forward to rest her arms on her knees. "Let me get this straight. You were an angel, and by Father, you mean...God?"

"Yes."

"You fell in love while you were here on Earth. What were you doing here, and how old are you?" Minetta asked.

Penny blushed, her cheeks going as red as her hair. "I was here as a guardian angel, and I'm rounding on four centuries, which is pretty young. I was always a freer spirit than the other angels. I guess it's fitting I end up not fitting in anywhere." Minetta sat back stunned, her hands falling into her lap.

"I'm sorry you felt that way, that you were forced to feel like you don't fit in," she said and meant it. She knew what it felt like not to fit in, to be different than the rest of the crowd, and always on the perimeter. It was lonely. "Will you ever age?"

"Yes, but very slowly. Like so slowly that I will still look this way when your great, great grandkids are born." A little mustard ran down Penny's face as she took a huge bite of her burger. Minetta couldn't help focusing on Penny's slightly forked tongue as it licked up the condiment. She'd always assumed the slight indentation had been a birth defect or some sort of accident.

"It's like you found the fountain of youth." Minetta stared at the abstract painting on the wall.

"I know this all sounds impossible, and if you can't handle anymore, I will just tell you what I absolutely have to and no more," Penny said, but Minetta shook her head no.

"Before you get into all the other stuff, tell me, what happened with the guy you fell in love with?"

Penny's face fell, her eyes instantly teared up, and she looked away. "He was more human than demon. He died a long time ago."

"Oh, Penny, I'm so sorry. I didn't mean to bring up something painful."

Penny smiled and shook her head. "No, don't apologize. It is life. Anyway, I haven't found anyone else, well I have, but he doesn't know I even exist."

"You mean he doesn't know as in he doesn't know about demons?" Penny laughed and then munched on a few more fries as her cheeks pinked. "Are you blushing? Who is this guy? Come on, girl, you said you'd tell me whatever I want to know."

Penny rolled her eyes. "Fine. He's Skye's brother, actually. His name is Neven, and he's...I just really like him, but he doesn't see me. In fact, I'm pretty sure he wouldn't even know my name even though we've met dozens of times over the years." Penny slumped into her chair.

"You don't know that."

"Trust me. He is like punching way above my weight class. I'm a nobody to him."

"Penny, don't you dare." Minetta held up her finger. "You're beautiful and funny and intelligent and so many other things. If he can't see that, then it's his loss, not the other way around."

A small smile curled the corner of her mouth. "Thanks, girl. So... should I continue with what you need to know?"

"Yes, keep going. I want to hear it all." Toby slinked up on the couch one paw at a time until his massive body was curled up beside her, his head lying in her lap. She gently ran her fingers through his fur on his head as she waited for Penny to continue.

"I went looking for you after I dispatched the ice demon back to Hell. I ended up finding you and Toby at the school. Just in time, too. You were drawing some attention from a few not-so-savory individuals. I took both of you home, and then I enlisted a little help from someone who owed me a favor and is really good at magically repairing stuff. We put everything back the way it was. I don't have much healing ability, but for the minor cuts the two of you had, I could wipe them away as well. I'm sorry I should've thought about your mom and how you'd take the strange night. I just kinda hoped you would think it was all a bad dream."

"It terrified me, almost more than the demon itself. To lose my mind so soon...I was just so scared."

"I know, and I'm sorry. Can you forgive me?" Penny pleaded and held out her hand for her to take.

Minetta took a moment to analyze her friend, but in her heart, she'd already forgiven Penny. She nodded and gave her friend's hand a squeeze. She flipped Penny's arm over and stared at the small tattooed symbol on her wrist. She'd seen this symbol in her searches of the different types of demons. It had intricate lines that looked like a cross between a pentagram and a sun.

"What does this symbol mean? Really mean not the, 'I thought it was pretty,' excuse you already gave me?"

"I was branded with it when I fell. It's to make sure that I can't cross back into Heaven. The only way I can get into Heaven now is if one of the archangels removes it and grants me permission." Penny lifted a shoulder, a shadow crossing her normally perky features. "It's kind of like a human ankle monitor, but I can't take this one off unless I cut off my hand. Trust me, I thought about it, but what is the point? Even if I could sneak back into Heaven, how long would I last before being noticed and kicked back out with a brand on another part of my body?"

"I'm sorry," Minetta said as she released her friend's hand.

"What do you have to be sorry for," Penny asked, taking a bite out of her burger that made her cheeks look like a chipmunk.

Smiling at the stupid look on Penny's face, she answered. "I feel like I somehow should've known. I mean, Heaven was your home, and to think what it must have been like to be kicked out. To be forced to live somewhere you didn't want to be and all because you fell in love. I had made some pretty silly choices when it came to James, and I can't imagine being kicked out of my home away from the family I loved because of it. How alone you must have felt. It hurts to think about Penny."

Penny blinked away a tear and looked away from her.

"Yeah, it was tough. I really went dark for a long time, bitter over what happened." Penny sighed as she rubbed her face. "Anyway, I will start by saying that I love my job, and I love you, Minny. You really are my best friend and my family now. But..." Penny paused, and her hands rubbed together nervously in her lap.

"But, what?"

"When I first came into your life, I was doing so as a mission and not as your friend. The mission was to keep you away from Riker Rhodes forever."

"What is it with this guy? I mean, I barely know him, and you and this Skye person are acting like it's the end of the world if I speak to him. Not that I want to, the guy is a real piece of work."

"Look, it's a very long and complicated story that I couldn't begin to get into right now, but basically, Riker is one of the original archangels that fell with Lucifer from Heaven. He is an original deadly sin. Greed, to be precise. Riker is Mammon."

Minetta smiled, waiting for the punchline, but Penny's face

remained serious. "You're not joking, are you?" Penny shook her head no, and suddenly the room felt too small like the walls were closing in.

She stood and paced to the far end and back again, stopping only to look out the window momentarily. From Penny's window, you could just make out the tall, imposing structure of Avidity Enterprises. His attitude suddenly made sense. How else would someone act whose sole goal was to create greed in the world?

Some of the lights were still on, and she wondered if Riker had gone home after dinner or if he'd gone back to work. And why had he taken an interest in her of all people? I mean, he literally had a line out his office door and down the hall of beautiful women, all of them wanting to have sex with the man.

"So why do I have to stay away from him?" She turned to face Penny.

Penny slowly rose and went to stand behind her lounge chair, her hands resting on the back. "Because...Riker needs to remain as is. He needs to be the sin greed. It is needed on Earth. I know that sounds nonsensical, but there is a balance between good and evil that is always at play."

"I'm not following."

"Have you noticed how Riker seems different around you?"

"If you mean an egotistical asshole, then yes, but I assumed that was his normal demeanor."

Penny smirked. "It would be difficult for you to see the change since you've just met him, but anyone that knows him can see the difference. Skye's reaction should tell you that much. You are a threat to the balance, and because of that, there are things coming after you, demons of all kinds—and they are coming because I failed to keep you away from him to start with."

"Whoa, you're saying that thing in my house isn't the last, that it wasn't a fluke, or it got hungry and stumbled into my house, but that they are purposely coming for me?"

Penny sighed. "I'm afraid so. I don't know what type of demon or when, but it's why I came to see you the night after the race. I was checking to make sure you were okay when I found the ice demon in your home."

"And that's why you're following me around?"

"Yes. Minny, I'm your friend. I promise you I don't mean you harm. I...I'm just sorry that I didn't do a better job keeping you two separated. I knew he'd be at the triathlon. He always competes and wins. It's his thing. I shoulda...I don't know...pretended I fell and needed to go to the hospital or something." Penny rubbed her face.

"That's why you were trying to talk me into doing something else. This...this is..." She couldn't find the right word and shook her head. The information swirled like a vortex of messed up going around and around. "Tell me, what can I do?" Minetta flopped back down beside Toby.

"They will only leave you alone if you stay far away from Riker. There will be too many demons for me to kill on my own. Hell literally has an endless supply. I hate to say this, but you should consider moving. Like to the other side of the world if possible. Now that he has met you, he will be drawn to you. You're unique, Minny. I know you don't think so, but your soul is kind and not filled with greed like everyone else. It was why the prophecy had chosen you, and he will crave to be near you."

This all seemed impossible. If demons and angels and whatever else weren't enough, now she had demon assassins after her because of some prophecy she'd never heard of? And all because this man she barely knew acted differently around her? There had to be another way other than moving. Maybe she could just tell the next one that she had no intentions of ever seeing the jerk again. He could happily remain the obnoxious sin, and she could live her life.

She sucked in a sharp breath as something occurred to her. Lifting her head, she stared at Penny. "So if Michael is not a demon..." Penny shook her head no. "And Riker is an archangel that fell, but he called Michael brother... holy shit, he's Michael, like Michael, Michael. The Michael in the bible, isn't he? The most powerful archangel, the one that cast Lucifer out?"

Penny nibbled on her bottom lip and nodded. Minetta's hands flew to her mouth, her head feeling dizzy. She'd had dirty thoughts about a freaking archangel and a Fallen one. Was she going to go to Hell? Would she never get the chance to go to Heaven now that she knew one existed because of her dirty mind? Oh, my, what if she'd slept with him? She sucked in a sharp breath. He looked at her boobs in a wet shirt! She flirted with him. Her heart galloped around in her chest wildly.

"Are you okay? You look like you're about to faint," Penny asked, walking a little closer. "Trust me he's not as awesome as the books make him out to be."

"I think I'm going to be ill. I had coffee and flirted with the closest thing that comes to God himself and saw another archangel, an original sin, fucking a girl. I can't even compute that at the moment. Excuse me." Minetta stood and made her way to the bathroom. She gripped the sink, and this time as she stared in the mirror, she wanted to run away from herself.

One thing was for certain, she wasn't seeing either of them ever again, not if she had anything to say about it.

CHAPTER
TWENTY-EIGHT

MINETTA dropped Toby off at home and got changed before heading to work. She and Penny had talked until she couldn't handle any more information and passed out on her couch cuddling her dog. He was the one and only thing that seemed to be as she always thought he was.

"Dad, you were right. Life definitely has a way of throwing you a curveball when you least expect it," she said as she got out of her car. The thing she still couldn't grasp was why her? Penny tried to explain it a couple of times, but there were so many great and wonderful people in the world that did far more than she ever could to help humanity, so the answer still seemed odd.

As soon as the elevator doors opened, she knew something was up. She couldn't see her desk, but a number of her co-workers were standing around, and they were all looking at something in her cubicle. Please don't let Riker or Michael be sitting in her cubicle. She couldn't handle that and was tempted to go hide in the lady's bathroom.

Yeah, that's gonna work cause an archangel can't reach you in a girl's bathroom.

"What's going on?" she said, nearing the group.

"Look, it's crazy!" One of the other girls said, smiling.

Minetta looked in her cubicle, and her mouth fell open. The entire space was full of flowers. There wasn't even space for her to sit because there was a huge bouquet on her chair. Flowers of every shape, size, and color, each arrangement was unique and beautiful. As the initial surprise began to wear off, the realization that this could only have come from three possible suspects. This wouldn't be James. He didn't have the money to pull off a gesture like this and wouldn't even if he had the money. It could be Michael, but this didn't seem like his style so that only left one person.

The arrangement of lotus flowers on the chair had a small card tucked in between a couple of the flowers. She leaned over the ones on the floor to reach it. Flicking it open, her heart pounded hard in her ears.

Minetta,

I'm sorry for Skye's behavior and if I made you uncomfortable. I'd like the opportunity to make it up to you. I promise you will enjoy what I have in mind. Call my personal cell 555-666-6969

Ri

"Well, looks like someone has an admirer. You must have been a really good fuck to get all those." Minetta turned and swung before she realized what she was doing. Her fist collided with Jared's smug face, and he stumbled backward before landing on his ass.

"Don't ever talk to me like that again." Minetta fumed as she stared down at Jared's shocked expression. "I mean it. I'm through with your attitude."

"I'll have you arrested for assault!"

"Go ahead and try. You've bullied me for the last time, Jared," she yelled.

Jared got up and took off with his tail between his legs, like the rat that he was. Her co-workers cheered, and their claps became deafening. Once he was out of sight, she shook her hand and rubbed at her knuckles. She was going to need ice and hoped she hadn't broken anything. That hurt more than it seemed to in the movies.

"It is about time someone laid him out for all the rude shit, he says. Good for you, girl," one of the older women said, giving her a smile.

The phones were starting to light up, and everyone quickly rushed off to get back to work. The small break from calls was a rare and coveted thing.

Turning back to the florist's store in her cubicle, she felt a smirk lift the corner of her mouth. She knew exactly what she was going to do with these because taking them home was not an option.

R IKER

"Do you think I should call?" I asked Shilo as I paced the length of the Olympic-sized office. "Then again, she may not have seen them yet," I said before Shilo could respond. "I mean, she should be at work by now. She should have seen them, right? How could she not see them? Maybe I didn't send enough, or maybe I should have her house filled with flowers when she gets home from work. Oh, I like that."

I unlocked the phone to call the florist. I'd already spent more than I ever had on anyone I was trying to impress, yet I was completely ready to triple it if needed. I paused for a moment. I'd never tried to impress anyone before—she was the first. Shaking off the thought, I thumbed through my recent calls to get the number.

"I think you sent enough, Sir," Shilo said calmly from where he stood by the door.

I looked over at Shilo and tapped the phone in my palm. "If that's the case, then why hasn't she called?"

Shilo watched me resume my pacing around the room. His eyes following me were unnerving, like one of those creepy paintings where the eyes followed you while you walked past it. I didn't like them. It always felt like the painting was holding onto secrets that I should know. I wanted to yell at him to stop staring, but that would only terrify the old angel. I'd made that mistake once in the early part of our working relationship, and it took over a month to get Shilo to feel comfortable being alone in the same room with me again.

"Sir, I think you should just let her be. If she is interested, then she will call."

"What, and let Michael win? Never. I need to make her mine. I need to get her away from that white-winged abydocomist." I made my way to the far end of the office and stared at the portrait of myself. I glanced at my Rolex. She should've called by now.

"Sorry Sir I didn't catch that last word."

"Abydocomist," I repeated, noticing that the new arrangement was uneven. "You know, he's a liar and a fake." Reaching up, I fixed the black and cream arrangement that I'd had delivered at the same time as Minetta's flowers. They were stunning but looked way too messy. I'd have to remember not to use that designer again.

"Sir, Minetta is at work. Maybe she is simply busy. Unlike yourself, she does not have the freedom to make her own hours or rules. She is much like the employees that work on the lower floors of this building."

I checked my phone again and then tapped my chin with it as I mulled over the best course of action. "Maybe, but she could've sent a text. I don't understand it. How could she resist my apology? I just don't understand how she can resist me? I saw interest in her eyes, Shilo, I swear to you I did, and yet she keeps her distance."

"Sir, she is not like the other girls that come here simply for pleasure. I feel you will need a different approach."

"I don't get it. I just don't get it and need to know. No, I can't wait. I have to know if she got them. Don't you think?"

"Are you asking me, Sir, or are you venting?"

I looked over my shoulder at Shilo. "I was asking you."

"May I speak freely, Sir?"

I turned and made my way over to the window across from Shilo, not sure if I wanted to hear what he had to say. The old angel had a tendency to be right more than I liked, especially when I was wrong, which was more than a little irritating. But if I wanted to win Minny over, I needed help. My stomach flipped at the mere thought of never seeing her again.

"Okay, Shilo, speak freely."

"Sir, please hear me when I say you need to do things differently and that your money is not the answer. You already mentioned she is different, that she is unique, and most importantly, she doesn't hold greed in her heart."

I could see Shilo in the reflection of the glass as I stared out at the ocean in the distance. "What of it?"

"Have you considered that lavish and over-the-top gifts are not the way to go?"

I snorted and turned to face Shilo. "Don't be ridiculous. She may not hold greed, but she is still a woman, and every woman likes to be dripping in gifts from their potential suitor. That is all I'm doing is apologizing for my rude behavior and making sure she knows how appreciated she is."

Shilo turned his calm stare away from me to look straight ahead. "If you say so, Sir."

"I think I should call her, but it might seem too desperate." I stared at one of the other smaller buildings. There was a man and woman kissing, and I was suddenly jealous of them. "I know. I'll say that I wanted to make sure she received the flowers. Maybe she didn't go to work today, and some other human got them. Yes, I'll call her."

I pulled out my phone and dialed the number that I had spent an exorbitant amount of time trying to locate—stupid cellphones and their unlisted numbers. Hitting send, I waited for the line to start ringing, but it went straight to voicemail. Another brain wave hit, and I dialed 911 and waited for someone to pick up.

"Nine, one, one. what's your emergency?"

"Yes, good morning. Could you please transfer me to Minetta Johnson?"

"This is not reception. You will have to call..."

I cut the woman off before she could continue. "No, I won't. I am the Riker Rhodes, and I'm the one who sent the flowers. I respectfully demand that you let me speak to Minetta immediately, or I'll make sure you never work another day anywhere in this city." Silence greeted me, and I stared at my phone to see if it was still connected.

"Okay, Sir, I will re-direct your call, but do not call this number like this again. It is for emergencies only."

No one told me not to do something. What kind of place was this 911 office? If they didn't know who I was, they were about to when I bought them out. I fumed as I waited for Minetta to pick up. The phone rang twice, and then her sweet voice came on the line.

"Minetta speaking, how may I help you?"

"Minetta, it's me, Riker."

"I should've known," she said, her voice sounding annoyed.

I wasn't sure what she meant or why she'd be annoyed but continued on. "I wanted to know if you received the flowers I sent?"

"You mean the jungle that greeted me this morning? Yes, I received them, and they are all happy in their new homes. Now, if you'll excuse me, I need to get back to work."

"Wait, what do you mean by their new homes?"

She sighed like she was frustrated, which was exasperating since I'd gone to so much effort to win her over. "Riker, I appreciate you went to so much trouble to apologize, but I would never want that many flowers, so I sent them to the hospital for those that are ill and don't have family visiting them."

"You did what? But I gave them to you."

"Yes, and I gave them away because they were now mine to do with as I pleased. Now, I'm asking that you don't call me at work. In fact, I'd prefer if you never contacted me again. I have to go. My boss is paging me. Take care of yourself, Riker. Thank you for the apology." The phone went dead in my ear, and I stared at it, my mouth hanging open.

"Are you kidding me? Has Michael made that much of an impression already," I asked Shilo, but the man himself answered.

"Don't blame me. She cut me off too." My head snapped up to stare at Michael, who appeared in the doorway. I hadn't seen him in over a century, and now it was like I couldn't get away from him. The fucker had turned into my personal stalker.

"What are you doing here again? Didn't I already tell you never to come back?" I marched across the room to the espresso machine.

"And here I thought we had a thing last night. You know, a moment where you didn't hate me?" He glanced at my coffee. "You could offer me one of those. I like double cream," Michael said as he sat in one of the black leather chairs I used for meetings.

"And waste my expensive blend on you? Not likely." Michael rolled his eyes at me, and I grumbled and found myself making the ass a coffee anyway. I hated him. I really hated him, and yet I missed him. How could both realities be true? We were once very close, best friends and spent a great deal of time together, and now I could barely stomach looking at his face.

"Here." I plunked the mug down on the marble table in front of him and proceeded to get comfortable since it didn't look like he was leaving anytime soon. "You can stay or go, Shilo, your choice," I said. Shilo hated to be in the same room as Michael even more than I did, and I wouldn't force him to stand inside the room with him here.

"Don't leave on my account," Michael said as he looked over at the fallen angel who refused to glance in Michael's direction.

"I will take my leave, Sir. If you need me, just ring." Shilo bowed and left, closing the door behind him.

"He never speaks to me. It's like I don't exist." Michael stared at the closed door like he might actually feel bad about that.

"Can you blame him? You did toss him out of Heaven and force him to leave his wife of almost a millennium and his three daughters behind."

Michael sighed and sipped at the coffee, obviously not wanting to discuss that particular situation. "Fine, don't say anything, but you know what I say is true, and you also know that he didn't deserve it. Now, tell me, what do you mean Minetta has cast you aside?"

Michael lifted one shoulder and let it fall. "Just what I said. She sent me a text this morning saying that she thought I was a great guy, but she didn't feel we were well suited for each other and didn't want to waste either of our time by going on a second date. Apparently, she doesn't find either of us appealing. Some archangels we are. Maybe our looks and charm are slipping."

"Ha! More like the girl has some sense, at least where you're concerned." I smiled over my cup. "Why are you here again gracing me with your presence," I said, my voice dripping with sarcasm.

"I came to see my brother and wanted to have breakfast. Maybe we can commiserate over a mimosa?"

My eyebrow lifted at him in question. "I find it very difficult to take you at your word Michael. I'm always looking for the other layer to your motives."

"I know, but I just wanted breakfast before I leave town." Michael stood and buttoned up his suit jacket.

"I'm not sure why I'm agreeing to this. Fine, I'll eat with you, but I'm driving."

The odd thing was that it should've become the perfect deterrent to stay away from Minetta with Michael out of the way. There was no longer the challenge of beating Michael to have her, yet it only fueled my interest more. She'd turned her back on myself and Michael? Who was this girl?

This Minetta was a challenge, and I loved it. The more I thought about it, the more I wanted to show Michael that I could win her over. More precisely, that I could have something he'd wanted and been denied.

Minetta might have thought she'd seen the last of me, but I was just getting warmed up, and I had the perfect idea how to get her attention next.

TWENTY-NINE

MINETTA swallowed hard as she walked up the stairs to her boss's office. She hated coming in here, and she'd only been summoned a few times. The office had an overwhelming smell of moist dirt, and she wondered if the place had a mold problem. It didn't help that she couldn't tell if Eric had a family or not. There wasn't a single personal item anywhere. Not even a fake beach picture on the wall, just bland grey surrounded him, and it always matched the emotionless look on her boss's face.

Eric rarely spoke to her. It was more like he preferred to never speak to her unless he was forced. Minetta knocked on the closed door, his deep voice barking out to come in.

Her initial trepidation turned into full-blown panic as she stared at the two officers in the room.

"Minetta, come in. We need to talk." Eric beckoned her forward with his meaty hand. His reddish face wore the same flat, emotionless mask it always had, giving nothing away.

"What is this about," she asked, keeping an eye on the two officers watching her.

Eric pointed to the men and leaned back in his chair, the thing squeaking under his portly stature. She turned her eyes up to the officers, their little notepads and pens in hand.

"Ma'am, I'm sorry that we're here. We don't take pleasure in questioning our fellow emergency members." The man that spoke had the name badge of Morris on his chest, and his eyes were shadowed under his hat. The handlebar mustache gave him an uncle-like appearance, but they were not there as her friend no matter how he looked. "Did you hit one of your co-workers today?"

Un-freaking-believable! Jared had actually done it. He was going to press charges. How many times had she let his shit slide, and this was what she got for it?

"Is this one of those moments I should be asking for a lawyer?"

"Only if you did something wrong."

Every swear word known to man ran through her mind, and she suddenly wished she knew more languages. It would give her a longer list to throw at them. Turning back to her boss, she leaned forward.

"You have to know this is wrong, don't you," she pleaded. The issue with not having a lot of money was that you couldn't afford things like fancy lawyers. If she was charged with assault, she could lose her job, have a record, and lose her volunteer positions. Eric's eyes were flat as he shrugged. There was no way this man was going to help her. What choice did she have other than to tell her side of the events? Maybe she could get ahead of this before Jared found a way to make the situation worse.

"I did hit Jared in the call center, but I only did it because he was sexually harassing me and has been for months. His comment would've made you want to hit him too. I felt threatened and highly uncomfortable," she said and watched as those pens began jotting down what she was saying.

"Have you ever reported any of these sexual harassment incidents to your boss?" Morris asked.

"No, I let them go. I didn't want to be a troublemaker. I was hoping he'd take the hint and leave me alone. He seemed like a typical bully just wanting to get a rise out of me, but today was different."

"How so?"

"For starters, he was in my personal space. Second, he flat out said I must have been a good fuck to deserve all the flowers that were in my cubicle."

"Is there anyone that can corroborate your story?"

"Ask anyone in the call center. They have all heard him at one time or another. The entire floor clapped and cheered when I hit him because he had been extremely rude to all of the girls on many different occasions. I think we even had a girl quit because of him, but you'd have to ask her to confirm that."

Minetta leaned back in the chair, crossing her arms as she pictured the look on Jared's face when he came crying into this office to complain. Such a weasel. Penny was right. She should've reported him a long time ago and kept reporting him until his ass was out the door. The problem with someone like him was they would just get a job elsewhere and continue to do the same shit.

"Unfortunately, we will have to take you down to the precinct to formally press charges," the officer said, and her mouth dropped open as she stared in bewilderment.

"You're kidding, right? The guy harasses me for months to the point I had to defend myself, and it's me that's going to jail?"

Officer Morris rubbed the back of his neck, he looked uncomfortable, and she hoped he knew this wasn't fair. "Since there is nothing on file and all we have at this point is a co-worker who you have admitted hitting wanting to press charges, we have to follow protocol."

"Eric, you have to do something. You know me," she begged her boss.

"I'm sorry, Minetta, but I can't interfere, and until you are cleared of the charges, you won't be allowed to come back to work."

"You're firing me?" She asked, exasperated.

"No, just suspending you until this mess has passed." Eric's chair groaned again as he leaned forward to place his arms on the desk.

"Please stand." Morris held up handcuffs, and bile rose in her throat. She'd never been in serious trouble for anything, and that puke Jared just got her suspended and carted off to jail.

"I'll come peacefully. Are the handcuffs really necessary?" In reality, she wanted to bolt from the room and keep running. All she could picture was being stuck in prison for the rest of her life with no way to pay for bail or get a lawyer and would end up rotting there as she slipped through the cracks in the system.

"As long as you promise not to run, we can accommodate that."

She nodded at Morris and followed the officers out when she stopped and looked back at Eric. "Can you call Penny and let her know what's going on? Please, she looks after my dog when I can't?" She stared at him until he nodded.

Minetta followed the officers out of the office, her back ramrod straight. She wasn't going to allow any of the looky-loos to see her scared. Least of all, Jared himself. She spotted him standing in one of the offices, his face held a fake image of shock, but his eyes glittered with evilness. She stared at him as she passed, a smug smile gracing her lips as he was the first to look away.

Her confidence was short-lived, though. The moment she saw the police car and was asked to get in the back, tears stung the back of her eyes. She knew this wasn't Riker's fault, and yet she couldn't help wanting to blame him for this as well. It was like a giant shadow of shit had decided to drop on her the moment they'd met.

Minetta looked out the window of the car as they pulled away from the curb and drove along the busy city streets. She felt like all eyes were on her, adding to the feeling of shame. They were probably all wondering what the girl in the back of the car had done. She could hear it now, she seemed like such a nice girl, or I never saw this coming from her, or I always wondered about her. She seemed too perfect.

The car turned off one of the more congested streets, and as they did, they drove right past Riker's building. As if it would help, she glared at the tall, imposing structure as she thought of every nasty thing she could.

She couldn't help the annoying little tingly sensation in her chest as they passed. Thankfully, the sensation went away as the moving police car put distance between her and the imposing black glass structure. It was as if it was reflecting the blue sky and fluffy white clouds, like the building itself rejected Heaven. She slumped back into the seat and let her mind wander as they continued to drive.

She sat up a little straighter as the tall buildings were replaced with subdivisions and strip malls. She looked out the back window as they turned onto the highway that led out of the city.

"Where are we going?" Morris looked in the rear-view mirror at her, and she bit her lip hard, trying not to scream. His eyes were like staring into black oil slicks, the light brown completely replaced with the eerie color. "I don't want him," she blurted out. "I swear I won't go near him. I just want to be left alone."

A chuckle-like sound that had her shivering came from the officer that had yet to say a word. He slowly looked over his shoulder at her, his neck turning unnaturally far. Minetta pushed herself back as far as she could into the seat as his lips pulled back, showing off jagged, pointy teeth. As her eyes met his again, a bloodcurdling scream ripped from her throat as his eyeballs made a disgusting sucking sound before they peeled open like sliding doors and two small snakeheads poked out.

"Help," she screamed, her fists slamming against the glass as her fear took over. Instinct screamed for her to get out and run. One of the small greenish heads stretched through the mesh cage, the red eyes twitching up and down as they looked her over. She wanted to vomit as the little forked tongues slipped out of their mouths and waved in the air. Her body shook uncontrollably as she yanked on the door handle, screaming like a banshee. She would rather take her chances with eighty-mile an hour road rash and a broken neck than spend one more second in this car.

Leaning into the door, she used her feet to slam into the back window, wishing she wore boots rather than sneakers to work.

"Enough!" Morris's voice boomed, the sound so much deeper than it had been in the office. "We will be there soon enough. Syliss, put your pets away. We don't want to give her a heart attack before we arrive."

"But her fear tasssts ssso good," the man, Syliss with snakes coming out of his eyes, hissed.

"Do it!" Morris barked out at Syliss, the sound turning very much into a deep rumbling growl. Syliss turned forward in his seat, the snakes retreating into his head. He stared directly at her as those eyeballs slid closed once more, leaving him with perfect-looking green eyes. His tongue snaked out of his mouth and stretched up far enough to lick at his eyes, and she covered her mouth as she forced herself not to throw up.

She turned her attention to Morris, who seemed to be the one in charge and somewhat sane. "Please, Morris, I'm begging you not to do this. I don't want Riker. I just want to go back to my life the way it was before all this craziness started."

"Mammon," he said, and she stared into the mirror, her blank expression likely giving way that she didn't understand. "His name is Mammon. Respect must be given to the sin of greed."

"I'm sorry, I didn't know that I needed to address him like that. This is what I mean, I just want to go home, and if you let me, I'll move, as far away as I can get. Just please don't kill me." Minetta clasped her hands at her chest as she begged. "I have an ill mother counting on me. There is no one else...I..." Tears clogged her next words.

"You should've already been dispatched. This was inevitable," Morris said.

She had no idea what he meant, but she did know that she didn't have much time and there was no way out. She felt her pockets and groaned as she remembered leaving her cell phone on her desk.

She couldn't die yet. She hadn't experienced so many things. She'd barely started to scratch things off the bucket list she'd made with her dad just before he'd passed. Hot tears slid in streams down her cheeks as she thought about never seeing her mother again. Even if her mom didn't know who she was anymore. She didn't want her in some home alone with no one going to see her, and what would happen to her once the payments stopped because there was no money in her account? Her bottom lip trembled, and she sucked in a strangled gasp as the fear morphed into something else. Other than Toby and Penny, would anyone even care if she disappeared?

Conserving her strength, she leaned her head against the glass and watched the landscape pass her by—she'd taken it for granted. It would be dark soon, the setting sun painting the sky with beautiful reds, pinks, and oranges. It was quite possibly the last sunset she'd ever see, and she stared at it with a renewed appreciation as she prayed.

She didn't think God would be bothered with her pitiful plea. He hadn't listened when she begged for her father's life. And he hadn't bothered to listen when she prayed for her mother's diagnosis to be wrong or to make the disease go away. He hadn't bothered to show up for her the night two boys decided it would be fun to take advantage of her while at a college party. She'd prayed through the tears that night, too, and it didn't help. No one came. It was an embarrassment she'd never told anyone. This so-called Father or God or whatever he was, had left her to fend for herself even though he had infinite power to help—her faith had been shaken long ago.

Where was this Michael, the master of manipulation now? Pushing the resentment aside, she closed her eyes and thought of her dad. He'd made sure she had survival skills, and she was going to need everyone to make it out of this alive. And if not, then at least she went out fighting.

THIRTY

MINETTA

The car had been unnervingly quiet the remainder of the drive. There was no music or two-way radio to listen to as a distraction. She'd watched the sun set, and the further they drove, the darker the night sky became, with only the stars and the sliver of a moon, lighting the surroundings. They'd long ago left behind any sort of help. The farms were few and far between, and for the last half hour, all she'd seen were trees. Nothing looked familiar, and it became glaringly clear that even if she did manage to escape, she had no idea which direction to head or if she'd survive the elements, but it didn't matter. If running were her only chance, then she'd take it.

The car slowed and turned off the dirt road they'd been traveling on, opting for an unkempt driveway. She couldn't see anything in the car's headlights other than tall trees, overgrown grass, and weeds. The shaking in her body started up again, but she worked hard to push it down. She could be scared later. Right now, she had to keep her wits about her. It felt like her teeth were going to rattle right out of her head as the car bumped and shook going over the rough terrain. They rounded a bend, and a dilapidated cabin lay before her, but what had her attention was that there was already a light on inside the place.

The front door opened before they came to a stop, and the tiny bit of courage she'd built up vanished as three other men walked out.

"Behave," Morris ordered, making her jump. His booming voice felt like a shot to the face. The two demons got out of the car and went to go speak to the other three men. She leaned forward and felt around frantically, trying to find anything that could be used as a weapon. Her hand brushed something under the seat on the floor. Wrapping her hand around it, she realized she had a pen, it wasn't much, but it was something. She shoved it into the pocket of her pants and sat quietly. The only thing that she could hear was the thumping of her own heart as it tried to pound out of her chest.

Morris turned and walked toward her door. Unable to help herself, she scooted to the other side of the car.

"Don't be a pain, and get out," Morris said as he held open the door.

She didn't move. She wasn't going to make this easy for them. His lumbering figure bent and reached into the car, and she screamed and kicked at his hands and face. He growled as her foot came into contact with his jaw. She screamed louder as his hands turned into claws wrapping around her legs. His strength was immense, the pain instant as he squeezed her calves, a whimper escaping her throat as the pain paralyzed her struggles.

With a hard tug, she was dragged out of the car, her head hitting the seat and then the frame of the car on the way down. She landed on the uneven ground, her tailbone screaming with the impact. She tried to flip over and pull at the ground as he continued to drag her along by one leg. As Morris reached the small group, he dropped her leg, and she lunged for freedom, but he was so much faster and jarringly strong as he jerked her back and upright to her feet. His clawed hand wrapped around the back of her neck and lifted her until her toes brushed the ground.

"Well, well...so this is the thing that is causing so much trouble," one of the new men said. He, too, was most certainly a demon, either that or his mother was a cat. His eyes looked identical to a tiger's, the yellow color glowing in the dark.

"I haven't done anything. All I want is to go home, and I will leave Ri...Mammon alone. I told them I'd move to the other side of the planet." She couldn't turn her head but pointed toward Morris and Syliss. "Please, don't do this. I will leave."

The demon cocked its head to the side as it stared at her. "How do you know so much," it asked.

"I only know what my friend, who happens to be a demon, told me. That I need to stay away from Mammon, and I will. I don't want anything to do with him. I don't even like him. He's an asshole, a complete jerk. I mean, who would want him?"

The demons erupted in laughter like she'd said the funniest thing ever. This was her life, and they were all laughing at her. She sucked in a deep breath and crossed her arms over her chest as she glared at the demon.

"You're certainly unique, but no matter, you need to die," he said calmly. He leaned in toward her, and she tried to back up, but Morris tightened his hold on her neck, keeping her in place. His nose touched her neck softly as he made little noises.

He was sniffing her?

His body was overly hot. It radiated off him like she was standing too close to a campfire.

"No worries, little human, you are going to get your chance to run," he whispered in her ear, making her shiver.

He took a step back and smiled, producing a pair of sharp fangs that turned the shiver into an all-out shaking throughout her body. All she could picture was those teeth sinking into her throat and ripping it open.

"We will give you say an hour head start—no, I'll be nice since you made me laugh, which is rare. I'll give you an hour and a half, and then the fun will begin."

Morris shoved her away, and she tripped, landing hard on her hands and knees, the stones biting into the soft skin. She stared up at the men as they walked toward the cabin. The one with the disturbing yellow eyes turned back to her, his eyes looking more disturbing, reflecting the light coming from the cabin.

"Run," he whispered.

Adrenaline spiked as she surged to her feet and ran. She needed to be smart about this and darted into the forest but angled herself toward the road. Within a few minutes, she burst out onto the dirt road and looked left and right. Left took her back the way they'd arrived, and she already knew that was way too far to anything or anyone that might be able to help. She could barely see the road or twenty feet in any direction. It was so dark. The old trees towered high into the sky and blocked out most of the moon.

Taking a deep breath, she turned to the right and picked up into a fast jog. She needed to put as much distance between herself and the demons as she could, and running like a bat out of hell wasn't going to get her far before she ran out of energy.

The night was humid, and it didn't take long for her to become soaked with sweat as it dripped down her back and soaked her underwear. She was tempted to strip her pants, but that would take time and leave an obvious trail. Her footfalls were the only thing she could hear, along with her rhythmical breaths as her legs pumped.

"Ouch," she groaned as a small stone ended up in her shoe. Taking the opportunity presented, she leaned over and tried to catch her breath. Hopping on one foot, she slipped her sneaker off and dumped the small pebble onto the ground. Her feet hurt, no, her entire body hurt. She slipped back on the shoe and froze as a strange noise could be heard in the distance. It was coming from the forest in the direction she'd traveled. She looked at the watch on her wrist. It couldn't already be time, could it? No, there was half an hour yet, but they could easily have lied to her. She looked to the tall trees and contemplated climbing to the top and simply hiding, but if they found her, she was a sitting duck. She had zero knowledge about what they could do, and sitting in one place seemed like a very bad idea.

Minetta resumed her jog and tried to picture the dark forest with its imposing dense trees as a pretty garden to calm the panic that was threatening to overtake her mind. A screech of an owl echoed through the night, and she jumped as her heart lurched. She stumbled with the sudden sideways movement and twisted her ankle.

"Shit," she softly swore as her stride became a limp. She needed to take up running. It felt like that was all she did anymore. If she got out of this, it was a pretty good guess she'd be running for the rest of her life.

Something was ahead of her in the murky darkness, but she couldn't quite make out what it was. It was something man-made—it had a distinct outline of a rectangle.

Drawing closer, she realized it was a bridge, an older style one with stone sides and wooden planks. It was narrow, only enough room for a single car to pass. She tentatively took a step on the wood plank, and it squeaked but seemed sturdy enough.

Like she was hit with an electrical charge, the hair stood up on the back of her neck, and she froze. Her hand gripped the edge of the bridge tight as she turned her head and looked over her shoulder. Her heartbeat quickened as her instinct told her she was no longer alone, although nothing moved in the endless dark. A soft breeze picked up, blowing her hair around her face, and she grabbed at the strands pulling them away from her face when something glinted in the middle of the road. It was a fair distance away, and when she blinked, it was gone.

She squinted her eyes as she focused on what she'd thought she'd seen.

Pound, Pound, Pound.

Her pulse thumped in her head. Then she saw it again, the flash of yellow reflecting in the dim light before it disappeared again like it had switched directions. Although there were many possibilities of what that yellow could be out here in the middle of nowhere, her gut screamed it was a demon. The same sensation from her house filled her, and her body shivered. She didn't think the demon saw her. It looked like it was moving around, maybe sniffing the ground.

Gingerly she stepped off the bridge and around the edge that led down the steep bank to the wide stream. She slipped under the bridge and stared at the dark water. She had no idea what was in there and probably didn't want to know, but between unknown water and demons on her tail....

She silently slipped into the cool water. It was deeper than she'd assumed, and it didn't take long before she was up to her chest.

She froze as the bridge above her squeaked, dust falling on her head. Swallowing down her fear, she tilted her head to look up at the narrow slats. Even with the darkness, she could make out the some-thing blocking out the tiny bit of moonlight that should be shining down. She held perfectly still and didn't even dare breathe as she watched the creature move further across to the other side. Her ears strained as she listened for any more noise, but the sound of feet running became faint and then disappeared. There was no way for her to know if it was going to circle back.

Biting her lip, she ordered herself to think. Her dad always told her that if she was ever lost in the wilderness to find water and follow it downstream. It would provide water to drink, which she could live off of for days if need be, and she would eventually find safety. She can honestly say she never thought that particular piece of information was ever going to come in handy.

Thank you, Dad.

Submerging herself in the water up to her neck, she allowed herself to drift with the gentle current. She hadn't traveled very far when the stream widened and picked up the pace. She hit more than one rock that she couldn't see coming and knew she was going to be black and blue if she lived at all. Each time she groaned but made sure not to yell out.

Minetta could see lights, they were little glittering dots in the distance, but it was hope. A small smile lifted the corner of her lip as she slowly drifted closer. The sliver of relief evaporated as something slid around her leg under the water. She kicked at it and made for the shore, but it gripped her harder this time and jerked her leg back. She gulped water as she was yanked below into the inky darkness.

Her arms reached for anything to hang onto as she kicked violently at what had her. She got just high enough that her mouth broke the surface of the water, and she coughed up the water she'd taken into her lungs before she was dragged back under the dark surface. Her legs kicked, and her arms flailed as her feet hit the bottom, and she used it to push with all her strength off the bottom until she reached the surface.

They'd continued to move downstream, and a rock came at her fast. She gave a hard pull against her assailant and gripped the rock tightly.

She'd never kicked so hard and fast in her life as she continually beat on something under the water as she yanked hard on the leg still trapped. The grip loosened just enough that she was able to scamper onto the large boulder. She stared at the thing that was still wrapped around her leg, and it looked like the tail of a snake. She slammed her foot down on the thing hard, squishing it between her shoe and the rock. It still wouldn't let go, so she brought her heel down two more times as hard as she could.

Syliss broke through the water not far away. A holler that came out like a loud hiss left his mouth. Her eyes grew wide as she took in the green scaly skin and multiple stubby tentacles protruding out of his body. Standing on the slippery surface, she jumped for shore, but her foot slipped, and she didn't get very far. Still, in ankle-deep water, she tried to run, but one of his longer tentacles torpedoed through the water and wrapped around her leg and pulled back.

She screamed as she landed face-first on the muddy bank. Her hands curled into the moist mud, and she flipped over before he could land on her back. Syliss crawled over the rock she'd been on as she stared into the green eyes of death.

Regaining her wits, she tried to pull herself out of his hold and pushed back with her feet and hands on the slick surface. It did no good. He held her firm and slid up her body like a snake. Grabbing handfuls of the soft mushy mud, she didn't hesitate and stuffed the mud in his face, making sure to grind it in his eyes.

It had done the trick.

He reared back, swatting at the dirt, giving her time to get her hand in her pocket and grip the pen.

Syliss hissed as loud as any lion's roar, a forked tongue hanging from his mouth. Those twin snakes pressed out of his eyes and stared down at her.

"Issss going to kill you," he said as four long fangs jutted down out of his mouth. He lunged for her face, and she screamed loud and swung her concealed weapon as hard as she could at the side of his head.

The mouth stopped short of her face by mere inches. The snake-like eyes shot back into his head, leaving vacant holes as the pen sunk deep into his ear cavity. His body went rigid, and before all his weight landed on her, she pushed back on the bank to get out from under his bulk. Adrenaline alone gave her the strength she needed to continue to fight.

She crawled as far as she could, with a tentacle still wrapped around her ankle. She gripped the closest rock she could find and lifted it above her head. Her arms shook, but her aim was true as it slammed down onto the disgusting thing. The long tentacle let go as Syliss's body convulsed on the ground, black foam bubbling out of his mouth.

Not knowing if the little pen would actually kill him, she stumbled to her feet. Feeling a draft, she realized that her pants had ripped during the struggle, leaving her with them hanging open and flapping as she moved.

Reaching down, she grabbed the sides and pulled, finishing the rip around her leg, giving her the ugliest bootie shorts ever. Dropping the material, she ran for the lights she'd seen. She didn't make it very far when something crashed in the dark forest beside her. She pumped her arms hard as she tried to get away, but the yellow-eyed demon jumped out into her path.

She skidded to a halt, almost falling on her ass once more. He looked like he was part cat and part scorpion with strange spikes all over his head. She stared at him for a moment as her eyes tried to make sense of what she was seeing. Minetta looked behind her only to see Morris on all fours, his body as black as his eyes, step out on the bank behind her.

"You got much further than I gave you credit for," the yellow-eyed demon said. "It's a shame we have to kill you. I'd have enjoyed playing this game with you again."

"Well, that only makes one of us," she said, his cat face pulling up in a strange smile.

Movement in the forest to her left and on the other side of the bank confirmed that she was indeed surrounded. This was not how she pictured her death, and it was not how she feared she would die.

Wrapping her arms around herself, she closed her eyes. If she was going to die, she didn't want to see it coming.

CHAPTER
THIRTY-ONE

MINETTA

There was the sound of a loud snarl, and her body tensed for the impact, but nothing hit her.

"Run!"

Her eyes snapped open at the sound of Penny's voice. She was as she'd seen her at her house, except now she had bright, fiery, red wings that looked like rubies glittering in the dark. Her unearthly sword had cut the demon across the bank, the body bursting into flames as Penny floated toward her, Morris, and the other two remaining demons. She was beautiful. Her pale skin looked like porcelain, her eyes glowing orange as her vibrant red hair floated around her shoulders. For a demon, she was breathtaking.

"I can't leave you to fight them on your own," she said.

Penny looked at her and smiled. "Do you think you can take on one of them?" A graceful eyebrow lifted up.

"I took that one out," she pointed back the way she'd come and watched in horror as Syliss stumbled to his feet. "Or, maybe not," she mumbled, stepping behind Penny.

"You're a traitor," the yellow-eyed demon growled.

"Run, Minny, and don't stop, not for any reason." Minetta stared into her friend's face and then grabbed her arm, giving it a quick squeeze.

"Thank you," she said. Doing as she was told, she bolted along the bank away from the action.

Snarling and roaring sounds grew louder behind her, but she didn't dare look. Penny said not to stop, but with each footfall, the guilt of leaving Penny behind to defend her clawed at her soul.

A woman's yell of pain sounded, and unable to help herself, she spun around to see Penny being held up by her throat by none other than Michael. The angel glowed in the darkness like a miniature moon. His massive, white wings were spread wide. His chest was bare except for a few straps of white leather that showed off his toned chest. His blonde hair floated behind him like a breeze was blowing while his blue eyes glowed. It took her a moment to get over the initial shock of seeing him in his natural form. Even knowing what he was, didn't stop the astonishment.

There was only one demon left, and it was running in her direction. But it was the smoke rising around Michael's hand as he effortlessly held Penny off the ground that scared her. She ducked as the demon leaped over her and continued to run away from the famous archangel. Michael lifted a great long sword in the air, and at first, she thought he was going to strike Penny down with it.

A silent scream ripped from Minetta's throat as she lunged forward. Without even looking Michael threw the long sword and she watched in awe as the shining, glowing blade spun end over end as it sailed above her head. It was with mixed fascination and horror she stared as the sword sunk deep into the last demon's back, the thing bursting into ash instantly.

Shaking her head to rid it of the million questions she wanted to be answered, she ran for Michael and Penny.

"No," Minetta screamed at the top of her lungs. Her muscles began to seize and revolt—her tired and unstable legs screamed in pain, but she ordered herself to keep going. She was reduced to hobbling but kept moving as Michael shook Penny by her throat and then threw her off to the side. Penny slammed into a large tree, the impact so loud it sounded like a shotgun had just gone off. Wood splintered and fell to the ground as Penny slid to her ass. She didn't see Michael move, but in the blink of an eye, he had Penny held up by the throat again and pressed against the tree. Penny's eyes were wide as she smacked at his unwavering arm.

Minetta screamed for him to put Penny down, but he didn't even glance at her.

Penny's eyes swung in her direction, and sadness mixed with undeniable fear lay bare. "Put her down, you fucking asshole," Minny yelled. She was angry enough to spit nails.

That got his attention.

Michael's head turned in her direction, and she bent to grab a handful of mud and hurled it at Michael as hard as she could. He may have been one of the good guys, but as his glowing blue eyes met hers, all she felt was cold fear. A cool power drifted over her skin and made goosebumps rise on her body. He looked at the small splat of mud that hit his side. It was the only thing to mar his glowing perfection.

Her anger beat back any trepidation that was in her chest as she continued to stumble on weak legs toward him with another handful of mud.

"Let her go! I mean it, you pompous asshat! Drop my friend right this minute, or you will have to deal with me!" Her fists clenched as she stared into the blue eyes, slowly losing their brilliant glow.

Michael laughed a hearty sound that shook the leaves on the trees. Penny stared at her with wide-eyed horror. It probably was the stupidest thing she'd ever done, knowing what he could do to her, but she didn't care. She wasn't leaving Penny.

"Again with the wet shirt. We really have to stop meeting like this." He glanced at her chest, and this time she glared back. She didn't find it cute or sexy, and she wanted to smack him. "I like this side of you. I can see why you were chosen now, Minetta. You have a fire that burns in your soul and a strength of character most don't exhibit."

"Don't talk to me like that. I'm no one's pet, not yours and not your Father's. Now let my friend go. She just saved my life."

"You know what she is, yes?"

"I do, and I don't care," Minetta said, as her legs finally gave out and she landed on her ass in the mud. Her hand fell open, unable to keep it closed any longer. She stared at the simple little dirt weapon and wanted to laugh at the ridiculousness of the situation.

Michael lowered the two of them to the ground and released Penny's neck. There was a massive red handprint around her throat, and she wanted to choke Michael for hurting Penny.

"Interesting. Did she happen to tell you why she is in your life? How a demon came to be your best friend?" Michael folded his great wings, the tops still rising high above his muscled shoulders. He stood with his feet apart, his toned abs on display as he crossed his arms over his chest that held thin silver lines that looked like runes embedded into his skin.

"Michael, please don't. Send me to Hell, send me to purgatory. I don't care, but don't do this," Penny pleaded.

Minetta looked at Penny and then back at Michael. "Penny told me that she came into my life to keep me away from Riker or Mammon or whatever the hell his name is. The friendship was unexpected but came after we met."

Michael smirked, and she had the strongest urge to get up and punch him square in that pretty face. And if she could've moved, she would have tried.

"Would you like to tell her, or should I," Michael asked Penny.

"Tell me what?" She looked at the horrified expression on Penny's face and realized that she was missing a crucial part of the story Penny had told her. "Penny, what is it? What didn't you tell me?"

"I'm so sorry," Penny cried and dropped to her knees, covering her face as she wept. Red tears seeped from her eyes that were shocking against her pale skin.

"Come on Penny, the truth will set you free," Michael mocked.

"Have you always been this big of a jerk," Minetta asked, which only made him laugh hard.

"I guess I will. Penny came into your life to kill you," Michael said flatly. Minetta looked between the two of them, and when Penny didn't refute the absurd claim or look at her, she licked her lips and stared up at Michael.

"Why?"

"Why do you think?"

"Really? A guessing game? Now I know why I didn't have any interest in a second date," she grumbled. Michael roared with laughter this time and smacked a hand off his leg which only annoyed her more. She was tempted to throw the dirt at him just because.

"Oh, you are perfect, alright. Fine, I will tell you. She sold the little that was left of her soul for something that she deemed more important than your mere life."

"I did not," Penny suddenly yelled. "I was approached and, yes, I agreed, but the prophecy says the apocalypse must happen. I thought I was doing the right thing when I agreed."

"And let's not forget the fact that you would be granted the opportunity to become human." Michael held up a finger. "Able to die." He held up a second one. "And a certain archangel granting you forgiveness to get back into Heaven had nothing to do with it?" Michael lifted the third finger as he cocked a brow at Penny.

"Is this true? Did you plan to kill me so you could get back into Heaven?" Minetta gawked at her, but Penny just looked at the ground.

"Don't forget the part where the apocalypse can take place. You see, Minetta, Penny here hated all humans before she was tossed from Heaven. They revolted her. In fact, she was so against the job she was tasked to do that she wanted everything on Earth to be destroyed. Isn't that right, Penny?"

"Please stop this," Penny pleaded.

Michael smiled, and she wasn't sure if he shouldn't be tossed from Heaven for being a Grade-A jerk.

"Humans were destroying the Earth. I used to think they didn't respect a thing. I really did think I was doing what was right." Penny looked at her. "But then I met you, Minetta, and I couldn't do it. We were like kindred spirits. Friends right from the first word spoken, and I couldn't follow through. I finally saw what Father had wanted me to see, but I had been too blinded by my own resentment and anger. So instead, I bargained for a deal to keep you away from Riker in exchange for your life, but the moment you met him, my deal was broken. Minny, please forgive me."

"You lied to me again. You had the chance to tell me the truth, and instead, you gave me a half-truth to make yourself out to be a hero, a savior?" Minny staggered to her feet, her legs seized, the muscles revolting against the movement. She sucked in a sharp breath as she stumbled but held out her hand to ward off Penny's help as she made to move in her direction.

"So then tell me this, why must I really stay away from Riker, Penny? What is the truth?"

"Yes, Penny, what is the truth," Michael mocked.

Minetta pointed a finger at Michael. "You shut up. I'm done

listening to your annoying, condescending attitude. You, sir, are nothing more than a winged version of shallow charisma! And it saddens me that God has made you his number one archangel. Manipulating me the way you did. You disgust me as much as anyone else, so don't act like you're some freaking saint for forcing this confession. I know it's not for me. It's only to further your own agenda." She pointed up toward the sky. "You have most certainly grown too big for those tighty whitey britches you're wearing." She pointed to the flowing white fabric around his waist. "I shudder at the thought of spending an entire day with you, let alone an eternity."

Penny made a snorting sound as Michael's eyes went wide. He opened his mouth to say something, but she held up her hand and cut him off. "And, you lied to me too. You cannot cast stones. The pleasure you're getting from sticking it to Riker—you should be ashamed."

She hobbled away from the two of them and stared at the black water. "Was your plan all along to show interest in me just to annoy your brother," she asked as she turned to face Michael.

He didn't refute the claim, so she turned to Penny once more.

"Now Penny, tell me this minute why I'm to stay away from Riker, and if you so much as leave one tiny detail out, we are done for as long as I manage to stay alive."

Penny swallowed and pushed herself off her knees to stand. Her tears had stained her cheeks red like a bad blush job.

"Riker is an Original Sin, and there is a prophecy that has been around for a longer than I can remember. It is hypothesized, and many believe that if the Sin's find redemption or fall in love with a human, it will stop the apocalypse from happening."

Minetta shivered, her damp clothes feeling very wet and cold against her skin.

"So let me make sure I have this straight. You wanted to keep me alive because I was your friend, but you were still working to destroy the world that I live in, which I suspect would also kill me?"

"I didn't look at it like that. The apocalypse could be years from now, another millennium even. You are human, your life expectancy is short, and I knew you'd be safe in Heaven with your family and with me."

Minetta stared at Penny and wasn't sure how she felt, but knew that their friendship was shattered. Could it ever be repaired? She had no idea, but the betrayal was painful.

"But it could also happen tomorrow, and what then?"

"I...I don't know, Minny, I'm sorry. I'd never want you to be hurt or killed, I...." Penny stopped talking and just stared at the ground. "I honestly thought you would be long passed by then."

"And everyone else dying, possibly my grandchildren, that would be okay?" Penny didn't answer and didn't look at her.

Minetta turned her focus on Michael. "Well, this at least makes more sense. Let me guess, you've been trying to goad your brother, the sin of greed, into wanting me in hopes that he will miraculously fall in love with me," Minetta asked.

He lifted a shoulder and let it drop, the action way too elegant for what it meant. "Maybe I wanted to see him again and happy as well. Riker has never forgiven me for my part in his fall, and if his happiness also saved the world, it was a win all the way around in my books."

"And Riker's interest in me is what exactly? Annoyance that you're interested?" She glanced at Penny. "A lie from another fallen angel?"

"No, his interest in you is real. The two of you are destined, and he doesn't know about any of this."

"You don't know that," Penny argued. "You think they are destined to be, but you don't know for sure."

Michael smirked. "Really demon, then why are you working so hard at keeping them apart? Why not let them spend time together and see what happens? If my theory is false, then there would be no harm, now would there?" Penny closed her mouth and crossed her arms over her chest. "Think Penny. There is a reason you were directed to Minetta and not any other random human. Riker's heart has already begun to shift, and you don't think your friend deserves happiness?"

"I...shit." Penny dropped her arms. "You talk in circles, Michael. You make my head hurt. You've always made my damn head hurt. It was the one saving grace of my fall, not to have to listen to you anymore scramble my brain."

"Okay enough, the two of you are worse than listening to political debates." She shook her head to stop the argument from escalating, which was where it was heading. "To recap, my choices are, continue living my life, and the apocalypse may or may not happen, but regardless I will be running for the rest of my life from every demon that decides I'm a threat. Or I go back and see if things can work out between Riker and myself and maybe stop a world-ending apocalypse, which will piss off more demons, but at least Riker's influence might protect me. Is that about right?"

Penny and Michael looked at one another and then back to her. She shook her head as she turned and hobbled along the bank.

"Where are you going?" Michael called after her.

"Anywhere that is far away from you two."

How was she supposed to make a decision like this? Who else woke up one day and was told they could be a key to saving the world? She looked down at her soggy feet. The sneakers sloshed with every agonizing step and felt disgusting and like lead weights on her tired legs.

She was no superhero.

"Minetta?" Michael called out, and she paused and looked over her shoulder.

"Would this be a good time to tell you that your father is proud of you?" She stumbled, and her ass found the mud once more. "I'm not lying to you. He is a good man and is proud of you and the woman you've become. I see the same strength in you that he did to make the hard choices in life, Minetta."

Her eyes found Michael's, and at that moment, she hated him. He knew exactly what to say to mold her to his wishes, and whether his words were true or not, she couldn't turn her back now.

"Can you take me home? I need a hot shower," she asked weakly, her decision already made.

THIRTY-TWO

RIKER

As I stood in the middle of my casino, I realized that it had been some time since I'd bothered to visit the place. Even on my last trip to Hell, I hadn't stopped in. It just didn't offer the same satisfaction that it had when it was first being built.

I'd received a note requesting my presence from my head manager, Skeet. I really wasn't a fan of coming to Hell twice this close together, and now, here I was having to listen to Skeet babble excitedly about all the changes he'd made. Normally, I would find the changes interesting at the very least, but I couldn't gather any enthusiasm today. The stage was more elegant. It stood out like a glittering golden ball of excitement as showgirl demons of all sorts strutted their stuff. Their ostentatious outfits sparkled as the crowd clapped. The next group of demons sashayed on stage, their skimpy outfits leaving very little to the imagination and some of it you didn't even want to imagine.

Take the always stunning and completely deadly Verendent demon. They were always magnificent up there. They had long legs, supple and curvy bodies, and a third tit giving you an extra handle to hold onto or suck. Their multi-colored hair and large gem-like eyes made them one of the most desired demons. They were known for giving exquisite orgasms that would last for hours or even weeks, but very few had the courage to follow through and find out.

And once their skimpy golden thong was stripped away, what lay underneath was a pussy full of razor-sharp teeth. Now, as I'd found out on more than one occasion, they truly were an unbelievable fuck. I'd also discovered there was a trick to making sure those sharp teeth didn't leave a being a member short.

My mind wandered to the last time I'd fucked one. I'd pressed her over the decorative wall in my palace's garden and fucked her ass hard until she turned into a sloppy sex kitten begging for all I could give her. It was her potent juices that placated the dangerous teeth and also provided an unbelievable high to any dick that slid home while she was climaxing.

I stared at the stage as they kicked their legs in the air and thought of fucking one, but it held no appeal. I turned to look at Skeet, who'd apparently stopped speaking and was waiting for a response. I had no idea what the little demon had said.

"Everything looks marvelous, Skeet. I couldn't be happier with the uptick in profits," I said, giving him a blanketed response.

Skeet's reddish face beamed, his small stubby horns glowing like a fucked-up Rudolph, then again, a reindeer with a glowing nose was pretty fucked up on its own.

"Thank you, Master, your praise is too kind. Come I will show you what I did to the swimming pool area. It was rarely used, and we have had a few unfortunate experiences, so I added entertainment instead. The guests have been delighted with the newest addition. The profits will blow your mind." Skeet scampered off, his short legs with cloven hooves clicking on the black marble floor.

"Are the torture rooms still doing well?" I inquired.

"Yes, the torturing of nasty greedy souls has been a hit from the installation. I have turned it into quite the sport and charge a ton for the experience. We can stop there next. I want to show you what I did with the soul Brill brought. I believe his name starts with a Nik. You will love the torture chamber I created for him."

I didn't really give a shit about the tortured souls at the moment, not even Nikolas. Before I built this palace and this casino, I'd simply tortured all the souls together when I had time. Now I had demons doing it and paying customers flocking for the right to get their hands on a soul. Not every demon got to torture, there was a hierarchy, and many greedy demons wanted the opportunity they'd normally not be granted.

I listened to the chimes of the machines and the cheers or crying at the different tables where those taking their chance at playing could literally lose their life. They played for more than simply money in this place. I tried to feel the same excitement I'd once had, so I took a deep breath as I walked and was only mildly aware of those I passed bowing and casting praise my way.

One particularly exuberant guest fluttered on small wings toward me and proceeded to wrap itself around my leg. Its ass humped my thigh as its short stubby arm groped for my cock. It made strange little mewling noises that wasn't any demon dialect that I knew.

"Guards, get this thing off me," I barked out, annoyed.

It looked to be half-demon and half of one of those fucked up angel things that Luci had made. He really needed to keep those fuckers on a better leash. If they were breeding...

I shivered at the thought.

The guards quickly rushed over and pulled the small female demon off my leg. Her face contorted as if in pain as she cried and wailed like a child the moment she was forced to let go.

Leaving it to whatever fate the guards deemed best, I continued my journey through the massive lobby. Skeet trotted along, his little head bobbing beside me, as we turned down Fuckers Lane. I'd given all the hallways fun names. It had been amusing to watch the new patrons run around to see what crazy name would be on the next hallway. I'd particularly liked this one as it was—it was where all of the solicited sex happened. I didn't give a shit if someone wanted to pay for sex with some demon, they normally wouldn't get the chance to fuck. The fact that I got all the profits was yet another stroke of genius on my part. It really was a tremendous situation financially. If you wanted the horniest, greediest, and most gluttonous, you needed to look no further than a foot in either direction. This place teemed with the most sinful.

There had been a number of unfortunate situations where the demons really didn't mesh well, which created a lot of blood and clean up, or on a few rare occasions, the patron's mate would show up. Nothing was as deadly as a demon mate scorned.

A door opened, and a tall, elegant demon stepped out. Erorite was the most profitable demons that worked in this section. She was very talented at her job, and males flocked to have time with her. I should know. I'd visited with her almost every time I was down here.

She smiled, her human-like face beaming as she caught sight of me. The only way anyone knew she wasn't human was because of her long tail that had a tiny spade on the end, and man, did she know how to use that well.

"Well, hello there, my ever so sexy Master," Erorite said.

She didn't just bow her head but got down on her knees before me. If I'd asked, she'd have sucked me off right there in the hallway, and her talented skills would normally detour me from my original mission, but not today. I was starting to wonder if I had a problem with my dick as it lay dormant in my pants.

"Erorite, you may rise."

As she stood, the loose material of her flimsy tunic slipped below her tits, giving me a delectable view. They moved up and down of their own accord, the tips seeping a sweet milk that I'd normally be bending over to enjoy.

But, like the rest of the casino I couldn't find any enjoyment in the sight of the stunning demon who was clearly offering herself up for whatever I desired.

"May I be of service," she asked but knew better than to reach out and touch me unless given permission.

"Not today. I have things I must attend to."

"Maybe later then, I am always at your service." She bowed her head and scooted around me, fixing her tunic as she went.

I was tempted as I stared at her lush ass to take my increasingly building frustrations over Minetta out on her. Maybe if I fucked her, I'd get over the human girl that was quickly becoming a plague on my mind and apparently my body. I stared down at my pants and my flaccid cock and growled. She was like a disease that I didn't know how to eliminate.

"Let's go!" Skeet jumped with the command and instantly picked up his trotting pace.

Grand, gold, double doors lay at the end of the long hall. I stared at the massive structure and took a moment to admire the craftsmanship. The doors had an image of myself engraved into them, the likeness astoundingly well done.

"Do you like them, Master?"

"I do, Skeet, excellent choice." The demon's horns lit up again with the compliment. Skeet tapped on the door in a rhythmic pattern, and slowly the massive gold door swung outward as a guard pushed it open. Cheering reached my ears along with screams and pleading before there was a splash. Thunderous cheers erupted from inside.

I stepped forward into a room that was built much like a human,

Roman coliseum, and wondered if Dai had a hand in the design. This was so to her taste. Rows upon rows of demons sat on the stone seats as they watched the show in front of them. A massive tank rose up out of the floor, the clear sides showing off the zombie-like, great white sharks slowly swimming around.

What the?

Their face and bodies were missing large chunks of flesh, making the large terrifying predator even more horrifying. Blood floated in the middle of the tank, but there was no sign of what they had killed.

A scream had me looking up, and high above the tank was a platform. A dark-haired human girl was screaming as she tried to run back from the way the guard was pushing her. She tried to dive under his arm but was easily scooped up and carried over the demon's shoulder.

"Is everybody ready?" Speakers boomed as the demon's voice echoed and was followed by thunderous cheers. Loud music began to play, the bass thumping with the eerie demon song.

Another loud scream reached my ears, and my attention returned to the girl that couldn't be any more than twenty at the most, her terror filled the room, and those sitting around roared with excitement. The demon slammed the human girl down face first on the platform and pressed a meaty knee into her back as he tied a thick rope around her feet.

Her eyes found mine in the crowd, and her blue eyes shimmered as tears ran down her face. My heart quickened as I stared into a face so similar to Minetta. The demon rose from kneeling on her back, and as it did, it gave the girl a mighty kick that would have easily broken ribs. She wailed in mixed pain and fear as she soared through the air. The rope caught her like an unforgiving bungee cord and jerked her by her ankles just short of hitting the water. She swung helplessly like bait on a line for the circling creatures inches from her face.

I couldn't take my eyes off the scene. The demon part of me was fascinated and wanted to cheer with the others, but a small part in my soul that had long ago died pulsed with dread.

"Please, help me," she pleaded quietly as she swung inches above the deadly tank. "Please."

The sharks moved in, circling in on the prey that was just above them, and as they did, so did I, my feet drawing me closer to the tank. The girl screamed again as one of the great hulking sharks hit the side of her head with the end of its nose. Her long hair that was hanging in the water lay across the shark's nose before he sank below the surface of the water. The girl curled herself in half and grabbed her legs.

My heart pounded hard for her, another face coming to my mind. She panted and groaned but managed to get her fingers on the rope when one of the sharks rose from the water. Time slowed, the image of the mouth gapping and teeth extending seized something in my chest. With a bone-crushing snap, the girl was bitten into three parts. Her feet stayed attached to the rope while her ass and back were devoured by the hulking shark that splashed back into the water. But it was her head and arms that floated slowly downward that had my attention. The head drifted to where I stood. Even in death, her eyes found me. They blinked once before another shark banged into the tank wall, taking the meal, the girl's face disappearing down the dark gullet of the demon shark.

"Master isn't it great!" Skeet screamed excitedly over the deafening noise. I looked around the room, and every demon was on their feet, betting chips in hand. "They bet on how long they will last before dying. They love it and come back again and again."

"That was a human, not a soul, but an actual living, breathing human," I said, my head turning to stare down at Skeet as the anger burned and twisted in my gut.

"I know! They cost a ton to get alive, but they make the best show, Master. Look around. The audience loves it. Not only do they pay for admittance, but they spend a ton on betting. We are making more on this one room than the entire rest of the casino. It's a real killing." Skeet laughed at his own joke.

I slowly turned in a circle, and sure enough, demons of all shapes, sizes, and ranks were still on their feet yelling and clapping. "To kill them down here will leave their souls in purgatory forever," I yelled at Skeet over the screaming crowd wanting more.

"I know, isn't it fabulous?" Skeet smiled and clasped his small hands in glee. "Look, the next one is getting ready." Skeet pointed across the room to a door where a guard was pushing the next human out.

"Were they sinful humans?"

Skeet tapped his chin and then looked up at me. "I don't know, Master. I don't ask. I just place the order for ten humans for every show. It does cost a fair piece to have them removed from Earth, but we are making enough that I'm thinking of increasing the show to twenty humans and splitting it into two different groups. The waiting list is that long, and we can charge whatever we want, and they will pay."

"Ten a show to date? How long has this been going on?"

"I'm not sure, Master. We don't have the same time you have on Earth." Skeet flipped through the clipboard and stopped on a page, his eyes moving back and forth as he read. "That last human pulled our number up to two thousand, three hundred and one. Oh no, now three hundred and three consumed. Profits have increased by over two hundred percent. We make more than any other palace. Not even the fight club can compete with this." Skeet giggled, the sound coming out like small, excited snorts.

"Who signed off on this," I asked, the first real threads of anger seeping into my voice.

"I did, Master. You put me in charge of creating new and exciting entertainment that would increase the profit of the casino. This fits both. It has never been done. It is exciting and highly profitable." Skeet smiled, and as he did, a wild fury consumed me.

Reaching out, I grabbed Skeet by one of his short horns, and with a heave, I tossed the demon into the tank. His stubby arms and legs swung wildly as he tried to avoid the water like a bird without wings.

"Let's see if they like a demon," I growled. My power surged, and I knew my eyes were glowing brightly, the golden hue cast onto those closest and reflected off the clear shark tank. Spreading my wings wide, I rose into the air.

"Get out or be next," my voice boomed and echoed off the stone with a mighty roar. The demons didn't hesitate and trampled one another as they scurried to get out before I followed through on my threat.

With a flick of my wings, I floated over the tank and stared down at Skeet, who was splashing and yelling for help. I could see the massive gray shape rising from the depths of the tank as it streaked for its next meal. It looked like a huge missile with teeth. It reminded me of the image on the film *Jaws* as it swam with increasing speed for Skeet.

Skeet screamed as the massive shark broke the surface of the water with the force of a train. The entire bus-sized beast breached the surface and hovered in the air like a whale at a show. I could still hear Skeet screaming as he disappeared into its mouth and was about to be swallowed whole. The shark froze as it reached the pinnacle of it's rise and everything slowed down. I pulled the flaming sword from the sheath at my hip, and with a mighty spin and swing, the shark was cut into two. The tail portion landed in the water and was quickly devoured by the others waiting below. Stabbing a hole into the belly of the beast, I reached in and grabbed a bloody, slime-covered Skeet—his small body shook, his eyes frantic as they stared at me. I dropped the remaining carcass into the tank and flew over the stairs of the now silent colosseum. The only sounds were Skeet's chattering teeth and hooves on the stone steps.

"Tell me, Skeet, was that fun?"

"N...n...no Master."

"I didn't think so. Destroy them. They are an abomination, and not supposed to be here. Fucking necromancers." I pointed to the tank and the zombie sharks that had been turned into mindless killing demons. "Find a better form of entertainment that makes as much money and doesn't involve killing live humans for sport." Skeet nodded and ran up the stairs toward the large doors. "Oh, and Skeet..." The demon stopped and looked at me. "You no longer have any signing authority. All entertainment must be passed through me first."

"Yes, Master." He ran off out the door.

I turned back to the tank, unable to shake the dead girl's image from my mind. I rubbed at the strange ache in my chest. I had to get back to Earth.

I didn't know why, but something told me that my Minetta was in danger.

CHAPTER
THIRTY-THREE

R IKER

    I practically ran out of the elevator and turned to jog toward my office. "Shilo! Where are you? I need you," I yelled. The man appeared seemingly out of nowhere from behind me. I jumped as he called my name. "I hate when you do that," I said and resumed my jog toward him.

"Sir."

"I need to find Minetta. I'll have to go out for a while, and I'm not sure where she is staying. I have connections, I can have them start searching." I pulled out my phone.

"Sir."

"I have this feeling that something isn't right. I didn't listen to my instincts once before, and I'm not doing it again." I pushed through the outer sitting area of the office and marched across the floor to the closed door of my office.

"Sir," Shilo barked out and jumped into my path. He held his arms out wide to block me from opening the office door. I pulled up, not sure what to make of the uncharacteristic behavior. "You have company," he said quietly.

"What kind of company?"

"Of a certain female variety. One you may have been wanting to find." Shilo's lip curled up, and my heart skipped a beat. Straightening my suit, I nodded and calmly walked into the office as Shilo opened the door.

And there she was, sitting in my office, a sweet piece of candy that I wanted to roll around in my mouth and taste. She was wearing simple attire, jeans, and a button-down blouse, and she was stunning. She was perfect. Swallowing hard, I had to force myself not to rush across the room, take her into my arms, and ravish that mouth.

She looked up, and her blue eyes locked onto mine. Like an iceberg slowly dripping into the ocean, so was the cold-casing around my heart. It had not beat like this since the last day I laid eyes on Callista. I sucked in a sharp breath as the emotion made me want to sink to my knees.

"Hi," she said quietly as she stood.

"Hello." Regaining my composure, I looked around the office and then back at Minetta. "Why have you come? I distinctly remember the last time we spoke, you said you never wanted to see me again."

Her eyes dipped to the floor and then back up. "What would you say if I told you I may have overreacted, and I'd like to try going to dinner? Just the two of us this time. No more weird double dates for a while."

My chest heaved, but I forced myself to appear relaxed. I closed the distance to meet her in the middle of the room, and the little electrical charge that accompanied her presence danced in my chest and under my skin. I watched her reaction like a cat with a mouse as I drew closer. She shifted from foot to foot, her hands rubbing at her arms—she had to feel the same thing I did.

"What about Michael," I asked as I stopped in front of her.

She made a disgusted face. "He's a jerk."

The laugh rumbled from my chest as her face turned into the cutest glare I'd ever seen. "Many would say that I too am a jerk."

"Maybe, but you're a jerk cut from a different cloth."

"So true." Unable to help myself, I cupped her cheek and ran the pad of my thumb across the bottom lip that was continuing to tempt me.

My hand itched to touch her, to see if she was as soft as she looked, and my body sighed with just that gentle touch.

"Little bird," I whispered. Her pulse leaped around wildly, the blood pounding visibly on the side of her throat. "Do I make you nervous?"

She swallowed hard. "Maybe," she said, making me smirk. "Okay, a whole lot. I'm really not sure how I ended up here."

Her body was stiff, and he could hear her quick, nervous breaths, but there was more to it. Under the surface of the apprehension was desire. I could see it in her eyes, yet she didn't paw at me or fall to my feet. She looked more like she wanted to run. But, it was too late now. If she ran, I'd catch her.

I lowered my head until my nose touched the soft skin of her neck. Her scent was divine and just as succulent as the rest of her. "Why do I make you nervous?" I whispered in her ear and loved that her body shivered.

"You just do," she said, her eyes fluttered shut as my lips hovered above hers.

"What is it about you that's so entrancing?"

I stared at her features that were so similar to Callista and yet so different. I could tell now she was completely unique whether she wore the same face or not, and I liked it more. Minetta had a fire in her belly and steel in her veins, yet a sweetness that would melt your soul. I had no idea how a human so unique could even be possible, but I didn't care as a searing heat spread throughout my body. My dick was working now. It stood up hard and painfully pressed against the zipper of my dress pants.

"I don't know," she whispered, her voice hoarse. "What is it about you that I'm drawn to?"

The corner of my mouth curled up. "I don't know, but I'm going to kiss you."

She nodded yes, her lips parting a little, and my control unraveled. Gripping her face, I gently touched my lips to hers, and the electricity between us erupted into a burning inferno of molten lava in my veins. She tasted like fresh peaches and cream. She tasted like innocence and purity, and the taste was sweet and addictive on my tongue.

I crashed my lips into hers and groaned as the pleasure shot through my body. She immediately yielded and wrapped her hands around my neck, deepening the kiss and pressing her body against mine. The feel of her body was pure pleasure as she wiggled against me.

All I could picture was getting her naked, feeling her body beneath mine. I didn't remember moving, but she was suddenly under me on the couch.

Rearing back, I pulled off the suit jacket and tossed it aside. I was starved for her touch—she felt like I'd finally come home and couldn't get close enough. She surprised me by pulling my head back down and sucking my tongue into her mouth. I moaned, pressing my cock into her harder as it throbbed in my pants. The need to sink into her, to claim her coursed through my body, making it shake with the effort not to become a wild beast of aggression.

"I want you," I gasped as I broke the kiss.

"Really? I couldn't tell." A saucy smirk played on her lips, and it made my heart pound in time with the raging pulse.

Dropping my head, I nipped at the nipple that was pressing against her shirt. She jerked, her body bucking up into mine. I smiled against the sensitive peak, this time sucking it into my mouth. Her hands gripped my hair, small whimpering noises escaping her mouth. She wiggled under me and wrapped her legs around mine, pulling me closer to her.

With anyone else, I wouldn't have cared how I took them or if I hurt them. It was usually fast and hard, or I was dispassionate in my task desiring nothing more than my own pleasure when I was in need of release. But, with her, I wanted her enjoyment as much as I wanted my own, and a part of me craved hers even more.

My tongue flicked over the moist material and swirled the hardened skin around with my tongue. "Oh yes," she moaned.

Breaking the suction, I ran my lips up her chest and across to her neck. She turned her head away, giving me better access to her soft skin. Her hands gripped my shoulders and pulled me closer even though we were already pressed together as if we were one. My muscles flexed under her touch, quivering with the thought of getting her out of her clothes.

My hands traveled down the sides of her body to pull her shirt off over her head, but I froze as she yelped and flinched away under my touch. Her face contorted in pain and I immediately released her side.

"Did I hurt you?"

"Sort of, I'm bruised."

I had to control my temper not to scare her as I pictured someone hurting her. My earlier fear stormed forward. "What happened," I asked, and she bit her lip but didn't answer. "Minetta, you will tell me, show me what happened, or you won't leave this office."

Her eyes flared like she was going to argue, so I laid a finger across her lips.

"Please." I kissed the tip of her nose and felt her body relax and meld against mine once more.

I sat up and helped her do the same. She slowly stood and pulled her long-sleeved shirt up to show me her stomach and sides. A low growl escaped my lips as I stared at the black and blue that traveled over the entire left side of her beautiful, delicate body.

Reaching out, I gently touched the damaged skin and looked up into her eyes. "What happened? Tell me, Minetta."

She sighed and took a deep breath. "I hit this jerk named Jared at work, he is always making rude comments and jokes, and when you sent the flowers, he was going on about how I must be good in bed. Anyway, I punched him in the face, and he got all whiny and had the police come and get me for assault. It all went sideways from there."

"What do you mean sideways? Did the police hurt you?"

"Yes and no. They weren't really police. They were just posing as some. I think Jared knew, I'm not sure, to be honest, but this only happened a couple of nights ago, so it will still take a few days for my bruises to go away."

My mouth fell open as she talked like this was all normal for her. "Why would this Jared go to such extremes to hurt you? And was it him that touched you like this?"

She sighed and sounded tired. "Look, it's been a really long, strange seventy-two hours, and I think I should go home and get some sleep. Can we talk about this another time? Maybe over that dinner, you offered?" She pulled the shirt into place and walked to the chair she'd been occupying earlier to retrieve her purse.

"Minetta, I don't understand." I walked up behind her as I gently touched her injured side.

"I know, and I'm sorry, but honestly, I just can't talk anymore about this right now. My body and my brain are exhausted." Raising up on her tiptoes, she gripped the front of my shirt as she laid a kiss on my cheek. I snaked my arm around her waist, savoring the feel of her pressed close. I wanted to tell her to stay, convince her to just let me hold her while she slept.

"I can't go back to work until I'm cleared of the charges. Charges from the real officers that I had to speak to this morning. So give me a call if you want to do dinner, and if you change your mind...."

She shrugged, and I studied her features closely, looking for more signs of injury. Only then did I notice her face had a few scrapes, and she was wearing makeup to cover a bruise by her eye. I glanced at her hand and her swollen knuckles. Whatever had happened, she'd put up a fight. The fury that thumped white-hot in my veins at the thought of someone touching her, hurting her, was enough to raise the demon in me. The tattoos along my back burned, and I could feel my power coming to life. I wanted whoever was responsible for this dead, and once they were dead, I'd make sure they continued to burn for eternity.

"I think I should take you home," I said, following her to the door.

"I don't think that is a good idea. I'll be too tempted to do more than we should yet." She paused at the door and looked back, her eyes unreadable. "Have a good night, and for what it's worth, I'm looking forward to your call." She slipped out the door, her eyes shrouded with an emotion I didn't understand.

I paced the office, torn whether to follow her home or not, but figured she'd hate that idea.

"Shilo!"

"Yes, Sir?" The angel poked his head in the door.

"Send one of the guards to make sure Minetta gets home okay and tell them to be discreet. I don't want her to see them. Also, I need you to find someone for me."

"Of course, Sir, who would you like me to find?"

"It is someone that works with Minetta. His name is Jared."

"Right away, Sir, I will see that all is taken care of."

Just the sound of this fucker's name angered me. No one treated Minetta the way he had. He was about to be very sorry that he'd ever even looked in my little bird's direction.

THIRTY-FOUR

RIKER

I stared at the naked lump of shit that was propped up and tied to one of my chairs. I evilly smiled as my gaze flicked to the tiny prick that lay slumped over. The man's head was cast down, his chin resting on his chest as he slumbered in his drugged state. I had no intention of waking him even a second sooner. I wanted the tranquilizer to be out of his system and Jared to be fully awake for what I had planned.

Shilo and his men had found Jared unsurprisingly with his cock in hand, stroking it off to a random porn of a dark-haired girl in a schoolgirl uniform. And of course, the girl happened to be screaming for him to keep going as he smacked her ass for being a very naughty girl. Not exactly original porn if you asked me, but it was very insightful into the inner workings of Jared's mind. My power had already seeped into his body and was reading him like an open book. Every dark and depraved thing was laid bare for me to explore and use against him.

The ice clinked a little as I took a sip of the decadent brandy, yet it could not even come close to comparing to my Minny. I could still feel her lips on mine, the peach taste lingered on my tongue, and I had yet to lose the throbbing between my legs that was also serving to fuel this particular bit of fun.

Jared groaned, his head lolling back and forth. "Wha..."

"Hello, Jared," I said casually.

The guy lifted his head a little, his lips smacking slowly as drool dribbled from his mouth. His eyes were still heavy with the cocktail of drugs that had been administered to assure his compliance.

"What..." Jared smacked his lips again.

"Would you like a drink?" I offered and stood to grab the glass of water I'd set on the table. Grabbing Jared's hair roughly, I yanked his head back, his mouth opening with a yell. I quickly dumped the large glass of water down his throat. He drank as fast as he could, but much flowed out over the sides and fell in streams down his cheeks to his neck and chest.

Jared tried to close his mouth and turn away, forcing me to pull harder on his head. His neck would now be painfully pulled further than it should. Delightfully, Jared's mouth opened wider, and I poured the rest of the remaining water into his mouth. I let go of the lump of shit as he swallowed the last of it and coughed as water bubbled out his nose. I sat the glass back down before wandering to the bar to refresh my drink.

"Who are you?" Jared asked and then coughed some more.

"Jared, you're asking the wrong question." I turned to face the man, getting a good look at him for the first time. He wasn't a terrible-looking human. He had dark brown hair that I was sure would normally be in a fashionably styled state. His hazel eyes were a unique shade, his square jaw giving him a cocky jock feel—while his body was toned in all the right places.

"I bet you get a lot of women, don't you, Jared?"

Jared straightened a little in the chair, the leather making a large fart sound as he moved. I smirked at him as his face went bright red.

"I do okay with the ladies," Jared finally said.

I tapped my finger on the edge of my glass as I thought. "I think you're being modest. I mean, look at you. You're quite the specimen."

Jared shrugged. "Like I said, I do alright."

"You certainly do alright with the porn anyway. Quite the collection you have. *The Naughty School Girl*, the complete set, *Spank Them All Sisters*, *Whip Her Til She Cums*...I could go on."

Jared looked away, his face darkening as I teased him, and as he did, I touched his mind. He was a Grade-A slimeball who had no game. The women that did foolishly go home with him quickly decided that was a bad idea. Shilo had found his stash of roofies in his bathroom, just sitting in a drawer like candy.

"It must've really burned your ass when Minetta wouldn't give you the time of day?" That got his attention, and his head turned to look at me, his eyes showing just the tiniest hint of worry. That was okay. I planned on having him full-on terrified before the evening was through, so worried was a good place to start.

"I don't know what you're talking about."

"Come now, Jared, we both know you have a thing for her, so I'm confused as to why you're pressing charges."

I wandered back over the large plush chair and sat down across from him. The guy wiggled a little in the seat but didn't offer any information.

"You have quite the obsession with her. All those bent-over ass shots, they are hot. A little far away, but hot, she is quite the piece of ass. You might as well speak. You're not going anywhere until you do."

"Who are you, and why do you even care?" Jared asked.

"Why don't we do this, you tell me what I want to know first, and then I will answer all your questions. So, I ask you again, what was your reasoning for pressing charges?"

Jared sighed and slumped in the seat. "I don't know. Seemed like the right thing to do. She made a fool of me after she teased me for months. She's nothing but a fucking cock tease, and she deserves it. You know teach her not to mess with me like that."

I smiled a little, loving that Jared continued to dig himself deeper into a hole. "You do realize that if she isn't cleared of all charges, then she'll never work in the call center again?"

"What do I care?"

"Well, Jared, if you haven't noticed, you're tied up naked in my office. I would think you should be even mildly concerned about my intentions and a little less worried about who I am or pretending to be a tough guy." I sipped my drink as Jared looked down at himself. It was as if the man had just realized his predicament. "Do I look like a man that doesn't get what he wants?"

"Are you the flower guy?" Jared finally asked. He wiggled again in the seat, and I smirked as I watched his flaccid cock twitch. It wouldn't be long before he was at full attention, and the real excitement would begin.

"Yes, I sent Minetta the flowers. She is mine and mine alone. I don't let anyone fuck with her, and you, Jared, are most certainly fucking with her." I smiled at him, but it didn't reach my eyes.

Jared swallowed hard. "What do you want from me?"

"I want you to call your boss and tell him that you instigated the punch and you deserved it for all the terrible things you've said to Minetta, and tell him that all the charges have been dropped. Then you're going to call the two-bit lawyer you hired and tell him the same thing."

"What the fuck do I get for doing this for that bitch?"

A growl rippled from my lips, making Jared's eyes widen. "Respect,

Jared, or I'll rip your beating heart from your chest and eat it in front of you before you die." Jared pulled on the bindings that were firmly holding him in place. I let my eyes glow their natural color, the gold color burning bright and reflecting off all the surfaces.

"What the hell are you?" Jared continued to pull and thrash back and forth in the chair, but it was no use, and he eventually stopped his struggle, breathing hard.

"I'm who you wished for." Jared's face scrunched up in confusion. "You know all those nights you prayed to Mammon, prayed to the god of greed to make you powerful, make you rich, make you the most desirable?"

"No... there's no way."

"Jared, I know all your secrets, every perverse and intimate detail of your deepest darkest desires." My voice was laced with a smooth intoxicator that bathed over Jared like a warm blanket. He rocked in the seat like I was a snake charmer, and his cock twitched again, rising to half-mast.

"This is impossible," Jared said and then sucked in a deep breath, his body bending back as he pressed up with his hips. The oh so much fun water elixir was working its way into his system.

"Oh, but it is. You prayed for me to show up, and here I am."

"I don't understand. Minetta is your girlfriend? She is dating a god?"

I loved that he was referring to me as a god. I was many things, but a god was not one of them, yet it was an entertaining twist to the game.

"Yes, she is Jared, and by hurting her, you hurt me. You hurt your god."

"No, I never, I didn't mean...I'm so sorry." He blinked and swayed a little more, his eyes glassing over. "What's happening, I...I feel..."

"Like you need to fuck? Like all you want is a hot, wet pussy sliding down onto your sub-average, rock-hard cock. Or maybe you want to fuck a certain raven-haired beauty's face while she chokes on your dick that's trapped in her throat."

I tapped my chin playing over the different fetishes I'd seen in his mind.

"No, I know what you want. You want to bend that girl over your desk and spank her ass hard before you slam that cock into her, thrusting so hard into her perfect ass that your balls smack into her sloppy pussy, making you wetter as sweat drips down your back. Wrap your hand in her hair and pull back hard so she knows who's in charge. Then pull out of her ass and force her to lick your dirty cock, because you're nasty like that, Jared. You want a nasty slut to do whatever you want, whenever you want it," I said and enjoyed the pained look on Jared's face.

He rubbed his legs together, trying to gain any sort of friction against the suddenly very hard dick between his legs, but unfortunately for him, all he hit was air. "Is that what you want, Jared?"

"Yes! I want it all," Jared yelled, his eyes frantic as he stared at me. He was panting now. Beads of sweat formed on his forehead, telling me exactly what level of distress he'd reached.

"You want the power and the money and the women, especially Minetta, don't you? You want to do all those dirty things to her. You want to teach her a lesson for shunning you all this time, am I right, Jared?"

"Yes! I want to fuck her so hard, in that tight, perfect, little ass. I want to tear that shit up. I want her to scream my name," his voice was strained. "I'm sorry I didn't know she was yours. I'd never disrespect you that way."

"Hmmm, I don't believe you, Jared. You're going to have to call your boss and your lawyer for me. And you're going tell both men what I've asked you to say. Can you do that, Jared?"

Jared bit his lip hard and groaned as his dick jerked violently, slap-

314

ping him in the stomach. A small drop of clear pre-cum slid out the top of his dick, followed by the tiniest stream of come that jetted from the tip of his cock and landed on his chest. Jared sighed and slumped in the chair.

I smirked, knowing that little bit of relief wouldn't last long. I'd taken the liberty of spiking the water ahead of time with the sweat of a demon frog. They were a terrible pain in the ass to catch and were highly sought after for their ability to make you hard for days. Way better than any little blue pill the humans like to advertise. One drop would make a demon hard for hours, and for humans, it could easily give them a heart attack with even a drop too much. I'd sacrificed a whole fucking frog for this occasion.

The flared head of Jared's dick was turning an angry shade of reddish-purple. I almost burst out laughing as he erratically thrust his hips up and down, his dick waving back and forth.

"Make it stop! Please make it stop. It hurts so bad! I need to come," Jared whined and begged pitifully.

"Because you've been a loyal follower, and I kind of like you, I'm going to make you a deal, Jared. One that I would not offer to anyone else."

I hit a button on my phone, and the office door opened. A moment later, what would look like the most stunning woman walked in, and shock of all shocks, she had black hair and blue eyes just like Minetta. The demon's more unusual features, like her third tit, were glamoured, but I could see them. Jared's eyes swung to the tall model, his mouth falling open as her graceful figure sauntered toward him.

"Jared, this is Illia, and she is going to do all sorts of things to you that you cannot even begin to imagine, but only if you make your calls."

Jared licked his lips. "Where's the phone?"

Jared was consumed with Illia and the exotic dance she was now performing for his benefit. Stupidly, he didn't ask what all she was planning on doing to him. The thought made me giddy with anticipation.

Standing, I retrieved the device and used Jared's finger to unlock it. I scrolled through the numbers until I found his boss's cell and hit call. Putting the phone on speaker, I held the device up to Jared so he could talk and I could listen.

"Also, add that you're going on vacation for a few days, last-minute trip with an exotic beauty."

"No shit?" Jared's excitement was palatable. I simply smiled at him and gave him a wink.

"Hello?" Jared's boss answered groggily.

"Hey Eric, it's me, Jared. Sorry to call so late." I nodded at him.

"What is it, Jared? I was in bed and want to go back to sleep." The deep voice rumbled through the speaker of the phone.

"I wanted to let you know that I dropped the charges against Minetta. I had been a real ass to her, and I totally deserved the shot to the face. She should come back to work. I feel bad that she might have lost her job." Jared smiled, laying it on thick.

"Are you serious? You stormed into my office and demanded that I fire her. Now you've dropped the charges and want me to bring her back to work?"

Jared sucked in a deep breath as his body went rigid with need. His back tensed, and he opened his mouth, but nothing came out. I nodded to Illia, who smirked before kneeling before Jared. His eyes grew to the size of saucers as she ran her tongue up the length of his cock.

"Oh fuck!"

"What?"

"Sorry, like I said, I overreacted, and I feel like a jerk."

"Alright, I guess. I'll call her tomorrow and let her know. We're going to have a talk about this, though. This cost me a lot of unneeded hassle," the man yawned.

"Oh, and I'm sorry for the short notice, but I'm taking the next few days off work. I met this woman, and we're going to go away, you know, a little fun in the sun." Illia smiled at Jared as she swallowed his dick in one swift motion, his mouth opened wide in a silent scream of pleasure.

"Fun in the sun? What the fuck Jared? You almost make me fire one of my best workers, and then you proceed to take off for a weekend of ass? You'll be lucky if I don't fire you when you return. Talk to you when you get back." The man ended the call, and I pulled the phone away from Jared's mouth.

"Am I really going to get fired," Jared asked but never took his eyes off the woman with his cock in her mouth.

"I wouldn't worry about that. I'll take care of you." I flicked through his contacts until I found the number for his lawyer. "Same speech."

I held the phone out to Jared again as it rang, but this time only an answering machine picked up. It took Jared a full ten seconds to stop panting from the incredible servicing he was receiving to speak. Sadly, I knew this was the best and the last blowjob he'd ever have.

Once finished, I took my place in my seat once more. "Okay, Illia, you can stop now." The dick dropped from her mouth with an audible slurping sound.

"No, no, please don't stop," Jared pulled on the bindings trying to get closer.

"Jared, I'm going to give you a very important life lesson. When you pray to a demon, make sure you know what you are signing up for and definitely understand any deal you make."

"I don't understand."

"I know you don't. That is my point," I said and then stood to replenish my empty drink. "Illia, why don't you show our young friend here what he's bargained for this evening." The screaming started before I'd finished filling my drink and adding the ice. I knew what

Jared saw, the beautiful, lush pussy lips that would tantalize him at first, and then Illia showed him what she held inside.

I turned to look at the scene and laughed hard as Jared pissed himself, the hot streams of yellow flying in the air and landing on his chest and in his lap. Just to witness that was well worth the extra clean-up. Illia had stripped down and was bent in front of Jared, spreading her pussy lips apart so he could see the sharp teeth that were waiting inside.

"Help! Get me the fuck out of here," Jared screamed.

Making my way back to my seat, I avoided the streams of piss spreading across the black marble floor. "Illia here is a Verendent demon. They can provide the most exquisite pleasure, but if you don't please them first, as you can see, their pussy gets a little hangry," I chuckled at the stupid joke.

Jared's breathing was so fast that I feared he'd stroke out before we got going.

"Please, I'll do anything. Just let me go. I swear I'll never talk to or even look at Minetta again." Tears joined the sweat streaming down his face.

"Once upon a time, I was a nice guy Jared, and I would've taken you at your word and let you go, hoping you'd learned your lesson." Jared nodded his head enthusiastically up and down. "But I'm no longer that man, and I have to say I'm looking forward to seeing you burn in Hell, literally speaking, of course." I turned my attention to Illia. "By all means, my dear, you may proceed."

"With pleasure Master," her voice was like silk as she spoke. She licked the side of Jared's neck, her three tits that Jared could now see hung in his face. He whimpered as he strained to try and put distance between them. Her hand slid down the front of his body until she was able to grab the dick that was continuously jettisoning small streams of semen from the tip. It was joyous to watch Jared fight his primal nature.

His hips thrust up into the delicate hand even though he swore and tried to pull away from her touch. The two sides of his mind and body furiously fought with the demon frog elixir running through his veins.

I already knew which one would win. His mind would break and yield to his body's basic desires causing him to beg for what he really did not want.

"What a big cock you have," Illia purred in Jared's ear. Her hand moved quickly over the slick and angry-looking piece of flesh. "Mmmm, you smell delicious." Her tongue snaked out and licked the side of his face.

"No, no, stop. Don't touch me," Jared cried out, and yet his body bucked faster in her grip.

"Tell me something, Jared, does the place you work for, this nine, one, one call center that is set up to help those at their most vulnerable, know you make phone recordings of them? Do they know you profit from others' pain and exploit their painful experiences?" Jared whimpered and then screamed in a mix of fear, pain, and pleasure as the first real stream of come sprayed like a miniature fire hose. "Do they, Jared?" I said.

"Noooo," he mumbled as Illia continued her work.

"No, I didn't think so either. You're definitely coming home to the right place. Everyone there will be so happy to have you." I sat back, and as Illia's eyes met mine, I waved her to do her worst. A glint of darkness crossed her eyes as she strolled around Jared, her long blue nails leaving a thin red line on his skin.

Jared's screaming reached new levels of fear, which I fed on mercilessly as Illia straddled his lap and began what would have been a seductive lap dance. Unfortunately, he now knew what lay inside those lush folds.

I could no longer see his face, but I closed my eyes and listened to his screams and knew exactly the moment when she sat on him and took him inside her for real. The terror-filled screams reached pitches that I didn't know were possible from a human as those sharp teeth severed this precious cock. The sound of more than fifty teeth crunching together through the muscle and veins was sweet music to my ears.

The screaming continued, and I opened my eyes just in time to watch Illia stand and bend over in front of Jared so he could see his own dick being consumed and eventually swallowed by the demon cunt. Blood flowed onto the floor, and I didn't even care that it was seeping into my expensive Persian rug.

Illia stood and smiled at me. "You did well, Illia. Consider yourself promoted."

"My pleasure, Master." She sucked her finger into her mouth. "Do you require anything else?"

"No, that's all." I waved my hand, dismissing her, my eyes never leaving Jared's pale face. He was still conscious, and I had to admit I was impressed. Soft whimpers fell from his blubbering lips, saliva meeting blood as he stared at the bloody stump that used to be his dick. After finishing my drink, I sat the empty glass aside and slid to the front of my chair to get a better look at Jared before he met his final end.

Placing my hand on the floor in front of me, I called upon my power, the darkness that filled me after my fall flowed out and down, calling on my pièce de résistance. The sound of a billion marching feet reached my ears long before Jared heard them. The room vibrated with the sound as my little pets drew closer. Jared's eyes flicked up to mine, the vibration strong enough now to shake all the furniture in the room, including the chair he sat on.

"Do you hear that," I asked. "Do you feel that?"

Jared looked around the room and then back at me. I didn't think he could look more scared, but I was wrong. The first of the demon centipedes stuck their head up from the register, a small shrill noise drawing Jared's attention. The nearly seven-inch-long creature with a sharp pincer-like beak would have been intimidating for anyone. But, seeing one while tied...well, that gave it a whole new hellish dynamic.

"What the hell is that?" Jared asked and once more resumed the useless struggling.

"That, my dear boy, is your death. Come my pets, come feast."

"No, please. Ahhh!"

What started out as one, quickly filled the room, their multiple legs scraping and thumping in time across the floor in a strange unison that only added to the dramatic effect. There was not an empty space in the room as they continued to fill it. They hung from the walls and the ceiling, falling onto one another as they surrounded their meal.

Jared's tears almost touched me as he continued to beg on a continuous loop of pleas for forgiveness. I stood and dusted off my suit jacket, the evil little pets moving like the parting of the red sea as I walked toward the office door. I reached for the handle and looked back at Jared.

"Oh, and Jared, I know you'll never hurt Minetta again. I'm going to make sure of it for eternity. You may proceed, my pets," I said and smiled as the painful shrieks filled the room.

I turned back just before I left and watched as my pets pried open Jared's mouth, as others crawled under his skin, making it look alive. The screams suddenly stopped, and I tipped my head to Jared as his soul separated from his body. The soul stared at him, blinking, and then looked at his old body, his old life now gone. This only lasted a moment before my soul collector demons rose from the floor, searching for their newest plaything.

I closed the door and took a deep breath as a calmness washed over me. I might have been Mammon, but tonight I was a man protecting what is mine.

CHAPTER

THIRTY-FIVE

MINETTA rubbed her eyes and yawned as she wandered down the stairs to the kitchen. She froze as the smell of bacon hit her nose with a tantalizing aroma that made her stomach growl. She rolled her eyes, forgetting that Penny was staying with her. It hadn't been her idea, it hadn't even been Penny's idea either, but apparently, Michael got the final say. So here she was, forced to live with a demon that she didn't know if she could trust, let alone ever call a friend again.

The fact Michael was trying to keep her alive and said that he believed Penny wanted to keep her safe was a small comfort, but she wasn't even sure she could trust him at the moment. Among the ever-growing list of things she never thought she'd think about, not being able to trust the archangel Michael was up there.

"I decided to make breakfast. I know it doesn't make up for what I did, but... hopefully you'll at least speak to me," Penny said as she shrugged and held out a plate.

Minetta had to admit the food looked amazing. Scrambled eggs, bacon, toast, and pancakes—who could refuse?

"Thanks," she said. Taking the plate, she wandered over to the already-set table and sat down.

"I have good news," Penny said as Minetta reached for the maple syrup.

"I no longer have a hoard of demons wanting me dead?"

Penny paused, spatula in hand. "Not that good, but that was a really good guess. You left your cell phone down here, and it started to ring. I know, I know...I shouldn't have snooped, but it's my nature."

Minetta stared at Penny and just shook her head. Of all the things that Penny had done, answering her phone was the least of her worries.

"Eric called while you were still asleep, and as of Monday, you can come back to work. I told him we wanted to be on the same shift again, for obvious reasons, and he seemed annoyed but agreed."

"Huh, I wonder what changed his mind." She stuffed the first forkful of fluffy goodness into her mouth and let out a little moan. Penny's pancakes were the best, such a sucker she was for the apparent food bribe.

"All he said was that Jared called and said the charges were dropped."

Minetta poured a cup of coffee from the pot on the table and took a sip of the dark roast. "I wonder how those demons knew to come and get me, they must have intercepted the original call somehow. Does that even make sense? Otherwise, how would they know I was going to be arrested? You've already said Jared isn't a demon, so...."

Penny leaned against the counter, her brow furrowed in thought. "You know, that is a good question. I'll look into that. There must be a demon that I don't know about working at the building with an agenda."

Minny paused with the next fork full to her mouth. "Wait, does that mean there are more demons at the call center?" Penny's face reddened as she filled a plate, which Minetta noticed. "Of course, there is. Why wouldn't there be demons everywhere. There are probably some at the grocery store and the bank, or where I like to shop."

"The cute little boutique with that amazing sweater you got last month doesn't have a demon there." Penny smiled, the sarcasm of her comment going over Penny's head.

"Penny, how am I supposed to stay safe when demons are every-where, like literally everywhere?"

"Oh, they don't want you dead. Not every demon wants the apoca-lypse to happen, and not every demon likes conflict. We're kind of like people that way. We're all different. And since many of the lesser demons are like mice that have been mixed in with a bunch of mean alley cats in Hell, they actually prefer Earth as it is. It's safer for them to live among humans than their own kind."

Her phone started to vibrate on the counter. The instant fear and then lip-chewing-worried expression on Penny's face told Minetta it had to be Riker, as Penny held the phone out

"Good Morning," she said and couldn't stop the flutter in her chest.

"Hello, my little bird. Did you rest well?" She could picture him sitting in his office behind his desk and looking every bit the deadly sin that he was.

"I did. How about you," she asked.

"I sadly didn't get much sleep."

"Oh," she said and couldn't stop the little flare of jealousy that flick-ered in her stomach.

"It's probably not what you think, although I wouldn't blame you. I had work, and things got a tad complicated, which required some clean-up." There was a hint of amusement in his voice, and her cheeks warmed.

"I wasn't thinking... okay, yes I was," she said. Riker laughed, and his hearty chuckle made her think of the sounds he'd make during sex. God, she'd bet it would be fantastic. She had to turn away from Penny's observant and disapproving stare. "Was there a reason you were calling?"

"As a matter of fact, yes. Tonight, for dinner, I will pick you up at noon."

"Noon?" She laughed, but Riker remained quiet. "Oh! You're serious." She bit off a piece of bacon and then stared at it, wondering if it was needed. "Wouldn't that be lunch?" That's pretty early for dinner."

"That is because we have quite the distance to go to get there. Trust me. You're going to love the spot. We just need to get going early."

Minetta bit her bottom lip, trying not to get too excited by a simple dinner. She was being forced into this to save humanity, she reminded herself. But her heart hammered faster in her chest, telling her she'd secretly been wanting this push. And yet her mind danced around waving a red flag that he was still the fallen angel of greed, and he could turn his back on her in a blink.

"Alright, noon it is. My address is...."

He cut her off. "No need, my little bird, I already know where you live. I'm looking forward to seeing you again." He hung up before she could say goodbye or ask how he knew where she lived. She simply stared at the phone.

"You do know you're playing with fire, right? Like actual demon Hellfire," Penny grumbled.

"Maybe, but I've rarely done something for myself. Even this date is to help save the world, so what harm is there in enjoying myself for a change. I could really use it." She didn't know if she should admit this but decided she didn't have anyone else she could share with. "Besides, I can't deny there is something between us, I felt it from the second we met."

Penny sighed and then sat down across from her, her plate in hand.

"You're right, Minny, and I'm sorry if I don't seem happy for you. It's just...this is all a very big risk, all of it." She pushed her food around on her plate with her fork. "I just failed so miserably already, and I don't want to see anything happen to you. No matter what you think of me, I love you."

She stared at Penny and knew that she'd forgive Penny. Maybe not today or tomorrow, but it would happen. She was already softening. Minny lifted her shoulders to her ears before letting them drop. "Okay, at least now I know the truth, and it's my choice to put myself in danger."

"Don't say I didn't warn you. It's not like Riker has a good reputation. I mean, you've seen the lineup of women, and he's a Sin, Minny, he has a dark side and...." Penny sighed. "And you already know all this, so just please be careful."

Penny had voiced exactly what she didn't want to hear and stared at the food as she pondered her situation. She wasn't backing out. It was worth the risk, but she had to wonder if her heart could handle another trauma. There was only so much one person could take.

The rest of the morning seemed to drag on and fly by all at the same time. All she could think about was dinner with Riker and what to wear. Even the usually relaxing walk with Toby hadn't done any good at being a distraction. Oddly once Penny realized this was happening and there was nothing she could say to talk her out of it, she was a lot of help with the outfit and hair.

Standing back from the mirror, Minetta smiled as she fastened her earring in place and took in the pretty updo that Penny had styled for her. Her new smoky makeup made her eyes stand out with the matching silver dress that Penny seemed to pull out of thin air.

Stepping into the bedroom, she smiled at Toby. He was in his favorite spot on the bed, eyes closed.

"You be a good boy for Penny," she said to him and gave the top of his head a rub and a kiss. A soft moan was all the response she got. "Yeah, yeah, I'll miss you too."

The doorbell rang, and her heart leaped into her throat as butterflies erupted in her stomach. She shouldn't be this excited to see Riker. Was she really ready to be the person to draw out his humanity, so to speak? And she really hated the idea of hiding what she knew from him. She understood Michael's rationalization that if Riker knew, then he would assume that any feelings he had would be fake, but it seemed conniving and wrong to keep something this big from him.

She made her way down the stairs just as Penny opened the door. "Penelope Mendroin, what an unusual surprise. What are you doing answering Minetta's door?"

"Penelope," she asked, giving Penny a look. Something else she didn't know about her friend, apparently.

Penny blushed, her cheeks reddening. "Penny, just call me Penny. I hate Penelope." Penny crossed her arms over her chest and stepped away from the door to let Riker in.

"That doesn't answer the question as to why you are here, Penny?" Riker emphasized her name like he was analyzing her response.

"Penny and I work together." Minetta said, bailing Penny out. "Penny mentioned you two had met, but I didn't realize you knew each other that well."

"Penny and I go way back, don't we, Penny?" Riker's intense amber eyes swung to Penny, and she backed away from his stare.

"Is there something I should know?" She looked between the two of them. She hadn't considered the two of them being an item at any time, but considering his reputation, it was highly plausible, and her stomach flipped.

Riker looked at her and a small smile formed. "Do you think I sleep with every woman I meet?"

"Honestly, I did wonder. Though I think I should know if my friend and my...date used to sleep with one another, it would ruin the first course if it came up, kind of thing," she said.

Riker stepped closer, and as he did, she had the urge to step back. His aura seemed to charge the air was with a potent electricity simply by being in the same room. Just as when she'd first met him, her body was alive with what felt like small electrical currents running under her skin, and she took a deep breath as he stopped a few inches away and stared down at her. She watched his hand like a worried animal as he lifted it to run his thumb across her cheek—something he seemed to enjoy doing. She bit her bottom lip to keep from fidgeting.

"No, Penny and I did not sleep together, my little bird."

"Why do you keep calling me that," she whispered.

"One day, I will tell you." His lips briefly touched hers, and she was tempted to tell him to screw dinner and drag him upstairs. He had a very carnal effect on her body, and destiny or not, she couldn't deny being drawn to him as a man. "You look ravishing," he said. "That should've been the first thing I said." He gave her cheek a soft kiss and then her neck, making her knees wobble.

Penny made a throat-clearing noise. She'd forgotten all about Penny standing in the same room. "Thank you for the compliment. You look very handsome, but don't we have a reservation to keep?"

Riker sighed but smiled as he took a step back. "Indeed we do. Come my little bird, our night awaits."

She waved at Penny as Riker escorted her out the door, making sure to call out Toby's food and schedule one more time. Penny gave her a thumbs up before closing the door. A distressed feeling settled in her stomach as she caught sight of the car. This was really happening. She was going on a date with this man, this archangel, this god-like demon, all alone. She swallowed the lump forming in her throat as Riker opened the door to a car that looked like a spaceship.

She slipped into the sleek silver vehicle and sat on the seat like it might bite her. She was terrified to touch anything because it was so clean. There was not a speck of dust on the dash nor a fleck of dirt on the floor. She was tempted to take off her shoes and hold her feet off the floor.

"Are you okay?" Riker asked. "You look like you're in pain. Are you still sore?"

"I'm all good." She was still a little sore, but that wasn't the issue. Minetta slowly slid back in the seat and put her seatbelt on as Riker pulled away from the curb. She quickly grabbed the door and the center console as he flew down the street, screeching to a halt at the stop sign. He whipped out in front of many lanes of traffic and then proceeded to exceed the speed limit by enough to make the world look like a blur.

She jumped as Riker grabbed her hand. "Relax."

"Little hard when you are driving like... oh dear god!" She closed her eyes as he veered into oncoming traffic to maneuver around a group of slower-moving vehicles. A horn blared as they swung back into their own lane. "This!" She finished and closed her eyes. Riker laughed and squeezed her hand tighter.

"You're adorable, little bird."

"Thanks, but if it's all the same to you, I'm going to keep my eyes closed," she said, getting a deep, chuckled response from Riker. He turned on the music, and she focused on the smooth jazz sound rather than the violent jerks of the car, which made her feel ill.

"We're here."

Minetta opened her eyes as they pulled through the gates of an airplane hanger. "Umm, why are we here?"

"This is my airplane." He pulled off to the side of the plane and parked. "So I need to be honest. I was already planning this trip to try and convince you to go on a date with me."

She looked between him and the plane. "Okay, and where are you planning on taking us?"

He smiled wide. "We're going to fly to Venice. I know the most amazing restaurant that serves spaghetti al nero di sepia, frittelle, and of course, it serves my wine. Did I mention I own a winery? It doesn't matter. We will land, take in the sites of the city, have dinner, and then I've arranged for a gondola ride before we head to my villa. Tomorrow I have a full day planned before we fly back."

"You thought that the flowers weren't enough, so you were going to fly us to Venice?"

"Yeah, it's really lovely, you'll see."

Riker smiled and went to get out of the car, but she grabbed his arm. "I can't fly to Venice. I have a dog to take care of, and my boss called. I'm to go back to work next week, and I have no clothes, that's really far to go, and...."

Riker stopped the runaway train in her brain as he leaned over and his lips touched hers. Cupping her face, he deepened the kiss. She moaned in his mouth. He tasted like rich nectar, sweet and thick on her tongue.

He broke the kiss and laid his forehead on hers—Minetta's breathing was as quick as her heart pounding in her chest. "Everything you're worried about can be dealt with. Now tell me, why are you really nervous?"

Turning her head, she looked at the large black jet with his company's logo on the side. "I've never flown before, and to be honest, it just seems rushed that our first real, get-to-know-you-date is like some big romantic getaway."

"I've never had a girl think anything I offered to do, be too much."

She rolled her eyes at him. "I guess I'm not like the other girls you've decided to impress by bringing them to your jet," she said and crossed her arms over her chest. She wasn't really jealous of the girls that had come before her, of which she knew there were countless, but the way he looked her over was upsetting. It made her feel like there was something wrong with her.

"Yes, indeed," Riker finally said. He sat back in his seat, and her heart sank that this was the end of their date. In one fell swoop, she'd ruined it. "Well, how about this? We will not share the same bedroom, and we can make arrangements for your work and dog while in the air. As for the clothes, that is the easiest fix. We can stroll the shops, and you can pick out a few new outfits. I'd planned that part anyhow." She kept staring between the plane and the man, the two things both so foreign to her.

"This still seems pretty over the top, Riker, like a first date is usually a dinner and a walk along the beach or ice cream in the park."

"We can do both of those things in Venice. Minny, I don't want this to sound like I'm an egotistical ass, but this trip is no more elaborate than a dinner here in New York for me. I have the luxury to do this." She lifted an eyebrow at him, not even sure how in the heck to respond. "You must have wanted to see more of the world at some point in your life?"

"When my dad was alive, we made this pact to see a new place every year. We were going to start with a city or part of the world that started with A and then move on to B and so on. He got sick much faster than the doctors thought, and we never made it past Boston, but we got to take in a baseball game at Fenway Park." She looked away from Riker, wiping away the tear sliding down her cheek.

He grabbed her hand, and his felt so warm and secure, it settled her instantly. Riker laid his lips on her knuckles, those amber eyes burning into her own. "Would your dad approve of you seeing Venice?"

She couldn't deny that he would, just maybe not with this particular man. But, from the time she was old enough to walk, he would point at places on the map in his old study and tell her a fact or story about each place.

He'd say, "One day, Minny, my girl, I hope you get to see the world and fall in love with every one of those places."

Locking eyes with the most intimidating person she'd ever met, she took a leap of faith. "Alright, let's do this."

THIRTY-SIX

RIKER

I was trying hard not to eavesdrop on my little bird's conversation. Those amazing blue eyes flicked up to me, a pink hew spreading across her cheeks. As she turned her head away, I quickly adjusted myself. From the moment I laid eyes on her, I'd been having trouble controlling the urge to ravage her, feel her body under her sexy little dress, and hell, I even wanted to kiss each of her dainty toes. I stared at the strappy heel she was wearing and pictured how good she'd look bent over one of the jet's seats in nothing but those.

"Yes, Penny, I know," she said. I could hear Penny say to be careful.

Like Penny could talk, she wasn't exactly known for being a straight arrow. There were good reasons for her being kicked out of Heaven, and in the many years since she'd been on Earth, she'd partied almost as hard as me.

"So you are okay to look after Toby for a couple of days? I don't want to put you in an imposition." Minny bit her lip, and I gripped the tablet in my hands, hard to keep from lunging across the short space. She had no idea what she was doing to me, and that was part of her allure. She genuinely wasn't after my money or what I could do for her sexually. It was strange, and I wasn't sure how to handle her behavior.

"Thank you, Penny. I owe you big time. I'll be sure to text and send pictures, yes, I promise, but I really have to go, the plane is starting to move. Okay, bye."

Minny smiled as she hung up from the call, and I watched as she dutifully switched her phone to airplane mode and then slid over to the window in the large seat that she was dwarfed by to watch us take off. I'd long ago lost the ability to be impressed by such mundane things—maybe I'd never been impressed because I could fly myself after all. Humans were generally archaic, yet I was fascinated by her excitement and interest in every little thing. She had an appreciation for life that was addicting.

She'd giggled when I showed her the mini bar that was stuffed full, and I thought she was going to faint when I held up the bottle of champagne and told her to order off the extensive menu for lunch. She'd decided to try a few of the appetizers and then blushed as she asked if I'd like to share with her. How could anyone resist that face?

"Riker? Would you hold my hand for the take-off?" Minny asked. Her hand was clutching the armrest in a death grip. Sitting the tablet aside that I'd been working on, I switched sides and sat down beside her. How many women had asked to hold my hand, and I told all of them to fuck off?

Yet, here I was, purposely holding out my hand for this unassuming human girl to hold. As her fingers laced with my open palm, I could feel sweat forming on the back of my neck. My pulse picked up as I stared at her profile—her lovely neck was begging to be kissed as her sweet peach perfume stirred something inside of me that I didn't think even existed since my fall. I quickly pushed the disturbing sensation away.

"Oh my." She sucked in a sharp breath and gripped my hand hard as the jet picked up speed. The nose of the jet tipped up and then pushed off the ground in a rush. Even her fear was endearing. "Oh my god, look at the clouds, and everything is so small." She smiled and peeked out the window. A child-like glow shone back at me as she pointed out things as the plane accelerated further into the air.

As soon as the plane was at cruising altitude, I stood and walked to the back of the plane to place the lunch orders, but I didn't return to her side. It was more unnerving than I thought it would be to be alone with the strange human temptress. Maybe Skye was right, and this girl was playing with me. I was most certainly not acting like myself. I sat down and picked up the tablet, not really seeing the latest growth projections.

"You said you have a winery. Have you been to Venice many times?" Minny asked.

"Yes, most of the time, it's boring now. I end up coming a few times a year for business and pleasure when it fancies me." As soon as the words were out of my mouth, I wanted to take them back, the smile slipping a little on Minny's face. She clammed up and simply stared out the window, the hurt naked in her eyes.

Fuck.

"I'm sorry, I shouldn't do work when I'm trying to enjoy myself," I lied. I held up the tablet and then turned it off and sat it aside. "I really am excited to take you to Venice." She nodded but didn't say any more. I opened my mouth a few times to say something, but nothing ever came out. This was new and weird, and I was at a loss for the first time ever in my existence.

The chef stepped out of the kitchen and nodded toward me.

"Lunch is ready," I said. Minny gave me a small smile, but it no longer reached her eyes. I didn't know how to fix this. Who the hell was I to try and soothe a woman's feelings?

You once knew how.

My inner voice berated me.

The chef pushed the silver cart down the aisle and spent a few minutes setting up a table before laying out the foods under their little silver domes.

"Everything smells delicious. Thank you for going to so much trouble," Minny said to my chef.

"It is my pleasure to cook for you, madam," he said and smiled. He looked shocked that she'd spoken to him, and frankly, so was I. "If you need anything else, just ask. I am happy to make anything you like."

"No, this is already too much, thank you." He gave her another smile before heading to the back of the plane. I didn't think I'd ever thanked the man for his work. I hadn't seen the need. I paid him to do the job after all.

"May I," Minny asked, pointing to the domes.

"Yes, of course. Help yourself, and eat whatever you like. I asked for a few more things than what you mentioned."

Her every movement was delicate and graceful, and I found myself once more captivated watching her unveil the hidden treasures. She piled a small amount of food on her plate, and my eyes watched as the first piece traveled to her mouth. Mine was suddenly watering as she bit a piece off and moaned. The sound traveled down my spine, making me take a deep breath—she licked the sauce off her finger, and I wanted to be those fingers. Unable to stand it, I stood and took off the suit jacket I'd been wearing. I didn't even care if she saw the raging hard-on I had going on. If she noticed, she didn't say and instead just continued to drive me wild with the sexy little noises she was making as she tried each new item.

"This is so good. Are you not going to eat," she asked.

I rolled up the sleeves on the dress shirt as I debated tossing her on the large bench seat and fucking her right there. Or, I could rip her stunning little dress in half and force her to sit on my lap. She was the only thing I wanted to eat. My mouth watered at the prospect of tearing off her underwear to take what I wanted. To have her scream my name—I shuddered as another surge of desire coursed through my body like a fucking stream of intoxicating drugs. This as well was new. I'd experienced pleasure. I had needs that I quenched weekly, but this...this was something I couldn't comprehend, and my brain felt like it was doing the backstroke in a passion-filled pool of desire.

"Are you okay," Minny asked, her eyes wide as she took in my flexed arms and closed fists. There was a sliver of fear in her eyes as I forced the carnal instincts down to a bearable level.

"I'm good. I'm just really happy you are enjoying the food."

"That's your happy face?"

I laughed hard. Soon she joined in until I gripped my stomach because it hurt and yet felt...good.

"I'm being weird, aren't I?"

"Well, I wasn't going to say it, but yeah, you kind of are." She ate another piece of the spiced sticky ribs, and a bit of sauce stuck to the corner of her mouth. I had no more control left. I leaned across the seat and loved that her breathing picked up. Her eyes went wide, a smoldering desire tucked under it all. She sat frozen in place, mimicking a wild little animal.

"I'm having trouble controlling myself around you." I kissed the corner of her mouth, my tongue quickly licking up the sticky sauce, but it was Minny that turned her head to capture my lips. My hand slid around to the back of her neck and deepened the connection. I sucked in that lush bottom lip, tasting her mouth. She moaned and surprised me again as she nipped at my lip. My little bird had a hidden sex kitten inside her just waiting to be lured out.

"I want to get you naked right now," I whispered, breaking the kiss. I could hear her pulse thumping over the sound of the plane engines. Each thump was in time to the throbbing in my pants. "Are you wet for me, little bird?"

A smile spread across my face as she wiggled in her seat, confirming what she hadn't said aloud. "Do you want me to fuck you?"

She placed a hand on my chest, she didn't push me away, but it felt like she was. I stared at her hand and then up to her cerulean blue eyes. "I do, but not now, not here. It's too soon."

"Patience has never been my strong suit, little bird. I have a tendency to take what I want."

She swallowed audibly, and the sour scent of fear emanated off her skin. The fear was too much to be from just my words, and I inspected her face. Her bottom lip trembled along with the rest of her body, and once more, I forced myself to stop before invading her mind. It would be so much easier if I did. I could coax her to do what I wanted, pull out all her deep dark secrets and desires, but I wanted her to share because it was her choice.

However, my greater concern at the moment was who had caused this fear. If it were James, the little taste that imbecilic ass had gotten from me, of who I was, would pale in comparison to what I would do when we returned.

"Who hurt you?"

She looked away from my eyes to stare out the window. I rubbed my thumb against her cheek, and her eyelashes fluttered, her pulse slowing, but she still didn't speak. "Tell me who it was, Minny."

"How do you know anything happened to me," she asked quietly. "It could be simply too fast."

"I just know. Now tell me, who was it?" The anger was already overpowering the erotic images that had been plaguing my mind.

"What are you going to do," she asked like she already feared I'd do unspeakable things. Unfortunately, she was right.

"I just need to know. Tell me what happened, Minny. I won't take silence as an answer." I could already taste death on my tongue, the darkness swirling around like a good brandy. The demon in me craved more. It craved the death of those who dared to hurt this beautiful soul.

"Can we not talk about it right this moment? I will tell you, but I want to enjoy these few days away and..." she shrugged. "It's not something I like to think about, and I don't want it to ruin this."

I sat back in my chair and contemplated her words. I wouldn't forget if that's what she hoped, and if I had to, I'd search her memories to find out who it was, and when I did...

"Okay, fine, let's enjoy the food before it's cold." Minny sagged as her body relaxed into the seat.

I managed to keep the conversation light, and when she yawned and nodded off, I stood grabbing a blanket. Lifting the armrest between the seats, I sat beside her and covered her with the material. She turned, mumbling something incoherent in her sleep, but cuddled into my side. It was my turn to sit frozen. I hadn't cuddled with anyone since before my fall. Even the bouts of sex that Skye and I had shared as fuck-friends, she knew to leave immediately after. I had no time or interest in cuddling. I had work that needed to be done, and sleep and sex were brief, timely distractions.

As the seconds ticked on, I found her body curled into my own, the heat she was generating and radiated through our clothes, to be something I didn't mind. I'd never admit it out loud, but I actually enjoyed having her close and laid my arm around her shoulder. She pressed closer, the top of her head settling into the crook of my neck, as her hand laid over my heart.

Giving the top of her head a kiss, I closed my eyes. I didn't know what it was about her, but I wanted this lowly little human for as long as she'd have my dark, pathetic soul.

CHAPTER
THIRTY-SEVEN

MINETTA

"Wake up, little bird. We're here." Soft kisses that made her squirm were tracing lines across her cheek and neck. "And the sleeping beauty awakes," Riker whispered in her ear before giving her cheek another soft kiss.

She rubbed her eyes and stared into Riker's smirking face. She could get used to waking up to that look. "Did I sleep the entire way?"

"You did, which is perfect since you will be well-rested for dinner and whatever the night has in store." She smiled wide and placed her hand in his as he helped her to stand. She paused as they reached the bottom of the stairs, and she stared at yet another sports car. "Don't worry, it is a short drive, and then we will have to walk or be in a boat for the rest of our time here."

"That's good, or lunch wasn't going to stay down." She laughed as he mocked a hurt expression.

"Shilo keeps telling me I'm a terrible driver, but I thought he was just being a fussy old ange...man."

She knew what he was going to say. Her secret wasn't the only one that was being kept between them. It was the second reason she'd been able to convince herself that not saying anything about what she knew was fine. It wasn't like he was jumping up and yelling who and what he was.

"I don't know who Shilo is, but I already like him," she teased.

Riker laughed, flooring the fancy Ferrari into action, the car leaping with eager abandon out of the private airport. She stared in wonder at the landscape. Even in the dark, the little bit she could make out excited her. Now that she was here, she felt like she was a kid on the edge of her seat at an amusement park.

Riker was true to his word because they were crossing a bridge toward Venice less than twenty minutes later. She stared out the window taking in the lights of the boats on the Adriatic Sea. She could barely contain her excitement as they stepped out of the vehicle.

"We'll be taking a boat to the restaurant, and then we'll come back tomorrow for the gondola tour."

"We're not staying here?"

"No, I have a villa in Padova. We'll go there for the night. It's not far," he said as he helped her down to the area where all the boats were docked. She couldn't get over how busy it was, the area was brimming with activity, and it was easy to tell that most of the people were not locals because of the cameras in their hands. No one took that many photos when they lived there.

"Signora, signore." The man at the boat said. She stared down at the long narrow boat and then around at the dark water. She wasn't sure what she was expecting, but this seemed like a dangerous idea.

"Francesco here has been manning a motoscafo for the past thirty years. He is the best driver I've ever had. We will be fine Minny," Riker said as he stepped in the boat, but she hesitated. She may be sick yet. She took Riker's hand and stepped into the black boat.

"What is a motoscafo?" She asked as they got settled.

"It means water taxi. Are you comfortable?" Riker wrapped his arms around her waist as he pulled her to sit between his legs on the little seat. She had to admit as Francesco pushed the boat away from the dock that she did feel safe and was extremely comfortable in his arms. She nodded and looked up at him. His eyes glittered in the darkness, the blanket of stars above not able to compete with them.

He laid a chaste kiss on her lips that felt like it meant so much more than the simple gesture. She snuggled into the warmth of his muscled chest and stared in awe at the buildings they passed. It was one thing to see these amazing structures on television or on the computer, but to see them in person was breathtaking. It took no time at all, and she was disappointed as the surprisingly smooth ride glided up to their location.

"Aspetteró qui. Buonanotte." Francesco said as Riker helped her out of the boat.

"Grazie," Riker answered. His accent was exactly the same as the man that lived here, and she had to wonder just how many languages he knew.

Her heels clicked along the sidewalk, all too aware of the stares Riker was getting from women and men alike. He had a commanding aura. You couldn't help but stare. She wondered how much of that was him and how much of it was the fact he was more than human. Did humans all instinctively know when they came across the immortals? Is that why she'd been drawn to Penny?

His hand was warm as it sat on the lower part of her back, and she could admit to herself that having him touch her like this made her feel special. They stopped outside a weathered dark door, the sounds and smells from inside already assaulting her senses and making her stomach growl.

"Signore, che meravigliosa sorpresa!" The man inside the door said, a massive infectious smile on his face. The glasses he wore only accentuated his brown eyes that could light up any room with joy.

"It's good to see you too, Giuseppe. I trust the business is doing well?" Riker responded, holding out his hand for the man to shake. She didn't know Riker well, but the little she did, she knew that he didn't spend any extra time with those in which he didn't see the value. To honor someone with the shake of his hand meant he thought highly of this man.

"Couldn't be better. I've saved your table as requested, but you did not tell me that you were bringing such a ravishing beauty with you." Giuseppe turned his eyes to her. "Signora, it is a pleasure." Giuseppe held out his hand, and as she put her hand in his, he leaned in to place a chaste kiss on each cheek. "You are quite the lucky man. One day maybe you will tell me your secret." His thick eyebrows wiggled comically at Riker.

"I do not believe Maria would like it if I shared that particular secret." Riker looked down at her as Giuseppe laughed. "Maria is his wife of thirty years," Riker explained.

"Almost thirty-two my friend, and I fear she will beat me to death with a rolling pin one of these nights, and I will certainly deserve it. Better not let her hear you speaking to me of beautiful women. It will only seal my fate sooner. Come let me show you to your table."

The place was right out of a magazine, picturesque and authentic in every way possible. And it was packed and filled with laughter and smiles from all around. She stared at the dishes, her mouth watering. Giuseppe stopped in front of a booth, and she couldn't help thinking of the last time they shared a booth together. She slipped out of the long light coat and handed it to Riker to hang up before sliding into the seat.

As soon as Riker was beside her, she jumped as his hand gripped her thigh. She looked over at him, and he looked at her out of the corner of his eye, a smirk on his lips.

She picked up the menu, stared at her choices, and tried to ignore the sensation of his thumb as it rubbed circles on the outer part of her thigh or the fact that his action was slowly pulling her dress up her leg. She bit her lip as heat spread all over her body, suddenly wishing she had a fan. She glanced around the room, and no one seemed to notice her unease.

"You don't give up easily," she whispered.

"Never."

Giuseppe was back before she could think of a good comeback.

"Have you decided?" He asked cheerily.

She had no idea what she'd like. Most of the items on the menu were foreign to her. "Why don't you bring me what you're famous for? I can't decide. It all looks amazing."

"I like you, Signora. You are wise." Giuseppe smiled and gave her a wink. "The usual for you, Signore?"

"Yes, and we'll also have one of each appetizer and dessert."

"I now remember why I love you. Always my best customer." Giuseppe walked away, and her breath caught as Riker's hand slid an inch higher.

He turned toward her, his hand never stopping its gentle and intoxicating swirl. "Tell me about yourself, Minny."

She couldn't stop the nagging fear that he was going to find her boring once he got to know her. James had always told her as much, and it was his patented reason for cheating on her. But, there was no point in making things up. Riker would see through it anyhow.

"I grew up on a small farm in Maryland. It was the best. I loved that spot. I sold it recently. It just didn't seem right to hang onto it now that no one was living there, and I needed the money for my mom's nursing home expenses. She has to have twenty-four-hour care, and it's part of the reason I stay at the call center in New York rather than going home. It pays a lot more. Anyway, my childhood was normal until my dad passed away. After that, a lot changed, and it took a lot of effort for me to find joy in my life again when my mother ended up ill as well. I liked to write and read to lose myself and of course, spending time with nature made me feel a little normal again. Kids don't really want to hang around the girl that spends all her time sitting in a hospital, you know?"

Riker stared at her, his expression unwavering, and it unsettled her more than if he'd asked a million more questions. Feeling compelled to continue talking, she cleared her throat of the frog that felt lodged.

"I like simple things. I read a lot. I love my dog and taking him for walks. I like to listen to music, sunsets, and the smell of rain on a hot summer day." She smiled a little. "I really love baseball, my dad was a huge fan, and I try to see the Yankees on his birthday every year. I dated the same guy most of my life and only recently told him to take a hike. I love my job, and one day I hope to have a family, and I sound really pathetic right now, I know." She looked away from his intense stare and grabbed her wine glass to take a healthy gulp.

"I don't think you're pathetic, you confuse me some, but you could never be pathetic." He tucked a loose strand from her updo behind her ear. "So, you and your dad were close?"

"Yes, we were. What about you?"

Riker snorted. "I would describe my father-son relationship as tenuous and abysmal at best."

"I'm sorry." She reached out mimicked him, and she rubbed her thumb against his jaw, earning her a smile.

"I have a confession to make," he said, and she froze, wine glass halfway to her mouth. "I was at your family farm."

"What? When? Why? I don't understand," she stuttered.

Riker held his tongue as the servers placed six different dishes on the table for appetizers, but she couldn't focus on food until he answered the question.

"You intrigued me, Minetta, right from the first moment you fell at my feet." He lifted an eyebrow as her cheeks flushed. The memory all too clear. "I wanted to find you, and you'd left town. I have many resources and tracked you to your family home, but you were already gone when I arrived. Unfortunately, shortly after that, you found me in a very compromising position at the office."

"That was a very tasteful way of saying sleeping with the neighborhood."

Riker laughed, his hand moving from her leg for the first time, and oddly she felt naked without his touch. "Yes, let's say I am not always the best person."

"So, is that what I am, another number? I pulled the little paper tab from the dispenser and will end up another conquest in the endless line of those that can't get enough," she said, dramatically and batted her eyes at him as she made fun.

"Quite the contrary, I can't seem to get you naked. I must be losing my touch," he teased back, placing a number of the delicious-looking items on a plate.

"It is most certainly an image that one cannot forget easily." She looked down at the food he'd given her, but his finger lifted her chin to meet his stare.

"I want to try a different approach with you, Minetta. I will not lie to you. I may not last long with this whole relationship idea because I haven't been in one in a very long time, but I'd like to try. If you are willing to try with me, of course?"

"If we are playing the honest game, you worry me, making me tentative to say yes. I have had enough heartbreaks in my life. I don't need another." She looked away from his eyes, unable to hold the intense stare. "Let's just see how these couple days go, and I will let you know." She looked up and almost laughed. His mouth was hanging open like she'd just given him the biggest shock of his life. "Are you okay?"

He sat up straight, a slow smile spreading across his face. "You should know. I love a challenge."

"And you should know, you can't buy my affections." She returned his smile before digging into the most wonderful meal she'd ever tasted.

CHAPTER

THIRTY-EIGHT

R IKER

As I anticipated, the meal was a success, I was certain that Minetta had enjoyed herself, but she was so genuinely nice and happy it actually made it harder to tell. She had Giuseppe wrapped around her finger by the end of the meal, and he came out from the kitchen once the doors were closed and enjoyed a dessert and coffee with us.

Her enjoyment was infectious, and I found myself smiling and laughing with her as she talked dramatically about the meal, the sites, and the countryside as we made our way toward my villa. Things I never noticed, she pointed out with exuberance.—

I pulled the Ferrari up to the gate of the outer wall surrounding the property, placing my finger on the little reader, and the gates slowly opened outward. I'd made sure all the lights lining the driveway up to the four-story villa were lit.

A gasp had me looking at Minny, and her eyes were as big as

saucers, her hands covering her mouth. I had to admit this was one of my favorite places to escape. I'd been an ass telling her this place bored me. The tall white pillars and staircase that led to the grand golden-colored doors reminded me of another time in my life.

"This is yours? Like the whole thing, not just a room," she asked, and the look on her face made me shift in my seat.

"Yes, do you like it?"

"Riker, it's stunning, but what do you do with all this space," Minny asked as I pulled the Ferrari under the carport area and parked. I wasn't sure how to answer the question.

"Do I need to do something with it?"

She didn't answer, just pushed open the door and stood to stare up at the expanse of the villa as it stretched before her. Following suit, I got out and came around to stand beside her. I wanted to see if I could understand what she saw, see it through her eyes.

"I guess not. It's just this must have cost a fortune, and you said you only come here once or twice a year, if at all? Just seems like an awful lot for one person."

"I didn't realize I needed to consult you on my spending." I glared down at Minny, annoyed that she kept throwing out how much everything cost. The jet, the car, the villa, the entire trip so far had her aghast at my spending habits, which I had every right to do if I wanted. It was my money. I could build a place three times this size for just myself if I wanted.

"You're right. You don't. I'm sorry."

She walked away to look at the flowers off to the side of the driveway, and I reined in my anger. I turned and stared up at the villa and tried to imagine what it would look like to someone seeing it for the first time. I didn't bring humans here, Skye and Neven had accompanied me and a few of the other demon females I didn't mind spending multiple nights with, but that was it. They all gushed over the place as they hung off my arm and promised all sorts of devious fun to be able to stay forever. All the lights burned brightly in the windows, but I knew the place stood empty other than a few servants.

"Did you want to go inside," Minny asked. Her voice was soft, yet it made me jump. I hadn't noticed she'd moved. I nodded and held out my elbow for her to take. "Just so you know, it's not that I don't think the place is lovely. I mean, who wouldn't?"

"I sense a but coming," I said sarcastically. I wasn't sure why her opinion irked me or why it seemed to matter so much.

She took a deep breath, gave me a small smile, and shrugged instead. "Forget it. I'm being a rude guest. The Villa is lovely, Riker."

I glared at her, and she looked away as we reached the massive front doors. I really wanted to argue. I wanted her to tell me exactly what she thought so I could tell her why the fuck she was wrong. I opened my mouth to tell her so, but the door opened, and Leeanne greeted us. She was one of the servants that lived here full time. She was a demon that opted to follow me to Earth and work here rather than stay in Hell. She took care of all the daily running of the Villa and served as a bit of fun when I was in town.

"Signore, it is good to see you again." Her eyes flared with the usual lust, but instead of being interested, I felt ashamed. I could feel Minny bristle beside me. Her small hands squeezed just a little tighter, and her body was rigid as she took in the other woman.

"Leeanne, this is Minetta. She is my guest for the weekend. I assume all is as I asked and that you will make sure Minetta feels at home?"

Always the constant professional, Leeanne bowed at the waist. "Of course, Signore, right this way."

I kept an eye on my little bird. She didn't say anything about the intricate floor pattern or the elegant gold crown molding. She glanced at the paintings that cost more than a home each and stared up at the crystal chandeliers that lined the hallways. I was overcome with a sense of shame for my home, and that only reignited my earlier anger. I didn't deserve to feel ashamed of what I worked so hard for—how dare she make me feel like this.

"I have prepared this guest room for you, Signora," Leeanne said, pushing open a door that led into a room I'd never seen. A four-post, king-sized bed stood as the centerpiece of the room. It was complete with shears that could drop down and shield the occupant. Windows lined the far wall, and like the rest of the home, it was decorated with gold accenting everything from furniture to the walls. Leeanne walked toward the closet and opened the doors to a walk-in area. "You will find whatever clothes you desire in here, and the bathing area is through that door. Would you like anything brought to your room, Signora?"

"Thank you for going to the trouble Leeanne. This is wonderful."

"No trouble at all. If you need me, there is an intercom that will page me directly." Leeanne pointed to the square beside the door. Bowing again, she left, and I was alone with Minny as she slowly wandered around the room. She looked like the little bird I called her, her movements light and unsure, as if nervous to touch anything. She was a bird in a gilded cage. I shook my head as the image disturbed me.

"I will let you get some sleep. If you need me for anything, I'm on the top floor at the far end of the Villa."

She stopped her inspection and clasped her hands in front of her as she turned to look at me. There wasn't anything different about the look on her face, but it felt like a small void had settled between us. "Thank you, Riker, it really is beautiful. Sleep well."

My brain was yelling for me to leave, but my feet remained rooted to the floor. The moonlight was shining in the tall windows and bathing her in its cool glare. She took my breath away. I swallowed hard and forced my feet to turn and leave before I did something more like storm across the room and convince her to let me take her up to my room.

The need that was coursing through my veins was like a wild beast making my pulse pound hard. I could smell her sweet scent from across the room, and I was almost able to taste her unique flavor on my tongue.

I marched to my room, and as I did, I realized just how far away her room was. It was probably for the best.

As I expected she would be, Leeanne stood in the middle of my room naked. She smiled as she sashayed her way toward me. She was a stunning demon, with long, lean legs, high perky tits, and a narrow waist. Her demon form was far less attractive. My dick kicked at the idea of finally finding a possible release. It felt like I'd been hard for weeks.

"Signore, I have missed you," she said as she ran her hand down the front of my chest. The shirt buttons popped apart with her expert touch. She rubbed her hand down the aching cock between my legs, and I groaned. Leeanne lowered herself to her knees, and her big dark eyes stared up at me with perfect submissiveness. When I didn't resist her touch, she quickly unhooked the belt and button on my pants. The zipper came mostly undone as my dick pressed against the opening, wanting to be free of its confines. Leeanne gripped the sides of my pants and boxers and lowered them to the ground, allowing me to step out of them.

She licked her lips as she crawled closer to the cock that stood tall against my stomach. I moaned loudly as Leeanne wrapped her hand around the shaft and gave it a few strokes through her silky fingers. As she did, another pair of eyes came to my mind. A smile that made my soul feel light for the first time, a pang of something that I didn't understand, lanced through my chest. I backed away before Leeanne could wrap her mouth around my aching shaft. I gripped her wrists and gently pulled her hands away, my cock screaming and kicking with need as I did so.

"I can't, Leeanne, not this trip." She twisted her head to the side as she inspected me and then stood in one graceful, fluid motion. She bowed deep, her tits with their hard nipples hung toward the floor. Her lithe ass swayed from side to side to side, and I stared at it as she walked out the door, closing it behind her.

"What the fuck is wrong with me," I growled and marched for the bathroom.

Flipping on the shower, I didn't care what the temperature the water was and jumped under the spray and ripped off my open shirt, tossing it to the shower floor. My hand immediately grabbed my throbbing cock and squeezed it tight in my fist. The angry head throbbed painfully as I stared at the tip.

I'd never had the need to pleasure myself, and I could've had Leeanne take care of this, but no, I had to feel... I didn't know what I felt. Was this guilt? Real guilt? I didn't like it.

The strokes were not slow. There was no savoring a release. It needed to be fast and dirty. I pictured spreading the thighs of the raven-haired beauty that was a floor below and slamming my cock into her as she screamed my name. I could almost hear her yelling my name as she came all over my shaft.

The first jets of my release splattered the wall, but I needed more. My hand never slowed as I finished. I tightened my grip further, almost to the point of pain, and sat down on the built-in seat of the shower. The drain made a slurping sound as the water swirled around, and I continued to beat out my frustration on my cock.

The sound made me think of Minetta and how I wanted her with her mouth wrapped around my cock, and just the thought had my back arching as another release threatened to make an appearance. My balls pulled up tight to my body, the shaft becoming more engorged a moment before the climax ripped through my body. So fierce was the powerful explosion from the tip that it lifted me off the seat, my wings breaking free of their tattooed state and taking up all the space in the normally large shower. I couldn't be bothered trying to figure out why I'd lost control as the need continued to rip through my body at a blinding pace.

My arm moved fast, my muscles burning as I yelled and thrashed against the shower until my ass slid off the seat, and I landed on the floor with my back pressed into the wall. I was closing in on a third release and gasped, heart pounding hard in my chest.

The earlier anger and frustration melted and folded in on itself. The image in my mind was of Heaven's gates as they closed in my face when I tried to return and seek counsel with Father. The memory brought pain to my chest, and then it morphed into something else, something stronger. The unusual emotion settled like a weight pressing down on me.

The potent mixture of pleasure and pain was coursing through my body as the strokes became more insistent. I jerked hard on my still rock-hard dick, my hand traveling over the sensitive head. I gritted my teeth and bucked against the movement, my ass slapping off the floor as my hand forced a third orgasm.

I screamed, the glass shower door and wall exploding outward as my wing smashed through it and sent small fragments flying. Sparkling pieces embedded themselves in the walls with the force. The rest of the shards made a tinkling sound as they fell to the gray tile floor.

Breathing hard, I slumped against the wall, the water traveling down the drain the only sound left in the otherwise quiet room. Whatever mess there was could be cleaned up tomorrow. Closing my eyes, I decided to stay and rest right here with the water beating against my chest and deflated cock still locked in my vice-like grip.

Nothing would ever cleanse my blackened soul, but there were cracks in the once pitch darkness. Little slivers of light were seeping through and creating a vein-like pattern in my mind. The warmth of the glittering golden hue throbbed stronger than my dick had a moment ago. It was impossible, yet I could feel parts of my old self, parts of a self I'd assumed dead and buried, trying to break free of the black prison.

Parts of myself I didn't know if I wanted to return.

CHAPTER
THIRTY-NINE

MINETTA sat in the garden, her feet dangling into the pool, a pink fruity drink in her left hand and a book in the other. She had tried with very little success to concentrate on the words on the page as her mind wandered over the last couple of days.

Riker had taken her back to Venice as promised, and they'd spent all morning on a gondola ride that allowed her to see the old buildings and learn about the history from the gondolier as he showed them around. She wandered Mark's Square and purchased a few trinkets. Well, actually, Riker paid for them, but she promised to pay him back.

They took a private tour of the Doge's Palace and ate on a patio overlooking the water for lunch. He then took her to his winery that was somewhere near Florence, and by some miracle, she didn't throw up all over his car.

When they arrived back at the Villa, she was wiped and decided to soak in the giant tub in her room. She'd kind of expected and secretly hoped that Riker would knock on her door, and when he hadn't, she paced her room until she was practically sleepwalking.

Riker had been oddly aloof all day yesterday, and now today, she'd yet to see him. He'd turned into a ghost. He'd sent Leeanne to tell her that he would be working for a few hours in his office, and he'd come to find her when he was done. It was now rounding on dinner time, and she had to wonder if she'd done something wrong or maybe there was more going on between him and Leeanne.

For all his talk of wanting to try a relationship, she was having a difficult time picturing it. You don't go from having sex with a lineup of different girls every week to monogamy. Could you?

What was worse was that she hated the idea of him being with another girl. She'd never been the jealous type, but this was different. He made her feel more than she wanted to analyze too closely.

Closing the book, she stared at the aqua water as the sun warmed her back. The rays glittering off the water's surface reminded her of the way Riker's eyes could unnaturally shine.

"Signora?" Minetta looked up at Leeanne. "Signore has sent a message to go ahead and have the chef make you dinner. He will be tied up for some time yet."

"Thank you, Leeanne."

"My pleasure." The woman bowed her head, and as silently as she arrived, she disappeared through the walls of greenery. Minetta watched her leave and a pain constricted in her chest. Why wouldn't he want the stunning sun-kissed beauty? She seemed to be exactly his type, beautiful, willing, obedient, content with his lifestyle. She rubbed her eyes as she played over all their interactions. Why did she always push his buttons? Why couldn't she be more like Leeanne and not question every decision he made?

No, he was going to have to like her for who she was and that was someone that questioned things. She'd never been great at standing up for herself, James was proof of that, but she couldn't do that again. She couldn't let someone steamroll her life. She wasn't sure what Riker wanted, he was a hard to read unless he was flirting or proudly showing off something he valued.

She stared at the sparkling water as she debated what to do. This was their last night here, they were going home tomorrow, and one thing was certain, Riker had decided to avoid her, or he'd decided to put the ball firmly in her court to make the next move. The question was, did she want to make the next move?

Pulling her feet from the water, she stood and stared up at the massive expanse of the Villa. Her dad's dying wish was for her to take chances in life. She wasn't sure if this was what he meant, but it was certainly the biggest risk she'd ever taken. She slipped on the little flip-flops and grabbed her towel as she marched toward the house with renewed purpose.

R IKER

"No! How many times must I repeat myself?" I gripped the dresser like it might give me the strength to deal with the incompetence that had decided to vomit all over my company while I was away for a few days. Was it really so difficult to do what I asked in a timely manner? I didn't think so, but apparently, I was unreasonable.

I may have been a little bit, but I sure as fuck wasn't going to tell George that. The last thing that idiot needed to think was that he might actually be right.

"Then call Neven. That is what he is there for," I growled.

My current state of mind hadn't been improved with the growing case of emotional yips. Minetta had my head all over the place, dancing back and forth between a lovesick moron and running scared. Not really a great combo for my personality type at the best of times.

Had I jumped into work to stay away from Minetta? I may have, but I would deny it until one of my brother's silver swords cut me down.

The electrical buzz that traveled like a swarm of bees under my skin announced Minny's presence a moment before she spoke.

"Riker?" Her voice was like velvet, warm and rich, and I stood a little straighter with the single word as a shiver raced down my spine. Composing myself, I turned to tell Minny I was busy and to go away, but that idea sputtered and died before my mouth opened.

Like a little sex goddess, she stood leaning against the door frame, her hair partially covering her face, but the blue eye I could see burned into my own. My eyes traveled up the sheer material that was loosely draped over her body. It somehow covered everything giving the impression of modesty, and yet it was clear as day she was naked underneath. A squawking sound was in my ear, and I looked at the phone in my hand, confused why it was there.

"Riker, are you still there?" George's grating voice came through the line.

"Call Neven. I gotta go," I barked out and tossed the phone on the dresser.

Reservations be damned, one look at that body, and I was ready to crawl to her on my hands and knees for just a taste.

"I hope you don't mind me interrupting you like this."

I shivered again as she spoke, her voice caressing my body as surely as any hand could. I was rooted to the ground, my brain unable to make my limbs work properly. Her lip curled up in a cheeky smirk as she pushed off the door frame.

"I was getting lonely all by myself," she said, biting her lip. That sexy fucking lip that I could taste from here.

My body vibrated, the tension building until I was a spring ready to explode as Minetta stalked me across the room. One elegant step at a time, she moved toward me, and my tongue moistened my parched lips. I watched with eager anticipation as her hands went to the tie at her waist. The aching desire that had plagued me raged forward from the depths where I had tried to bury it—so potent was the force that my ears rang with my power trying to escape. The wing tattoos burned along my back, and I had to concentrate on making sure they didn't make a sudden and unwanted appearance.

With agonizingly slow movements, she pulled on the one end of the sash. She smiled and paused, her feet stopping with her hand, and I almost cried out, 'no, please don't stop.' The vibration turned into a tremble as she gave the sash one more tug, and the delicate material parted like a sacred curtain. The veil that kept all her treasures hidden fell open, leaving me incapacitated from logical thought. I'd never been one to ignore the pleasures of the body, yet as my eyes glided over Minetta's toned and petite form, it became staggeringly clear that I'd been missing something.

Her nipples stood proudly, hard peaked buds on her breasts that rose to attention. She wore strappy little heels that screamed to be fucked while wearing them, and her long, lean legs were slightly crossed, hiding the last bit of treasure that I intended to have tonight.

The demon in me was not letting her leave this room. Like an unexpecting animal walking into a trap, my little bird had flown into the cat's clutches, and I fully intended to devour her. She'd awoken the beast, the carnal and visceral part of my personality that alone would get me kicked out of Heaven all over again. Like a mirage, her hand reached toward me, and as she made contact with my chest, the man became the sin.

I shuddered out a breath as my cock ached with a pounding need the likes I didn't know possible. The all-consuming sensation within my body was more than the last few nights put together and it made me suck in a sharp breath. "Do you have any idea what you are doing to me? What you're awakening in me?"

"What I know is that I want this. I don't know about tomorrow or the next day, but right now, here with you in this magical place, I want all the pleasures you are offering me."

Her hand slid up to my cheek, and I leaned my head into the soft contact. Her other hand replaced the one that had been on my chest, and as she did, the dam broke loose.

I gripped her by the waist, and with no more effort than lifting a feather, I picked her up and sat her on the dresser. Minetta squealed as her ass came into contact with the cool surface, but I didn't give her time to adjust as my lips found hers. The kiss between us deepened and became frenzied as hands pulled at material and slid across skin. She opened her legs, and I stood between them, gripping her ass in my hands to pull her as close as I could get her.

The rich peach scent was strong in my nose, the sweet aroma mixing with the scent of her arousal. A deep rumble close to a growl left my lips as my mouth watered to taste more of her. Breaking the kiss, I swiped my arm across the long dresser sending everything flying to the floor with a crash.

"Lay down." The words were a command, and I thought she might argue, but the passion that burned in her eyes told a different story. She did as I asked and shifted around so she could lay on the hard surface. "Keep this leg down." I tapped the leg closest to me.

She dropped it immediately to hang over the edge, her dainty foot in that sexy heel swung like a metronome with a nervous energy that I could feel thrumming off her body. I held back the smile. Her energy soaked into my skin, feeding the demon a different meal than it normally craved but just as satisfying. Her dark hair splayed over the pale marble of the dresser, those blue eyes staring up at me, the bravado slowly slipping.

"Are you scared, my little bird?" My fingers worked at undoing my dress shirt, and the fact that she watched every move was not lost on me.

"No," she said quietly, but she didn't look me in the eye.

"It's not wise to lie to me." Her skin was unbelievably soft, my fingers skimming up the inside of her leg and making her breath hitch.

Minetta licked her lips, her eyes locking with mine. "I'm not scared of you. I'm scared of opening myself up to you."

"Why would you be scared of that?" Her stomach muscles flexed as my hands slid over her hips, her breathing quickening as my thumbs grazed the bottom of her breasts.

"I'm not stupid, Riker. I know a woman like me can't sustain you for long. I will be a new shiny plaything for a while, and I have no doubt you will try to stay committed, but you will want more at some point. It is simply your nature to consume what you want and spit out the rest."

My hands stilled as I locked eyes with Minetta. Her words echoed around in my head—they were the truth. I couldn't have put who I am any more plainly than she just had, but the words cut like a knife. Seconds turned into minutes, and all I could do was stare at her beautiful face. I couldn't imagine her with another. Just the thought made my blood sing as hot as Hellfire itself.

"And yet you are willing to sleep with me knowing what I'm like?"

She broke the stare, her eyes looking up at the ceiling, a ghost of emotion traveling over her face.

"I haven't known much happiness since my father passed away, Riker, but what I've learned the last couple of days is that when I'm with you...you make me smile. You make me believe that one day there could be more for me."

Her eyes found mine again, brimming with emotion that stopped my racing heart in its tracks.

"I don't think about what I'm not or what I've lost, only how you make me feel when I'm around you. That may not make sense to you, but it's important to me. So, if this only lasts a week or a month or just tonight, I will take it." She gave me a small smile that spoke more of a deep sadness than happiness. "Don't worry, Riker. I'm going into this with my eyes wide open, and I don't expect anything from you."

I swallowed the lump in my throat that was like jagged glass. The cracks that had already formed in my soul broke open wider, chunks of it flaking away, leaving a blinding brightness underneath that choked me with long-forgotten emotion.

"I won't hurt you, Minetta. I will never hurt you." Dangerous words to be spoken, yet I meant every one. The barren truth of it was as shocking as what I almost said next. Three words I never thought I'd say again.

FORTY

MINETTA wasn't sure what she said, but Riker's face had become emotionless and frozen in place. She wiggled on the cool surface, not sure if she should get up and leave or stay where she was.

"Did I say something wrong," she asked.

Riker blinked, his eyes focusing on her once more. "No, you didn't say anything wrong."

He lowered his head, his lips touching hers gently, yet there was no denying the power behind the act. She sucked in her breath and wrapped her arms around his neck, unable to get close enough. Riker's arms snaked under her body and raised her back up, lifting her into his arms.

He never broke the kiss as he walked across the room and laid her down on the oversized bed. The heat pressing into her body from his own was a physical force. Riker's hands resumed their journey of her body but were much more controlled this time. The passion was still licking through her, but he didn't rush as he touched her like he had been. She gasped and arched into his hold as he tweaked her nipple, his thumb and finger expertly rolling it around. The sensation sent a stab of pure pleasure to her core.

Minetta was light-headed by the time Riker broke the kiss and stood beside the bed—he looked menacing with the fading light at his back, casting shadows on his face. She trembled under the intense stare, and her body wiggled with uncertainty while craving more of his touch.

"You're so beautiful," Riker said. He slipped the shirt off, and it was the first time she was able to get a good look at the man beneath the suit. Like Michael's chest, Riker's was covered with paper-thin lines with similar runes but different from the ones she'd seen glowing on the archangel. He was not a huge hulking man, but he was muscled in all the right places. He reminded her of a swimmer or maybe a lacrosse player, with wide-cut shoulders that tapered into a well-defined V. His abs were no slouch either, she was easily able to count eight distinct dips, and she licked her lips, wanting to taste every one. "I like that look on your face. You seem to enjoy what you're staring at."

Riker smiled, making her blush. She could feel the heat going straight to her cheeks, and she was unable to hold his amber stare. "Do not look away, Minetta. I want you to stare. I will be the only man you look at from now on. Do you understand?"

Her eyebrow lifted in defiance of his command. "Only if I am the only woman you look at from now on."

"Fair is fair. I agree to your terms."

The khakis he'd been wearing pooled around his feet, and she swallowed hard as she laid eyes on the erection that was standing tall against his stomach. He hadn't taken his boxers off, but it didn't matter as the head of his shaft poked above the top as if trying to escape. The head was wet, with droplets of clear fluid on the end, and she followed that stream until it hit the waistband of his boxers and disappeared.

Minetta sat up, drawn to the sight of him, her tongue tingling, a pull in her gut wanting to taste him and drink him down. She'd never been into oral sex with James. In fact, she couldn't remember a single time she'd craved to touch anyone like this.

"Ah, ah, ah." He waggled a finger back and forth at her like she was a child being scolded. "Lay down, my little bird."

She was tempted to see what he would do if she reached out and grabbed what she wanted instead, but that seemed like a game for another time. Was she really considering his words to be true? That there would be more than this moment between them? Minetta had no idea, and it really didn't matter right now.

Obviously, not moving fast enough for his liking, he reached out and grabbed her legs, giving her a hard tug and forcing her to flop backward. A small scream left her lips as he pulled her to the end of the bed and placed his hands down on either side of her.

"When I ask you to do something, you do it. Do you understand?" She swallowed hard, but instead of fear, a powerful burst of desire wracked her body. She could feel the moisture running down the inside of her legs and closed them, embarrassed by her flagrant arousal. Riker shook his head at her as he stood straight and lowered the black boxers to the floor. She wanted to answer, but when she opened her mouth, nothing came out. All the air had ceased to move properly in her chest.

The erection she'd only been able to see the tip of, made her eyes bug out as he revealed the whole length and girth. It became extremely clear why women lined up to be used by him. It had been a mutual using, she'd assumed he was simply an overly horny individual, but it was crystal clear now that they'd been using him too.

Riker gripped her knees as he lowered himself, pulling her legs apart. "Don't hide from me. I want to see all of you, taste every inch of your body, bury myself deep inside you, and make sure you keep your promise to never look at another."

"You were serious?"

"Very much." His hands were just as commanding as his voice, and he pushed on the inside of her knees, her weak resistance giving way to his insistence. "I love these. From now on, when we are together, I want you in heels." Riker kissed the top of her foot, and surprisingly a bolt of pleasure traveled up her leg. She'd never expected such a simple act would cause this kind of a reaction. Then again, it probably had more to do with who it was than what he was doing.

His tongue swirled around the ankle of her left leg before he switched and repeated this action to her right. The licking and tongue work continued up the inside of both legs, his hot tongue mixed with the cool air creating a tantalizing sensation. Her core was aching, the muscles gripping and releasing as her body begged for more. She craved to feel an orgasm the likes of which she'd only known in her dreams.

Gripping her ass, sheer material and all, he jerked her closer to the edge of the bed. Her ass was almost hanging over the side, and she grabbed fistfuls of the sheets. Before she could say a word, his tongue licked up the inside of her thigh, lapping up the wetness she'd been trying to hide.

"You taste like warm milk with honey on a rainy day," he said.

His tongue continued to work along both legs until they were clean of her juices, but in doing so, all it did was create more. She cried out with an explosion of pleasure as his mouth finally landed on the most sensitive part of her body. Riker's tongue invaded her, fast and rough, like he was trying to lap up all the honey that her body was producing.

"Oh god," she yelled, not thinking as his tongue suddenly flicked over her swollen exposed clit. He chuckled, and she covered her mouth, not only to stifle the next yell as he continued to assault her with his hot tongue, but so she didn't say something she shouldn't. She could only imagine how awkward it must be for him always to have women yelling his Father's name. It brought the meaning of the word strange to a whole new level.

She was extremely close to a climax, her body arching off the bed as another wave of heat seared through her system. Minetta had no idea if it was her own body or something about Riker that was doing this to her, but it left her panting and craving more. Unable to help herself any longer, she sank her fingers into his soft, golden hair and gripped it hard.

"Yes, let go," Riker groaned, his words coming out mumbled.

The vibration was all that was needed to push her over the final edge of bliss. She yelled, and this time, she screamed his name, her hands pulling his head harder into her body. Minetta had never felt so wanton before, and her body bucked against his face as he moaned and continued to suck on the sensitive folds. The wave was continuous and wracked her body, and she tried to flinch away from Riker as the sensitivity almost became too much.

He chuckled as she wiggled in his tight grip. "You are so sweet, my little bird. I could eat you every day and never have enough."

Minetta flopped back, breathing hard as Riker nipped at the inside of her thighs. As Riker shifted and slowly rose to his full height, she swallowed hard. The look on his face was raw and as primal as she'd ever seen. His muscles were flexed and showing off exactly why he was considered a gift to behold.

"Roll over onto your stomach."

Limbs a little shaky, she did as he asked, and she was shocked as he moved up her body until he was straddling her legs. His weight was delicious, but as he touched her lower back and kneaded the tight muscles, she relaxed and let him work away all the stress that had plagued her. He was gentle with the side that was bruised. Although

Penny helped them heal, there was still a soft shadow, a reminder of what was still after her.

She moaned and gasped as his hands moved from her shoulders down so he could squeeze her ass in his large hands.

"Do you like this, my little bird?"

She nodded, her eyes closed as he expertly relaxed her body, and with a soft touch here and there, the spark of desire was beginning to burn inside her again. She wiggled a little as his hands retreated from her shoulders once more to work on her butt cheeks. He chuckled a little and slipped a finger between her legs.

"And how about this?" His voice was rough, and her heart jumped around as his finger teased playfully over her pussy folds.

Riker pressed his hips forward, and she moaned louder as the motion rocked her body and craved more than the little tease.

"Are you ready for me?" His voice sounded like gravel.

That was a question she didn't have the answer to but found herself eagerly nodding her head, yes. No matter what happened between them tonight, there was no doubt left in her mind that she wanted him. She wanted all of him—the sin, the archangel, but most of all she wanted the man.

CHAPTER
FORTY-ONE

MINETTA looked like an angel laid out before me, and I was one of few that could confirm that for a fact. The moonlight was shining through the window, blanketing her in a spotlight of cool white light. Her skin was like porcelain as if she was one of the great statues that had been carved and laid upon my bed. I couldn't look away. She completely mesmerized me, my heart pounding harder than a thousand galloping horses.

I had to be mindful because she was human. I didn't want to hurt her. Pulling back from her body, I stood to give myself a second to get my need under control. I was on edge, flexing my hands, digging my nails into my palm.

"Riker, is something wrong?"

"Come here."

I held out my hand, and Minetta's fingers shook as she placed her hand in mine. As soon as her feet touched the floor and she stood before me, I cupped her face and dropped my lips to hers. Pushing the edges of the delicate material off her shoulders, it slid to the floor, pooling at her feet. Goosebumps rose under my fingertips as they traveled over her skin. I loved this reaction from her. She gasped into my mouth as my fingers ran gentle lines down her back. I could almost feel the pounding of her heart through the kiss.

Since my fall, I hadn't been one for romance, but with my little bird, my Minny, I wanted her to feel nothing but pleasure. That thought had become the center of my focus. I wanted to show her the world and everything it had to offer, starting with tonight.

Cupping her ass, I lifted her up my body and groaned as the softness of her skin slid against my own. I didn't trust myself and turned to sit down on the bed with Minetta sitting on my lap. I could feel her body igniting like a fire under my touch, the remnants of her release were gone, and the massage had left in its wake a woman that wanted more. She wiggled in my lap, small whimpers escaping her lips as her slick sex rubbed against me. My cock kicked hard, trapped between our bodies. It was taking every ounce of control to keep from ravaging her.

Her nails dug into my shoulders as she rose up on her knees, our eyes locking as she looked down at me.

"Do it," I whispered.

My body tensed as she reached between us, taking my cock in her small hand. She tentatively gave it a stroke, and a shudder rippled through my body.

"Oh fuck," I moaned out as she positioned herself right over my aching shaft—so close that I could feel her heat pressing into me. In one agonizingly slow movement, she sat down, taking me into her warmth, her tight walls gripping me like a vice.

I couldn't have taken my eyes off her if I wanted to as she arched her back and sucked in her lower lip. She clung to my shoulders, and I was mesmerized by her.

With every aching inch that she took inside her, the power simmered higher within me. I was dangerously close to losing control and showing her what I was. I wasn't even sure what would happen if it rippled out like this, but I couldn't stop. I wouldn't. Now that we had crossed this line, there was no going back for me—I had to have every inch of her. Every fiber of my being demon and otherwise had to have all she offered.

Her ass bottomed out to sit fully in my lap, and I sucked in a deep breath as my desire only increased to higher and more dangerous levels. She felt like home, and this was where I was always meant to be, which was outrageous. She was a human, a mere human, yet the effect she had on me was undeniable.

"You're in control, my little bird, do what you want," I whispered into her neck. I didn't trust myself yet to take over. I kissed her neck, and she groaned, her pussy clamping down harder. My hands shook and sweat trickled down my spine as I forced myself to remain still. She arched back once more, her breasts rising to eye level. Taking advantage, I moved to allow my lips access to one hardened nipple and sucked. She whimpered in pleasure as she began to move.

"Fuck, you feel amazing," I said.

I switched nipples, my tongue swirling around the sensitive hard nub, and bit down gently as she picked up the pace. She was making little noises of pleasure that were addictive to my ears. The power seeped out a little as my control frayed around the edges. It hovered low to the floor, creating a shimmering golden fog snaking across the room. Minetta didn't seem to notice since her eyes were closed, her head was back, and her mouth was open. She was the perfect picture of erotic beauty.

"Oh Riker," Minetta yelled, my name, and it was music to my ears. I gripped her body close as her pace picked up, and it didn't take long before I could feel her body tremble as she closed in on her release. Our mutual panting mixed with the distinct slap of wet skin against skin joined the insatiable whimpers that escaped our lips.

I pushed back the damp hair from her face. The heat rolling off her skin in waves seemed to attract the attention of my leaking power. It swirled up off the floor and wrapped around her body. Minetta shivered and screamed as she came—the orgasm was so powerful that I yelled along with her as her walls flexed and rippled around my cock.

I fell back onto the bed and bucked up hard into her, her release coating me like a sweet nectar. "Ride me hard!"

I was surprised she had the energy to do as I asked, but she bounced faster. Gone was the timid bird, and left in her place was the woman that had passion in her veins. The view of her body bouncing, her breasts rising and falling with her movement was hypnotic. My hands gripped the sheets tightly, balling them into fists, so I didn't hurt her human body. I had to close my eyes and focus on my breathing as my control slipped another notch, but no matter what I did, I knew I was going to fall.

She screamed my name, her fingers digging into my skin. "Riker, I...I...."

My eyes snapped open as her pace slowed a little. A feral need to release and claim her body as mine rose like a demon from the depths of Hell within me. My mind broke as another climax ripped through her body. Taking her waist in my hands, I flipped us over and held her legs out to the sides.

"Yell, stop if I hurt you," I bit out breathlessly.

She reached up and laid her hand on my cheek, and I kissed her palm. "Let go, Riker," she whispered. My body shuddered with her words, the power rippling like waves as my muscles did.

I growled a guttural sound that was not human, yet she didn't look away. I'd never experienced anything like this and didn't know how to keep the raging sensations in check. "Let go," she said again.

And I did.

My hips were like a piston as I sank home and back out at a blinding pace. She screamed and arched her back, lifting off the bed as her head pressed back into the pillow. The sound of skin slapping against skin, mingled with her screams and my grunts as my release drew closer, was music to my ears.

My arms flexed, Minetta's nails digging hard into my shoulders as she came once again. The throbbing feel of her release pushed me over that final cliff as I gripped her legs tight. The orgasm was so wonderfully violent that a roar was ripped from my mouth. The power I'd been trying to keep a lid on finally broke free like an explosion punched outward from my body.

The world around me froze. There was no sound, no smell, just nothing—the bedroom walls dissipated into dust, the entire top floor of the Villa turned to specks of glittering nothingness. Something big had just happened. The world only stopped when a new fork in prophecy was created. I didn't give a fuck what it meant. The pleasure was so immense that Michael could have taken my life at the moment, and I would be content. I'd been touched by real love, and to have tasted it, my heart beat stronger in my chest. I felt alive for the first time since my fall.

A storm of power swirled around the two of us as we clung to one another through the surge of ecstasy that felt Heaven sent. Minetta screamed as her body constricted around mine, forcing another soul-shifting release from my jerking cock.

The particles of glittering dust began to move faster and faster. They spun around us like a vortex until the walls slowly took shape. The roof and windows were next, and the furniture, including the bed we were lying on, had all disintegrated, but it was reforming before my eyes and leaving them looking as perfect as they'd been before. I had no idea why this was happening, and I didn't care.

I closed my eyes as another burst of power ripped through my body. My wings tore from their tattooed cage, fanning out and stretching almost from one side of the room to the other. I couldn't stop it, any more than I could stop the next release from gripping me as I came again, the hot seed flowing out of my body in streams that never seemed to end. The runes that coated my skin and had gone dormant with my fall glowed brightly along my chest, the warm sensation and thrum of power long forgotten until this moment.

Opening my eyes, I realized that the entire room was now bathed in a bright golden glow. I knew my eyes would be glowing golden, and I tried to rein it all in before Minetta opened her eyes, but I knew it was far too late as I glanced down. She stared at the walls a moment before her eyes found mine. They were filled with a mix of surprise and wonder, but there was no fear.

Panting hard, the last of my climax settled. My arms were shaking, barely able to keep me from collapsing on top of her. "You're not scared?"

She shook her head back and forth, her hand reaching for one of the wings. A smile lifted at the corner of her mouth as she stroked the soft raven feathers with their golden tips. "I already knew who you were," she said, and my eyes went wide. "Penny told me, it's why she didn't want me going away with you. She was concerned."

"So, you know what Penny is?"

"Yes. I have for a while now."

I lifted an eyebrow at her as a smile spread across my face. "You are much braver than I gave you credit for, and I already thought you were brave. To willingly sleep with a demon is no small feat. I could have killed you. I'm sure I almost did."

She blushed the pink making her already flushed cheeks glow brighter. "I don't see you as a demon, I see you as Riker, and I believed you when you said you wouldn't hurt me." She casually lifted a shoulder. "Can we go again, but leave these out?" She drew her hands along my wings, the sensation sending a strange quiver down my body.

"We can go as many times as you want. I can stay hard all night."

Minetta's mouth fell open, but a smirk crossed her face. "This I have to see."

Dropping my head, I kissed her deep and slow, savoring her flavor on my tongue. I couldn't tell her that I loved her, but it was confirmed in my chest and my mind. She was meant for me. She was my little bird, maybe a gift or an olive branch from Michael or my Father, but she was my only chance at love.

She wrapped her arms around my neck, and I lifted her body enough that I could wrap the great wings around her. She was mine as I was hers, and I intended on keeping her.

CHAPTER
FORTY-TWO

R IKER

Hours later, I lay on my back, holding Minetta to my body as she slept. Her slow, deep breathing was a comfort to me. Two things plagued my mind now. The first was how different I felt. I was still Riker, still Mammon, and yet I wasn't. My soul was lighter, more akin to when I was a warrior of Heaven when my name had been Maddix, and I was a beloved son and brother.

The second thing that gave me cause to sweat and worry was how little time I had with Minetta. As an immortal, I didn't give time much thought. I would wake up every day the same way I did the day before and the one before that. I'd seen history shape itself, humans advance, and the world change, but I'd taken it all for granted. Minny was human. At best, she had another fifty good years. At worst, she could die tomorrow. The thought made me hold her closer and kiss the top of her head. I couldn't lose her. I just couldn't.

I stared at the ceiling slightly terrified to close my eyes and try to get some sleep. I didn't want to lose a single second with her and had this crazy urge to stand over Minny and growl at everything that came near her. I pinched the bridge of my nose and pushed the images aside. As my eyes fluttered shut, I was pulled under and taken back in time.

I'd never thought I'd have to cut down a fellow angel, but as I flew into the chaos that had erupted in Heaven, I found myself drawing my golden sword and defending myself from an onslaught of attacks. The sound of metal-on-metal clanging and the roar of the dragon echoed off the ivory palace—the once bright green grass and white clouds had become a disturbing abstract blanket of blood red and grey ash.

I dropped to the grass and laid my hand on Dai's shoulder. I'd never seen her cry. She was a warrior, an archangel, and one of the strongest angels I'd ever known. Yet, tears streamed down her face as her hand lay on her bloodied best friend.

"I'm sorry, I'm so sorry," Dai said as she rocked back and forth.

I spun with the sound of wings and cut down a small hoard of the black demon things that were flying around, causing chaos and mayhem.

"Come, you must move from this spot, Dai. It's not safe."

Her tear-stained cheeks turned up to me, and anger that burned bright in her violet eyes caused me to swallow hard.

"I'm going to kill them all." With a mighty thrust of her wings, she soared into the air with wild furye, and I took flight after her, fearful of what she would do.

"Stop this madness!" I heard someone yell and looked down to see Shilo as he grabbed a fallen sword and held it up, his arms shaking as he tried to fend off an attack from an angel guard. I no longer knew who was on whose side, but the angel's face was twisted into a mask of rage as he swung his weapon at Shilo. The sword Shilo had been holding sailed out of his hands harmlessly, and I quickly averted my original path to land in front of my old friend. I glared at the angel I once considered family.

"What are you doing?" I said, my sword up and at the ready.

"His family is part of the traitors!" The angel screamed and pointed to Shilo's son, who was indeed dressed in the same black leather as the rest of Lucifer's army. "He must die with the rest!"

"He doesn't even have a weapon, so you consider an old angel and not even a warrior a threat?" My question was lost on deaf ears as the angel lunged. Sighing with sadness, I smacked the sword away from the much less experienced guard. He looked down and began screaming hysterically as he realized that I'd taken his entire hand. The bloody stump spat blood like a fountain, and he turned to leap into the air and flee. I swung my sword again. The blade easily sliced through his wings, the large white feathers landed on the grass in a bloody heap, and the angel crashed to the grass.

"What have you done," the guard yelled as he gripped his bloody arm to his chest and tried to push himself backward on the ground. I stalked him, following his path, my boots squishing in the bright red grass.

A hand grabbed my arm before I could make a killing blow. "Do not kill him. You will be no better than the rest." I looked into Shilo's concerned face and nodded.

"Are you okay here? I must go see if I can stop this."

"Yes, go. I must do the same, and thank you, my boy."

With a flick of my wings, I joined the chaotic fray of battle once more and spotted Michael and Lucifer facing off at the far end of Heaven that had turned into the raging battlefield. I dodged blades and spears from both sides of the battle a I sliced my way through wings and armour no longer certain which side I was on.

Rising higher into the darkened sky, I soared toward the two archangels, my two brothers, and my family that was tearing this place asunder.

The distinct reverberation of their silver swords rang out like a bell toll sounding the beginning or maybe the end. With lightning-quick motion, they flew around one another, blade meeting blade, black versus white as their skin and eyes glowed with power. Fire rolled along the ground as the great dragon roared and stomped closer to the palace, its mighty breath consuming all in its path with blood-curdling screams and wails of pain.

The dragon reared, and as it did, it unwittingly knocked the two fighting above it away. Michael and Lucifer tumbled toward the ground, landing hard. They rolled their wings and became saturated in bright red blood, making them look like bleeding marble. Michael recovered a split second before Lucifer did, and a wicked smirk spread across Lucifer's face as the sword lowered for the killing blow.

Neither had seen me moving in, and just as the blade would have taken Luci's head, my blade landed between Michael and his mark. My arms strained to hold Michael off and to keep him from doing something he'd regret.

Michael's eyes met mine, his glowing blue orbs locking with my own. "What have you done," he asked softly.

I watched the slow trickle of blood running down his cheek from a cut I knew would scar. The silver made in Heaven was a killing blow to all it touched, and an angel cut would never heal clean. The blemish would become a constant reminder that another angel had touched them with aggression.

"I stopped you from killing your brother. Look around you, Michael. Is this what you really want? For Heaven to be divided, and for your hand to lay waste to your brothers?"

"He brought this war upon us! Look at that thing. It is an abomination and has destroyed our gates. It has killed many and marches on Father's palace. How can you protect him?"

I looked down into Lucifer's face, who still had two blades touching the skin of his neck in a deadly V. He'd done an egregious thing, but all I could see was my family.

"I see my brother, as you are my brother. I cannot let you kill him any more than I could let him kill you, Michael."

Michael stepped back as a massive boom, a voice of their Father reaching the furthest corners of Heaven and maybe beyond, sounded. "Enough!"

All fell silent and stilled regardless of position. Even the dragon stopped to stare. And as they did, soft sobbing reached my ears. My eyes found Shilo holding his dead son in his arms as he rocked back and forth. A deep sadness filled me, a pain that I couldn't comprehend as I stared at the man's grieved expression.

My last image of Heaven was that of Callista standing with a group of other angels huddled near the badly damaged palace. Tears dripped from her beautiful eyes, but the look on her face was one of disgust. I looked down at my body dripping with blood and other things, and as I looked up, she turned away and disappeared into the crowd.

I awoke with a start, my body jerking back to the now. But my eyes immediately found another set of blue eyes staring down at me. Concern etched into Minetta's beautiful features.

"You were dreaming, are you okay," she asked and laid a soft kiss on my cheek. Tears pricked the back of my eyes, and I turned my head so she wouldn't see it.

"It was only a dream. I'll be fine."

"Maybe you will tell me what happened one day because dreams don't cause the pain I see in your eyes."

Turning my head, I pushed her dark hair out of her face before claiming her mouth. So sweet, she was always the same. Rolling us over, I sighed as I settled between her legs. "Right now, I don't want to remember."

Wrapping her legs around my waist, she kissed me hard and nipped at my lower lip. "Then, let's see if we can make you forget," she whispered.

I'd never felt more at peace. Not even the grander and warmth of Heaven's touch could compare to her.

FORTY-THREE

MINETTA slept most of the plane ride home, and to say she was sore would've been the understatement of the century. When the man said he could stay hard, he hadn't been joking or bragging. At least not falsely bragging anyway. She ached in places she didn't know was possible, yet all she could think about was climbing on his lap in the jet for more of that delicious pain. She couldn't stop the silly glowing smile as she reflected on the last couple of days. Had she really taken off on a romantic weekend getaway with a fallen angel? The idea seemed preposterous and felt oddly right, like it was fated to happen. She'd felt a calm flow over her and seep into her soul as they'd made love and for the first time, she felt like she was exactly where she was supposed to be.

"I think we should go to Spain next weekend or maybe Ireland? Do you prefer tropical? I know a great location to do some scuba diving," Riker said, holding up his tablet to show her a stunning island with crystal blue waters. He flicked up, and the image changed as he went through the list of different locations. "Or if none of those interest you, then how about an Orient cruise? I have my own yacht, so we can leave whenever and just live on the boat and see the world."

She gripped his forearm to stop his excited rambling. "Riker, please stop for a moment." His smile faded as he looked at her face. "You're doing it again."

"Doing what?"

"Trying to buy our happiness, or my feelings maybe. I don't know, but I don't need or want a fancy trip every week. I don't want you buying me anything, really."

He ran his hand over his face. "Then what do you want, what would make you happy?"

"Do I not look happy?"

"Yes, but we were just away on vacation."

"So, you think that I need a vacation every weekend to make me happy? Is that how shallow you think I am?"

His mouth opened and then closed, no sound coming out. "I don't think there is anything wrong with wanting to spend money on you."

"That's fine, but doing this 'going overboard' thing is overwhelming. It's like you think if I'm not being lavished on, then I'm going to lose interest in you. Riker, I'm happy because of you, not because of what you can purchase. I'm a simple soul to my core, and that doesn't mean we can't see the world, just not all in a month. If you want to spend the money, then do it to help others. You don't need to impress me."

He stood and walked away before turning and marching back. "I have worked very hard for what I have, and there is nothing wrong with me wanting to spend some on you. Why do you make me feel bad every time I open my mouth?"

"It's not the spending the money that bothers me. It's why you want to do it?"

"You're not making sense." He stormed off to the bathroom, the little occupied light glowing. She sighed and slumped down into her seat. Why couldn't he see that she would want him even if he was penniless and had nothing but himself to offer? It was like she was speaking a language that he couldn't comprehend.

When he returned, he sat across from her and didn't speak. In fact, he didn't look at her at all. As the captain's voice came on over the cabin speaker, she stared out the window, "Please buckle up for landing."

As soon as the wheels touched down, she turned off the flight mode on her phone to find it full of messages from Penny.

Pressing the voicemail button, she listened to the first message. "Minny, it's me, Penny. Call me back, there is something wrong with Toby, and I don't know what to do." Her heart sped up with the message. She quickly pressed end, not bothering with the rest, and dialed Penny.

"Minny! Why did it take you so long to call me back? I'm freaking out here."

"We were in the air and just landed. What's wrong with Toby," she asked as she grabbed her stuff and headed for the still closed plane door.

"I don't know. He just started throwing up and wouldn't stop. He wouldn't eat or drink anything and hasn't had a bowel movement for an entire day."

Her heart pounded hard in her chest, but as Riker placed his hand on her, she took comfort in his steadiness. "Where are you now?"

"At some emergency vet. I called the number you gave me, but they sent me here. The vet took him back to examine him, but I haven't heard anything yet."

"Okay, text me the address, I'm on my way." She hung up the phone, her hands shaking as her adrenaline hit her system. "I don't want to lose him," she said softly.

"You won't. He's going to be fine," Riker said calmly as his hand rested on her back. She sucked in a steadying breath and wanted to yell for them to move faster and get the plane door open. A ding sounded and she looked at the address Penny sent her. A knock sounded, and Riker leaned forward. With a click and hiss, he pushed the door open. She rushed down the stairs and then remembered that her only ride was the man behind her.

"I know it's out of the way, but could you drop me off at the vet's instead of at my home?"

"Of course, come on."

She'd never been more thankful for his crazy driving and heavy foot as they tore out of the private airfield onto the highway. She gave him directions, and it took half the time it normally would for them to pull into the parking lot. She bolted from the car before it had completely come to a stop.

"Thanks for the amazing trip Riker. Um, I..." she paused. "I'll call you." She closed the door and ran for the front door of the vet's office. The scent of dog, cat, and cleaner invaded her nose as she burst inside. Penny stood from her seat, and the two of them embraced, hugging one another tight.

"What is it? What's wrong with him," Minny asked as the door behind her opened again. Riker walked in, surprising her that he'd stayed.

"He's in surgery. He has some sort of bowel blockage. I told them to do the surgery. I'm so sorry. This is all my fault. Maybe I fed him too much, or maybe I should've made sure he went to the bathroom." Penny blubbered, tears steadily running from her eyes. Minetta rummaged around in her purse and pulled out tissues to wipe away the red tears before she scared the people working there.

"It's not your fault. Come on, let's go sit down," she said, handing the package of tissue to Penny.

Riker was a silent shadow as he followed her, but she couldn't deny that it helped to have him here. Just his closeness was enough to make her feel stronger. He sat down beside her and didn't say anything. He laid his hand on her leg, and she quickly laced their fingers together.

They waited in silence for the vet to emerge from the back. Time had never ticked by so slowly before. She held her head in her hands, aware that Riker was rubbing circles on her back. One of the large double doors opened to the back area, and she stood fast. Rushing toward the vet, she wished she hadn't as she stumbled on her feet. Only Riker's hands held her upright.

"Please tell me Toby's alright," she said softly. "I'm his owner."

The vet removed the surgical cap as he stepped forward. Her heart pounded hard in her ears, the pulse thumping wildly. She wanted to shake the man and order him to speak.

"He's in recovery, but he's not out of the woods. He had a perforated bowel," the vet said. Her knees shook, and Riker wrapped his arm around her waist.

"But, he's going to live?"

"The next few days are crucial. He was in a state of sepsis when he was brought in, and he is not a young dog anymore for his size, so the surgery has taken a toll, but I am hopeful that he will if he makes it through the night."

"Can I see him?"

"He is on strong medications so that he will sleep, and our visiting hours are almost up. I will call you if there is any change, and you can come back tomorrow to visit."

"No, I'm not leaving him here alone. He needs to know that I'm here."

"I'm sorry, but...."

"There are no buts. If she wants to stay, you will let her stay as long as she wants. I'll donate a hundred thousand to this place to let her be with her dog, but let me be clear, we are not leaving." Tears filled her eyes as she stared up at Riker's stern expression. He stared down at the vet, his expression that of stone.

The vet swallowed hard. "That is very generous of you for night visitation. Alright, I cannot say no to that offer. The money will help a lot of animals in need. Follow me."

"I'll call you, and thank you," she said to Penny, giving her a quick hug, and then followed the vet into the back of the clinic.

She ran across the room as soon as she spotted her sweet boy lying on the mat on the floor. He had a tube going into this shaved leg, his eyes were closed, and his breathing was slow. The bright white bandage wrapped around his body had the tears pricking her eyes once more. She buried her face in the fur around his neck.

"I'm here, Toby, I'm here," she whispered into his ear. "You fight, Mister. I don't want to lose you too." She stroked the soft fur on his head and rubbed his ears just the way he liked. She grabbed a towel and folded it up to put under her head as she laid down and got comfortable. She immediately resumed her gentle attentions.

Riker stood for a long time like a guard and stared at her before finally sitting cross-legged on the floor. It seemed strange to see the imposing man, a prince of Hell, sitting on the floor like a child in his expensive suit.

"You don't have to stay if you don't want to," she said, her eyes finding his.

"There is nowhere else I want to be."

She reached out and squeezed his hand. "Thank you. It means a lot that you're here." She bit her lip as a tear dripped off her cheek.

· · ·

"What's going on?" She asked her dad. He smiled but didn't answer as he led her across the farmyard.

"It's a surprise, Minny."

She crossed her arms and stopped walking. "Dad, I'm not in the mood for a surprise. You should be resting."

"Minny, look at me." Her dad smiled and laid his hands on her shoulders. "You can't stop living just because life throws you a pitch you don't like."

"Dad, stop with the baseball metaphors, please. This is serious, you're sick, and you need to keep up your strength."

He chuckled, which annoyed her further. "I'm feeling good. I'm having a great day, and I need to take advantage of all the good days I have left. Now come on, don't be a poopy head."

"A poopy head? Really Dad." She dropped her arms and rolled her eyes but followed her Dad into the barn.

She heard the whimpering noise before her Dad opened the stall door. As soon as the wood swung out of the way, a chubby little puppy bounded out at her. She dropped to her knees as the bundle of wiggly cuteness ran to her, his pink tongue lolling out the side of his mouth.

"Dad! He is so cute! Whose puppy is he?"

"Who do you think, Minny?" Her Dad laughed as she picked up the pup to be assaulted by wet kisses.

"He's mine," she asked excitedly. The first real smile she'd had in weeks spreading across her face.

"Yes, Sweetheart, he is yours. I think the name Shortstop would work well," he laughed as she rolled her eyes at him.

"Thanks, Dad! Mom is going to hate him." The two of them laughed as they pictured the horrified look on her mother's face about having a dog in the house. "How about Toby? For Toby Harrah?"

"You want to name him after my favorite baseball player?" Her Dad *squatted down and rubbed the head of the pup. The extra dark hair around his big brown eyes made it look like he was wearing a mask.*

"Yeah." She lifted her shoulder, not able to meet her Dad's eyes. Knowing he was going to die and to look him in the face while she said it was too much. She wiped away the tears in the pup's fur as he licked her cheek.

"I love you, Minny. Always remember that."

"I know, Dad. I love you too."

S he jerked awake and realized she'd fallen asleep. Toby was moving, his large body violently jerking. "Help! Help," she screamed, and Riker jumped up from where he was slumped over, sleeping. He bolted for the door and began yelling for the vet.

Staff came running in and ordered her out of the way. Riker wrapped his arms around her and pulled her body into his as she watched them work on her Toby.

"Please save him," she begged as she pulled against Riker's hold to get back to her boy. Riker picked her up to take her out to the waiting room. "Put me down. I have to go to him. He has to know I'm here. I can't lose him. I just can't."

"He knows you're here." He held her tight as she pushed against his chest, trying to get away. His strength was too much, and she stopped fighting and buried her head in his shirt as the tears consumed her.

She heard the door open, and Riker let her go to turn and face the vet.

"No." She held up her hand as if that would stop the pain that was going to rip her heart out. "No, don't you say it." Grief wracked her body as the vet simply looked at the floor.

"I'm sorry, but the surgery was just too much for his body."

Her knees gave out as she collapsed onto the floor, but Riker scooped her up into his arms as the pain lanced her heart. Her best friend and the last piece of her dad were gone. She hadn't even been here when he needed her the most. She could hear Riker and the vet talking but had no idea what was being said as she sobbed and clung to Riker.

It felt like her dad had died all over again. It felt like her heart was being ripped out of her chest.

"I need to say goodbye," she suddenly said, interrupting the men. "I need to say goodbye," she said again.

"Okay." Riker kissed her forehead and sat her down on her feet. Gripping her hand, she sucked up her pain to put Toby first.

Her lower lip trembled, tears clouding her eyes as she dropped to her knees beside her dog. "I love you. I love you so much. Thank you for being the best friend anyone could ask for. You saved me so many times. I only wish I could've done the same for you now."

She leaned over and buried her face in the soft fur as she kissed him for the last time.

CHAPTER

FORTY-FOUR

R IKER

I drove Minny home, and the look on her face broke my heart. I wanted to wipe the pain away, comfort her, but she barely responded to me when I spoke to her. I had no idea what to do. I wanted her to come to my place, but she wouldn't hear of it and insisted that she needed to be in her own space. Her eyes were red and swollen, and the tears hadn't stopped once since Toby crossed over.

I couldn't wrap my head around her connection to her dog when all I saw was a dog that could be replaced with another. I'd never had this kind of closeness or connection with anyone, not even Callista. What we now shared was the only experience I could draw on to understand her grief. If I lost her, I realized I would be like this. I would be worse. I may not even survive. I gripped the steering wheel tighter and pushed the thought aside.

It was clear that Toby had meant so much more to her than simply being a pet, and I wanted to understand, but the only thing she said

405

was she lost her dad before she broke down into uncontrollable crying again.

I pulled into her driveway and shut the car off, but she didn't move. "Do you want me to come in with you?"

She gave a noncommittal shrug, but I took that as a yes. Opening her door, she slowly looked up at me, and I wished that I had the power to take away pain for the first time. I'd have saved the animal if I could, but saving souls was not my specialty. Breaking them, taking them, and warping them was what I could do, but saving....

I didn't bother to ask and bent over and picked her up out of the car as if she were a child. Giving the door a nudge with my hip, it closed as she wrapped her arms around me and buried her head into the crook of my neck.

Penny met me at the door, and she looked like she'd been crying just as hard. Her red-rimmed eyes met mine, and then she fell on her friend before I could step back out of the way.

"Follow me," Penny said and turned to walk further into the small home. She jogged up the stairs ahead of me, and although I already knew which room was Minny's, I followed her as if I didn't. Penny pulled the comforter down on the bed, and I gently laid my little bird down. She rolled onto her side and curled up in a ball.

"Do you want me to stay?" I whispered in her ear.

She shook her head no as a fresh wave of tears filled her eyes. "I just need to be alone right now."

"Okay." I gave her temple a kiss, my lips lingering as I did something I'd been holding off on doing, and started to dig through her memories. I wanted to see why Toby meant so much to her.

"What are you doing?" Penny hissed and pulled on my arm, breaking the connection I was trying to establish.

I glared at the young fallen angel turned Erinyes, and she took a step back, but she was right. I needed to stop. I'd managed to be good about not invading her private thoughts so far, and to cross that line would most certainly upset her. The thing was, Minetta shut me out. It was like a door had been slammed in my face, and the panic it was causing in my chest was new, and I didn't like it at all.

"I'll come by tomorrow," I said to Minny, and she nodded but didn't move from her fetal position.

Grabbing Penny's arm, I dragged her out the bedroom door and closed it softly. I didn't stop dragging her along until we were in the tiny living room. I gave the girl a shove, and she fell on her ass in the big chair.

"Don't you ever question me again, Erinyes. I will pluck your wings one feather at a time." She swallowed hard, but her chin tilted up in defiance.

"Then so be it, but I was looking out for my friend, and I'd do it again, from you or anyone."

Crossing my arms, I studied the demon girl, my power reaching out and feeling her soul. Her caring was not bravado. She really did care for my Minny. "And is looking out for your friend what you were doing when you told her that I'm a fallen archangel?"

Penny gasped, her hands covering her mouth. "You know that she knows?"

"Of course, I do. I didn't have much choice to admit it when my wings made an unexpected appearance, but that's beside the point. She was not scared like I'd expected her to be." I squinted at the girl as she nibbled at her bottom lip. "What is it? Why do you look so concerned?"

She stood and went to the bay window that looked out over the street. "It's dangerous for the two of you to be together, Mammon."

"Call me Riker, and what do you mean dangerous?"

"Just what I said. There are many that don't like the idea of the two of you being together. They fear you're going to turn soft, stop being the embodiment of greed, and most of all, stop the apocalypse."

I crossed my arms over my chest, my forehead drawing down as I studied Penny's face. She was telling the truth, or at least the truth as she saw it. "You're talking about the prophecy? That's ludicrous. Everyone knows the prophecy is a wild card. The forks are constantly shifting, someone could have a bowel movement the wrong way, and they will shift. Why do you think no one takes them seriously?"

"Riker, there are those that believe you're an important key to this particular prophecy. A stabilizing link between yourself and the great war to come."

"Why?"

"Think about it. Would you really want to see the Earth destroyed and all the humans on it crushed if you were to fall in love with one?"

"First." I held up a finger. "Love is a powerful word, and no one is slinging it around," I said, but the voice in the back of my brain refuted my words. "Second, even if I was to fall in love with her and what you claim is true, the likelihood that the great war will happen between now and her life expectancy as a human is somewhere between zero and none. Not only that, but I am one archangel of seven that have fallen. What am I going to do on my own to stop Lucifer, other than nothing?"

"I'm just telling you what they believe. Demons on all plains are not happy about the two of you spending time together. Word is spreading that you are siding with humans over your own kind. Even here on Earth, I heard about the anger you showed over your newest exhibit."

"That was different. We are not supposed to take humans alive to Hell for our amusement. You know what kind of reign of terror that could cause. I was simply stopping it before it got any more out of hand. And I haven't sided with any human over my own kind because I never chose any of my kind to start with." I leaned against the wall giving a relaxed impression, but Penny didn't look convinced.

"Not even Skye?"

My brow furrowed. "Not even Skye. Her and Neven are friends and yet we've been intimate, but not emotionally, not like what you're insinuating."

"The point is Minny is my friend, and I want to keep her safe, and I thought if she knew who you were, she would stay away. Apparently, I was wrong. The girl is way too good and understanding for her own damn good."

Now, I agreed with Penny about that, and I tapped my chin as I thought. This was a problem for another night. My head hurt thinking about the stupidity of this conspiracy theory. How could one human create so much havoc if their existence meant nothing? Isn't that what we preached? That humans were nothing more than an annoying speck that Father created and rubbed in our faces.

I shook my head, annoyance boiling in my gut. No one was going to order me to stay away from my little bird. Not Luci, not Father or Michael, and least of all, this red-headed Erinyes and her mysterious band of demon rumors.

"I have somewhere to be, but I assume you're staying here?"

She placed her hands on her hips and cocked an eyebrow. "That's it? That's all you have to say on the subject?"

"Careful with your tone, Penny. Be thankful you're not in one of my torture cells for your disrespectful tongue...because you're Minny's friend, and she needs you."

Pushing off the wall, I took a step toward her, and she jumped from the chair to put it between us, like that would stop me if I wanted to kill her.

"Mark my words Penny—your rope is not as long as you imagine. Do not cross me, or you'll be dragged to Hell, and I'll toss you to my pets." Her eyes were wide, fear shining through. Next to Luci, I had the most terrifying demons at my beck and call that were loyal to only me.

"As I said, I have to go, but I'll be back tomorrow." Taking a moment, I looked around the space that Minetta called home. The place seemed practically unlivable, yet she did and did so happily. This is just another thing to add to my list of things I had issues understanding. That seemed to be happening far more than I would like recently.

Marching out the door, I grabbed my phone to call Shilo. Maybe he could shed some light on this prophecy nonsense. Pausing, I looked back at Penny. "Tell me something, why did that dog mean so much to Minny?"

Penny looked to the carpet and then wiped away tears on her cheeks. "Her dad gave him to her."

"So Minny and her father were so close, that a dog would mean that much?"

"Yes, they were very close, but he passed nine years ago, not long after he gave her Toby. I think he knew she was going to need something to focus on after he was gone." Penny shrugged. "I wasn't there, but that's what I know from what Minny told me."

"I have one more question, Erinyes."

"Can you please just call me Penny? I hate what I ended up becoming." The red strands around her face floated, announcing without words what she was. He could relate to the girl, and he would agree to her request only because she'd proven to be helpful.

"Alright, Penny, I have one more question. How did her father die?"

"Brain tumor, cancer. Why?"

"That is none of your concern."

I marched out of the house and hit dial on Shilo's name. I was going to need the man's help for a couple of things.

CHAPTER
FORTY-FIVE

Minetta stared at the ceiling, her hand on the space where Toby would have occupied. Guilt ravaged her mind. She wasn't here when he needed her. It was the only thought that kept circling her brain.

She sniffed and wiped away the latest bout of tears, not sure she was going to get over this blow. It seemed insurmountable. A soft knock had her eyes going to the door, and Riker poked his head in.

"Hey, my little bird, how are you today," he asked softly and squatted down in front of her. His voice was so kind and worried that it brought on another wave of tears.

"I'm sorry I'm such a mess."

He cupped her cheek, wiping away the tears with his thumb. "Don't be sorry. You need to grieve, but it's been three days, and you need to eat, but before that, a shower because you're getting ripe."

"I'm that bad?" She picked up her shirt and sniffed it, and then nodded. "Yup, that bad."

Before she could say she didn't care, he'd scooped her up and walked out into the hallway and down to the bathroom. He sat her on the counter and went about turning on the water and grabbing towels. Who was this man, really? Kind and thoughtful or arrogant and self-serving, he was like an unreadable map that kept moving.

"Lift your arms." Taking a deep breath, she did as he asked, and with skillful movements, she was completely naked. "Once you're clean, I have a surprise for you."

She fixed Riker with a stern glare. "I don't want a surprise."

"Trust me. This one is going to make you feel a bit better." He kissed her forehead and knew she was going to give in because there was no point arguing.

She paused as she stepped into the shower. "Are you not joining me?"

"I will join if you want me to," he said. His face was calm, but his body was rigid, including the tent in his pants. She bit her lip and nodded. He was exactly what she needed to wipe away the lingering pain for a short while.

She watched as Riker quickly undressed, and once more, she couldn't help admiring how sexy he was. He seemed so much larger in her small bathroom.

"I really do love it when you stare at me like that." Those amber eyes filled with so much mischief it had her smirking back.

She held out her hand to him as she stepped into the cramped space. "Come on, lover. It's your turn to help me forget."

"How long would you like me to help you forget? Maybe a month?" He asked, and she couldn't help looking down at the raging hard-on that was ready for action.

"Are you trying to kill me with pleasure?"

Riker laughed, the sound echoing off the tiles as he pulled her into his body. "I guess we can afford a few breaks for food and rest, but if I had my way, you'd never wear clothes again. And locking you away from the world where I can keep you safe and only for me doesn't sound bad either." A shiver ran down her spine as he nipped her neck, his lips tracing her collarbone and making her pulse race.

Riker grabbed her bottle of liquid soap and poured a large quantity into his hand. She closed her eyes, as his hands worked over her body. His touch was soft and her desire continued to grow as the soap was massaged into her skin. A soft gasp escaped her mouth as his fingers delicately slid between her legs. She spread her legs further for him, her body trembling as he carefully cleaned every inch of her flesh like he was worshiping her.

Her eyes fluttered open as he stopped. The sly smile on his face was so sexy not for the first time did she wonder why her?

Riker smoothed back her hair and softly kissed her lips until she felt like she couldn't put two words together in the same sentence. "Rinse off Little Bird."

Stepping under the spray the water ran over her skin, the heat of the water pinking her skin.

Riker smiled as she stepped toward him once more. "Tell me what you want, Little Bird?"

A wet heat that had nothing to do with the water beating down on them hit her core. "Be rough with me. I don't want soft or kind right now." She looked into his captivating stare, the weight of the heat forming already making her head swoon. "Use me, Riker."

A dark passion flared in the amber color of his eyes as his jaw tensed. "Get down on your knees," he ordered.

His voice was commanding and made her shake with anticipation as she lowered herself to the tub floor. He held out his cock to her, and she licked her lips, staring at the tip. "I'm going to fuck your mouth, little bird. Now open up."

She swallowed hard and yelped a little as he twisted his hand in her hair. The pain was sharp, but it was exactly what she craved. She wrapped her fingers around the thick length, and Riker jerked back on her hair hard. "Did I say you could use your hands?"

"No," she whispered.

"No, what?" he growled, and she'd never been more terrified and turned on in her life. She didn't know what to say and simply stared up at him. "Give me a name. Who am I to you? Who do you want me to be?"

She licked her lips as she ran through all the naughty possibilities and remembered all those she'd met, calling him Master. It had sounded perplexingly sexy when they said it. "No, Master," she said tentatively.

His eyes glowed a little brighter as his nose flared with a sudden intake of breath, and she wasn't sure if he was excited or angered by the name.

"Put your hands behind your back and keep them there. You don't move them again until I tell you to." She did as she was told, her eyes watering with the tight grip on her hair.

He roughly jerked her head back, so she was forced to look up at him. "Is this what you want, Minetta? Is this what you want from me?"

"Yes, Master, make me feel better." He lifted a brow at her, and that one small action alone made her squirm with building anticipation of what he had planned.

"Open your mouth. Do you have a strong gag reflex?"

She didn't think so, but she'd never tried taking one down her throat. "I don't know."

"Fine we will go slow...for now. Now open up." She swallowed hard as she opened her mouth, eyes fixated on the large cock in front of her face. He didn't move to put it in her mouth, but she didn't dare move either. Her instincts told her not to do any more than what he asked. "Good girl," he praised her. "Now put my cock in your mouth, and other than moans, you don't speak unless I ask you a question. Do you understand?"

"I understand, Master."

Raising up higher on her knees, she licked the tip and moaned at the taste. He didn't taste anything like she'd expected. He was sweet to her senses, and her tongue eagerly lapped off the clear liquid before sliding her mouth down the long shaft. She only made it halfway when he hit the back of her throat. She retreated and took a breath before sucking hard until her cheeks hollowed out and taking him deep into her mouth again. Once more, he hit the back of her mouth, and this time she swallowed and tried to relax, but he only got partway past when the panic hit, and she pulled back.

He groaned loudly. "Good, my little bird, try again."

She looked up at him, and the eagerness in her eyes made her determined to do this. She swirled her tongue around his shaft and loved how it flexed in her mouth as if begging her for more.

She took a deep breath just as he hit the back of her throat, but she pushed past the opening into her throat, and this time she didn't stop and pushed through the awkward pain until her nose met his abdomen. "Fuck, little bird, you have a hot mouth."

Minetta pulled back slowly, her eyes watering as she took him down easier this time.

"Ready," he asked, and she had no idea if she was but nodded as she looked up at him. He didn't give her any more warning as he pulled back and slammed home into her mouth. Her nose hit his body, and fresh tears sprang to her eyes. He tested her again, and her eyes rolled up to his as her nose bumped into him once more.

"Fuck, little bird, you're hot."

Pride and confidence swelled in her chest as he praised her. She held perfectly still as he picked up the pace, the sound of slurping and soft groans mixed with the running water. His hand tightened in her hair every time his hips pulled back and pushed her forward, lancing her throat once more. The initial nervousness was wiped away as her own desire soared and overrode everything else.

She wanted him to come. She wanted to drink him down. "Fuck yes," he mumbled, his pace picking up and making it harder to breathe.

She forced down the thread of rising panic, her nose flaring to take in as much air as she could. His movements became jerky, the rhythm she'd found to be able to breathe disappeared. Fortunately, she didn't have to wait long to get her wish as he pulled back, so just the tip was in her mouth.

"Suck hard," he ordered, his voice rolling over his skin and making her shudder.

She sucked with all she had, her cheeks hollowing out with the force. "Swallow it all," he said a second before he came in her mouth. Even knowing he was going to come hadn't prepared her for the force of the first shot. It slipped down her throat before she had time to contemplate swallowing, and when she didn't choke, figured it went the right way. Sucking harder as he continued to release, she gripped his hips hard and pushed him a little further into her mouth. Her throat feverishly worked on drinking him all down and marveled again at how good he tasted. Riker was genuinely sweet with a touch of tang like fresh oranges. She moaned around his dick as his body settled.

"Stand up." Her legs were stiff as she stood, but she'd endure the pain anytime to do that again. Her nerves were tingling as she stood and stared into the softly glowing eyes that made her want to melt. Grabbing her waist, he turned them around in the tight space, so she was facing the back of the tub. "Bend over," he whispered into the side of her neck.

She wasn't sure what to expect, but her knees buckled as his tongue found her sensitive folds. A hard crack sounded, and she yelped with shock as his hand came into contact with her ass. "Keep your legs straight, or you get another one."

She panted hard. Her arms shook as the pleasure raced through her body—she almost broke the rule and cried out as his fingers pressed into her heat while his mouth latched onto her clit.

He stopped and looked up at her and she wanted to scream never to stop. "You like that, my little bird?"

"Yes Master," she mumbled, barely able to form the words. His fingers worked feverishly, pressing on all the right places, and she could feel her orgasm building. She involuntarily jerked and pushed back into Riker as the climax started to ascend through her body. Minetta whimpered as he stopped. His mouth and fingers slipped from her body, leaving her feeling empty—she shamelessly waved her ass at him in a silent beg to continue.

"Don't you dare touch yourself, or you will be punished." She nodded, but the pressure was painful as her body throbbed for release. "Stand up straight."

"Hang onto the rod." She cheekily raised an eyebrow at him. Riker smirked, a small chuckle leaving his mouth, knowing exactly what she was thinking. "That one." He pointed up, and she wiggled her ass at him, daring him to smack her again as she maneuvered herself to stand with her back to him and grip the shower curtain with both hands.

She was having way more fun than she should be teasing a demon.

Her body shivered with anticipation as his hand hovered over her body, close enough that she could feel the heat from his skin, yet he didn't touch her. Minetta arched her back as the nervous energy coursed through her body and hummed along her skin.

Riker placed his hand on her hip, and she softly moaned with the simple contact. As he slid his hand around to her stomach, her breathing picked up a little more. He was slow and meticulous with every inch as his fingers skimmed over her sensitive skin until he reached the delicate nub that was begging to be touched. He rubbed her swollen clit for a few seconds, and it took everything in her not to make a sound. He knew exactly what he was doing to her as his other arm wrapped around her body to tweak her nipple.

The heat from his skin pressed into her body, and she was so tempted to rub against the cock she could feel pressing into the cheeks of her ass. Her chest rose and fell quickly as she fought to remain compliant. He continued to roll the nipple with his fingers and once more rubbed her clit. She looked back at him, and a wicked smile played across his lips.

Riker did it all over again for the third time, but this time added a soft smack to her mound. She groaned with the slight sting that didn't hurt but made her want to cry out for more. A moan vibrated in her throat as she laid her head back on his shoulder. By the fourth strike, she cried out in pleasure, and she could feel him smirking even with her eyes closed.

She was a mess emotionally. She couldn't help it, but no matter what he did to her, only heightened her arousal. And just as she was nearing that beautiful peak of her orgasm, he let go of her body altogether, his hands falling away, driving her insane. She wanted to scream in anticipation, she had to have the release soon, or her body was going to combust with this need.

"Do you want me to fuck you, Little Bird?" Riker's tongue made a wet line up the side of her neck, and he nipped her ear. "I can't hear you."

"Y...yes, Master."

"Are you sure?"

"Yes, Master," she practically yelled, and she could feel his lips smile against her skin.

"Then call me by my real name when I fuck you. I'm not your

Master." She looked over her shoulder at him, and her heart swelled with the simple statement that said so much about how he saw her.

"Yes, Riker." She grinned as his eyes flared with the same passion she was feeling.

"Say my name again."

"Yes, Riker!"

With a single movement, he thrust himself up into her and her breath caught in a gasp in her throat. "You feel so good," she cried out.

He pulled out and slammed home again, and her strung-out body was so taut that she crested the peak and tumbled down the other side of her orgasm on his third thrust. Her arms shook as she panted out his name again. With every thrust, another small climax burst inside of her until her legs couldn't hold her up any longer—it was Riker's hands alone keeping her on her feet. The water had cooled and was beating down on her heated skin, creating a sensual mix of hot and cold along her skin.

"Fuck Minny!" Riker growled out.

The sound had a direct line to her heated core, and she screamed as she came harder than she ever dreamt possible. As her walls clenched down around Riker, he came a moment before she yanked a little too hard on the flimsy shower curtain, and they tumbled out onto the floor with a resounding crash. Riker had somehow maneuvered himself to take the brunt with a loud thump and thud with her sprawled on top of him.

"Is everything okay in there," Penny called out from the other side of the door.

Minetta pushed the shower curtain off them and stared into Riker's face as they burst out laughing at the same time.

"Yeah, we're fine," she called out to her friend, which only enhanced her laughter.

"Well, I can honestly say that has never happened before." Riker pulled her up so she was lying fully on his chest.

"I'm sure it hasn't." She kissed his chin and then wiggled up so she could capture his lips. "Thank you, I really needed this."

Riker's eyes were soft as they stared back at her, and her heart swelled with emotion as she stared into his amber depths. He wrapped his arms around her and held her tight. "Anything for you, Minny, not that fucking you senseless is really work."

She smacked his arm as he kissed the top of her head. "Come on, we better get in the shower and use what's left of the water before it turns ice cold. I still have that surprise for you."

As he helped her stand, she realized that she was falling for this man, demon...archangel. Whatever and whoever he was, she was falling hard, and that prospect terrified her.

CHAPTER
FORTY-SIX

RIKER

I couldn't remember the last time I was this nervous about something. My legs and hands were jittery as I drove Minny to the surprise I'd arranged. She seemed better after the shower, but she'd withdrawn in on herself once more as time passed. I glanced over at her and could just make out her reflection in the glass, her face was placid, but her eyes made my heart hurt. There was so much sadness staring back at me. It was the same look of despair and loss that Shilo had given me when we'd been tossed out of Heaven. The old angel had lost more than I had that day. Not only had his son died, but he'd been ripped away from his wife and daughters, banished from ever seeing them again.

I glanced over at Minny again, and I had to wonder how he got up and worked for me every day. My anger burned brighter for him than it had for myself.

I turned the final corner to our destination, and Minny's brow furrowed as she stared at the hospital entrance.

"Riker, why are we at the hospital?"

I wiped my hand on my pants, the strange ball of nerves worsening until I would have sworn that Luci's stupid little angels were flitting around in my gut. "This is where your surprise is."

"My surprise is in a hospital. Why am I suddenly worried?" The suspicious look on her face made me laugh.

"I swear, it's nothing horrifying. Do you think demons only do terrible things?" I teased as I reached over and gave her knee a squeeze. I wouldn't tell her that the percentage was skewed toward a yes as she smiled back.

"I told you I don't see you that way."

"Not many would agree with you, but this is not about me." I wheeled into one of the only spots left and shut the car off. Why did they never have enough parking in the one place it was sure always to be full? "Are you ready?"

"I guess. It's hard to be ready for something when I don't know what I'm to be prepared for." She looked up at the bright blue letters and red cross. "But I am intrigued."

Smiling, I jumped out of the car and made my way around to help her out of the low vehicle. She looked so pretty in her summer dress, the blue flower pattern a perfect match to her eyes. I held out my hand and walked her toward the front doors. The glass double doors opened as soon as we were close enough, and the sudden burst of cool air had Minny shivering beside me.

We stepped into the lobby, and as with all hospitals, the place was humming with activity. There was certainly no shortage of sick, mean, and stupid humans. I spotted the inconspicuous sign I was looking for and wandered along the corridor, her hand in mine. Being around Minny was like experiencing Earth and the people around me in a whole new way. She'd randomly stop and talk to people she didn't know and would smile and wave at others. An elderly lady stood leaning up against the wall in obvious distress, and no one noticed but my Minny.

She let go of my hand and helped the older woman sit in a wheelchair. I stood there in shock as Minny pushed her over to the nurses' desk and told them off in her soft, direct manner. I wouldn't even have noticed that there were people here unless they got in my way or had something I wanted. But she had a gentleness that reminded me of someone I used to be, someone who burned to ash as a meteor would when I fell from home. I smiled as she bent down, picked up a teddy bear, and jogged after the mother and little girl, who had dropped it. The mother and child smiled brightly when she handed the stuffed bear back.

"Sorry about that," she said, her voice a little breathless. I couldn't stop staring at her, a disease that was worsening the more time we spent together. "Is everything okay? Do I have something on me?"

I laughed as she looked down and smoothed her dress. Cupping her delicate cheeks in my hands, I laid a chaste kiss on the lips I'd never grow tired of. "I watch you, and I see the world through a whole new lens. One that sees everything with a rosy view."

"Isn't that usually a bad thing?"

"In your case, it is endearing and as beautiful as you are." Her cheeks flushed instantly, warming beneath my hands. "Come, we are almost there."

The long corridor opened up into a much smaller lobby. This one held a number of doctors, nurses, and other hospital staff as they stood around drinking sparkling cider and nibbling on the gourmet brunch I had delivered. Tables were decorated with flowers and balloons, and a massive drape hung from the ceiling covering the main event. A wooden podium was situated near the stairs, and I nodded to the head of the hospital.

"What's going on?" Minny leaned in and whispered. "Is someone special speaking?"

"Wait and see." I offered her a small smile, and she didn't question me further, but the raised eyebrow she gave me said plenty. The fluttering in my stomach turned up another notch, making me wish I'd ordered something stronger than the fake champagne.

"Ladies and Gentlemen, now that our guest of honor has arrived, I'd like to get started." The man who I only knew as Roberts was the one who had spoken, and the room quieted down, all eyes turning toward the podium. "This hospital has always strived to provide the best care to its patients—care that often, even with our best efforts, ends up falling short. The ever-increasing costs that many cannot afford and the lack of equipment that has been too expensive to replace have caused far too many to go without the critical treatment that they so desperately need. It is only through the donations of very generous individuals and companies that have allowed us to keep our doors open. Every year it has become more difficult to meet our goals, but this year we had a new sponsor step forward out of the shadows and become not just a donor, but a major contributor to this hospital."

Roberts stopped and smiled as people clapped with the news.

"Yes, please do clap," Roberts said and clapped himself. I smirked as Minny began clapping as well. "Not only has this new sponsor offered to build a new cancer wing for this hospital complete with all the newest and cutting-edge equipment that will undoubtedly save countless lives." Roberts stopped and made sure the clapping had died down before continuing. "This sponsor has also offered enough annual funding to hire fifteen new doctors, a hundred new nurses, and...." He paused again as a gasp rose from the crowd. "This generous person has also offered to fund five thousand surgeries for those that otherwise couldn't receive treatment." Roberts clapped, and everyone paused and started looking around to find the source of this donation.

Minny, on the other hand, was smiling up at me. I gave her a wink and turned my attention back to Roberts. The best was yet to come.

"Without any further ado, we are honored to name the new cancer wing in honor of this charitable person." Roberts walked over to the tie that released the drape, and I couldn't help but stare at Minny. Her face went from a smile to one of shock, and then she quickly covered her mouth as tears welled in her blue eyes.

"Minetta Johnson, it is with great honor that we name the new cancer wing and all those lives that will be saved in the memory of Douglas Johnson. Your father was a cancer fighter that lost his battle, but his legacy and memory will forever live on with your unbelievable kindness. Thank you, from all of us to you."

Claps erupted, and people turned in our direction as Roberts pointed to Minny beside me. I slowly stepped away, clapping and smiling wide at the woman that had a heart made of the pure gold I'd coveted for so long. She looked to me and then back up at the golden sign proudly announcing Douglas Johnson Cancer Wing. People swarmed in to shake her hand and offer their personal thanks. For as long as I had lived and watched this world change, I knew I would never forget the happy smile on her face and the appreciative look in her eyes.

I gave her space to talk to those that approached her before I wandered over and smiled at the handsome surgeon that was spending a little more time than necessary with my Minny." Excuse me, but I must cut in." I smiled at the man, but my eyes clearly shouted, 'back off, she's mine.'

Taking the hint, he shook Minny's hand, and we were blissfully left alone. "Are you really okay with this? I know you're not a fan of me spending great gobs of money on you," I asked, tucking a piece of her hair behind her ear.

"Riker...I...I have no words to tell you what this means to me. You gave me this, but really you gave something far greater than either of us. Do you even comprehend how many lives you will change with this?" She pointed to the sign. "You're an amazing man Riker. I don't care what you think of yourself, or who you were, or even how you ended up here on Earth. What I see, what I know is that the man before me is a man that has a beautiful soul. Tarnished maybe, but beautiful nonetheless." A pooling of warmth spread from my stomach to fill me up with a strange giddy sensation. I hadn't smiled this wide in so long, and it was all her fault. "Kiss me," she whispered.

"Gladly." Placing her hand over my heart so she could feel it pound, I lowered my lips to hers. As always, they were warm and soft and tasted divine. I didn't give a shit if the entire hospital saw us, and I deepened the kiss as if no one could see. Breaking the kiss before I pulled her to the floor, I stared at her swollen lips then into her glazed eyes. I opened my mouth, trying to say the words, but nothing would come out. How could three little words be so difficult to speak?

Minny placed a finger over my lips and smiled. "I know," she said. Rising on her tiptoes, she kissed my cheek. "You're amazing, Riker. Never forget it."

CHAPTER

FORTY-SEVEN

MINETTA hadn't been this happy since before her dad passed away, and her entire world shifted. Even with the sadness of losing Toby, what Riker had done would ensure the kindness and warmth of her father's heart would live on forever. In essence, they would both live on since Riker was also increasing the funding to the therapy dog program in honor of Toby.

She hadn't even known what to say to him. It was way over the top, which was totally him, and yet it was done in a way that would help others. She didn't need expensive things, but this...now this she could accept. She glanced up at him as they walked and realized that he'd always be greed, yet he was different. She hadn't believed Michael, but what he'd done today was proof that he could be a better version of the sin, a better version of himself. And suddenly, she wanted to be here for every second of it.

They stepped outside, and the night was perfect. The heat of the

433

day was gone leaving the warmth, but the gentle breeze in the aftermath of the humidity left a freshness behind.

"Wait here, I'll go get the car," Riker gave her lips a quick peck, and he began weaving his way through the large, busy parking area.

Minetta took a deep breath, the joy of the day filling her. She was sure she was glowing because she was that happy.

A sound reached her ears, and she looked to her left, not seeing anything, but she was sure that she'd heard crying. When she didn't see anything, she turned her attention back to Riker and could no longer see him among the throngs of endless cars. The sound reached her again, and her head snapped in the direction of the crying. This time she did see movement. Off to the side of the building, there was a small, huddled figure in the shadowed area.

It looked like a small girl, long hair hanging around her face. She couldn't make out all the features, but the child was certainly in distress.

"Hey there, are you okay," she asked and stepped toward the child. "Do you have parents around here?" She looked around and didn't see anyone that seemed to be missing a child. In fact, there were only a couple of people, and neither was close. No one was running out the door looking for a missing child. Did she wander over here all on her own?

Minetta took another step toward the child, and she sniffed and wiped her face with the back of her hand. "Can you speak?"

The dark-haired child looked up with wide eyes and darted away. Not giving it a second thought, she took after the child. She was way too young to be out here all alone.

"Hey, stop, I won't hurt you," Minetta called out as she jogged around the corner of the hospital into the darkened alley. "I promise I won't hurt you. Did you need the hospital? Is that why you're here?" She could just make out the small shape crouched by the dumpster. She took a few small tentative steps toward the terrified child. When the little girl didn't bolt, she took a few more steps.

"My name is Minetta, but everyone calls me Minny. What's your name?" She mimicked the position and crouched down, keeping some distance not to scare the frightened girl.

"Rabbith," the voice hissed. Minetta froze—the voice was way too deep to be that of a little girl. A coolness brushed over her skin as she shivered, and the hair stood up on her arms. The small shape of the child began to morph and twist, and shock kept her paralyzed in place. Her eyes were glued where the small child had once been.

Standing, she took a step back as the dark smoke-like substance swirled and grew taller. She took a few more steps back, and her heart hammered in her chest as the thing that was clearly not a child continued to reform. The bones snapped and made a crunching noise that churned her stomach. She blinked a number of times as she tried to make out what the thing was as it took on a new shape.

She swallowed the bile in the back of her throat as the smell of sulfur hit her in the face. She took a step back and then another. Her eyes transfixed on the shadowy yet hideous creature. The blood-red eyes flashed and then glowed in the dark as the creature reached its full height and stared down at her. It stretched and rolled its large shoulders.

"Time to die," it hissed, those red eyes fixed on her.

Minetta spun on her heel and managed to get a few sprinting strides in when the darkness around her came alive like a living, breathing thing, the shadows peeled away from the walls and descended upon her. She looked up at the ceiling of dark, and the coolness turned to a bitter cold as it washed over her body.

A shadow wall sprouted out of the pavement and blocked her exit. She skidded to a halt, little pebbles of asphalt rolling in all directions. Losing her footing on the small marble-like objects, she landed hard on her ass and yelled out at the hard impact. She could no longer see the street or the hospital's parking lot. It was as if the night sky had consumed her.

She looked over her shoulder, and the creature's long tongue hung from the wide gaping mouth. It would've looked like it was smiling if it wasn't for the multiple rows of jagged teeth. The asphalt beneath her began to shift like a whirlpool, her hands sunk into the dark substance, and she screamed at the top of her lungs. She managed to get onto her knees and wished she wasn't wearing a dress. She kept stumbling and getting the material stuck under her feet as she tried to get up off the spinning ground that was threatening to suck her in.

She clawed at the pavement but kept falling to her side at the whirling sensation that was like a crazy floor in a carnival funhouse. Getting on all fours, she lunged forward, but her hands slipped out from under her when she landed, and she smacked her head off the ground.

"Riker," she screamed at the top of her lungs as hysteria clawed at her mind.

She sucked in a breath to scream again when a tendril of the black slinked around her throat, choking off all air to her lungs. She clawed at the shadowy arm, but her fingers slipped right through. Unable to get a grip and unable to breathe, cold terror seized her.

"You must die human," the creature hissed once more.

It jerked her to her feet by her neck until just her toes touched the ground. Minetta opened her mouth to try and draw in a breath, but pain exploded behind her eyes as her chest burned from the lack of oxygen. She was dying, she thought, as she struggled in the immensely strong grasp of the demon, black dots flickering in front of her eyes dimmed her vision.

All she could think of was Riker and what he would think when she was gone. She slumped in the demon's grasp, her limbs giving up the fight as a hot tear trailed down her cheek.

"Let her go." It was Riker. She'd know that deep voice anywhere. The rumble of his anger filled the space, but hope exploded in her chest.

"No, Mammon, she must die."

She managed to suck in a ragged breath as the demon changed position, but the hope was short-lived as the demon leaped into the air and did a nose dive for the swirling pavement. She had no doubt where it planned to take her. For just a moment, it was if she was staring through a window into another world. One where everything was dark with vibrant streaks of red and then a shot of light that could have passed as a small atomic bomb exploded in the alley.

She was instantly blind, and she yelped as she hit the ground hard, her knees and hands screaming in pain. The demon screeched an ear-splitting sound, and she covered her ears. Something heavy crashed near her, and instinct alone had her rolling away. She knew her eyes were open, but everything was just a bright white light.

"Leave this place, now," Riker's voice was so commanding.

"I cannot, Lord Mammon. She must come with me."

Something grabbed her ankle, and she screamed as she was jerked hard, her stomach scraping along the ground. Her fingers dug into the blacktop, but it felt like she was being dragged over the edge of a cliff. She reached out and searched for anything to hang onto but came up with nothing. Using all of her strength, she pushed up with her arms and pulled her legs toward her. It was like she was caught in a strange tug-o-war. The demon screeched loud again, and she was hit with something wet that she could only assume was blood but didn't want to know.

She cried out as the tendril that had let go of her neck was suddenly back and squeezing, blocking off her air supply once more.

A loud roar that was not the demon sounded right beside her, along with another flash of the blinding light and a thunderous boom. The stronghold it had on her ankles and neck slipped and gave her just enough room to take a breath and pull her legs away. Another deafening shriek turned into a wail and could only come from a creature in pain as the tendril around her neck let go. Rolling onto her ass, she pushed herself away from the noise with her hands and feet until her back slammed into the brick wall.

Minetta covered her head and closed her eyes, but it didn't stop the steady stream of tears that ran down her cheeks and dripped onto her chest. She was shaking and jumped as the terrifying noises lessened and finally disappeared, the sound of her panting the only sound she heard.

"Shhh, it's okay, I've got you." Riker wrapped his arms around her, and she wrapped her arms around his neck clung to him. She never wanted to let go. It seemed like the only time she was safe anymore was when he was with her. She could feel the softness of the immense wings on his back, and she stroked the butter-soft feathers, the action calming her fear. "Come on. I'm taking you to my place for the night. Hang on."

"Wha...Ahhhh," she yelled as Riker pushed off the ground, and in a powerful rush, she could feel them rising into the air.

She yelped as the woosh of the powerful wings propelled them forward. Slowly the white cleared from her eyes, and then wished she'd left her eyes closed.

"Oh shit," she squealed and gripped his neck tighter as they soared above the city. She wrapped her legs around his waist and felt like a little spider monkey as she hung on for dear life. "Oh my, oh my, oh my," she said, her voice hoarse.

Riker laughed, the rich sound vibrating against her chest. "You are the cutest thing I've ever seen, even when you're trying to choke the life out of me."

"I'm sorry, but you don't tend to wake up thinking today is the day I'm going to fly like a bird." Minetta coughed and knew her throat was going to be sore for days.

"I keep telling you—you're my little bird, my raven-haired beauty of hope." Riker pulled up and hovered over the tallest building. She dared to lean back enough to look into his brightly glowing eyes making her heart race as she stared into their depths. "Are you okay," he asked, kissing her forehead and then glaring at the mark that she knew without looking was on her neck.

"Yeah, I'm bruised, but it's nothing a fashionable turtleneck can't fix." His fingers touched her throat, his eyes glowing a little brighter.

"I'm sorry," Riker whispered.

"For what?"

"For not believing that you were in danger. Penny mentioned it to me, and I told her she was being ridiculous, but it seems she might be right after all. That demon attacked you because of me."

She looked away from his eyes, unable to hold his stare when he was being so truthful with her, yet she couldn't bring herself to tell him that she already knew.

"Don't worry. I'll keep you safe from now on." He smoothed back the hair that was blowing around her face. "Do you like it up here? Sometimes I like to stretch my wings, but I mostly fly over the ocean. It's peaceful out there."

"It's beautiful, Riker," she said and laid her lips upon his cheek. "Thank you for saving me."

"Always, Minetta. Would you like me to show you the ocean?"

She was sore and tired, but as she stared in the direction of the dark water that glittered with the moonlight, she could only smile and nod.

She may not have gone to him of her own volition, but she couldn't picture her world without him now.

CHAPTER

FORTY-EIGHT

R IKER

I laid still, holding Minetta to my chest, but couldn't fall asleep. No matter how hard I tried, I couldn't get the image of the shadow demon trying to drag her to Hell out of my head. I would have torn the place apart looking for her and wouldn't have stopped until every last demon responsible was destroyed. She murmured something in her sleep, her muscles twitching.

"You're okay, my little bird, I have you," I whispered, and her body settled.

"Why aren't you sleeping?" She yawned and looked up at me. Her dark hair draped around her delicate features, my heart swelling with the unspoken emotion.

"I could ask you the same thing."

"This really sexy guy woke me up." She smiled wickedly, and even though it hadn't been that long since I had her screaming the walls of my penthouse down, my cock was ready for more.

"How about you tell me something you promised you would but

have conveniently been quiet about ever since?" I raised an eyebrow at her, and she groaned, making me smile.

"Do I have to talk about it? Can't you just ravage me again?"

This time I laughed. "Oh, I plan on ravaging you again very soon, but first, let's talk. You don't seem like the type to go back on your word."

She slowly pushed herself up into a sitting position and wrapped the blanket around her shoulders. "Fine, but I'm only going to tell you the short version."

"Deal." I pushed myself up to lean against the decorative backboard attached to the wall.

"It was my first year at college, and it was a typical frat house party that got a little out of control. I was there with three girls that I was rooming with and who I thought were friends. I mean, they were in a sense, but just not the way I thought."

"I don't know what you mean," I said.

"Girls have a code at a party. We're supposed to look out for one another. You know, check on each other and make sure our drinks aren't spiked or that if one of us is missing, check and make sure we're okay. That sort of thing."

"I'm assuming they didn't look out for you?"

"You would be correct. I'm sure you can put the rest of the story together. You don't need me to go into all the details." Minetta played with the edge of the sheet. She was obviously uncomfortable talking about this, yet I had to press a little more. I needed to know who had hurt her.

"Who was it?"

She sighed and turned her gaze to the massive window that stared out at the dark night sky. "Why do you want to know?"

"Because I need to know."

Her eyes that never missed a thing swung back to mine. "And what do you plan on doing once you find out?"

I decided a politically correct answer was best. "I'm not sure yet, but whoever it is, needs to be punished in some fashion. If not for yourself, Minny for anyone else that has been hurt since. I'll find the answers, and whoever it is will be marked."

"Marked?"

"It's a demon term. It means that upon death if the human has been a particularly terrible human, they go straight to Hell. Usually, it's when they die, but if the person continues to be...troublesome, then sometimes the Hellhounds are released to drag them to Hell early." Minetta shivered and sat a little straighter, her face paling. "What is it?"

"I...I think I heard someone being dragged to Hell. I think I heard Hellhounds."

Reaching out, I rubbed her leg. "Maybe, but I doubt it."

She nodded but didn't look convinced. "You're saying that you're going to mark this person to go to Hell for what they did?"

"Minny, I won't promise anything. But, what would you like me to do if I find out this person has turned into a serial rapist?" I watched as she mulled that thought over as she characteristically chewed on her lower lip. "I could find out by looking in your mind, Minny, but I haven't out of respect for you. Please just tell me."

"You can do that," she asked, her eyes going wide.

"I can, but before you ask, I haven't looked, although I've been very tempted. I really want you to tell me because you trust me with the information." I leaned forward and reached out, running a strand of her hair through my fingers. Minny's eyes closed, and she leaned her head into my hand, the little movement making my heart swell.

Taking a deep breath, she grabbed the sheet and slowly stood to wander over to the window. She stared much like I had many a night. The moon was bright and illuminating the dark water in the distance— the way the light played on the dips and plains of her features almost made her painfully beautiful to look at, and I could feel tears forming at the back of my eyes. I had an urge to get down on my knees at her feet and beg for forgiveness for all that I'd ever done. The idea was prosperous, and yet the sensation burned in my heart.

"Anthony Kent and his friend. I never knew the other guy's name," she finally said. Minetta turned and looked at me. A tear shimmered and slowly traveled down her cheek. I realized at that moment that no matter what I promised to her, this Anthony Kent and his unknown friend were as good as dead.

FORTY-NINE

M INETTA

> R: I miss you already.

Minetta smiled at her phone as she read the text from Riker.

> M: I've only been gone a couple of hours. Don't you have business to take care of? You keep saying you're soooo busy with all these high-powered business deals.

> R: I do, and I know, but it's still too long to go without your touch. I always knew there was a reason I aimed to be a top exec. If I can't play hooky every now and then to play with my... hmm would you call yourself? My girlfriend? No matter, if I could, I'd keep you in bed with me all day. How did you put that? It was so eloquent...oh yes, you wanted me to ravage you.

Minetta's cheeks warmed as she pictured exactly what they'd been up to until the wee hours of the morning.

R: Are you still there, my little bird?

M: Yes, I'm still here, and yes, I miss you and want you to ravage me, but not until tomorrow. I need some actual sleep tonight.

R: You do know you never need to work again if you don't want to?

M: Riker!

R: Fine, fine, work away, my little bird, but be prepared to have that sexy body of yours worshiped the next time I see you. I have a few new positions I want to try out on you.

M: Such a devil.

R: I think you mean demon, but yes. I wish you'd reconsider moving in with me.

M: I'll think about it, but I feel like it's too soon, and I can't have you getting sick of me.

R: LOL! That is impossible, but fine, we can look at something maybe more to your taste in a couple of months, but I should remind you I'm not a patient man.

M: You're impossible.

R: I know, but you might as well give in now. I always get my way. Looking forward to seeing you again.

M: Same.

She chuckled and sat her phone down on the desk.

"Minetta!" She jumped out of her seat, her heart almost following suit out of her chest. She turned to look over her shoulder at her boss Eric.

Pulling the work headphones off of her head, she swallowed hard as she gave the stern man a small smile. "Yes, Sir?"

"Have you seen or know what happened to Jared? I haven't heard from him since he called about dropping the charges against you."

Minetta looked around as the rest of the people on the floor, who weren't on a call. They'd all turned their attention toward the action. She was pretty sure he wasn't supposed to yell personal information across the entire floor like this. No wonder Jared had a warped sense of what was right and wrong.

"No, I haven't seen him or spoken to him since the incident here. I'm not sure why you'd think he'd talk to me of all people."

"Thought maybe he called to apologize or something—fucking shit show." The man snorted and mumbled something about a beach beauty as he walked away. She shook her head and sat back down as Penny came over.

"Why the fuck would that man think you would have anything to do with the jerk that harassed you and then tried to have you charged? I think he drinks. I could sneak into his office and find out, or I can give him a demon special," she whispered and smirked.

Minutia laughed hard and held up my hands.

449

"Don't do that on my account." She paused as a thought occurred to her. "He's not a...you know...is he," she asked, keeping her voice low.

"You'd think so, wouldn't you, but no, he's just a very angry person."

"Do you know what happened to Jared," she said.

"Me?" Penny put her hands on her chest, her eyes going wide. "Why would you think I had anything to do with him not showing up to work?"

"Just cause of what he did, but I guess not." Suddenly, a thought came to her, and she swore under her breath. "Do you think Riker could've done something to him?"

Penny laughed, and then her face sobered when she didn't laugh along with her. "Oh, you're serious. I mean, maybe, but he didn't know Jared, though." Penny looked around and then squatted, getting in close. "Look, the thing is, Riker is always going to be Riker no matter how much nicer he becomes, so I guess it's possible." Penny shrugged. "Not really a loss if you ask me."

"Penny, he's still a person, even if he is a douche canoe."

Penny laughed hard. "Best insult ever. Fine, feel bad for him, but if he is roasting, I'm not going to shed a tear." Penny wandered back to her cubicle and picked up the next call.

The more she thought about it, the more it made sense that Riker would have a hand in Jared's miraculous dropping of the charges and disappearance. She was going to be paying him a visit after work to get the answers.

She shook her head and looked at the screen that was surprisingly quiet. How do you get a demon to stop killing people and taking them to Hell? He was an original sin. It seemed like an impossible task. Her head hurt with confusion as she put her headphones back on.

R IKER
　　I stepped out of the private elevator to the lower levels of the penthouse I owned. It was an area that no one other than a select few were ever allowed to use. It wasn't even on the building blueprints, but every now and then, I needed a fun place to torture people. In this day and age of technology and cameras on every street corner and phones that recorded everything, even I had to be careful. Plus, I had no interest in my office needing another deep cleaning so soon. The stench of Jared still lingered in the air.

My feet echoed on the stark metal hallway as I marched toward the cell. This Anthony Kent had been far too easy to find. His friend, on the other hand, I was still in need of a lead. Anthony's trail of abuse had been far greater than I could've ever dreamed and gave me the perfect excuse to kill him. Not that I needed one, but if Minetta ever asked, then at least I didn't look like a total monster, only a partial one.

All I knew was that I didn't want her to see me that way, the thought of her looking at me the way Callista had...I sucked in a sharp breath as I pushed that image out of my mind.

Skye stood leaning against the wall outside of the cell. Her black leather outfit was like a second skin and was already speckled with blood. There were only two things in this world that Skye and Neven truly loved other than each other. The first was sex, and the second was torture.

"Hey, thanks for including me. I kinda thought you'd never call again after our last conversation," Skye said. She was referencing my harsh scolding of her telling Minetta to stay away from me. Minny had let the little episode slip while away in Venice. It had been a good thing I had some time to cool off before seeing Skye again, or else she may be visiting an entirely different set of torture cells. Ones that were far hotter and one she most certainly wouldn't enjoy.

"Whether you agree with my choice about Minetta is inconsequential to our friendship as long as you don't go butting your nose into my business." I crossed my arms over my chest and glared at the demon.

Skye rolled her eyes at me. "So does this mean you won't do any more of our fuck friend sessions?"

"Skye, what did I just tell you?"

"That you're in a relationship with that twerp of a useless human flesh, and you don't want to screw it up by screwing me." She rolled her eyes and sighed dramatically at the statement.

"I'm pretty sure those are not the words I used, but the general idea is correct. Minetta means a lot to me, Skye, don't go messing with her or me or else."

"Fine, whatever, you made your point. Neven is inside, and he is having way too much fun with this human."

Smiling, I reached for the door. "Well then, we better join in before there is nothing left to play with."

I pushed open the door, and screaming met me, making me smile. There really were some days I enjoyed being a fucking Prince of Hell.

CHAPTER
FIFTY

MINETTA

By the time work was over, she'd graduated from mildly annoyed to downright pissed off. If Riker had anything to do with Jared's sudden change of heart, he was going to get an ear full. She understood his nature. Well, most of it she did. But, seeking out and possibly hurting Jared just because he was a tool wasn't right. On the other hand, Riker was a demon, a fallen archangel, and knew that there were certain aspects she'd never be able to get him to see differently.

Traffic was light as she traveled the short distance to Riker's building and pulled into the visitor's parking area. She stared up at the large structure, her hands gripping the steering wheel a little too hard.

She didn't have any proof that Riker had anything to do with Jared, so why was she so quick to judge him? Jared had made her time at work terrible, and he'd been cruel to many others, so again why did it bother her that the man may have found a different punishment than jail time?

Minetta turned the car off and rubbed her eyes. She was always so quick to think the worst of Riker, yet that was prejudiced and based solely on the fact she knew what he was. If he was any other man, would she throw him under the bus like this?

"Shit, no, you wouldn't," she said aloud. "You gave James a million chances, and you knew he was screwing around under your nose."

Minetta stared at her reflection in the rear-view mirror and shook off the lingering anger toward him, and was more annoyed with her own attitude. She would ask him about Jared, but she wouldn't go in there, guns blazing and accusing him like she'd been all fired up to do. If his answer was yes, she would simply ask him not to murder people in her name. She couldn't live with that on her conscience.

Grabbing her purse, she locked her Mini Cooper, made her way into the building, and waved to the security guard. The man nodded to her. "Ms. Johnson, it's good to see you again."

She was a little shocked the guard remembered her name. "Same, have a good night." She smiled and made her way to the elevators.

Riker had given her a key, not that she planned on using it. Her stomach lurched as the elevator practically flew upward. She grabbed at her stomach and reached for the railing. What was it with him and the elevators that took off like rocket ships?

She felt green by the time the elevator came to a stop and stumbled out of the thing. Okay, if she could get Riker to change even one thing, it would be the speed of that contraption.

She stopped in the hallway and fixed her hair before making her way to his door. There was music playing, and she knocked hard so he would be able to hear her. She knocked again a minute later, and a female voice called out to wait a second.

As the door swung open, all the air in her chest and hope in her heart evaporated. Skye stood holding the door in nothing but a T-shirt. The shirt hung to her knees. Clearly, one of Riker's and her hair was wet like she'd just gotten out of the shower. She even smelled like his body wash, the scent hitting her in the face. Pain unlike she'd ever experienced before seized her in its grasp. She should've known better. She should've trusted her instincts when they screamed that a man like him could never be satisfied or love one woman no matter what promises and pretty words he said. She promised herself that she would take what she could get and move on but figured it wouldn't be so soon. To be pushed aside so quickly. It shouldn't have mattered how long it took, but for whatever reason, it seemed worse.

"Are you going to say something or continue to stand there all night looking like a guppy," Skye asked.

Skye's voice kicked her mind into gear, and not bothering to say a word, she turned and marched toward the still waiting elevator.

"Was there at least a message?" Skye called after her, and she looked over her shoulder. The woman now stood in the hallway, a smile on her face. Skye's arms were crossed over her chest, the action pulling the T-shirt up enough to show she wasn't wearing any underwear.

Tears pricked the back of her eyes, and she quickly looked away so she didn't have to stare at the pretty demon and be reminded of what she and Riker had just been doing.

How could she even have been considering moving in with him?

"Fucking humans," she heard Skye swear as she stepped into the elevator and pressed the lobby button. The tears flowed as soon as the doors were closed. The faint tingling in her chest only made the tears fall faster, knowing that he'd definitely been inside the penthouse. She'd promised him that she would be fine with however long this lasted, but that was a lie. Her heart was already too involved. But, she promised herself she'd never let another man treat her like James had, which meant turning away even he was one she loved.

How could she have thought that they had a possible happily ever after? She'd convinced herself he was different than when they first met. He'd certainly put on the act of a lifetime. She quickly wiped away the tears as the elevator dinged.

She jogged past the guard in the lobby and ignored him as he called out to see if she was alright. As soon as she was outside, she ran for her car, and even though she most certainly shouldn't have been driving, she sped away from the curb for home.

But was it really her home? She no longer had Toby to share the space with, and she would forever be on the run from one demon or the next, and for what? No, this wasn't her home any longer. She had nothing to keep her here. The little car revved as she floored it, wanting to get as far away from Riker as fast as possible.

RIKER

Stepping out of the shower I paused with the faint tingling under my skin fluttered and then disappeared. Pulling on a pair of track pants, I walked out of my room, rubbing my hair with a towel. I couldn't hear anything except Skye's terrible singing.

"Was someone at the door?" I asked as I wandered into the living room.

"Nope, just me and my terrible rendition of Chicago, great musical, I got to fuck some of the cast members," Skye answered as she made her way to the couch.

"I'm shocked." I looked around the room. "Are you sure no one is here? I could've sworn I heard knocking, and I...." I paused and rubbed at my chest.

"I what? I know that I don't know how you hear anything in this place. It freaking echoes, and I still can't hear from one side to the other."

I shook my head and wandered over to the bar to pour myself a glass of wine before plopping down into the leather chair. I kept staring at the door, and finally, Skye turned to stare at the door as well.

"What are you staring at? You're freaking me out?"

"I just can't shake...." Was it that I wanted to see her so badly that even my body was telling me to go and see her. I rubbed my eyes as I thought. The sensation had been faint and fleeting, but still....

"Okay, you're acting super weird. It's just me here. Ri, for fuck's sake, relax. We just had the best torture session in a long time, and we have a name to do it all over again soon." Skye smiled wide, and I nodded but couldn't find the same sense of enthusiasm she was showing. "Oh, and Neven is cooking steak for dinner. I hope he does the double-baked potatoes. Is Shilo joining us?"

I couldn't help feeling like something was wrong. A small pain in my chest and a knot in my stomach had developed for no reason, and feeling wouldn't go away. If something were wrong with Minetta, then Penny would call. The demon said she and Minny were hanging out tonight and she'd stay with her until they could figure out a different living arrangement. Penny wasn't my first choice for protection, but even I had to admit the fallen angel had skills. She wouldn't have survived this long otherwise.

Trying to push the anxiety away and relax, I turned my attention to Skye just as Neven walked in from the kitchen. "Did you have a good shower?" I sipped my glass of wine.

"You know, it was the best shower I've ever had." She smiled wide, her grey eyes dancing with an impish glint.

"What are you up to, Skye? I already told you we are not fucking again, so you can wipe that look off your face."

"Oh, I know, but the torture was fun, and Neven filled the rest of my needs for the night." She looked up at Neven, who rolled his eyes. "I'm just in a really good mood. Did you want a refill? I think I'm going to get myself a glass. This night calls for a celebration! Neven, would you like a glass?"

I watched Skye jump up from the couch and skip to the bar. Glancing down, I stared at the red wine and swirled it around. Unable to set my mind at ease, I picked up my phone, and saw that there were no messages.

I tried to call Minny, but it went to voicemail. "It's me, Minny. You know what to do. I'll call you back as soon as I can."

Beep.

"Hi there, my Little Bird. I was just thinking about you. If you change your mind and want to come over tonight, I'd love the company. I know I said I wouldn't push, but I miss you. Talk to you later."

I hung up the phone and tapped the cell on my knee. I was being unreasonable. The woman was allowed to have her own space and time to breathe without me hovering. I needed to learn to be patient. Sitting the phone down, I stood and made my way toward the kitchen, pushing the notation that I needed to rush over to her house out of my mind.

Anthony had a very loose tongue once the pain started, and I now had a Mr. Kupp to visit very soon. Taking a deep breath, I turned my attention to Neven and Skye, who were bickering over who got to do the best part of the torture. I smiled as I watched them, but my normal keenness for the topic just wasn't there.

CHAPTER
FIFTY-ONE

RIKER

I woke up late, and the light was already streaming through the window. I groaned and flopped my arm over my face, tempted to roll over and not even bother to get up. I had meetings to attend today and someone else to ream out for their incompetence. What would normally bring me joy and rejuvenation felt like a weight around my neck trying to pull me down.

How many years had I been building this empire? Too many when the zeros barely fit on the bank balance of your statement. Maybe Minny was right. Maybe I needed to look at doing more with my funds and my talents. It had felt surprisingly good to give the money to the hospital and not simply because it was in honor of Minetta's father. It had also stirred a longing in my gut, something that hadn't happened in a very long time.

The phone rang, and I grabbed it smiling, hoping that it was Minny, but instead, it was an unknown number. I was tempted to let it go to voicemail but figured they'd keep calling if I didn't tell the telemarketer to fuck off.

"I'm not interested in anything you're selling."

"Is Minny with you?" I sat up straight in bed as Penny's worried voice drifted through the line.

"No, why would she be with me? She said she was going to be too tired to see me last night and was going to be staying home with you."

"She changed her mind at work and told me to go home instead, that she was going to see you," Penny said. "What did you do now, Riker?" Penny fumed, and I was tempted to reach through the phone and choke the young demon.

"And you didn't accompany her here?"

"No, I...just tell me what you did."

"I've warned you before about your attitude, Penny."

She sighed and cleared her throat. "I'm sorry, I'm just worried, and you're the only reason she would take off."

"Whoa, back up. What do you mean take off?" I jumped out of bed and put the phone on speaker as I marched for the closet.

"When she didn't show up for work, I went to her home. Her suit-case was missing, along with most of her clothes and her picture of Toby. Her car was gone...Riker, if she's not with you, I'm worried. She shouldn't be alone."

"I have no idea why she would take off. Yesterday we texted, and all seemed well between us." I pulled on a pair of jeans, and as my hand reached for a black T-shirt a thought occurred to me. "Could she have received a call about her mother or something else to make her take off?"

"She'd tell you or me something like that."

"What time did you get off work last night?"

"We were working the three to eleven. Why," Penny asked.

"Fuck me! That fucking bitch! I have to go. Figure out where she would have gone and call me back." I hung up on Penny and stormed across the bedroom.

"Skye," I hollered so loud the walls and windows shook. "Where the fuck are you?" I leaped over the railing of the top floor and landed softly on the lower level. "Skye," I screamed again. Shilo came running, his face that of a ghost, he looked so terrified.

"Sir, what is it, what has happened," Shilo asked.

"Skye," I bellowed again.

Neven and Skye ran from the end of the penthouse, which was where they'd been sleeping. My bare feet slapped against the floor as I stormed across the room, leaving golden footprints with every step. My rage was rolling out of me in a rush as I laid eyes on the manipulative demon. Her eyes went wide as they met my glowing ones. Wisely she backed away and then turned to run for the door.

I rarely used my supernatural abilities, but I blocked her way in a blink. She swallowed hard as she stumbled backward and landed on her ass with a thud. She pushed herself back along the tiled floor. All I saw was red. I wanted her blood, the demon in me could taste it.

"Ri man, what's going on," Neven asked, but wisely didn't touch me or block my path.

I didn't answer Neven. My focus was on the demon on the floor, her grey eyes wide with terror. "Did you really think I wouldn't find out?" I kept my voice calm as I watched her shiver.

"Skye, what the fuck did you do?" Neven looked between myself and his sister.

Skye bumped up against the window and whimpered as I reached down, picking her up by her neck. Small mewling noises escaped her mouth as my hand burned into her skin. "Answer me!"

"I didn't do anything," her voice came out small and pathetic.

I yanked her in, so our noses were touching. "I would recommend not lying to me right now, friend." I accentuated the word like it tasted terrible in my mouth. "Your friend status is the only thing keeping you alive, but Skye, I will summon Brill right now if you don't start talking."

"Riker, please." Neven started to say until I glared in his direction.

"Did you know?" I glared at Neven.

"Know what," Neven answered, but his eyes told me all I indeed to know. He had no idea what was going on.

"He doesn't know." Skye's voice came out rough around the fingers pressing into her throat.

"So, you do admit you did something to Minetta."

"Oh fuck me, Skye! Seriously?" Neven flopped into the leather chair and rubbed at his eyes.

I turned my attention back to Skye, and my hold tightened around her throat a little more. Her feet kicked, connecting with the window as smoke slowly rose into the air. She shook her head no and tried to speak but was unable around my grip.

"Sir, may I suggest you take a moment to let the girl speak, or you may never find out what happened. If you still choose to kill her, you can after you hear what she has to say," Shilo said. His voice was calm and soothing and exactly what I needed.

My heart pounded like a drum in my chest. If something happened to Minetta, if she had left me for good because of Skye, I wasn't sure I wouldn't tear her limb from limb.

Releasing my hold, she dropped to the floor, her hands going to the bright red handprint round her neck. "Speak, Skye. This is your one chance to tell me the truth, all of it, or I will rip the memory from your mind and send you to one of my torture chambers for the rest of eternity."

"The human came by last night."

"And?"

"That was it, she saw me and left. I asked her if there was a message, and she didn't say anything. She looked at me and got in the elevator."

"Let me make sure I understand this in its entirety. Minetta came over last night, and you answered the door in nothing but Neven's shirt, hair wet from just being fucked and having a shower?"

"Yes."

"Did you tell her that you were here with me?"

"No, I swear, I didn't say anything like that. She must have drawn her own conclusions. I can't help what she thought."

My knuckles cracked as a growl rippled from my lips. "Do I look like an idiot Skye? Didn't I just say not to fuck with me? Do I look like I'm joking about killing you?"

She shook her head slowly back and forth. "I didn't lead her on, but I didn't correct her assumption either."

"And then you lied to me about someone being here." Skye pulled her knees up to her chest and wrapped her arms around her knees.

"Yes, I lied to you," she looked down to the floor. I turned and looked at Neven before I changed my mind. "Get her out of my sight before I kill her. And I don't want to see her ever again. If she crosses my path, I can't promise that I won't kill her."

Neven looked to his sister and back to me. "I'm sorry."

"Don't apologize for her. She knew exactly what she was doing and chose her own desires over our friendship and what I wanted. I pulled the two of you from the Pits of Despair and called you friend." My eyes found Skye. Red demon tears trickled down her face, staining the white shirt she was wearing. "She is no longer my friend, and if you're not my friend, you're my enemy. Get out."

"Please, Riker, I'm so sorry," she blubbered.

"Stay away from me, Skye. I never want to see you again, but know this—the only reason I'm not sending you to Hell where you belong right now is because of the woman you chased off. Minetta wouldn't want me to kill you, isn't that fucking irony for you?" I ran for the stairs to finish getting dressed and left Neven to deal with his crying sister. I had bigger issues to deal with, like finding Minetta and then trying to convince her I hadn't been fucking with her emotions.

FIFTY-TWO

MINETTA yawned as she stared up at the nursing home sign. It hadn't been a long drive to get here, but as she crossed the state line, she realized she had no home left to go to and decided to nap in the car outside the nursing home.

Stupid, she'd been so upset she hadn't even remembered she sold the farm. She stretched and then sipped on the cold coffee, choking down the burnt disgusting taste.

"Yuck." She gagged. "That's what I get for buying gas station coffee."

She needed to make a plan, she wasn't sure where she wanted to live, but she needed to see her mom first. Maybe, she could have her mom moved to a new location so she could live as far away from Riker as possible without having to fly to see her mother.

She pushed open the car door and rolled her shoulders. Minetta walked up to the glass doors, and the only word that came to mind was tired.

She was tired of feeling beat down. She was tired of feeling used and abused and lied to by the people she loved. She did feel bad about not telling Penny that she was leaving or where she was going, but if Penny knew, then she would try to stop her from going or would want to come with her, and honestly, she wanted to leave the entire situation behind.

Why Michael ever thought she was this chosen person, she had no idea. But she was stupid to think that she could be the one person to help stop an apocalypse and save the Earth. Or change a demon's heart from pure black and see humans as more than pathetic husks of flesh. Michael had to find a new savior because she'd failed.

The outer automatic door opened, and the scent of the lemon-smelling cleaner they used invaded her nose. If the coffee hadn't already made her gag, this scent would.

"Good morning," Minetta said as she stepped up to the nurse's station.

"Darlin, you do know it is too early for visitation?"

"I know, but I'm hoping you will make an exception. I'm in the process of moving and wanted to make sure I see my mom before that happens. It may be a while before I can get her moved to an opening close to me."

"Oh, who is your mom?" the woman asked, her fingers flying across the keyboard.

"Shelly Johnson."

"Oh, she is such a sweet lady. Some of those with Alzheimer's can get nasty, but not your mom. She is so kind to everyone."

"Sounds like my mom. Do you think I can see her? I can help her get dressed and eat so a nurse can be freed up for someone else."

"The apple didn't fall far from the tree with you." The woman smiled warmly. "I will let them know to expect you. Head on over to the door, and I'll buzz you in."

"Thank you so much." Minetta made her way to the locked door and waited for the patented click before giving it a pull. The place hurt her heart every time she walked through the doors, and not because it was likely she would end up here one day. It was because so many of them didn't have anyone. Their wails of fear from the deadly disease left behind confusing images in their minds, and they had no one other than these kind employees that made sure they were taken care of in their final weeks, months, or years.

Her mom's door was at the end of the hall. She'd paid a little more to make sure her mom had two windows. The one looked out over the still undeveloped farmland, and she hoped it would bring her a sense of peace to see something familiar.

"Hey, mom, it's me, Minny," she said as she pushed open the door. Her mother was already out of bed. She was wearing her long night-gown with the pretty pink flowers—it was her mom's favorite, so Minny made sure she cleaned out the Walmart, so she would never run out. "Hi mom, did you hear me," she asked quietly as she walked toward her. She didn't want to scare her. "Mom?"

It was strange for her mom not to respond at all. She could see her mom's reflection in the window, but her eyes were unfocused and didn't track her. Minetta swallowed hard, tension racing up her spine. "Mom, are you okay?"

A snake of fear traveled throughout her body, the hair standing on the back of her neck, which made her swallow hard. Her hands shook as she reached for her mom's shoulder but stopped just as her hand was about to touch her.

There were noises from a loud commotion coming in from the hall-way, and she sucked in a sharp breath and spun to stare at the door as the yelling got worse.

The door burst open just as a hand touched her shoulder, and

Minetta screamed, jumping off to the side. Her mother's confused eyes stared at her while Riker stood in the doorway, looking just as unsure about what was going on as she felt. She was going crazy. All the demon and angel appearances were making her insane. She grabbed her chest and then glared at the man in the doorway.

"Go ahead and call the cops, but I'm not leaving," Riker snarled at the nurse in the hallway.

"Mom, I'll be right back," she said and marched at the man she wanted to smack at the moment.

"Do you want me to call the police on this jerk," a woman who looked like she was the head nurse asked as she reached Riker.

"No, trust me, it will go smoother if you just let him stay."

"Are you sure? I have no problem hauling his ass out of here." The woman crossed her arms over her chest and stared at Riker.

Minetta smiled at the nurse. "No, really, it's okay." She glared up at him. "I'll deal with him."

"Alright then, but you're both out of here if there is any more commotion." The nurse stomped off and ordered the other residents back into their rooms.

Grabbing Riker's arm, she pulled him into the room and closed the door. "What the hell are you doing here?" He laid his hands on her shoulders, and she jerked away. "Don't touch me," she whispered harshly.

"Minny, I didn't sleep with Skye. I know that's what you think, I know that's what she led you to believe, but I need you to trust me. Nothing happened."

"You really expect me to believe that? Do you just happen to have all your friends over for shower parties?"

"Who..." Minetta looked to see her mom shuffle closer. She sighed and rubbed her face.

"Riker, this is not the place or the time for this conversation." She left him at the door and made her way to her mom. "Hey, mom, everything is okay. You don't have to be scared."

"You, you," her mother said, her arm raised to point at Riker.

"This is a friend of mine. He isn't staying," Minetta said. She patted her mom's hand as she linked their arms together and started to guide her to her chair, but her mom tugged against her.

Her mom pointed at Riker again. "Angel," her mother said, and Minetta froze.

"What did you say?" Minetta stared at her mother's face, but her eyes were trained on Riker.

"It's nice to meet you, Mrs. Johnson." Riker slowly walked toward them, and as he did, tears burst forth from her mother's eyes. Unhooking her arm, Minny watched with fascination as her mother, who hadn't recognized anyone for years, reached for Riker. Her mouth fell open as her mother wrapped her arms around Riker.

"Have you come to take me home," her mother asked, the first full sentence she'd spoken in years, and it was her turn to cover her mouth and blink away tears.

"Soon. You will go home soon, but not today. Today we are here to visit," Riker said, his voice soft and calm as he stroked the grey braid laying on her mother's back. "Would you like the chance to speak to your daughter, to say a proper goodbye?"

"Yes, the fog...it's clear. Am I going to be alright, or am I dying?"

"I'm sorry, Mrs. Johnson. I don't have the power to heal you, but I can give you some time with your daughter to say what you want to say before you travel home to see your husband."

Minetta sniffled and wiped at the rampant tears running down her face. How did he always have the power to melt her heart, even when she wanted to punch him in the face? Her mom reached up and gripped Riker's cheeks in her hands.

"Thank you, dear boy. I've been waiting for you." Her mom turned and looked at her, and she couldn't hold it back anymore as she stared into eyes that actually saw her. "Look at you, sweet girl, you're so grown up. So beautiful."

Minetta rushed forward and gripped her mother in a tight embrace. "I've missed you so much, mom. There is so much I want to tell you, so much that has happened. I...I don't even know where to start." Her mom pulled back, and they laughed. "Here." Minetta grabbed the box of tissues and held the box out for her mom to take some.

Minny watched as she dabbed at her eyes. She'd always been so proper, so lady-like. Minetta and her dad always had so much fun poking at her mom and how everything had to be perfect. Not in a mean or snobbish way. She just had a particular way of doing everything.

"Well, for starters, why don't you tell me where you happened to meet this handsome angel? Good choice, my baby girl."

Minny's eyes locked with Riker's, and the kindness she saw in his face broke her all over again. She mouthed thank you, and he gave her a wink. "Would you ladies like to sit in the garden? It's lovely right now."

"Now that sounds wonderful. Can we, Minny?"

"Of course, mom, let me get you your sweater and slippers first." She rushed around the room and gathered her mother's things before holding out her elbow for her mom to take.

Her mom blushed a bright pink and looked up at Riker. "Would you mind taking me down to the garden? It will drive all the other women here crazy that I have such a stud on my arm."

"Mom," she said and laughed as Riker smiled wide.

"I would be honored." He stepped up beside her and held out his arm like a true gentleman. "Now tell me, Mrs. Johnson, how naughty was Minny as a little girl?"

"Oh, do I have stories for you. She wasn't always so sweet and inno-cent, don't let that smile fool you."

Minny walked behind the pair, and her heart felt like it was going to burst right out of her chest. If nothing else, he'd just earned himself a conversation. It was the least she could do for this gift.

FIFTY-THREE

RIKER

I didn't have the heart to tell Minny that her mother didn't have much longer. It was the reason that she was able to see me for what I was. As a human, she wouldn't be able to tell the difference that I was a fallen angel. Mind you, angel was not the word I expected her to use. A number of people close to death had called me the reaper or worse.

Once situated in the garden, I let the women have their space and sat on a bench nearby. I could just make out Shilo leaning against the car in the parking lot. He'd been the closest thing that I'd had to a Father since being kicked out of Heaven. In this quiet moment of self-reflection, I watched those that lived and worked here. Most of those that were residents had some sort of strange illness.

I never had to worry about illnesses, but the thought that Minetta could get one of them and cause her frail human body to perish was terrifying. Was this what his Father had seen in the humans all along? Was this what Michael had meant when he said, "we as angels didn't understand the meaning of the word gratitude." I'd been grateful for many things and never thought of his message as anything more than Father's whispering nonsense.

It was like there was something in the air that was giving me clarity. I blinked and looked over my shoulder as Minetta laughed with her mother. There was this glow about her, a happiness in her eyes that spoke to how much having this time with her mother meant. Her eyes found mine, and she still appeared hurt when she looked at me, but the coldness was gone. This time was a gift, a gift I'd never needed and therefore never understood.

I had to wonder if there was a clarifying remedy to help me find a way to convince her that I hadn't betrayed her.

Mrs. Johnson yawned, and Minny signaled that they were going inside. I stood, but she shook her head no, and I sat back down to wait. There was a storm on the horizon. I could smell the rain in the air and feel the slight electrical charge that accompanied the lightning riding the clouds.

Minetta rounded the corner of the bench and sat down beside me. I was tempted to grab her hand and pull her close. I wanted so badly to make things right between us.

"Thank you. Whatever you did, to give me that time with my mom." She looked up at me. "I will always be grateful."

"You're welcome, Minetta."

She took a deep breath and slumped against the bench. "Okay, why was Skye at your house dressed like that?"

"First, I will tell you that she did have sex, just not with me. She did have a shower, as you've seen I have over a dozen showers in the place, and again it was not with me. I'd specifically told her that nothing was going to happen between us anymore, and she agreed, but when you showed up, she took advantage of the situation. I didn't sleep with her, Minny."

"How am I supposed to believe you? You said you wanted to try a relationship, but you openly admitted you didn't know how long it would last."

I turned and laid my knee on the bench and rested my arm across the back of the stone structure. "Look into my eyes. You've grown to know me well enough to know when I'm lying to you." I reached out, feeling compelled to touch her skin, and ran my thumb across her cheek. "You mean more to me than I can put into words, Minetta."

"Shit!" Minetta stood and walked away toward the small decorative pond. I wasn't sure what to make out of her sudden outburst.

"I can't do this." She turned to look at me, and I swallowed the massive lump in my throat as I waited on her next words. "I can't continue to have a relationship with you, and you not be completely honest. I need to get this off my chest."

"I don't know what you're talking about," I said. It was obvious she was nervous. She was nibbling on her nail, and she seemed jittery. "Just tell me, whatever it is, we will get through it."

"Do you remember when I told you that Penny already explained to me who you are, and that is why I wasn't scared?"

"Yes, what of it?" I stood and took a step in her direction.

"I wasn't a hundred percent truthful, and I hate myself for it." She walked in a small circle and then stopped as she seemed to prepare herself to say what had her so tied up in knots.

I couldn't imagine what would be so terrible. "What you don't know is that I had no intention of dating you. Penny said that demons would continue to come after me if I did, so I had full intentions of never going near you again."

"Continue to come after you?"

"I had one attack me in my house and then again when Jared had me arrested by the police or the fake police. What I didn't say that night when I came to your office was that I got injured by a group of demons.

481

They had me in the back of a cruiser, and I couldn't escape and...." She stopped talking and rubbed at her arms. "They took me out to the woods to meet up with other demons to play this crazy game of 'chase the human' through the woods as they tried to kill me."

"Minny, what the? Why wouldn't you tell me that?" I put my hands on her shoulders and could feel the tension in her body. Her eyes showed how torn up she was about telling me any of this.

"Because Penny and Michael showed up and saved me. They told me that I had two choices. The first was that I could try running for my life and stay far, far away from you, but it would mean that there was a good chance some apocalypse would happen. Or I could give you a chance, and there was the possibility that we would work, and it would help save everyone."

My hands dropped from her shoulders. "So, Michael tells you that you should date me to save the world, and that is the reason you came to my office?" I walked away from her and thought this through. Anger burned in the pit of my stomach. Michael had been orchestrating all of this the whole time. He'd danced around the question like he always did, but I knew he was up to something.

He'd manipulated me, and here I thought I'd actually fallen for a human? None of this was real. She'd never been interested. I shouldn't have been so blinded by my desire and listened to the warning bell that told me her attitude change was unusual.

"Was this all an act? Your feelings? The pretending to not want anything from me? All the while, you were secretly trying to make me... what? Become a different person, a better person? Or at least a better person in your mind. Minny to the rescue to save all the human souls," my anger bubbling over into my voice.

"No, I haven't been faking anything, Riker. I didn't tell you why I changed my mind, but that was it. I'd already been hunted twice by demons. I couldn't imagine the entire world being taken over by more with the sole purpose of killing everyone."

"You wanted to save all the pathetic human lives, and it didn't matter that you were screwing with my feelings, as long as you got what you wanted."

"Riker, you're not hearing me. It wasn't like that." She grabbed my arm, and I jerked it away.

"I can't believe I almost told you I love you. Michael is always manipulating me. He must have been having a great old laugh over this one." I marched away, but Minny ran in front of me and held her hands up to stop me. I held out my arm and pushed her to the side.

"Riker, please, he didn't manipulate you. I chose to give you a chance. It was my choice to see what you were really like."

I spun around and looked at her beautiful face, and my rage hitched up another notch. "But, would you have, if Michael hadn't said it would supposedly save the world and whatever else he dressed it up with?"

"I don't know, you weren't exactly the kind of guy I'd date, and after the office incident and my track record, I honestly don't know."

"No, you prefer soul-sucking losers that don't bother to work and cheat on you because you know what to expect. That is safe in your world." She took a step back like I'd slapped her. "Stay away from me, Minetta. Maybe you seeing Skye, jumping to a conclusion, and choosing to think the worst of me was the sign we were both needed to see we were making a huge mistake."

Tears welled in her eyes, and even angry, I couldn't stand to look at them and wanted to pull her into my arms.

"Goodbye, Minetta." This time she didn't follow or try to stop me, and an ache formed in my chest and got worse with every stride. I growled as I got to the car and hopped into the driver's side.

Skye was right, Michael was playing with me from the moment he got to town, and I was blinded by a pretty face that he knew would remind me of Callista.

Fucker.

No more, I was done playing his game. The world could burn for all I cared.

CHAPTER

FIFTY-FOUR

MINETTA stood on the edge of the grass to the parking lot and watched the sports car as the tires squealed and then sped out of the parking lot. The painful sobs hit the moment Riker was out of sight. What had she done? Why did she tell him? She'd always thought that the truth was better, but right now, it didn't feel that way. Instead, it felt like her whole world had crumbled around her. He was right. She'd thought the worse of him and had the moment she drove to his home. Jared, Skye, it didn't matter. She'd been ready to implode things because the feelings were too real. She was terrified that she would lose him, so she was gearing herself up to end it no matter what and classically pushed him away.

She straightened her shoulders and wiped the tears off her face. "I had to tell him the truth. I was honest, and he ran." That told her all she needed to know.

By the time she got back to her mom's room to gather her purse, her mom was sound asleep. She could never hate him, there was no doubting she loved him, but it was time to move on. Minetta kissed her mother's forehead and made her way out to the car.

Slipping inside the Mini, she pulled out the map she'd purchased at the gas station. She'd decided that she was going to fulfill the journey she and her father hadn't got to do.

"Okay, dad, where to?" She stared at the map and smiled as she made her decision. She pulled the small car out onto the road as the storm rumbled closer, the dark clouds in the distance announcing it was going to be a bad one.

She hadn't gone very far when the rain began to hit her windshield. What started out as normal drops quickly turned into a blinding torrential downpour. The car shook violently from side to side. The wind was so strong she could barely keep the car on the road, and the sound was as loud as she'd ever heard. Everything echoed inside the little car, and with the loud boom of thunder, she would've sworn ripped the roof clean off.

Minetta leaned forward over the steering wheel as she tried to gauge where the lines on the road were. She flicked on her four-way flashers as the rain turned into massive ice pellets and decided that if a tornado was coming, she better be parked. She pulled over and put the car onto the shoulder, and came to a stop. She'd never seen a storm like this. The sky was darkening further, blocking the sun completely with a strange inky hue that made her shudder.

She yelped as a particularly large pellet hit the car with a bang, shaking it. The thumping on the roof had her looking up and worried if it would hold. A dark shape out of the corner of her eye had her looking out the front windshield, but nothing was there. Her eyes scanned the growing inky darkness closing in on the vehicle and wiped the sweat off the palms of her hands.

"No, you're imagining it. They wouldn't want you now. It couldn't be," she said out loud, trying to calm the building nerves in the pit of her stomach. She hit the on-button on the radio and jumped, covering her ears as the loud screech and crackle sound of no channel blasted through the speakers. The hair stood up on the back of her neck a moment before she caught a glimpse of something out the side window.

This time as she looked up, she screamed, a massive fist of a creature that was certainly from Hell slammed through the glass of the passenger side window. Instinct alone had her slamming her foot down on the gas. The demon held on to the side of the door as it growled and spit at her as she sped recklessly down the road. She yelped as a sharp claw scraped across her arm as she reached into her purse. Her hand wrapped around the small canister of pepper spray she kept. Not even caring if she got the thing in the face, she pulled out the bottle and pressed the button.

The demon roared and fell away from her car, but she could see more lumbering beasts running along the shoulder beside her. No, no, no this was not happening again!

"Go away! He left me. It's over," she bellowed out the open window. Only red glowing eyes and the sound of snarling greeted her. "Please go away!"

Tears like the rain outside streamed down her face as she coaxed more speed out of the small vehicle. What looked like waves of water sprayed up either side of the car and flowed through the broken window, soaking her to the bone.

"Please just leave me alone," she whispered as her foot pressed to the floor.

R IKER

"What is wrong, Sir," Shilo asked as I streaked down the road.

"It was all a lie, all a fucking lie!" I slammed my hand on the steering wheel.

"What was Sir?" Shilo gripped the door and the center console, his knuckles going white with the death grip.

I filled Shilo in on everything that Minetta had just told me. When I finished, I looked over at him, and he simply stared back. Slowly his face darkened. I couldn't remember a time the man looked at me with such anger.

"Pull over," Shilo said.

"What?"

"Pull over now," Shilo suddenly yelled, his hand smacking on the dash. The look on his face was fierce, his blue eyes shimmering with a power I hadn't seen since before his fall.

Thrown off by the outburst, I did as he asked and watched in confusion as he got out and paced on the gravel shoulder. Luckily this was a quiet road, and there was no car in sight. I slowly got out and stared at the old angel. His face was almost as red as a tomato, his body vibrating with anger. I thought his wings were going to make an appearance next.

"Boy, you're an idiot!" Shilo finally said as he pointed a finger at me.

My eyes went wide, and I took a small step back from the words that were as strong as any physical blow. "Shilo, I..."

"I mean it, you're stupid, and I never thought I would say those words to you. I mean, seriously, after all this time and all these years, I thought you would have some common sense about you."

"How have I angered you? It was me that was wronged."

"Oh please! Spare me. Wronged you, my old wrinkly angel ass." He made a gesture with his hands like he was done with me and walked a few strides away before whipping around to face me once more. "Tell me something, how many people have you wronged since you fell from Heaven? How many people have you purposely set out to ruin their business, ruin their reputation, or life without a second thought? How many people have you tortured or lied to if it suited you? Can you even fathom a guess? I can't. I lost count after our first year here alone." Shilo raised his hand and shook his finger at me, but the rage in his soft blue eyes held the real threat.

"That girl is the first real and good thing that has happened to you. She put her own fragile life and heart on the line to save not herself but millions and you. Can you comprehend that? She didn't set out to scam you or hurt you, and she tells you the truth about why she came to see you, and you turn your back on her?" Shilo shook his head. I'd never seen disgust in his eyes for me before—nothing I'd done earned that look until now. "She is a kind and sweet person who was torn up about lying over one single thing to you, one thing that in the grand scheme of things means a piddle of shit! Shit! Do you hear me, boy?"

I held up my hands. "Yes, I hear you."

"No, I don't think you do. Me, of all people, has the right to hate Michael, and that hate burns hotter and brighter than any Hellfire, yet in this, he was not wrong. His obvious scheming aside, I've seen you and Minetta together, and the love that is between you is unique and special. That connection, that soul melding type of love, is one of a kind. I should know. I had that once." His face fell, the hidden pain from all the years showing.

"I loved my wife and children more than my own life, and it was all ripped away from me. You have a chance to have that kind of love, and her time is fleeting, but to have even a few fragile years is worth more than all the buildings and fancy cars in existence." He held his hand out toward the car to make a point. "Does this piece of shit love you back? Do your fancy buildings and expensive clothes make you feel whole?"

"But she lied and wasn't even planning on seeing me again."

"Ha! I wouldn't have either."

"What?"

"Maybe you haven't looked in the mirror and really seen what was staring at you, but the man she met was a fucking asshole of the first order."

Shilo pulled off his suit jacket and threw it into the dirt, stomping on it with his foot. He rolled up his sleeves, and I thought for sure he was going to throw a fist but instead, he pointed back the way we'd just traveled.

"That girl is the human embodiment of kindness and selflessness, something you used to know about, Maddix. Why would she have given the biggest asshole in the state a chance? Think about it from her point of view. If it had been me, I would've run as far as I could get and never looked back. And you know what? Human lives on the line or not, I still wouldn't have given you a chance to hurt me and especially not at the cost of my own peril at the hands of Hell itself. I can tell you right now that she knew you'd hurt her, or she'd die for her efforts, and she swallowed the fear down to open herself up and give you a chance. That is real, that is...brave, and it's more than you deserved when she met you."

Shilo twisted his foot on the jacket, smashing it into the dirt, and pulled his perfectly tucked shirt out from his pants.

"And since you're sitting so high on your pearly white horse there, did you tell her about Anthony Kent you had me go get?" I looked away from his eyes. "Or how about that guy Jared she worked with? Have you told her about any of the terrible things you've done or how you wanted her simply because Michael showed interest?"

"Okay, fine, I get it. I'm still an asshole."

Shilo walked around the car and shocked me further by placing his hands on my chest. "My boy, you are the only thing that I have left in this world that I love and care about, and I'm telling you right now I will leave and never speak to you again if you don't fix this right now."

"You're serious?"

"I swear it on my son's death."

"How am I supposed to know what is real and what is fake between us?"

"Think about it, my boy." He tapped the side of my head. "Every touch and look you two have shared, even an old decrepit angel like me could see what was happening. She stared at you with so much love—it was like you hung the moon. Yes, Michael very well could have put the idea in her head to come to you, but he didn't do anything else. For all the puffing of his annoyingly arrogant chest, even he doesn't have that kind of power. He can't make the two of you fall in love."

I stepped back as the reality of his words sunk in. The anger lifted, leaving fear in its wake. What had I done?

"You're scared, boy. Scared of the emotion that she has invoked. Scared to let someone in, and I don't blame you after what happened, but you can't let her go. The man I see before me is the man I always knew you would become, not that shell of a thing you've been for centuries."

Loud thunder rumbled in the distance just before a sharp lightning crack. I looked back the way I'd come and into the storm. I stared at the black that was as dark as Hell itself, and a shiver raced down my spine. I sniffed the air and looked at Shilo.

"Do you smell that?"

Shilo nodded. "Demons, lots of them."

"Minetta, no!" I ran a few strides and jumped into the air, my wings ripping free of the confines of the jacket I'd been wearing. "Sword." I summoned my great sword that had laid dormant since the day of my fall. I'd protect her with my bare hands if I had to.

With Shilo by my side and the wind loud in my ears, I streaked across the sky toward Minetta and could only pray to someone that I never thought I would again, that I wasn't too late.

FIFTY-FIVE

R IKER
      The searing pain of dread in my chest only worsened the closer I flew. Minetta's small car looked like a mangled piece of metal, the front end and roof smashed in as it lay up against a tree. Penny stood on with her back to the roof of the upturned vehicle, flaming sword in hand as she tried to fend off the massive swarm that was descending on the car.

Brill, I need you.

I sent the telepathic message to the captain of my army. There had to be hundreds of demons, far more than the three of us could take on. My sword reached my hand just as I descended upon the hoard. Sweeping low, I cut a path through the throngs, the gold blade flashing in the darkness as red and black and green blood flew in all directions. I landed with Shilo beside Penny, who was panting hard, but her face was resolved to the task of saving her friend.

I gripped her shoulder and allowed some of my power to flow into the girl. She sucked in a shuddering breath, her eyes glowing brighter. "Thanks. Where the hell were you?"

"Later." I jumped up on the side of the car and dropped to my knees. The side window was broken. Minetta hung like a doll on strings from the seatbelt, her dark hair cascading over her face. Hand shaking, I reached in and touched Minetta's neck. She was still alive. The ball of dread eased a little with that little thumping under my finger.

"There's just so many!" Penny yelled over the noise of the hoard.

"Do you know who's controlling them," I asked.

"Give up! This has to happen!" I looked up and stared into Raphael's face as he slowly floated toward the ground.

"Brother, what are you doing," I asked, shocked to see the archangel and the wild look in his silver eyes.

"You're no longer my brother, and she needs to die." He pointed at the car. "The prophecy has to continue, the war must happen, or balance will never be restored." Raphael raised his sword in the air as he preached. "And you Erinyes, you disappoint me. You'll be sent back to Hell where you came from for your betrayal."

"Fuck you, Raphael!" Penny spat on the ground. "I'm done being manipulated by you."

"So be it." He laughed, and I was torn as to what to do, go after Raphael or help Minetta out of the car.

"You must know the prophecy is volatile? Anything can change the course of a crossroads or simply create a new one that will come to the same conclusion. Killing one human will make no difference," I tried to reason.

"These are lies. This prophecy has stood in the book of creation for millennia. You will stop the war, you are the closest to Lucifer, and I cannot allow you to stop him from rising. Only in the final battle will peace be restored to the way it was."

I laughed, the sound bitter. "You really think I have any control over anything Luci does? Then you don't know your brother very well."

"It is written! She must die!" Raphael screamed hysterically. I knew not what to make of his erratic behavior. This was so not like the angel I remembered.

The ground began to vibrate, the car shaking like they were in the middle of an earthquake, and it was my turn to smile. "You underestimate me, Raphael."

Brill's distinctive battle roar ripped through the air, his twin swords raised as my army charged toward the hoard of demons Raphael had gathered. Raphael spun to see what was coming just as Skye and Neven suddenly appeared in a puff of smoke. They wore their red battle leathers and twin swords in hand.

"What are you doing here," I yelled at her.

"We followed the sword. Look, I'm sorry for all the shit I've caused, but nothing is keeping us away if you're in trouble. You can stop speaking to me again after." She spun gracefully and took the head of a demon.

"Fine." I nodded at her.

"Kill them all," Raphael bellowed as a ripple of thunder and bright light rolled across the dark sky, breaking a hole in the dark. The sky glowed brightly, and what looked like a star fell from Heaven, but I recognized Michael's face long before he would've been recognizable to anyone else. He used the battle trumpet to call angels to arms as he descended upon them. One by one, the glittering pride leaped from their fluffy perch and dove toward the Earth.

Like the past had never finished, a war erupted all around me, the car shaking violently on its side. I needed to get Minetta out of here. Michael's appearance had distracted Raphael, and he rose into the air, their silver swords clashing loudly. The sounds were so much like other battles as screams of pain, and the sound of bones being crushed was all you could hear.

Brill leaped over the car. "Protect Mammon!" he ordered.

The army did as he asked, a wide circle of multiple rows forming around the car, the snarling fangs of his Molyneux an imposing force. Their great size and muscled bodies were enough to have the closest demons take a step back. "What do you want, Master?"

I looked to my Captain. "Kill any demon that stands with Raphael. Leave everyone else alone."

"You heard the order!" They roared as a unit and pressed out from the car, death the only thing in their wake.

"Is she okay?" Penny yelled up at me as another clap of thunder boomed.

Standing, I stepped to the side of the door and hooked my fingers around the mangled edge. I growled, muscles flexing as I ripped the door from its hinges. Tossing the door aside, I knelt and reached in the car. Gripping her body so she wouldn't fall, I pulled hard on the straps, but they wouldn't give without hurting her. "Do you have a knife?"

"Here." Penny tossed up a small red blade. Catching it, I reached back in and cut at the straps holding Minetta. With a snap, the seatbelt let go, and she was free. "Come on, my little bird, let's get you out of here."

As gently as I could, I pulled her from the small car. Jumping to the ground, I laid her down and Penny knelt beside her, checking on her... for what exactly I didn't know.

"What are you doing?"

"It's called first aid. We had to learn it at work. She's breathing, and her airways are clear. That's good. Move out of my way. I need to check for other injuries." She gave me a little push, and I surprised myself by moving. I watched in fascination as Penny felt down all of Minny's limbs and then lifted her shirt to check her stomach. A dark bruise was easily seen on her stomach. "Shit! She has internal bleeding. She needs a hospital now."

"It's just a bruise."

"No, not to a human. That is life-threatening. She could die from this and soon." Penny's eyes were wide with fear, spiking my own panic.

Minetta's eyes fluttered, her eyes slowly opening as she mumbled something.

"Minny?" My hand went to her face to stroke her cheek. Her face was splattered with blood from a cut on her forehead, but it didn't look like she had anything worse.

"What happened?" She licked her lips, her words coming slow.

"You were in an accident. We need to get you to a hospital."

"Okay," she said and rolled onto her side, wincing.

"What are you doing? I'll carry you," I said as she stumbled to her feet. I wrapped my arm around her shoulders to help her stand when a pair of demons broke through the line and charged. Skye and Neven stopped the first one, but I had to let go of Minny to fight off the second. It was a mammoth beast, with fists larger than the car, and it swung at me as it tried to get to Minny.

She screamed as she saw what was coming and stumbled backward. "Get her out of here!" I yelled to Penny.

"I can't carry her far. We'd be sitting ducks out there alone," Penny yelled back as she stabbed a smaller snake-like demon through the head.

Time. More time.

Time was of the essence was all that was running through my head as my sword cut through the beast's tough hide. Rolling out of the way of another fist, I sliced at the creature's wrist, the sword cutting clean through. A geyser of black blood shot in all directions, coating the field and making it slick.

"We can take it from here," Neven said as he and Skye worked in perfect tandem. Neven jumped on the demon's back while Skye sank one blade through the creature's eye. "Go! We got this," Neven barked out.

I jumped into action and turned back to Minny. I reached for her, and everything slowed down—the sounds disappearing around me. I looked to my left as Brill was yelling to get down as he came for my side and pushed me to the ground just as Raphael's silver spear streaked through the air.

I screamed a blood-curdling sound as I was toppled toward the ground. I reached for Minny, her body bowing back and eyes wide as the spear pierced her chest.

"No," I roared as I felt the pain rip through my chest as surely as the spear had found me. Minetta looked down at the thing protruding from her and then looked at me.

"Riker?"

"Are you okay," Brill asked as I continued to scream hysterically and fight his weight and the three other demons that piled on top of me. I didn't need their protection.

"Get the fuck off of me," I roared, and Brill and the others jumped at the order. My arms wrapped around Minny just as she started to crumple to the ground. "No, no, no. No, please don't die."

Tears slipped down the sides of Minny's face as I gripped her to my chest. I went to my knees, the grief crushing me as I stared into her beautiful blue eyes.

"You came," she said, her voice soft. A sob gripped me. I'd never known agony like this. "Hey, don't cry," she wheezed. Her hand touched my cheek the way I always did to hers. A small smile formed on her lips. "You're so beautiful."

"I'm not the beautiful one. I'm sorry I left. I'm so sorry I left you alone." The words poured out of me as I rocked her body. "I'm going to get you help. You're not going to die. Michael! Michael!" I screamed.

"Shhh, it's okay." Blood slowly trickled from the side of her mouth, and I wiped it away with my thumb. She cupped my cheek and smiled like I was everything to her and the look made the anguish worse. "Promise me something," she gasped again, and my body shook uncontrollably.

"Anything, it's yours, name it."

"Don't." She paused, her chest barely rising as she tried to take a breath. "Slip back, don't be... who you were," she coughed, and more blood dripped from her mouth. "Be this version of you, be the man I fell in love with."

"I...I..."

"Promise me, Riker," she said, her voice softer.

My lower lip trembled. "I promise."

She smiled wide, the same smile that captured my heart the first moment we met. "I. Love. You." Her hand slipped away from my face and fell onto the blood-stained grass.

"No, no, this is not happening." I picked up her hand and laid it against my cheek. "Don't leave me, please."

When she didn't move, her eyes stared blankly up at the sky, a roar ripped from my chest that shook the ground. My power flowed out in a mad rush as the pain enveloped me, seizing me in its grasp. I couldn't breathe. Every limb shook with the crushing sadness as I wailed. The power exploded and tossed everything to the wind. Demon, angel, car, and trees were driven back by the blast.

"Father! Please help her!" I yelled to the Heavens. It was the only time I'd asked for anything since my fall, but I'd do anything he wanted if he'd let Minny live. "Please, if you ever loved me, save her!"

The sky remained quiet. No words of comfort came from above. More tears fell from my eyes, landing on her still form.

A hand gripped my shoulder, and I looked into Dai's tear-filled eyes. So similar was the look on her face as when I'd comforted her so long ago. "Get her out of here. We'll finish this."

I lifted Minny as carefully as I could. Penny and Shilo stood close by, both wearing the same expression. I wanted so badly to rip out the stupid spear from her chest. Michael stepped forward, his sword bloody, but his eyes sad as he stared at Minny's still form.

"I'm taking her to a hospital."

"It's too late. She's gone, my brother," Michael said quietly.

"No! I don't believe you." My mind didn't want to believe what I already knew to be true. I soared into the air, my wings taking me faster than they'd ever done before.

"Brother, stop!"

"No!" I hollered back at Michael, who was following not far behind. "I'm not letting her go."

As we neared the tall hospital with its glowing H, Michael grabbed my legs and hauled me toward the roof.

"Stop it, let me go!" I tried to kick him off, but I couldn't fend him off properly with Minny in my arms.

Michael let go at the last second, and I barely got my feet underneath me, but we didn't crash. "What the fuck? I'm trying to save her!"

Michael grabbed my shoulders and shook me. "Look at her face, brother. She is gone." He gripped my shoulders harder. "She is gone," he said softer.

"No," I said but couldn't bring myself to look at her face knowing he was right. "Save her, please save her." I held her out to him. "You want me to beg?" I dropped to my knees, his hands falling free of my shoulders as I held her up to him. "Please, save her. I will do anything you want."

"I can't. I wish I could." Michael said and reached out to wipe some of the blood off her face. "I really wish I could."

"What good is being an archangel then?" I growled out bitterly.

"I don't know," Michael whispered, his eyes moist.

"You did this. You put her in my path, and you made this happen! You killed her." I laid Minny down on the ground as gingerly as I could and called my sword to me once more. "You commit more sins than I ever could, and yet you remain at Father's side as the loved child."

The sword slammed home into my palm as rage flowed through my body. The demon that was part of me rose from the pain and growled at the archangel, the sound rippling from my lips.

"I didn't kill you all these years, but I won't hold back now." Gold met silver as our blades collided and wings flapped hard.

"I don't want to hurt you, brother," Michael pleaded.

"You already have. Her blood is on your hands." The clanging of the swords grew as we swirled in the air above the hospital, our arms moving faster than any human eye could see. "You wanted to break me? Well, you've done it. I'm broken, Michael." Sparks flew as the deadly metal met and the handles locked together. "I hate you. Everything you touch turns to ash, and yet you live. It's not right," I growled in his face.

"I didn't kill her, Riker. I didn't put her in your path."

"Lies!" Gold and Silver streaks swirled, and the noise of the blades grew faster. More sparks rose into the night sky like little bits of ash from a fire.

"Truth! I swear to you, Ri, I only got involved after the two of you met, and the spark in the prophecy began to glow. I didn't want her to die, brother, I swear to you." Michael ducked a killing blow, but I managed to get a boot up and kick him hard in the chest. He rolled over backward and crashed to the roof as he lost his sense of direction.

Swooping down, I landed beside him and touched the point of my sword to his neck. "You must die for the pain you caused, the pain you continue to create!" Pulling the blade back, I swung, and the sword streaked toward Michael's neck, his eyes closed, knowing the end had finally found him.

"P*romise me something.*"
"*Anything, it's yours, name it.*"
"*Be this version of you, be the man I fell in love with.*"
"*I promise.*"

P anting hard, I screamed in agony, a deep sorrow splitting me in two like a cavernous fault line. My arms shook as the blade touched Michael's neck and stopped. I dropped the blade with a clang as my knees found the rocky surface of the rooftop. I gripped handfuls of the hard stone as tears ripped from my body in waves. I crawled over to Minny's still body and gently lifted her into my arms. Reaching up, my hand shook as I closed her eyes for the last time.

Arms wrapped around my shoulder. "I didn't want her to die. I didn't want any of this, brother, I promise you on my own life and on my faith that his is not what I hoped for."

I sucked in a sharp breath, my head snapping up as I jumped to my feet, shaking Michael off.

"The Ether...take care of her, I'll be back."

"What are you going to do?" Michael called after me.

"To get her back," I yelled as I streaked for the Ether.

"Don't do it, brother!" I could hear Michael yell, but I was too far lost in grief and my hope to listen to him. I needed to get her back. That was all that mattered.

CHAPTER
FIFTY-SIX

R IKER

I could see Lucifer and Leviathan as I swooped down into the Ether. They were probably wondering why my army stormed out of Hell, but I didn't have time to explain right now. I raced toward the cavern of River Styx and veered into the wide opening. The inside of the tunnel was dark, but the ghostly spirits of the humans eerily glowed under the dark water and cast luminescent shadows along the ceiling.

I curled my wings down so that I could drop low over the water that would consume a demon or an angel for all eternity if one was so foolish as to try and swim. I hovered over the water staring at the thousands of faces that were passing by. With a flick of my wings, I made my way back and forth from the river's entrance to where they divided and went to Hell or Heaven. I flew in a back-and-forth pattern from one side of the sandy shore to the other but didn't see her beautiful face among the others. She couldn't have passed by, could she?

My shadow reflected back at me as I made another pass, frantically looking for my Minny. I was making my third pass when a ghostly hand slowly rose out of the glittering water toward me. Veering around, I gripped the hand reaching for me. Her beautiful face came into view just below the shimmering surface. Pulling her from the water, it dripped in long streams from her body as I flew for the shore. With a gentle thrust of my wings, I lowered us down, my heart soaring as I clutched her to my body.

Her arms wrapped around me, and I buried my head into her damp hair. My body shook, the wet tears falling and mixing with her soaked gown. The simple material that was given to all those entering the river to wear looked stunning on her. She could've worn a paper bag, and she'd still be just as beautiful.

"I thought I lost you." I cupped her cheeks and kissed her hard. I poured every ounce of emotion into the kiss, every unsaid I love you, every you're my forever that I'd ever thought. She was my everything. My heart no longer wanted to beat on its own. "Please stay with me," I said, breaking the kiss breathlessly. "Please."

"My time had come," she said simply and lifted a shoulder. "I thought I'd have more time to, but it wasn't meant to be."

Minetta mimicked my position, her hands lying upon my cheeks.

"But it doesn't have to end like this. You can stay here with me. We can live here in Hell. I have a palace."

In that moment, it was painfully clear how she didn't belong here. Her soul glowed brightly against the dark grey of the rock walls of the cavern while the sand shimmered like black diamonds in her presence. She was a beacon of pure light. Before she opened her mouth, I knew what she would say.

"Please don't say it." I kissed her soft lips, savoring her flavor. Nothing could stop the sweet peach scent that would forever remind me of her. "I have never begged for anything." I slowly fell to my knees at her feet. "I'm begging you now, as selfish as it is, for you to stay with me. You make me a better man, you make me someone I like, you make me feel again. I love you. I love you so much. Just stay. Please stay."

Her blue eyes softly glowed in the dim light as she lowered her face to mine. "I love you more than anything, Riker, but I do not belong here. You must know that." She kissed my nose and then laid a soft kiss on my lips, and a whimper escaped as I contemplated just taking her and keeping her regardless of what she said. "Look at me, Riker," her voice was soft and yet as commanding as any captain. "You have always been great, and you never needed me to be so. I just reminded you of who you were and what you let get buried in here." She placed a hand over my heart.

"No, I was horrible. I've done so many terrible things. You don't understand. You are my angel. You are the love of my life. I don't want to breathe in a world without you. Please, Minny, I'm sorry I left, I'm sorry I didn't see how much I meant to you, I'm sorry...." She placed a finger on my lips, and everything inside me fell apart all over again.

She smiled wide, and it was the most stunning thing, that look on her face of pure joy and love. It was something I'd never forget. "Everyone is watching you, Riker," she whispered.

I glanced around at the demons at Charon's. All the faces pressed to the glass as they watched the show. "I don't care. Let them watch. Let them see me beg."

She smiled a little wider, her sweet laugh warming my broken soul. "Don't you see, that is the point. You're admired. You're more important to Hell, Heaven, or Earth than you could imagine. This version of you, this version I fell so hopelessly in love with. I'm sorry I kept what I knew from you, Riker. I never should've don't that."

"No, don't apologize to me. I shouldn't have been so quick to run. I could've saved you. I could've...."

"Riker, what you fail to see is that this was going to happen. If not today, then tomorrow or next month, but this was always my fate." Her lips touched mine, the taste of salt from our tears mixing with her sweet flavor. Standing straight, Minetta looked around again. "Please don't ask me to stay here, I love you, but I don't belong here, and...." She stopped and looked off toward the direction of Heaven. "I want to see my dad again."

I sucked in a ragged breath, my wings drooping to lay on the black sand. She lifted my chin with one delicate finger. "Look after those that follow you with loyalty. They love you wholly. And please look out for my mom until she passes, I know she doesn't have much time, but I don't want to see her alone. I hate to ask this of you, but you're the only one I can."

"You're leaving me alone. I don't want to be alone anymore." My hands gripped the dark sand, and I was tempted to throw myself into the river and be lost forever.

"No, Riker, I will always be with you." She looked toward the fork in the river again. "I can hear the gates calling. I need to go."

She kissed me then, hard and passionate, filled with all that was between us—the touch of her lips lingering long after she walked into the water. Our fingertips held on as our eyes locked.

"I love you," she whispered as she lowered herself back into the water. "I'll always love you, Riker. Always." And then she was gone, below the surface and drifting away once more.

The grief and sadness turned into a white-hot rage that blinded me as I knelt there and watched her disappear. Bursting from the ground, I bellowed, shaking the walls of the cavern. Jumping in the air, I burst out the opening and veered toward my palace. My fist met the golden gates, the impact busting them wide open. The frenzy only increased with the pain that exploded in my arm.

"Ahhh!" I screamed as I grabbed the first thing I could get my hands on and threw it across the courtyard. Worse than any raging storm, I tore at the doors, the walls—my fists beat the side of the black onyx.

Large chunks of the expensive rock and gold inlay ripped away from the building that I'd poured so much into—gone. I didn't care. Nothing mattered anymore. I didn't stop when I couldn't feel my bloody hands any longer, and I didn't stop when I could no longer stand.

Exhaustion and the overpowering grief had me stumbling back and landing on my ass in the middle of the rubble. I looked up as someone squatted down beside me.

I stared into Skye's grey eyes. "I'm so sorry, I'm so, so sorry," she cried and pulled me into a hug. "I didn't know what she meant to you. I didn't understand. I'm so sorry." Neven gripped me from the other side, and I just couldn't cry anymore. All that was left was this aching numb sensation that filled me and left me feeling like an empty shell.

I hated my Father and yet understood him more at that moment than ever before. The only thing that kept me from taking my own life, and ending the pain, was my promise to Minny. I wouldn't break that. It was her last wish, her dying wish, and it was all I had left. After that, I had nothing.

I'd been born a powerful archangel, and reborn a prince, the sin of greed, but my fall was from a woman's touch that showed me the meaning of love.

FIFTY-SEVEN

RIKER

I'd never understood the power of immortality, nor what it meant to have such a delicate life, what it meant to wake up each day and be thankful for the gift of life. Being an immortal, I had no concept of time. I never valued the time we shared, the moments we made or even appreciated those in my life. Not the way I was supposed to, not until Minny had come into my life and showed me what it was to really love and long for more. What it was to experience loss.

Me, Mammon, longing for more of the one thing I couldn't have. More time with her. It had been two months since her death, and every single day was a struggle. I struggled to breathe, eat, or even sleep. I'd lost all motivation, and my will to continue on weakened with each passing day. Simply getting up or doing simple tasks like getting dressed was an effort that took everything out of me.

I did keep my promise to my little bird. The plans for the hospital were well underway, and now the sign read in both her and her father's memory. I'd also moved Shelly Johnson closer, making it easier to take care of her. I'd hoped that Minny would be okay with that, but when Shelly cried with joy as she stared at the ocean, I figured Minny would've been happy. Sitting with Shelly, we spoke about Minny, and I learned stories of her youth. It was the single highlight of my day, and those couple hours were the only reason I pressed on.

Minny's funeral had been small but beautiful, just like the woman herself. I'd never attended a funeral before. A group of people standing around an open grave, dressed in black as you cried over a loss. I'd always wondered what kind of peace doing this brought to people?

But, as Minny's shiny casket was lowered into the ground and Shilo read a poem about everlasting love, I understood while Penny cried and Skye and Neven hugged. For better or worse, I was forever changed by the short time she'd been in my life.

I sat on the edge of Shelly Johnson's bed, her frail and boney hand lying in my own. It wouldn't be long now, and mother would be reunited with daughter. The corner of my mouth lifted in a small smile as I pictured their reunion. I sat with her until she took her final gasping breath and then laid a kiss upon her brow.

"Tell her I miss her and that I love her," I whispered in her ear. Turning my attention to the nurse in the room. "I'll have the funeral home call with the details."

Walking outside, I stared at the bright blue sky and took a deep breath, and yet it never felt like I could take in enough air. The ache in my chest was an old friend now, one I took everywhere. I had to hand Neven the reins of my company. I couldn't even look at the building, let alone walk inside.

"Are you alright, Sir," Shilo asked.

I nodded and walked toward the angel that I now thought of as a father.

"Yes, she passed peacefully."

"Very well. What would you like to do now?"

"Just take me home. I'm feeling tired today," I said and slipped into the car's passenger seat. Laying my head against the window, I watched the world go by. My penthouse had suddenly turned into a commune, or at least that was how it felt with Shilo living there and Penny, Neven, and Skye all taking rooms and proceeding to stay.

They all said that they didn't want me to be alone, and each took turns trying to get me to engage in meals or conversation. I thought they were ridiculous, but I let them do what they wanted. I didn't have the energy to fight them. I wandered past the kitchen, where I could hear their voices laughing.

"I'll be in my study if you need me."

"You should eat something, son," Shilo called.

"Later, Shilo, I'm not hungry." I didn't bother to look at the angel. I didn't want to see the concerned look in his eyes. Closing the door, I tossed my jacket on the rack and grabbed a whisky before sitting down. My great sword shined like the day it was made. There was not a scratch on the golden blade that hung on the rack behind my desk, but I couldn't' say the same thing for my soul.

I stared at the massive bowl of fresh peaches on the table and took a deep breath as I closed my eyes. It didn't quite do her scent justice, but I could almost pretend she was here with me. Laying my head back on the leather, I did what was becoming a habit. I played over every moment we shared. My finger ran across my lip as I remembered our last kiss.

A soft knock sounded at the door, and I sat up, wiping away the tears. "May I enter," Shilo asked.

"I told you I'm not hungry right now."

"I know."

Sighing loudly over the interruption, I answered, "yes, come on in." I stood and made my way to the bar area to refresh my drink. "I'm not sure why you're so insistent that I eat Shilo."

"Because he loves you." I froze with the decanter in hand. My heart picked up its pace and beat wildly in my ears. Her scent invaded my nose as I slowly turned around. I blinked, the decanter and glass dropping to the ground. She covered her mouth and winced as the crystal smashed into a million little pieces.

"Oh shoot, I'm sorry I should've called first or had Shilo make sure you were sitting."

"It's really you. You're here?"

The smile that could light up any room spread across her face. I'd missed that smile. No, I'd missed her. I rushed across the room, scared that she would disappear again if I didn't grab her. Her body was warm and perfect as I wrapped her up and spun her around. She squealed and kissed me hard, our tongues entwining as our kiss said what words couldn't.

"How is this possible? How are you here?" I peppered her face with an assault of kisses and wrapped her up in a hug, scared to let her go. "I'm not going crazy, am I?"

She laughed hard. "No, you're not going crazy. I am really here."

"Then how? I don't understand how this is happening."

"Well, if you let go of me for a moment, I'll show you." She looked up at me and gave me a sly smirk before stepping back. Unable to help myself, I licked my lips as her fingers worked at undoing the blouse she wore. It dropped to the floor, and I groaned at the sight of her body and the adorable lace bra she was wearing.

"If I'm dreaming, never wake me up," I mumbled.

"You're not dreaming, silly." Her body shimmered, the soft white and golden light emanating and casting shadows across the room. I gasped as delicate white wings rose behind her and slowly spread out wide. My eyes stared at the white wings and swallowed hard.

"You were made an angel? A human-made angel?" She nodded, and a tear rolled down my cheek. "You deserve it, you always were one anyway, my little bird, and now you have your own wings. How often can you visit?"

Her smile turned into a sexy smirk as she undid her bra and held it out, dropping it to the ground. I stopped breathing, my mind going blank, my eyes glued to the rise and fall of her chest. "What if I told you that I was made into a guardian angel and was to stay here on Earth?"

"Really?" Hope burst inside my chest as I took in her smiling face. "Who's the lucky person?"

She lifted her arm and pointed it at me.

"Me?" She nodded. "Father made you my guardian angel?"

"It was Michael's idea, actually. Apparently, you've redeemed yourself enough to deserve a little happiness. Besides, he said I was a positive influence on you. You should know that Michael got down on his knee as he asked for this favor. He said you had the chance to kill him, and you didn't. No secrets this time between us." She smiled.

"No secrets and no running."

"Oh, and in case you want to know, Raphael was super pissed and has been banned from coming to Earth until Father forgives him." She laughed, and the sound was infectious, making me laugh along with her.

With a yell, I grabbed her around the waist and lifted her over my shoulder. "Oh, my little bird, we have so much time to make up for," I said as I ran for the bedroom, she laughed and smacked my ass.

I ignored the laughter and cheering spectators in the living room as we ran past, slamming the door in my wake. Sitting her down on her feet, I leaned in until my lips found hers and didn't stop until we were both breathless. In the span of one heartbeat and the next, my soul mended back together like she was the needle and thread I'd needed, and I was never letting her go again.

"I love you more than words can say, Minetta Johnson."

"I love you more than words can say, Riker Rhodes. Now ravage me already."

"Yes, ma'am."

EPILOGUE
FIVE YEARS LATER

MINETTA ran around the large yard of her family farm chasing their four-year-old, Maximus, while Riker rocked the newest addition, Aliyah, in his arms. Max was the spitting image of her with his large blue eyes and midnight black hair, while their sweet little Aliyah was definitely daddy's little girl with his unique amber eyes and blonde hair that verged on gold. There was no way to tell if the children would grow up immortal and have abilities or remain human since they were born on Earth. Either way, they were happy, they were a family, and the kids got to experience the same loving childhood she had.

Riker talked the owners she'd sold her farmhouse to into finding another place. It probably involved a lot of money being tossed their way. But she and Riker moved out to the farm shortly after her return. Shilo insisted on moving with them, and honestly, she didn't know what she would do without him. He seemed rejuvenated, helping look after the kids and organizing the renovation that was currently underway. Riker was set up in the small spare bedroom upstairs to continue working, but it gave her great access to distract him when she wasn't on shift. She took great pride in tearing him away from an important Zoom meeting with just a whisper in his ear.

She'd got to see her mom and dad in Heaven, and although she knew it was goodbye again, this time felt different when she'd agreed to become Riker's guardian. They were happy and together, and she knew they were safe and she could visit a couple of times a year.

But this here and now was her time. It was her time to make her own dreams a reality, and she was given that chance. Maybe a little of the greed had rubbed off on her while some of her kinder nature had been reborn inside of Riker, but together they balanced.

Penny, Skye, and Neven opted to live in the penthouse, but they were not allowed in the master bedroom. She'd made sure they didn't have to contend with anything weird if they decided to stay in the city for a few nights. The parties they were throwing were apparently off the charts, so there was good reason for her concern.

Minetta decided she still wanted to work part-time, much to Riker's dismay, and picked up a fill-in 911 operator's position in their new area. Work was where she was heading when their little troublemaker smacked her butt and told her she was it.

She scooped up Max and swung him high into the air. "You are just like your daddy," Max squealed as she swung him around like an airplane, his hands out wide, a smile as bright as the sun shone back at her.

"Hey, don't blame that on me. I think Shilo has been showing him that trick," Riker said, earning a raised eyebrow from Shilo as he rocked slowly in the fancy new rocking chair—Riker's newest addition. He still liked to have a few obscenely expensive items around that she shook her head at, but he was the sin of greed. There was only so much corralling one could do. Riker handed over Aliyah to Shilo and walked down the front stairs to meet the two of them.

"Yes, Shilo has been wandering around smacking my butt, seems so like him," she teased and heard a small laugh from the porch.

"Hmm, alright fine, you win. It might be my fault. I have something for you," he said and reached into his pocket to pull something out. "Here, I'll trade you." Riker reached out to take Max.

She handed their high-spirited son over to Riker and held out her hand. He opened his fist, and a slim gold chain with a red ruby landed in the palm of her hand.

"Riker, it's stunning. What is this for?"

He shrugged and smirked. "Just because you deserve it."

"Should I be worried about the smirk?"

Riker laughed, and the warm, rich sound rolled over her skin and warmed more than the sun ever could. "No, my Little Bird, you have nothing to worry about."

She held it up to the light, and it was the most beautiful stone she'd ever seen other than the amber diamond in her wedding ring. Smiling, she undid the clasp and clipped it around her neck. Raising up on her toes, she gave both her men a kiss. Her lips lingered on Riker's, her hand on his neck as she took his kiss before she whispered in his ear.

"I'm off for the next few days, and I have a couple of ideas on how we can spend them." Riker groaned low in his chest, his eyes finding hers as she stepped back, and as always, the look in them had her heart racing.

"Now that is an idea I can get behind. Did you want to see Ireland?" He smiled wide as she laughed.

"You know what, why not. I still needed to see a place that started with an 'I.' "

"The jet will be ready for when you get off work."

She could tell he was having trouble containing his excitement, and there was going to be a whole trip planned by the time she got off work, but it didn't bother her now. He'd proven over and over that he could be both the sin of greed and have a selfless heart. A dance that was part of his condition so that she got to stay was that Riker must remain the sin on Earth.

"I'll see you in the morning, little man. How about we have a special breakfast before our plane ride, like have chocolate chip pancakes?"

"Yes!" Max yelled, making us all laugh.

"I'll see you after work, don't let him talk you into staying up past his bedtime." She gave her two men a stern look but only got innocent smiles in return. "Mmhmm, you both look guilty. That is a deadly duo right there."

Making her way to the car, she stopped to stare back at Riker, and her heart swelled as both he and Max waved goodbye, wide smiles on their faces.

"I love you," she called out and blew them a kiss that Max pretended to catch and place on Riker's cheek. Her heart almost burst with happiness.

"I love you more, Little Bird."

This call center was much smaller and a lot quieter than the one in New York, and at the moment, there was only herself and two others working. She yawned and stretched as the clock on the wall showed she had a couple more hours to go. She did miss Penny. The couple of times she saw her a month just wasn't enough girl time. And she hated to admit it, but Skye and Neven had grown on her now that Skye wasn't trying to interfere in her relationship with Riker.

The phone rang, and she was startled out of her dazed thoughts. She reached for the button, but the ringing stopped. She looked at the light that was still showing a call and her computer and realized that nothing was moving, not even the air in the room.

Minetta slowly stood and stared at the girl that was on her way back to her desk with a coffee and was frozen mid-stride. Not sure what was coming, she reached back and pulled out the two swords that were invisible to humans. The soft ring of the metal pulling from their leather sheaths was loud in the sudden quiet.

The front door of the building opened, the little bell announcing that someone had walked in, but she couldn't see who it was. She stepped out of her cubicle and prepared herself for the potential threat. She learned early that just because she was now an angel and more powerful than she could've imagined didn't mean they didn't have enemies.

A shadow graced the door a moment before Lucifer himself walked in. He marched across the floor, looking every bit the badass she remembered from when Riker took her to Charon's to meet the man that started the fall. Other than being clueless about a great many things, he was actually entertaining. He was apparently going through a leather fetish at the time, and the outfit was a little unusual, to say the least. Skin tight leather pants, black combat boots, with a black T-shirt were one thing, but it was the long cape with fur on the collar that had her wonder what the heck?

The only thing was Lucifer rarely came up to Earth. In fact, he only did so when he was bored or wanted to cause some sort of mischief. She was terrified to find out why he was here with her alone at work.

"You can put your toys away. I'm not here to hurt you." Lucifer walked past her and held out an entire tray of coffee and three boxes of donuts that would have fed twenty people.

She slipped her swords away and took the offering. "Thanks, I think."

"What? Isn't that the standard food for cops?"

She was tempted to correct him that she wasn't a cop and that the comment was very prejudiced, but then again, it was Lucifer, was there really a point?

"It's great, thank you, I'll sit everything over here." Before she could move, he grabbed a coffee and a couple powdered doughnuts, and she had to stifle a laugh as she placed the boxes down and turned around to face the devil. Lucifer had a powdered mustache and it was obvious he didn't know or care as he grinned and stared at the jelly center. Minetta made her way across the floor and sat down across from the devil, a little terrified to see why he'd come to visit her.

"So how can I help you, Lucifer, Prince of Darkness?"

"Call me Luci. You and Riker are doing the horizontal mambo we are past the formal stage."

"Okay, Luci," she said, and there were no words to describe how strange that felt to say. "How can I help you?"

He pointed to her chest, and she looked down, terrified to see what was wrong. "That's a really nice ruby."

"Thank you, Riker gave it to me." She smiled wide and rubbed her hand over the stone.

"It looks like the ones on my throne. The man has good taste." Lucifer smiled, and as he did, she swallowed hard, remembering all too well the smirk on Riker's face. The man was going to have his ass tanned. Then again, he'd like that.

Shit.

"Anyway, I need your advice." He leaned back in the chair and chugged down the coffee.

She prepared herself for what he said next because whatever this was about, it could not be good.

The End

Would you like to know what Lucifer wants? Be sure to read Pride by T.L. Hodel for the answers you seek.

BROOKLYN

If you like it dark and edgy then look no further. Brooklyn Cross has always had a deep passion for writing that stemmed from a wild imagination. When she is not busy typing away about the next character you will fall in love with, you can find her walking with her dogs on the farm and sipping a hot cup of coffee.

In addition to getting her degree in business she was highly competitive in the equestrian sport of dressage, with aspirations of an Olympic dream. She is an entrepreneur at heart and has coached and trained many of a riding enthusiast or their wonderful mounts, but always found herself drawn to writing full-time.

"Writing is what I love. I just want to be authentic with my characters. To tell a story that others can immerse themselves in and enjoy, but also relate too. If I can make you smile, laugh, cry, or your heart pound then I have done my job. To drop people into my worlds and for a short time have you live alongside my characters, is what I have always wanted."

CROSS

www.ingramcontent.com/pod-product-compliance
Lightning Source LLC
Chambersburg PA
CBHW051306190726
48290CB00001B/30